"We're supposed to be newlyweds."

"We are newlyweds. Marriage is hard. First twelve hours is the hardest." Leah continued typing away, not looking at him.

"So it seems. But we must attempt to make this look real."

"It is real. As you pointed out, I signed a license, I took vows. It's all real."

"You know what I mean."

"Love," she said, looking up at him. "You want it to look like love. You want me to gaze at you in adoration so no one doubts my happiness or your penis size. I got it."

His throat tightened, a strange kind of heat prickling his face. "You do not normally talk this way."

"Maybe I do, Ajax, how would you know? We don't know each other. I didn't think you were as big of a jerk as you played it this morning—but, hey, I learned something new. And you think I'm a child, but you're wrong about that too."

Maisey Yates was an avid Mills & Boon® Modern™ Romance reader before she began to write them. She still can't quite believe she's lucky enough to get to create her very own sexy alpha heroes and feisty heroines. Seeing her name on one of those lovely covers is a dream come true.

Maisey lives with her handsome, wonderful, diaper-changing husband and three small children across the street from her extremely supportive parents and the home she grew up in, in the wilds of Southern Oregon, USA. She enjoys the contrast of living in a place where you might wake up to find a bear on your back porch and then heading into the home office to write stories that take place in exotic urban locales.

Recent titles by the same author:

THE COUPLE WHO FOOLED THE WORLD
HEIR TO A DARK INHERITANCE
 (Secret Heirs of Powerful Men)
HEIR TO A DESERT LEGACY
 (Secret Heirs of Powerful Men)
HER LITTLE WHITE LIE

Did you know these are also available as eBooks?
Visit www.millsandboon.co.uk

HIS RING
IS NOT ENOUGH

BY
MAISEY YATES

MILLS &
BOON®

First published in Great Britain 2013
by Mills & Boon, an imprint of Harlequin (UK) Limited.
Harlequin (UK) Limited, Eton House, 18-24 Paradise Road,
Richmond, Surrey TW9 1SR

© Maisey Yates 2013

ISBN: 978 0 263 90703 2

Harlequin (UK) policy is to use papers that are natural, renewable and recyclable products and made from wood grown in sustainable forests. The logging and manufacturing process conform to the legal environmental regulations of the country of origin.

Printed and bound in Spain
by Blackprint CPI, Barcelona

HIS RING
IS NOT ENOUGH

To my support system of writers:
Megan Crane, Michelle Willingham, Jackie Ashenden
and Lisa Hendrix. Friends are so important,
and I'm glad you're mine.

CHAPTER ONE

"It's officially time to panic." Leah Holt finished reading her sister's text message and looked up at her father.

The expression on his face could only be described as shock, and Leah really couldn't blame him. She felt the same way. Everyone was here. Everything was planned. The decorations were in place, the cake was made. The media had been alerted and was out in full force. The groom was present and ready.

And the bride was gone.

"Why is it time to panic?" her father, Joseph Holt, asked.

She took a slow breath. She found she didn't want to tell her father. Didn't want to expose Rachel to censure. Because as upsetting as the text was, Leah knew Rachel well enough to know she wouldn't have done this without a very compelling reason. "She's gone. She's…she's not coming."

"Who is not coming?"

Leah looked up and her heart stopped. Ajax Kouros had chosen that precise moment to walk into the room, already dressed in a dark tuxedo, perfectly fitted to his masculine physique. He looked as untouchable as ever. A god more than a man.

Seeing him made her think of summer days at the estate. Of following him around and chatting his ear off. Her sister away at school, her father busy with work, her mother having tea with friends.

But Ajax had always been there to listen. Her sounding board. The one person she'd felt had understood her.

A lot of time had passed between then and now. She wasn't that girl anymore. Not foolish enough to think that a man like Ajax could be interested in her, or what she had to say. And he wasn't that boy, tanned from working shirtless in the sun.

He was a billionaire now. One of the world's most successful businessmen.

And today was the day he was marrying her sister. And officially gaining control of Holt Industries, along with a hefty piece of *her* own business, since so many of her shares were owned by her father's corporation.

At least, it was supposed to be the day he was marrying her sister and gaining control of Holt.

But Rachel was gone. Gone and not coming back, if her text was an indication. And it should be, since it said she was gone and not coming back.

It was so out of character for her bright, beautiful sister. The eternal hostess and darling of the media had never once set a toe out of line. She was always gorgeous and graceful, a walking photo-op.

So very unlike Leah, who was a walking photo-op for a whole different reason. And the press loved to play it up. Loved to highlight her every shortfall, her every imperfection.

Leah swallowed hard and met Ajax's eyes. They were dark, hard. They always had been. Even when he'd been a boy, there had been no laughter there. No lightness. But the darkness was compelling to her, just as it had always been.

"Rachel isn't coming," she said, her voice barely a whisper, but deafening in the empty sitting room of her family estate.

"What do you mean she isn't coming?" he asked, his voice soft, a vein of granite running through it.

"It's just… She texted me. She… Here." She handed the phone to Ajax, nearly dropping it when his fingers brushed hers. "It says she wants to be with Alex, whoever that is, and that she can't marry you. Not now. She's sorry."

"I can read, Leah, but thank you." He handed the phone back to her, and she curled her fingers around it, holding it down at her side. He looked to her father. "Did you know?"

Joseph shook his head. "Did I know what? That she was having second thoughts? Not at all. I never pressured her to do this, Ajax. You know I wouldn't have. I was under the impression she was completely on board with this."

Ajax nodded once, then looked at Leah. "Did *you* know?"

"No." If she'd known, she would never have let things go this far. She would never have let Rachel leave Ajax like this, without warning. With the world watching.

"Alex who?" he asked, his tone sharp. "What other information is there?"

"I…" Leah scrolled back through her phone's messages. The look on Ajax's face was fierce, feral, like nothing she'd ever seen before. Usually he was so controlled, so unruffled. But now he was frightening. A different man entirely. "She doesn't say."

"Text her. Now."

"Ajax, if she needs space…" Her father spoke tentatively.

"I'm not overly concerned about that," Ajax bit out.

Leah texted as quickly as she could, her fingers shaking. Alex who? Anyone I know?

You don't know him. Alex Christofides. Unexpected. And I'm sorry.

"Alex Christofides."

Ajax and her father shared a look that said volumes. The hair on the back of her neck prickled, goose bumps rising on her skin as she realized the full implication of the name.

"Alexios," Leah said slowly. "Alexios Christofides."

"That would be the one," Ajax said. "Not content with at-

tempts to destroy my business, the bastard has to destroy my
wedding, as well. And make a grab for Holt, I imagine."

"Why, Ajax? Why does he have it in for you like this?"

A shadow passed over Ajax's face. "I don't know. Just business, I suppose."

"But she… Does she know that? Does she know who he is?"

"She wouldn't," Ajax said. "This isn't her world."

No. But it was hers. She knew about Alexios Christofides
and his attempts to bump Ajax's retail and manufacturing con-
glomerate off the map, via covert stock purchases and reporting of illegal activities that hadn't even existed, much less been
provable. Alexios had been a headache for Ajax in an increasingly alarming way over the past five years.

"And you never mentioned him to her?"

"As I said," he replied, teeth clenched, "it is not her world."

Leah sent another text to Rachel, while her father and Ajax
continued talking.

He's an enemy of Ajax's. Didn't you know that? What if he's
using you?

It's too late, L. Can't marry Jax now. I need to be with Alex.

The day of your wedding?

I'm sorry. Trust me. There isn't another way.

"If Rachel has chosen him," her father broke in, "then she's
chosen him."

"Even if he's out to hurt Ajax? And what about the company? My business is rolled into this. I am going to get steam-
rolled by his heavy machinery tactics."

"You're making the assumption that he doesn't care for
Rachel. And that Rachel is a fool. I don't believe that, Leah,"
her father said.

No. Of course not. Rachel would never be so foolish. At

least, that's what everyone would think. Sparkling, poised Rachel, who did so well in every social situation, would never be seduced away from the man she was meant to marry through lies and deceit. She was too savvy.

Leah didn't buy it. Her sister was wonderful. And as such had been coddled by the media. Rachel didn't see the ugly things in life. And the idea that a man, Alexios, might be lying to her, using her, made Leah's stomach churn.

"Sign it over to me," Ajax said, his attention on Joseph. "Revise the agreement."

"I would," Joseph said. "But the company is something that was promised to my daughters. To the husband of the first to be married."

"It was always meant to be me," Ajax said. "You made the offer with me in mind."

"Yes. Naturally, I assumed it would be you. But what can I do? I gave my word, and I would not have Rachel feel I was holding the company hostage to make her marry the man I wanted her to. And if this is her choice, it's her right to have the company in this matter if she chooses. She knows the agreement, too."

Leah knew the agreement, the promise, had only ever been intended for Ajax and Rachel. Joseph loved Ajax like the son he'd never had, and he and Rachel had seemed like a logical and clear match from moment one. As though Ajax was always meant to be a part of their family.

But now everything was falling apart. And Leah's stores, her business, her entire life, were all wrapped up in the package that might now be delivered into the hands of Ajax's enemy.

If Alex was making a grab for Holt, intent on wrapping his hand around it and crushing it for vengeance against Ajax, then he was going to crush Leah's dreams along with it.

She wasn't the media darling. She wasn't the beautiful one. She wasn't the one who attracted men. She had Leah's Lollies. Her business was on the upswing, building and becoming a sort of trend. Candy from one of her stores was fast becoming one of the most popular gift items in the world. Tiffany Blue might be iconic, but Leah Pink was starting to gain momentum.

She wouldn't lose it. She couldn't. It was who she was.

"I need to talk to Ajax alone," she said, before she could fully process her request. "Please," she said to her father.

He nodded once. "If you must." He looked at Ajax. "I am sorry, my son. But I cannot force her down the aisle. No matter that I wouldn't have had her leave you today, I won't force her. And if she has chosen Alex, no matter who he is to you, if she is intent on him, I won't stop that, either."

"I would never ask that of you," Ajax said, his voice hard.

Her father turned and walked out of the room, and Leah fought the urge to follow him. To try to reason with him. It would be easier than dealing with Ajax. But her father wouldn't bend on this. He had given his word, and in Joseph Holt's world, one where men had honor, one where men didn't stoop so low as to use a woman as part of a business firefight, your word was all that was needed.

But that wasn't the real world. She knew it. Ajax knew it.

Ajax pushed his hand through his hair and looked out the window again. "The question is, what is to be done? There is an agreement, drawn up and ready to sign. There is a wedding planned. There are a thousand guests coming in only three hours. The media will be there. This has been hailed as the wedding of the century. So the question is—" he turned to face Leah "—what is to be done?" His control was fraying slightly, an edge to his voice that Leah wasn't accustomed to.

She looked at his face, at the hard lines around his mouth. At the worry in his eyes. Ajax Kouros, worried. And the answer hit her. So clear, so simple. This was how things worked in business, and what they were dealing with was a business-related problem. A contract that needed signing.

Or to be specific, two contracts that needed signing.

"What was the extent of your deal? What did the contract say?"

"Ownership of Holt was to pass to me upon signing the wedding agreement, contingent on the fact that the marriage last for five years. Otherwise, ownership returns to your father."

"And the names on the document?"

"No names. Interchangeable. That's the issue."

"Five-year minimum?"

"Yes."

"I'll do it," Leah said.

The words hung in the room, too loud in the emptiness.

For one fleeting moment she felt exposed. Awkward. No. She wasn't that girl anymore. She was stronger than that. She'd learned. Never expose yourself. Never let them see you cry.

"You will do what?" Ajax asked, dark eyes now trained on her.

"I…" Insecurity rose up and grabbed her by the throat, choking her. Past Leah, the Leah who had idolized Ajax. The girl who had made a fool of herself chasing after his attention, his affection. The idiotic teenager who had nearly declared herself just before he'd declared his love for Rachel.

It's for Leah's Lollies. It has nothing to do with those feelings. It's for Holt.

She wasn't a slave to those old feelings anymore. Sure, she'd dreamed of Ajax when she was a girl, but then, like everyone else, he'd chosen Rachel. And she'd learned never to expose herself like that again. Had learned how to cover up pain under a layer of armor. Because the alternative was to show it to the world, and damn your pride.

Well, she was quite fond of her pride.

"I'll marry you. And then the guests and the companies, yours, mine and Holt, and all of that will be fine. And no matter what, no matter if Rachel marries Christofides next month or…tomorrow, it won't be him that gets his hands on Holt. It will be okay. All of it."

He laughed, humorless, dark. "It will all be fine, will it? Perfection. Just a slight hiccup."

"I'm well aware this is more than a hiccup. But it's better than nothing, right?"

Ajax was not an expressive man. He'd been good to her sister, but not overly affectionate. She'd wondered more than once exactly what sort of relationship they had. If it was more convenience than passion. But just then, she had to acknowledge that Ajax looked very much like a man who'd lost the love of his life.

Ajax put his fingers through his hair again, the look in his eyes so different to what she was used to. Lost. It reminded her of a younger version of him. Of the boy he'd been before coming to the Holt Estate. A boy she'd never known.

She still remembered the moment she'd met him, when they'd come to the estate for the summer. It was like the world had fallen away. Like *she'd* fallen away.

She'd been so young, but there had been something about him that had pulled her to him. He'd, in an instant, been so many things to her. And he'd listened. He'd made her feel important. Special. And she'd clung to him, followed him around like a lost puppy. Obvious. Just thinking about it made her skin crawl with embarrassment.

He looked at her, that lost look in his eyes fading as suddenly as it had appeared. Now his gaze was unreadable, unexpressive. Like he was looking over a new yacht, or sports car. Well, no, not even that. He got a bit more passionate over sports cars. And dark chocolate. That was one thing they had in common. Or at least something they'd had in common.

Handy, because she was short on sports cars, but she did have a lot of dark chocolate. Occupational hazard. Although, she'd stopped trying to tempt him with treats a while ago. About the time she'd realized she was staring at him like an idiot and he only had eyes for her sister.

"You will have to do."

The way he said it made her want to melt into a puddle and slither out of the room. She was being compared to Rachel, again, and being found utterly lacking. "Thanks. And you're welcome."

"Don't expect me to be happy about any of this." He started to pace. "My bride has walked out on me. Chosen my rival over me. And she didn't even have the courtesy to text *me* about it. Rather she contacted you."

"I'm her sister."

"And I'm the man she was supposed to love," he bit out.

She put her hand on his arm, a flash of heat racing from her fingertips and through her body. She pulled back as though she'd been burned.

She hadn't expected that. Hadn't expected to feel that intense, scorching heat. After all, she'd stopped carrying a torch for Ajax years ago. Though, that didn't change the fact that he was an incredibly handsome man. The heat was only due to a physical attraction. She was only human. She imagined any woman who touched him would feel the same way.

Thank God she knew how to hide that moment of insanity. She'd spent years cultivating her mask, one that kept the press at a distance. One that kept her from getting hurt. One of indifference. A smooth, cutting smile on hand whenever she needed it. One that said: *Oh, you again. Can't be bothered.*

Oh, dear Lord. I proposed to him.

That thought made her smile slip.

But it wasn't as if she'd done it for herself. Not for herself personally, anyway. Everything was on the line. The future of Holt, of Leah's Lollies, and Ajax's dreams and hard work. And that mattered to her. She wasn't in love with him anymore, hadn't been for years. But she cared. About Holt. About her own business.

"Why, Leah? What are you getting out of this?"

"Well, jeez, Ajax, Rachel has clearly lost her mind. She's run off with this man that you and I both know is probably not with her by coincidence. A man who would do this just to hurt you. He would, wouldn't he?"

"Yes," he said.

"My father loves Rachel, but he's frankly blind to her faults."

"Does she have them?" Ajax asked dryly.

"She's far too trusting, I think, which you and I know full well is a fault. Alexios would take advantage of that to get to you and to get his hands on Holt to keep you from expanding your business. He'll hurt her. And I can't allow that. I doubt you can, either."

"Of course not."

"So then it's settled. We have to marry before she does. You can still graft yourself into my family tree, which we both know you want. Otherwise we both lose Holt. You especially lose. You lose Rachel, *and* Holt, to Christofides."

"I didn't know Holt mattered to you so much, Leah."

"In terms of it being my family legacy, it does. I can't just let it pass into some stranger's control. But more than legacy, my father owns half the stock in my business, and it's all rolled into the Holt corporate umbrella. Suddenly a stranger has control over me and my business."

"And if Rachel wants Holt?"

"She doesn't. It doesn't mean to her what it means to you and me—you know that. She was going to be your right hand socially, but I doubt she ever spent a day in those offices of her own free will."

"True enough. But I didn't require that of her. A hostess, someone to give me a softer face—*that* I needed."

She looked at the granite lines etched by his mouth, his eyes. Yes, he most certainly did need a hostess.

She took a breath, putting her hard, practiced expression in place. "Well, that's not happening now. And do you want some other man to have your wife and your business?"

Ajax took a step toward her, dark eyes trained on hers, and she felt something inside her melt.

"Other than Holt, Leah, what do you want?"

"To preserve Leah's Lollies. Holt owns a quarter of my stock. And in addition to my candy stores being linked to Holt, I *am* a Holt. It's my legacy. It's ours, not just yours."

"It was meant to be mine and Rachel's."

"I know."

"And you trust me with your stocks, do you? Alexios is quite the financial genius—perhaps he would serve you better than I would. Rachel seems to think so."

"You'll do right by me and my shops, Ajax. I have no doubt."

"I don't know. Perhaps I'll sell my stocks off. You think they'll be profitable enough for me?"

"Of course I do. I sell things that are expensive and bad for you. I think I'll be in business forever."

He arched a dark brow, something in his expression changing. "A sure success, then. There is very little some people love more than indulging a vice."

"Yes. Well, and if I may, allow me to continue my argument for marriage."

"Please," he said, no emotions on display.

"You're right. Everything is in place. Everything. You taking the reins at Holt. The guests. The minister. The cake. There's… I donated a lot of candy. A gift."

"Nice of you."

"Well, now I'm donating a bride. Which might be a bit more than nice."

"If I accept."

"Oh."

Ajax looked at Leah, the woman who, up until ten minutes ago, had been about to become his sister-in-law. Now she was talking about being his wife. Leah. He scarcely thought of her as a woman. In his mind, she was still a round sixteen-year-old girl with curly hair, braces and a sweet tooth.

He could remember, very clearly, having a piece of candy waiting for him with his gardening tools every day when he'd first started working at the Holt Estate. And what had started as a childish game had continued as a tradition. When he'd started interning at the corporate headquarters in New York there had been a piece of candy on his desk. And when he'd branched off on his own, an entire bouquet, and yes, it could only be described as a bouquet, of chocolate had been waiting in his office.

Yes, whenever one of her little gifts showed up, he pictured Leah, the girl. Sweet, uncomplicated Leah, who looked at him and saw someone worth smiling at. But that vision didn't match the reality standing in front of him.

Now she was a woman, he supposed. She was twenty-three. Some of her roundness had melted away, but not all. Her hair was still a mass of dark curls, albeit sleeker than when she'd been a teenager. And there was a hardness to her that had never been there before.

Still, she was nothing like Rachel. Beautiful, willowy Rachel.

Rachel, the woman he'd set his sights on so many years ago. The woman he'd spent so many years planning to marry. She had been standing there, at the end of his path, his goal, for so long that having her removed left him feeling lost. Aimless.

She was the only woman he'd ever loved.

And she had left him. Along with her, she would take Holt, and every piece of the plan, of his life would be broken off in chunks and scattered around his feet.

If he let it happen. If he didn't accept Leah's offer.

It was a bad day for his pride. That he needed help saving a deal he'd spent years working toward because his bride had decided to skip the wedding, burned. She'd left him to be with someone else. His biggest business rival.

This wedding, their union, made it feel like pieces were finally fitting together. Like the pieces of his life had united into one smooth picture, the end of the plan in sight.

Everything he wanted. Everything he'd worked for, in his

grasp at last. His reward for rigid control, for never deviating from the path since he'd first put his foot down on it.

But Rachel hadn't seen things that way. Obviously.

He supposed, if he thought about it, it made sense. Rachel was passionate. About life, about everything. But she'd never been passionate with him. And she'd never been bothered by his reserve with her. He'd imagined she was responding to the way he was naturally. Now he wondered.

Still, pride wouldn't see his plans come to fruition. They wouldn't bring Rachel back, either. Refusing Leah was of no benefit to him. It simply wasn't logical.

However, he had a hard time thinking of her as a wife. As the sort of woman he would share his life with, take to events, take to bed.

Leah was not the woman he'd imagined himself with. Not ever.

"Well, come on, Ajax, don't keep a girl waiting like this," she said, a small smile curving up the edge of her lips. As though she were unruffled. As though all of this was just an interesting diversion. He wondered when she'd become so calculating. When she'd traded in that sweetness for the hard, cutting edge of a businesswoman.

"I accept." There was no logical reason not to. And above anything else, he was a man of logic. Emotion could never be allowed to rule. "I will make a call and have the seamstress come and fit Rachel's dress to you."

Leah's cheeks turned pink, although her expression remained stone cold. "Could you cut a foot off the hem and add the fabric around the middle?"

She was exaggerating and yet, she had a point. Rachel was long and angular, while the top of Leah's head came just below his shoulder. It could not be ignored; she was certainly a larger size than her sister. Though she wasn't proportioned unattractively. Round in the appropriate places. He'd just never given it much thought.

"What size, then? I will order you a new one."

"I'll make a call," she said, her cheeks still pink. "It will have to be off-the-rack, of course. We only have two hours, but it's doable. All things considered, the fit of my dress will be the least scandalous thing about this wedding."

"You are still a Holt heiress," he said.

"Yes, we're practically interchangeable. Except, clearly, for the dress size."

"That is not what I meant. You are not interchangeable." He gritted his teeth. "You are not Rachel." Rachel, who, in his mind, was the embodiment of his perfect life. He'd imagined that when he reached this day, when he reached her, standing at the head of the aisle, his struggle, his fight to stay on the path, to stay in control, would be over. That he would finally have reached a destination instead of walking endlessly.

He'd never touched her, not beyond a casual kiss, but things between them had been understood, for the past six years. They hadn't spent all of their time together, hadn't acted as a couple. Rachel hadn't wanted to feel tied down. She'd wanted to live her life. But he'd been confident that in the end she would come back to him.

He had been wrong. And he hated being wrong.

"I'm sorry about that. Not that I'm not her, but that she left. I am."

"Of course you are. Now you're stuck with me."

She looked up at him, whiskey-colored eyes glittering. He didn't know why she looked like she was about to cry. Because of the situation? Though she had been part of creating it, it wasn't like he had asked for her to stand in. Or because of his comments? Either way, he didn't like it.

Joseph Holt had become a mentor to him when he'd been a teenager, and his family had, in many ways, become his family. He would never do anything to hurt the Holt family. Ever.

"It is not too late to back out, Leah. I will not hold you to a rash statement made in the heat of an emotional moment."

"It *is* all very emotional."

"I meant for you."

She blinked. "For you, as well. Do you feel nothing?"

"I feel—of course I do. But I do not make decisions based on emotion, which is why I'm prepared to marry you instead of Rachel. It's logical." It kept his plan going until he could shift things. Until he could get everything re-sorted in his mind. Planning kept him on point, in control, and control was everything.

He knew what happened when control was lost. Knew what happened when a man lived for feeling.

"Yes. Well, while the situation overall might be emotional, I didn't offer out of a sense of emotion."

"Holt is mine. By right. By promise. I'm not family by blood, but your father trained me for this."

"I know. And I've worked too hard to elevate Leah's Lollies to this position to see it mowed down in a firefight."

He looked at Leah and wondered if he'd underestimated her. He knew she had a business mind, whereas Rachel most certainly put the *social* in socialite and had used the money her father had given her to become a silent partner in a few ventures that helped expand her web of personal connections.

It was one of the reasons Rachel had been such a valuable prospect for a wife. She did what he did not. She connected with people, made friends easily, and used charisma to make happen what she wanted to see done.

She was, in essence, the perfect accessory to his life. Leah on the other hand, was more focused on the business end. She would possibly want a hand in the decision making at Holt, which would be her right, since ownership was to be shared between him and his wife.

But then, he would get a stake in Leah's Lollies, which, in spite of his line of questioning, he knew was quite successful. And with his assets? Mass production of her products was entirely possible.

In terms of how he would benefit, there was the chance it could be very profitable for him. As for Leah…it could be extremely profitable for her.

"What else do you know, Leah?" he asked.

"A lot. I see things. I know how much this means to you. I know you didn't spend years working under my father to not end up as head of Holt."

It was true. Joseph Holt had become his mentor when he'd been a sixteen-year-old boy with little schooling and no money, working on the grounds of the opulent Holt Estate in Rhodes. He'd only just left his father's mansion, fled the island he'd grown up on, which was filled with so much corruption not even the police could help him. He'd been rooming with other teenagers who'd been disowned by their families, for varying reasons. Working. Paying rent. And he'd protected them all, because he'd known about the evil that was out there waiting.

They'd lived and worked like that until better jobs had taken them better places.

For Ajax, that better place had been provided by Joseph Holt. Every summer and winter, the Holts came and stayed on the estate. Unlike other wealthy families he'd worked for, they'd been kind, friendly with their staff. Especially Joseph Holt, who had taken the time to speak with everyone, get to know everyone.

And he'd taken a special interest in Ajax. Had, in many ways, become the father he'd never had. But more than that, he'd taught him an interest in business. Had sent him to college. Had, like he'd done for his daughters, given him money as venture capital. Ajax had spent three years working at Holt in the United States, and after that, he'd gone on to get his own business off the ground, dealing in retail stores, rather than manufacturing.

Ajax had made his success thanks to Joseph, knowing all the while that in the end, Holt would be a part of his stable of assets. As would Rachel.

He had lost one of those things today; he would not lose the other.

"You do see a lot, Leah. And I think you have inherited your father's ability to spot a good business deal. And his inability to pass it up."

She lifted her chin, dark hair shimmering in the light, the glossy curls sliding from her shoulders to tumble down her back. "I am a Holt, Ajax."

"As is Rachel."

"I am not my sister. Not even close. That you will have to remember."

He looked her over. Still, he couldn't help but see that image of a young teenager, sitting in her father's office with a book on her lap, her hair, not glossy or gently curled, but frizzy and barely contained by a rubber band. Or her following him around the estate, chatting his ear off about a new idea she had for a business, asking him if he thought it might work.

If you put your mind to it, Leah, it will work.

That was what he'd always told her. He hadn't realized how true it was. Just how dangerous she could be when she set her mind on something.

"I am in no danger of forgetting."

"I'll need…" She cleared her throat. "Well, that is, I have to get ready now."

CHAPTER TWO

LEAH'S HANDS SHOOK as she picked up the bouquet, the one that was meant to have been her sister's. Thank God she never could have in a million years worn her sister's dress or shoes.

And this was the first time ever she'd been glad she couldn't have. She didn't want her sister's flowers, groom, dress *and* shoes.

As it was, the dress and shoes were Leah's. The flowers and groom...they weren't.

Her stomach cramped painfully and she looked in the mirror. Her eyes looked overly large for her face, and as frightened as she felt. She didn't have her mask up. Because she was very suddenly confronted with the reality of what she was doing.

On paper, in the moment, it had been very black-and-white. Alexios couldn't be allowed to succeed in gaining access to Holt. If he was using Rachel, it couldn't be a reward.

But here, standing in a wedding dress? It was feeling more real. More insane.

She reached down and took a tissue off the vanity and pressed her lips to it, leaving a crimson stain behind. She stared at it for a moment. Would her lips leave red marks on Ajax's?

And it hit her with the force of a wrecking ball. She was going to kiss him. Today. She sank down onto the chair that was positioned in front of the mirror. She was actually *marrying* him. A legal marriage.

Worse, and more worrisome, since it was in her immediate

future, she was about to expose herself to the press, and their ridicule, again. Her least favorite thing ever.

This wedding was huge. A major event. Rachel was so popular, a style icon for the masses and a favorite on the cover of magazines worldwide. And Ajax…he exuded dark sex appeal and mystery, plus there was the whole billionaire thing. That made this wedding, their wedding, a very big deal.

And she just didn't match up to the fanfare.

She stood up and tried not to topple over as she looked in the mirror. She put her hands over her breasts, barely contained by the bodice of the strapless gown. Not her first choice, but it had been an emergency, and that meant she'd had to take the smaller size, and she'd had to take the one that showed a bit too much of her curves. Which were abundant. And she wasn't big on putting them on display.

So, yay, of course now she'd be doing it in front of an audience of a thousand. Plus photographers. As a replacement bride for the lovely Rachel, who the media showed such favor. Who men, all through their lives, had shown such favor.

It reminded her of the time she'd gone to an event in a dress Rachel had worn earlier in the year. So there Leah was, having the sort of fashion misstep sixteen-year-olds often did, but in front of the world. Her less-svelte figure was too much on display thanks to the dress being too small, and the color washed her out. It had been put in a fashion magazine under a Who Wore it Better? heading. And Leah had been savaged in both the article and online.

Borrowing clothes from her sister's closet was a lot more fraught for her than it was for other teenagers.

She remembered so clearly sitting down and crying in her father's office when she'd seen it, and Ajax coming in. He'd been visiting, taking time out from his own corporate empire that was making a serious statement in the business landscape. But he'd always made time for them. He'd always felt like a part of the Holt family.

"I'm so humiliated, Ajax!" she'd wailed. "How will I ever live this down?"

Ajax had looked at her, dark eyes impassive. "If you don't want to be compared to your sister, stop putting yourself in the position. You're different. You will never be her, so stop trying." He'd knelt in front of her then. "And you must never let them see you cry. Never give them anything they can use against you. An unbreakable target is not a satisfying one."

He was right, then and now. She wasn't Rachel. Not even close. And so she'd made an effort to look as different as possible from her sister. And she'd never let them see her cry.

Leah had become the snarky one, the one with the acerbic wit, the businesswoman who didn't care what the press said and didn't waste time trying to court them.

She'd become her own person. Her own very guarded person.

Unless she was with Ajax. With him, she'd felt free to show herself. She'd poured her heart out to him. Hours spent tailing him at the estate replaced with spending time in his office after school.

And she'd left him treats. Ajax wasn't demonstrative, but she always saw the candy wrappers in the trash bin the next morning. And it always earned her a smile. A small one, but from Ajax, it had been gold.

And with those small smiles a girlish crush had turned into love. She'd been so close to telling him, too. One night when there were few people left in the Holt building and they'd been alone in his office. But she'd lost her nerve.

And by the end of the week, he'd announced that he intended to marry Rachel.

Never let them see you cry.

His words had played over and over in her mind that day, as her dreams, her fantasies, had been crushed like a rose in an iron fist. She hadn't gone to his office after that. She hadn't left any candy on his desk again.

She hadn't shown a crack in her facade since.

But no matter how she played it, she still didn't like what the press wrote about her, and she knew this would be no exception.

Round-ish Candy Tycoon to Wed Man Way Out of Her League in Desperate Last-Minute Substitution at Wedding!

There was a headline she could live without.

But it was likely unavoidable. All right, it wouldn't say round-ish, but still. There would be an implication. Especially since she owned candy stores. They loved that about her. That she'd grown up to sell candy. It made for such delightful headlines, filled with the suggestion that she overindulged in her own product.

And she would be standing there, next to Ajax, who was physical perfection. She was sure she would look like a little marshmallow in comparison. A little marshmallow with cleavage.

"Leah." Her father walked into the room, and Leah whirled around toward the sound of his voice. He looked as shell-shocked as she felt. "Are you ready?"

"Yes."

"Are you sure?"

Leah nodded slowly. "Yes."

She felt dizzy, light-headed.

You know what this is. You signed the agreement. There will be an end date on this marriage. He'll probably never even touch you.

But fantasy and reality were having a head-on collision and it was hard to remember how she was supposed to feel. Who she was supposed to be. It was hard to keep her mask in place while the world shook beneath her feet.

"I want to do this," she said, her voice hushed.

The expression on her father's face changed, as if he was seeing deep inside her. "I see." He extended his arm. "Then let's go. I confess, I was not ready for you to be married yet."

She wanted to shout that he didn't see. Because there was nothing to see. Instead, she cleared her throat. "I'm twenty-three."

"But still. With Rachel I knew it was coming. I was much more ready for her to marry. And I knew…I knew Ajax's intentions for a long time. The moment his feelings toward Rachel changed, he told me."

"Six years," Leah said, knowing the exact moment, the exact hour. Because the memory was still so raw, no matter that it shouldn't be.

"She wanted to live more first. She was only twenty-two when he fell in love with her. And you don't want to live?"

"I can still live with a husband," she said. "I'll be married, not dead." And probably not married for that long. Or in truth.

"That's true. But you are still my baby."

She breathed in deep, fighting against the tight ache in her throat. "Dad, I haven't lived at home in years."

"I know."

"And Ajax is like a son to you."

Her father stopped walking and looked at her. "And if he hurts you, I will personally see him undone."

She blinked. "He won't." She would make sure he wouldn't. Her armor was solid; it wouldn't break now. In spite of her moment of flailing insecurity back in the dressing room, she would make sure her armor held.

Anyway, Ajax didn't have a foothold in her life anymore. Not in her emotions at least. She might still find him physically attractive, but she wasn't hopeless over him anymore.

They stopped talking then, because they were in the foyer, and just beyond that was the courtyard, where everything had been prepared for the wedding. Rachel's wedding. None of it was to her taste. Leah was more whimsical, her sister a sophisticate. Everything was white at Rachel's wedding.

Too damn bad she hadn't shown up.

Leah swallowed hard as the doors opened and the sunlight

poured in, painting her in white, too. The only color was the sea beyond the stone-covered courtyard, a blue jewel against the sun-washed sky.

She started descending the steps, and the guests stood, a gasp and ripple of whispers rustling through the crowd, audible even over the string quartet that was playing. She knew what they were saying. They were wondering why. Why her?

Why not the beautiful sister? Surely, everyone would know Rachel had left. Because there was no way Ajax would have preferred her. And everyone would know that.

She'd always imagined she would marry here. In Rhodes. But it hadn't looked like this in her mind.

She raised her eyes and saw Ajax, standing at the head of the aisle, and her heart just about burst through her chest, nerves, remnants of old dreams converging on her, making it hard to breathe. Ajax had always been in her fantasies. Always. Of course, in her fantasies of old as she drew nearer to him on her trip down the aisle, he had smiled. He hadn't looked at her like she was judge, jury and executioner come to hand him a terrible sentence.

But that's how he looked now. Grim. Like a man at the gallows, not the altar.

She tightened her hold on her father's arm and continued down the aisle, looking anywhere but at Ajax. What was she doing? She couldn't back out. She was halfway down the aisle, the man had already been jilted once today. And as they drew closer, the ache in her heart intensified, a swollen mass of emotion growing in her, choking her.

And logic couldn't talk her out of it. Her mind telling her that she shouldn't feel anything for him, did nothing to stop it.

Where was her armor? How had this sneaked beneath it?

They stopped at the head of the aisle, and Leah just about stopped breathing.

"Who gives this woman to this man?" The pastor's voice was thin, distant. Like he was underwater.

"I do."

Her father sounded the same way, so maybe it was just her.

And then he kissed her cheek and she was moving toward Ajax. He extended his hand, and she took it. He had never held her hand before. Now that she thought about it, she didn't think he'd ever touched her skin.

Heat assaulted her, starting at her cheeks, spreading to her ears. Oh, good. Now she was blushing. What was wrong with her? Why couldn't she get a grip?

Why did this feel so real?

It's not real. It's just business. It's for Leah's Lollies. It's for Holt. It's not for you.

He took her other hand, too, turned her to face him. Terror streaked through her, and on its heels, an emotion so big, so real, she couldn't deny it. Couldn't push it down. It grew, it bloomed in her, alive, strong.

In that moment, reality melted away, and fantasy won out.

Surely this was only a fantasy. With her in a wedding gown and Ajax, looking like perfection in a tux, how could it be anything else? It couldn't be real. This was a dream, the dream she used to have when she was a teenager. It wasn't real.

He said his vows, his voice steady. Strong, without emotion, but then, that was how he was. She spoke hers without stumbling, and there was this strange, underlying conviction that each word was the truth. That there would be no one but him, forever.

There never had been, not for her. It was Ajax. Always.

She could feel the walls inside of her start to quake. Start to crumble. All of that supposed hard edge she'd cultivated. All of her defense.

"You may now kiss the bride."

Leah's heart stopped, and for a moment, so did the world. Her focus dropped to Ajax's lips. How many times had she thought about kissing those lips?

It was her last thought before he wrapped his arm around her waist and dipped his head, his mouth covering hers.

She hadn't been prepared. Not for the heat, the flash of pure fire that raced along her veins. She found herself lifting her arms, curling her fingers around the lapels of his suit jacket.

She'd expected something chaste, something appropriate for a thousand pairs of eyes, for two people who had barely ever touched, but that wasn't what she got. What she got was a real, full-on kiss.

He slid his tongue along the seam of her lips, and she opened eagerly, tasting him as he tasted her. She felt as if she was falling, but Ajax was there to hold her up, his arm a strong band around her waist, her fingers curled into his jacket like claws.

She'd never been kissed like this. Not ever. And she'd never felt like this, either. Like she would die if he stopped touching her, like her skin was on fire. Her breasts ached, her heart fluttering like a trapped bird. And the ache, low and strong between her thighs. An ache she knew only he could satisfy.

And all of her expectations about the marriage were blown apart. And all she had were questions. Well, questions, a thundering heartbeat and the feeling of being horribly, hideously exposed.

And then, suddenly, he pulled away and she nearly lost her balance. The guests were clapping, and the pastor was making his pronouncement, but she couldn't pay attention. Her head was swimming, her legs shaking.

"Smile," Ajax whispered in her ear, and it kick-started her brain again.

Never let them see you cry.

So she did smile, a bright, false smile she didn't feel, and he led her down the aisle as the band played.

They went back up the stairs. Into the house.

The doors closed behind them, and Ajax started loosening his tie.

"Don't we need… Should we… The photographer."

"Do you honestly think I want pictures?" he asked, his voice rough.

"I...I had thought... It's our... We paid for the photographer."

"I'm sure the press in attendance got enough. I am not interested in posing for photos. What I would like is alcohol."

"You don't drink."

"Not usually."

Never. She'd never seen him drink. That wasn't the best for her ego. That marrying her was driving him to drink.

"What about the reception?"

"I am far too eager to take you back to my villa and consummate the marriage," he said, his tone dry as sand. "We'll have to skip it."

"Wh...what?"

"We're leaving. Now." She didn't want to leave now. Not while she felt so...shaken.

But they were.

He took her hand again, and they went out the other direction, out the front doors, where there was a limo idling. He opened the back door for her and she got in. He gathered up the skirt of her dress and put it in behind her before getting in and closing the door.

He looked out the window and she followed his gaze to the photographer standing on the step. "Let's give him a picture," he said, his voice nearly a growl.

"The windows are tinted."

"He'll work around that. It's his job to get the shot after all."

He hauled her to his body, her breasts, precariously close to making an exit from the bodice of her dress, pressed against his hard chest. And then, for the second time in the space of five minutes, she was being kissed by Ajax Kouros.

After consigning Ajax to the "fantasies that were never going to happen" bin, two kisses in such short succession were shocking.

His tongue delved deep, tasting her, sending a shock wave through her, straight to her core. And again, she found herself responding, helplessly, intensely. She speared her fingers through his hair, held on to him for all she was worth.

She couldn't pretend she didn't feel this. Couldn't pretend that the touch of his lips against hers didn't light a fire in her body. Couldn't pretend that no matter what her emotions were doing, no matter how she'd shut them down, she'd never wanted a man the way she wanted Ajax.

He removed his lips from hers and pressed a kiss to her neck, down lower, lower…oh…yes.

Then he lifted his head. "Drive," he said, the order clearly meant for his driver and not for her. He kissed her neck again, his tongue tracing a circle over her skin before the limo exited the driveway of her family's estate and went out onto the main winding road that led back down to the highway.

Then, he moved away from her, all of the heat from the earlier moment completely gone. As if cold water had been thrown on a flame.

"What was…all that?"

"I was not in the mood to deal with questioning—were you?"

"I… No, I suppose not."

"We'll need to get a story together, one that matches, before we talk to the press."

"Right, okay, I see the merit in that." Her lips felt swollen and hot, and she felt dizzy. What had just happened to her? She looked down at her hand, where he'd placed a ring only moments before, and she wondered if she was involved in some kind of weird dream.

"There will have to be an explanation for why it was you and not Rachel who walked down the aisle today."

"And the truth won't work? That she realized she loved someone else?"

The expression in his eyes could only be described as fierce. "No, it does not. Would it be so simple for you?"

"I suppose not. But please let's come up with an answer that doesn't completely burn my pride. I've had enough of that in the media."

"We both have issues of pride, it seems. I do not intend to hurt you, Leah, but none of this was part of my plan."

"Clearly."

"I imagine it wasn't a part of yours, either."

"Well, this morning I was getting ready for my sister's wedding, and it turned out to be *my* wedding. And now I'm married and sitting in a limo on my way to…I don't even know where. Maybe you told me, but I forgot because that's just the kind of day it's been."

"My home. We weren't planning on going on a honeymoon until things had started settling at Holt."

"Are you going to New York?"

He shook his head. "Not yet. But I will be working from my office here on getting things in order. Your father has left everything in magnificent working order, and the transition has been well under way for a while, but even so…"

"Business first. I don't have anything to wear," she said. "I have this dress. I don't have…panties." The words sort of slipped out, horrifying her as they did. She didn't feel savvy, or self-contained, or well-protected. She felt dazed. "I don't have deodorant. My suitcase is back at the house."

"I will have all new clothes sent over if you like. And your things from New York."

"My things from… What?"

"You'll be living here with me. We will of course travel to New York, but we'll stay in my penthouse there, not in your apartment or flat or whatever it is you have."

"It's a very nice apartment."

"We will live together. We are husband and wife after all."

"Oh. Right. Yes. We are."

"You sound shocked."

"Are you not?"

He looked her over, dark eyes assessing. "I am a hard man to shock, Leah, but all things considered, I am a bit."

He was so dry, so condescending. It wasn't fair that he was so in control. That his mask never slipped. Because she was confused and a little freaked and kind of in internal upheaval and he just…wasn't.

He was all cold and calm and stare-y.

Blessed reality was starting to trickle in. Cold. Unflinching. It provided a harsh portrait of her slipups over the past few minutes. Over how stupid she'd let a couple of kisses make her when she knew better than to let that happen. Or, she at least knew better than to let anyone see it. She knew better than to reveal anything.

"You really want me to live with you?" She crossed her arms beneath her breasts, then thought better of it when she realized just how effectively that hoisted them up.

"*Need* is the better word," he said. "I will not risk this appearing to be anything but real." He put his elbow on the armrest of the car and put his hand on his forehead. The first sign of him truly not being all that okay.

They were silent for the rest of the ride to the house. And while they climbed the mountain, anger built inside her. Blessed anger that helped her armor feel fortified.

The limo wound its way up the mountain that would carry them to Ajax's home. She realized she hadn't been there. He came over to the family's estate for parties in Rhodes, and he visited her family's penthouse in New York, but she'd never visited him here, not after he'd got a home.

She'd never seen where he'd lived as a teenager working on the estate, either, but she'd been a child then so it wasn't all that surprising.

Double gates came into view, then they parted as the limo approached. And beyond them was a sleek, modern home with windows that opened it all up to views that surrounded it. Mountains behind, the ocean, glimmering bright in front. Bright pink flowers climbed the walls, the only nod to a traditional Greek villa.

The rest was all new. Clean lines and exceptionally expensive construction.

"I've never been here before," she said.

"Have you not?" A strange look passed over his face.

"No. I haven't. You've never invited me. Well, it's not like we really hang out." *Anymore.* "We just happen to make a wide circle around each other at many of the same gatherings, and kind of, pass close enough two or three times in an evening to say 'lovely to see you, how about this shrimp cocktail? Delightful? Yes, delightful!' But no, we don't hang out."

Not by accident. After her big Ajax-induced heartbreak she'd needed to push him away. Needed to give herself some time to erect stronger barriers.

"And I don't have parties," he said, his voice comically serious.

"So, that mystery's solved. That's why I've never been here."

The car stopped and she scrambled out of it, not willing to wait for Ajax or his driver to open the door. The further away the wedding got, the weirder she felt in her dress. The edgier she felt in general.

Every time he'd kissed her, the fog of fantasy had closed in around them and it had seemed a dream. Now, standing in front of his glass-and-steel house, the sun's harsh light bathing her skin in heat, the breeze coming up from the sea blowing the skirt of her wedding dress around her ankles, it all felt much too real.

"Can we go inside?" she asked. "I'm overheated."

"As you would be in that dress." He led the way to the house, and she followed, relief washing through her when they entered the cool stone foyer.

"Are you all right now?"

"Better, thank you." She folded her hands and put them in front of her, the folds of her skirt hiding them.

"Hopefully your things will be here soon. I imagine that is quite uncomfortable."

She looked down and took a breath at the same time, her breasts trying to escape the bodice. Again.

Her things. Because she was expected to live here. To drop everything for this. For him. Because he wanted it to look real.

"So," she said, her voice tight, her next words escaping before she had the chance to think them through, fueled by her nerves, by her need to know what he was thinking. What he might ask of her. "Are we about to consummate this marriage?"

"What?"

"You said…you said you were so eager to consummate, and you're having my things sent here. You want to get on that?"

"I think not," he said, dark brows drawn together, his grasp of her sarcasm clearly loose at best. "Certainly not tonight."

"What exactly is the marriage going to be? And if not tonight, do you see it happening in the future?"

"I wanted to present a certain front to the press. That's all. Per the agreement we signed this afternoon, we have to stay married for five years before the deal is finalized, or ownership of the company defaults to…"

"It would go to Alex, wouldn't it?"

"Considering your father's health? And if he stays with your sister that long? Likely. That means whatever happens, this marriage is not going to be quick and easy. Even then… even then perhaps it would be best for us to consider making this arrangement permanent. However, you have just stepped in at the last minute—I'm hardly going to force you upstairs to ravish you."

Her breath caught in her throat. "That's not what I…"

"You were the one who asked," he said.

"Just making things clear. We *did* get married today, and you did make a comment about consummation," she threw back.

"So you're offering me your body, as well? Right now? How about here? I could dismiss my staff, or hell, they're paid to look the other way, why bother dismissing them? Would you like me to tear your dress off and have you against the wall?"

His voice was rough, unsteady, like nothing she'd heard from him before.

She'd pushed him to a place she hadn't intended, the conversation not seeming as absurd as she'd imagined when she'd first spoken the words. There was an edge of danger, reality to all of this. She'd never seen him like this. This close to losing grip on his control.

Being in the path of it was almost frightening. But she was close to the edge, too. She felt vulnerable and at a disadvantage, two things she hated. And pushing at his control made her feel like she had even more of it.

"I could, Leah. Some women like that. Or, if you prefer I could take you upstairs and make you my wife for real. But the thing is, I would be doing it because I'm angry. At her. I would think of her. She is the only woman I have ever loved, and she walked away from me on our wedding day to be with someone else. Someone I despise. If I were with you," he continued, his voice rough, "it would be to get back at her. I'm a man—never forget that. I could think of anything and get it up while I parted your thighs. It would hardly make you special. Yes, I could have you. But the question is, right now, would you want me?"

His words shouldn't hurt. But they were so cold, so hard, they cut through her defenses, straight to her heart.

But she wouldn't let him see.

"You loved her?" she asked.

"I *love* her," he said. "Years of loving someone isn't erased by one act. As convenient as it might be."

"I suppose not."

The whole thing made her pride burn. How adamant he was about not wanting her. And at the same time, she looked into his dark eyes and realized his own pride was savaged. Realized how hard this was for him.

He'd lost the woman he loved. He had married someone else. Someone he had no feelings for. He was looking at her and seeing a broken dream. No matter how strong her armor, she felt the impact of that like a battering ram against the steel.

"I think I'll go to my room then, since you're not interested in a quick consummation," she said, her tone tart, her expression as neutral as she could get it. "Good night."

He nodded once. "Tomorrow, we'll come up with a plan."

"I look forward to it."

Maybe a night of sleep would help her figure out what she was doing. Help her figure out what had happened to her.

And what they were going to do about it.

CHAPTER THREE

AJAX WOKE UP without a hangover. Because he hadn't been able to bring himself to drink. As Leah had observed, he didn't drink alcohol. He prized his control far too much. Vice was the downfall of man.

The need for a certain high, whether it be from alcohol, drugs or sex was responsible for much of the evil in the world. Something he'd lived at one point in time. Something he'd witnessed in horrific detail. And something he'd done his best to destroy, even if it was only one small piece of it.

He did not let vice own him. Not anymore. He didn't even give it a foothold on his soul.

Rachel leaving wasn't reason enough to give that up. But, *Theos,* it burned his pride. He hadn't imagined pride had such a place in his life, but apparently it did.

He stalked down the stairs, wearing nothing but a pair of black pants, not bothering to get dressed. He was not in the mood to deal with much of anything or anyone.

He stalked through the house and into the dining room, where the one thing he couldn't avoid dealing with was sitting, perched on the edge of a chair, a cup of coffee in her hands, her whiskey-colored eyes round. She looked very like a lost child. And he had no patience to deal with it. Any of it.

"I trust you slept well?" he asked, attempting civility because regardless of his feelings it was the appropriate way to treat one's wife. Or so he imagined.

"Not in the least," she returned, her voice crisp.

Her dark, curly hair was tied up, a little puffball on top of her head, and she was wearing a baggy sweater, the sort that made generous breasts blend into a woman's waist, concealing any nice attributes her figure might possess.

Not that he cared. Her figure was the least of his concerns.

"If the mattress is a problem for you, a new one can be ordered."

"I don't think it was the mattress so much as the unexpected acquisition of a husband, but I could be wrong. Maybe the sleep surface was too firm."

"You seem a bit off this morning."

Her fingers flexed around the cup, giving the impression of claws. "Do I?"

He found he wanted to push her. He was spoiling for a fight and he couldn't say why. He'd never tried to pick a fight for no reason in his life. He'd grown up in such a volatile environment, and he'd learned early on that the quickest way to an early death, or at the very least a world of pain, was to cause trouble.

Keeping his head down, doing as he was told, all while planning, planning and strategizing, finding a way out—that was the way to survive.

Today, he didn't just want to survive. He wanted to fight. It seemed a perfect substitute for getting drunk.

"Hardly the blushing bride," he said. "You look like hell, to be honest."

"Are you always such an ass?"

Good. She was getting angry. That was what he wanted. What he craved right now.

"Perhaps you've never had the chance to really get to know me before now, though, in the interest of full disclosure, I am in a bloody bad mood this morning."

"I'm glad to know this at least qualifies as a bad mood. Why are you taking it out on me?"

He didn't know. He didn't know why his control was fraying. Why he wasn't being self-contained. Why he was suddenly incapable of maintaining an iron grip on emotion. "Because you're here, *agape mou*. The lucky replacement bride."

"Would my sister be on the receiving end of this treatment? If so, I can certainly see why she ran out on the wedding."

"If your sister were here, I daresay we might still be in bed. And I would certainly be in a better mood."

Something flashed in her amber eyes that he didn't like. Pain? He had gone a step too far in venting his anger. Saying things he wasn't even certain he felt just to simply let the anger continue. Indulging emotion for once rather than sublimating it.

He didn't know how sleeping with Rachel would make him feel. The idea of it…it had made him tense. But that was to be expected, considering the nature of their relationship, and everything else.

But sex with his wife was half the appeal of marriage to him. Everything in life had a place. A fire burning in the fireplace was all well and good. But when the fire spread outside of it, that became a problem.

Yes, things had their place. And he had been looking forward to having everything where it was meant to be.

But now the plan was upended. And he wasn't certain of his next move. For a man who liked to plan ahead, it was disconcerting at best.

"I am sorry," he bit out. "That was crass of me. I'm frustrated, and it has very little to do with you personally." Except, somehow, the frustration, or rather, his inability to manage it, did seem tied to her.

She blinked, and he could see some of the tension release from her body. "Of course not. Of course. None of this really has anything to do with me personally, does it?"

"I'm glad you have such a good grasp on the situation."

"I don't, Ajax, not even close. What, if you'll excuse me, in hell do you want from me? Do you want me to just hang out for the next five years, living in your house, and then go on my merry way like none of this ever happened?"

"Clearly that cannot happen," he said.

"Clearly?"

"I would not disrespect you that way."

"Oh, honey, after all the crap you said to me last night, you're saying you don't want to disrespect me?"

"I was angry."

"Great. So was I. So am I."

"I apologized."

"An apology isn't a magic healing potion, it's just a bandage. It covered up some of my pique nicely, but it's hardly healed."

"Well," he said, shifting his weight to the balls of his feet, "perhaps we can set it aside in the interest of figuring out what it is we need to do?"

"All right," she said.

"We're married, and we really had no other choice, all things considered."

"Yes."

"And we have to stay married for at least five years."

"Uh-huh," she said.

"And I planned on marrying into your family. On keeping Holt in your family. I want to be married. I would like to have children. A real marriage suits me."

"Oh, indeed?"

"Yes. I wanted a wife. A wife was always my end goal."

"Except she was tall, blond, a size four and named Rachel?"

"Yes," he said, teeth gritted. "But in the end, what difference does it make?"

"Is that really how you feel? Do I matter that little… Does she?"

"It isn't you, Leah. I have had a plan for my life from the moment I left my father's house. I planned to work my way up, and I did. To make a new start for myself with nothing but hard work, honesty. To never, ever set foot back on the path

I was born to walk. And I have done that. I met your family, and your father and mother made me feel welcomed. Like a son. And then there was Rachel. Everything fit. It all seemed perfect. I knew the first time I saw her she was my end goal. That she would be my wife. She is the first part of my plan that has dared not to fall into place."

"Yes, well, that's because she's a woman and not a business venture."

"But we would have been perfect," he said.

"No, Ajax, you wouldn't have been. You would have been fine, but not perfect. Because she's not perfect. *You* certainly aren't."

"But it made sense," he said. "In my head…in my head she made everything fall into place."

"She's not a business venture, and she's not an ideal, either."

He rubbed his temples with his fingertips. "I know that."

"Well, you don't seem to. You talk like marriage to her was your end goal and then…and then what? It would just be perfect? Your life would suddenly be perfect?"

"I can't… It's hard to… I've been working, Leah, so hard, all of my life. I came to your family's home, and your parents treated me more like a son than an employee. They took me in, gave me focus and purpose. Your father set me on this path. He taught me things, taught me how to be a man, to be strong. He gave me goals. He sent me to school. I have been walking that path he set me on, tirelessly, never looking away from the goal, from the end."

"To where you would make Holt continue on for him. Where you would be part of our family."

"I've been walking for a long time," he said.

"And then you reach the end and you rest?"

"And then maybe I don't have to work so hard to stay in control all the damn time because I'll have arrived at a more stable point," he bit out. "My…everything would be in place."

Because things weren't now. He'd made money, obtained

power and connections. He'd used all of the resources at his disposal to bring down his father's drug and human trafficking ring. And he still couldn't rest. He still didn't feel he could stop working. Stop trying to distance himself from his past.

From all he had done.

"Why do you need to hang on to control so tightly, Ajax?" she asked, her eyes filled with…sympathy. Pity. If she knew who she was talking to, if she knew the beast that lived inside him, she wouldn't look at him like that.

He stood and started to pace the room. "It's nothing. This is nothing. It can still be fixed."

Leah studied him, noticed the tension in his jaw, in the lines of his body. He was uncomfortable, and thrown off. And she had to take into account that he could very well be heartbroken.

He said he loved Rachel. But for the first time she wondered. Wondered if he'd ever known her really, or if she'd just been symbolic for him.

"I have a plan, Leah," he said.

She crossed her arms beneath her breasts. "Oh, good. Let's hear it."

He stopped moving, his hands locked behind his back. "First, we must show a united front. I am taking over a massive corporation here, changing the layout in some respects. We need to show solidarity—I will not appear weak."

"No, you wouldn't." She couldn't imagine him appearing weak anyway.

"And I will not be seen as a man forced into this situation."

"Pride is a beautiful thing. At least I think it is. I don't know that I have any left."

"I find myself in short supply, as well." His expression turned fierce. "And I will turn my focus to helping mass produce Leah's Lollies products, as soon as time allows."

She ignored the leap her heart took and looked down at her fingernails. "Payment for services rendered?"

He looked stricken for a moment, and his face paled. Then,

as soon as the reaction occurred, he covered it again. "This is not that sort of arrangement. You are my wife. Not a woman I have purchased."

"And how long will I be your wife?" That was the one bit left undiscussed. Undecided. Would she be his wife on paper, or in reality.

"I made vows," he said. "I intend to honor them. Do you?"

"In what regard?"

"In all regards. What's the sense in divorce when this union could serve us both?"

"We're missing the love bit."

"You don't strike me as the kind of woman who's overly romantic."

He was right. Now. It hadn't always been true. But over time…over time all that sunny optimism had bled from her, an open vein that had truly begun the hemorrhage the moment she'd first seen Rachel standing by Ajax. The perfect couple, so beautiful, so poised. The embodiment of her heartbreak.

"I'm not especially. But what do I get out of this, Ajax? Beyond a husband who is bitter toward me and will think of other women if we ever make love?"

He looked her over, slowly, and something changed in his eyes, heat sparking in their dark depths. Heat that lit an answering fire in her stomach. Heat that reminded her just how strong a pull Ajax had over body.

"What do I get?" she repeated, her voice a whisper.

"What do you want?"

As they'd both pointed out, their pride was all but destroyed. So why cling to it now? She wasn't going to sit around, angry over not getting what she wanted because she hadn't asked for it. She was going to make her own demands. If he wanted a marriage, she would give him a marriage.

She had her armor now—she didn't need love. She didn't want it. Didn't want emotion. But a business partnership, cemented by marriage, that she could handle. And sex with Ajax?

Well, she was attracted to him. And frankly, she was over being a virgin. This was a convenient way to deal with both her attraction to him and the virginity. A win-win situation, really.

And yeah, kissing him had knocked her defenses a bit, but it wouldn't happen again. Not when she was the one making demands. Not when it was expected.

She would make this a marriage that would work for her, not just for him. To hell with his plans, she had plans of her own. If he said no, maybe he'd release her.

But if he said yes...

"If we're going to stay married, then I want a marriage. I want you, in my bed, every night, and never with another woman. I want you to support me personally and professionally. I won't live a half life forever because of a rash decision I made."

"Naturally," he said, "I want children, as I said already. It has always been a part of my plan. And you?"

She hadn't given it a lot of thought, because marriage had seemed a far-off event. But part of her had always taken for granted that she would be a mother someday.

"I want them," she said, trying not to think too deeply about it.

"And as you are my wife, sleeping with you seems only logical. What is the point of seeking physical release elsewhere?"

"I'm relieved you feel that way." Though not overly flattered. "Better for our health, wellness and media image, I imagine."

"However, I stand by my original statement. You and I may figure out the finer points of our relationship after this whole thing has been smoothed over in the public arena. While we're attending events as blissful newlyweds, it would be best if our personal relationship was kept as simple as possible. I don't want Christofides thinking there might be a weakness he can exploit. I don't want him to get desperate and decide he should come and seduce you."

"Me?"

"He may very well if he sees that Rachel is a dead end to destroying my goals."

"Oh, seduced for revenge from my marriage that's for business only. I am such a lucky girl."

"It's the reality, Leah. I don't say it to insult."

"Of course not."

"Also in favor of waiting, you need time to adjust."

"Time to adjust? What do you... What?"

"Yesterday you were to be my sister-in-law—today, you're my wife, I doubt you're prepared for the change. In spite of what I said about you not being a prisoner, and while I know you entered into the arrangement of your own free will, it was an emotionally heightened moment, and there were a lot of reasons why our marriage made sense in terms of business. But just because all of that made sense, does not mean you and I make sense as a couple. Naturally, you will need time before you're ready to consummate."

She blinked, unable to wrap her mind around what he'd just said. "Need...time?"

"Naturally."

She felt raw. Her ego wounded and scrubbed with salt. And now he was telling her what she wanted. To hell with that. "You have no idea what I'm ready for, what I want. Don't you dare think you can tell me. I'm quite okay with sex, the idea of us having sex sits very well with me. I didn't agree to marry you thoughtlessly, I know what being married means."

"You're young, Leah, naive. I will not take advantage of that. A little time for everyone to adjust to the situation is necessary."

She felt defiant now, her pride, that pride she'd decided only a moment ago she didn't care much about. "I don't need time, Ajax. You could have me on this table right now if you want. Think of my sister. Hell, think of England, I don't care. I know what I want. I said exactly what I wanted. I want you."

The words hung, heavy in the silence of the room. She'd admitted it. That she wanted him. That she wanted to sleep with him. Something about the admission made her feel stronger. Made her feel like her armor was back in place.

"The thing is," he said, his voice a growl, "I don't want you. You are a child to me. I look at you and I see a girl. I do not see a woman."

His words didn't hurt as badly as they might have, not with her armor on. Not when she could see, so easily, that he was lashing out because of pain in him. Not because of her. "I'm twenty-three. I am not a child."

The anger in his eyes dissipated, and he just looked tired. "I…I have not had time to adjust to the new plan."

Just then she found it hard to be mad at him, in spite of the cutting edge to his words. "And the plan is everything, right?" A new thing she'd learned about him in the past twenty-four hours.

"Yes, Leah, the plan is damn well everything," he said, each syllable rough and hard. "How do you navigate life without one?"

"Follow your heart. Your passions…"

"Passion," he spat, as though the word tasted terrible on his tongue, "is the single most destructive element in life I can think of."

"You don't feel passion?"

"I deny it."

"Not even for Rachel?"

He shook his head, dark eyes blank. "For nothing. For no one."

"I thought you loved her."

"What does that have to do with passion?" he asked.

"Everything."

He shook his head. "That's where you're wrong, Leah. Passion is all about self. All about pleasing yourself. And that path…that path can get very dark."

And then Ajax turned and walked out of the room, and the last bit of fantasy and mist that had hung before her eyes evaporated.

There was nothing more than cold reality and the realization that the man she'd thought she'd known for most of her life was nothing more than a stranger.

CHAPTER FOUR

AJAX NEEDED A new plan. All things considered, the plan wasn't as derailed as it seemed at first. He was still married to a Holt heiress, and he still possessed Holt Enterprises. He had a wife, albeit not the wife he'd wanted, but from that wife he would still get the children he needed to continue on his legacy. A legacy he had reason to feel proud of. In theory.

As for Rachel…his feelings for her were not essential to the plan. Love, however nice it had been as an idea, was not essential to the plan.

As far as the sex went…it had been Rachel in his mind for so long, it was hard to transfer the desire to Leah. Leah, who was ten years his junior. Leah, who had so much softness in her. At least, she'd had it in her. Back when they used to talk, she'd been so open. She'd connected with him on a level that was so different from anyone else. But in terms of wanting her? That could wait. Until he'd got used to the idea at least.

Sex was, by the account of some, a basic human need, much like eating and drinking.

He disagreed. He'd done well without it for more years than he cared to recall. Just as he'd never needed alcohol. He valued control over all else, and anything that might distract him had been weeded out as unnecessary. That said, he couldn't lie. He'd been looking forward to that part of marriage.

The acknowledgment of it nearly made him laugh. He liked

to think of himself as being entirely above desire, but that wasn't the case. He was simply very good at keeping it on a leash. The hours he spent working out late at night were a testament to the fact that he was sublimating desire, rather than absent of it completely.

Leah was his wife. His real wife, per the new plan outlined this morning.

He repeated that, over and over in his mind, trying to make it real. Trying to incorporate it into his vision for the future. Trying to figure out where she fit in with his end goal.

There was a fund-raiser tonight, for one of Ajax's favored charities and that meant that the personal things would have to go on hold for a moment. He would worry about the physical piece of the marriage later. For tonight, they would simply have to put on a show for the people and press attending the fund-raiser.

He closed his thoughts down, narrowed his focus. He walked through the house, his footsteps loud on the tile. He hadn't seen Leah since their argument that morning.

He finally found her in the study, her laptop on her lap, dark hair piled on her head. She'd ditched the baggy sweatshirt in favor of a T-shirt and yoga pants. She had a pen in her mouth, four bags of candy in front of her, with the highly recognizable pink-and-green-polka-dot logo associated with Leah's Lollies, and she was typing furiously.

"I see your things arrived."

She paused and looked up, golden eyes round. Then she straightened and tugged the pen from between her lips. "Yeah, and I had a few issues to deal with."

"Chocolate emergency?"

"You'd be surprised. Some quality control stuff. I had to go and grab a few random bags of product to run an unofficial check. I haven't found any problems, but I guess some deformed butterscotch high heels went through to the boutiques.

I'm not very thrilled about it. Actually, Holt is my manufacturer, you know. I pay them, it's all aboveboard, not a nepotism thing."

"So you're a client in addition to the Holt Corporation holding shares."

"Indeed."

"But now you've married into part ownership of Holt. I would suppose that means the shares are passing back to you in many ways. And now you own more of Leah's Lollies."

"One of my wins. One of the very few."

"Perhaps few in this situation, but in general, it seems you've had quite a few. This is what you always said you wanted. You were always telling me about your ideas for a store. Pink, you said. It would be pink. Now they make paint that comes in Leah Pink, don't they?"

She cocked her head to the side, a line creasing her forehead. "How did you know that?"

"I read about your work." If there was a news article about her on a website, he clicked it, naturally. And occasionally, he was enticed to do an internet search to see how things were doing. Because it was nice to see how things were going for her. Because she was Rachel's sister. It was only natural.

"Oh. Huh." She looked back down at her screen, then back up. "Sorry, did you need something?"

"I forgot to mention that there is a charity event tonight Rachel and I planned on attending. Given the circumstances surrounding our marriage I'm certain the media will be there, and they will be waiting for the story."

"You mean…we have to go to this?"

"Yes. If we miss it…if we miss it we're inviting speculation. I will not give that to the public. I'll not give it to Christofides."

She put her hand on her forehead. "Oh, jeez."

"Yes. Have you got a gown?"

"I have several. It's a bad habit of mine, buying dresses that

I don't really have any reason to wear. Don't judge. Everyone needs a hobby."

"Well, in this case it seems it's served us both well."

"I suppose."

He looked at her, and more specifically, at the way she wasn't looking at him. Not really. Not the way she usually did. Usually when he looked at her, he saw the girl with sparkling eyes.

She looked different now. No glitter. Her face a bit more drawn, sculpted. And she seemed tired. He'd never seen her looking tired before. Leah was a woman of endless energy, at least she'd always seemed so to him. A constant sugar high that never seemed to end.

But it had ended sometime. She was so much harder now, but he hadn't seen it till the past twenty-four hours.

"You will need to be ready by six."

"Okay," she said, not looking back up at him.

"And you will need to not look like you're contemplating putting my head on a pike."

"No guarantees, darling," she said, her words carrying a razor-sharp edge.

"We're supposed to be newlyweds."

"We *are* newlyweds. Marriage is hard. First twelve hours is the hardest." She continued typing away, not looking at him.

"So it seems. But we must attempt to make this look real."

"It is real. As you pointed out, I signed a license, I took vows. It's all real, man."

"You know what I mean."

"Love," she said, looking up at him. "You want it to look like love. You want me to gaze at you in adoration so no one doubts my happiness or your penis size—I got it."

His throat tightened, a strange kind of heat prickling his face. "You do not normally talk this way."

"Maybe I do, Ajax…how would you know? When was the

last time we had a real conversation? Six years ago? We don't know each other. I didn't think you were as big of a jerk as you played it this morning, but hey, I learned something new. And you think I'm a child, but you're wrong about that, too. We're learning new things. What do you know about that?"

"I think you're having a fit because you're angry at me."

She shot him a deadly glare. "Fits are what little girls have. I'm a woman, I'm in a mood."

"Is that it, then? I'm not accustomed to dealing with women and their moods."

"And why is that?"

"Because I'm not accustomed to living with a woman. When a woman is in a mood, I am able to avoid her."

"Oh, how charming. You only deal with them when they're all sweet for you."

"That is not it. I was not being insulting, I was making an observation."

"Oh." She looked down again. "Well, anyway… Look, I get that tonight is a big deal. I don't want to screw it up, either. I'm already being called the backup bride by the press, and I'm not all that enamored with the title so it suits me just fine if everyone thinks we've fallen into a mad passionate affair."

"That is part of the plan. My plan."

"The new plan?"

"We did need one."

"You know…everyone will think that we betrayed Rachel."

"Will they?"

"With a bride switch two hours before the wedding? It's either she betrayed you or you betrayed her."

"Betrayal doesn't need to come into it. What if we realized we really loved each other, while Rachel and I were merely marrying for convenience?"

Leah felt like she was being stabbed in the heart, slowly, each new inch he pushed the blade in burning fresh like a new cut. And she didn't know why it hurt. Why, after managing as well as she had with every other slight, this went so deep.

It was nothing to do with Ajax specifically, but with coming in second to Rachel again. Every boy she'd ever dated had nearly got whiplash watching Rachel walk by. And Ajax…Ajax had preferred her, too.

Her mother and father had always loved them both, and treated them both well, but Rachel had an ease about her. An elegance that people responded to instantly. She was beautiful, poised, long and lean.

Leah had always been awkward by comparison. Her life had not been the social whirlwind Rachel's had been, not ever. There had never been too many party invites, or lots of cute boys. She was the Other Holt. She was the incidental, the afterthought. And that realization always hurt, no matter how many layers of armor she put between herself and the world.

"Do you think people will buy it?"

"Why not?" he asked, shrugging.

"What about what Rachel might say?"

"It's Christofides I worry about. What has she told him? And what might he entice her to say?"

"Oh. Yes. That's right. The evil boyfriend of doom."

"Perhaps one of us should…"

"Me," she said. The idea of Ajax calling Rachel was a bit much to handle. "I'll do it." She closed the laptop and stood, tucking her computer under her arm, ignoring the slight awkwardness of the position. "And then I'll…get ready for tonight."

"Okay."

"Great."

Something changed in his expression, a strange look in his eyes. "Tell her…tell her I said hi."

She clutched the computer more tightly to her body, and tried to ignore the strange wave of sadness that crested and crashed over her. For him. For her. "I will."

* * *

She shut the door to her new room behind her and took her phone from her bedside table. She clicked on the text her sister had sent yesterday and hit reply.

You ok?

She paced, the phone in her hand, and when it buzzed, she jumped a little before looking at the screen.

I'm good. Is Jax ok?

Her sister's nickname for Ajax always made Leah bristle a little. Perhaps because it was a reminder of their special relationship.

He's ok. Leah sucked in a sharp breath and typed the rest of the message. He married me, BTW.

She winced and hit Send. Then waited. Her sister's response came quickly.

Holy crap. Just saw it on Google.

Leah waited for more. For anything, but there was nothing. So she started a new message.

You're happy? You didn't love Ajax did you?

Her phone pinged.

Not like that. Not the kind you need to marry a guy. You know?

Do you love Alex? Leah sent the message.
The reply took longer than the ones before. I need to be with Alex.

No declarations of love. Or even of happiness. It made Leah feel heavy

You're really okay?

I'm tougher than you think.

If anyone asks—Leah stopped typing and thought for a second before continuing—tell them that you and Ajax were marrying for the company. Tell them we fell in love and you let us get married.

Why?

Leah blew out an exasperated breath.

For his pride.

Tell him I am sorry. And I'll tell the press and curious people whatever you want. I have my own problems to deal with.

I'll tell him. And he says hi. She hit Send on it before she could delete the last part. She almost wanted to. Almost wanted to hide that bit of his vulnerability.

Thanks. I don't know when I'll be back. There are things that I need to take care of. I love you.

Leah sighed. Me too.

Leah threw her phone down onto the bed and let out a long growl. She noticed her sister did not return Ajax's hi. Which she found annoying, for no good reason. She was trapped between feeling protective of him and feeling angry at him, and somewhere between that, she was just mad for herself. Upset about the entire situation.

Well, there was no time for that. It didn't matter how she

felt, not right now. She took a deep breath and stalked over to her closet, which had been all arranged for her over the course of the day by Ajax's very helpful staff.

Nope. No sulking allowed. She had a dress to choose, and she had to look appropriately amazing. She had to get her mask on. Because no matter the story, she was still going to be Ajax Kouros's backup bride.

Because it was going to be a high school flashback all over again. Instead of *Who Wore it Better?* It would be *Who Hung on Ajax's Arm Better?*

Hmph. She was done with this.

If she had anything to do with it, she would be Ajax Kouros's fabulously sexy backup bride, who didn't flinch against the flashbulbs, or the comparisons. She only hoped her defenses held.

CHAPTER FIVE

THE WOMAN WHO walked downstairs to greet him that night was an entirely different woman from the one who had been on the couch in the study earlier.

Frizzy, mahogany curls had been tamed into softer waves, whiskey-colored eyes were lined with dark makeup, making them glow. And unlike her T-shirt and sweatpants, her black dress didn't hang off her curves. The one-shouldered, Grecian-inspired gown molded to her curves, revealing no skin but giving everyone an insight into the figure beneath.

Her lips were painted cherry-red, the perfect accent to a showstopping ensemble. She was playing her part well. She looked every inch the woman in love, the woman trying to appeal to her new husband.

It wasn't just the clothes that made her seem different. It was the way she looked at him. Or rather it was the way she didn't look at him. Her chin was tilted up, her expression cool. Haughty. Always Leah Holt had looked at him with a special glitter in her eyes. No one else had ever looked at him that way. No one else had ever smiled at him as she had, with open affection and warmth. No one else had ever left chocolate on his desk, just because.

He'd lost that somewhere along the way. And it wasn't until now that he missed it.

"You look beautiful," he said. It was true. She did. He realized the truth of it as he spoke it. He'd always put up a block where Leah was concerned. She was too young for him to look at her like that.

And he had been looking at one woman for years, a woman who was wholly different in looks and personality, and it was not an immediate thing, to want to look at anyone else.

Though Leah's transformation was startling enough that he had to look, was powerless to do anything else.

Startling, not necessarily welcome. It seemed to him that the chill emanating from her like mist over frost would be obvious to anyone who saw them.

And then she smiled, red lips parting, and he could see how false it was.

"Let's go then," she said, extending her arm.

He took it, drawing her close to his side and leading her out the front door where the car was already waiting.

She leaned into her step, her body coming into fuller contact with his. He paused, and for a full second, he was unable to look away from the lush outline of her breasts. Fire kicked through him, a quick burst of it, like kerosene being thrown on a match. It was like nothing he'd felt for years. Nothing he'd let himself feel.

Nothing he'd felt since he was a boy. Surrounded by all of the women he could have. No one to tell him no. Until…

He let out the breath he hadn't realized he'd been holding. No. He wouldn't think of that. He wouldn't look at her that way.

He gritted his teeth and moved away from her, rounding the car to open her door for her before going to the driver's side and getting in.

They might have been a couple who'd been married for years. They were comfortably silent on the ride, Leah keeping her eyes on her phone while he kept his eyes on the road, taking the time to enjoy the way his car handled the turns.

It was one of his few indulgences. Cars. He liked different cars. The way they handled, the rate at which they accelerated. Driving was the one time he could keep a blank mind. The one time he could loosen his focus on the plan and simply see what was in front of him.

He was almost feeling relaxed by the time they pulled up to the front of the hotel where the event was being held. This could work. This sort of side-by-side existence.

It was only when he got out of the car and rounded to her side, when the flashbulbs started going off, and when he reached in and took her hand, helping her out, when he saw the frost in her eyes, that he felt the ease slip.

The blast of light from the camera revealed a flatness in her gaze. And tomorrow everyone would see it. They would have to be blind to miss it.

It took him a moment to realize she was smiling. Because he had only been looking at her eyes. And there was no smile there.

"Ready, darling husband?" she asked, the brittle steel in her voice carrying over to her posture, her body rigid, tense.

"Ready, *agape mou*." He slid his arm around her waist, pulled her up against the side of his body. He'd held her close yesterday, kissed her lips. But then he'd been high on adrenaline, completely disconnected from his body. He'd been focused only on one thing: getting out of the wedding venue before questions had started pouring in.

And he'd succeeded. But there had been no time then, to think of her lips, of her curves, how soft and warm she felt up against him.

Suddenly it was the only thing he could think about. From shouting at her this morning, to the wave of lust he was battling with tonight, Leah seemed to make a mockery of his control.

Marriage had been intended to make everything easier, but so far, his was just making things more difficult. Made him feel like he was being dragged backward. Back to the place he'd started. Back to the man he'd been.

Back into hell. Where he wasn't one of those suffering eternal damnation, no. That would be too kind. In his hell, he was the one meting it out.

He closed his eyes for a moment, blocking out the camera flashes. Blocking out the memories.

He led her up the steps and into the hotel, all the while smiling, at her, not at the photographers. It would look much better in the photos. Make a better headline.

He would close it off. The desire. The heat. He moved his fingers, gently, over the indent of her waist. He was used to going places with Rachel like this, with his arm around her like this. But Leah was different. Her waist nipped in a bit more, her hips flaring out wider, where Rachel was flat and slender.

An observation, that was all. And yet he did find it interesting. He moved his hand down slightly, to the rounded curve of her hip. Yes, very interesting.

"Do you have to do that?" she said, her voice choked.

"Do what?"

"Touch me like that?"

"You are my wife. And if I'm not remembering wrongly, you told me yesterday that you wanted me in your bed. Every night. In light of that I should not think my hand on your clothed body would be an issue."

"I didn't think we were worrying about our personal relationship until after we got our public one under control."

"This is our public relationship, *agape*."

"Sorry," she said. "Felt like personal territory."

"And it disturbs you?" he asked. God knew it disturbed him. This entire change in her physical appearance disturbed him. She wasn't conforming to the box he'd put her into, and he didn't like it in the least.

They passed through the double doors that led to the glittering antechamber of the hotel ballroom. The white marble floor was edged in black, the design echoed on the walls. White pillars were stationed throughout, a nod, albeit a highly glossed one, to an ancient Grecian temple.

"Yes. No. I don't know."

"You are prepared to sleep with me and yet personal disturbs you?"

"Will you stop bringing that up?" she hissed. "This is not about our personal lives. This is our public life, right?" She smiled at a passing photographer.

"Unless our personal life starts to affect the public facade, which was the entire point of us leaving it as it is for now."

"I don't know, seems like it was never the best idea. I'm not sure our personal life is all that great."

"I'm not sure we have one."

He felt her go stiff beneath his touch. "No. I daresay that is what you'd think." Her words were as stilted as her posture. "After all, I've never been to your house. When you practically grew up living in mine."

"Your father's."

"How many Christmas parties have you been to at my penthouse in New York?" she asked.

"A few," he said.

"Yes, and yet I had never been to your house once until yesterday. So of course you don't think we have a personal relationship. I guess I'm the one who thought we did. The one who thought we at least had respect between us. I won't be so stupid again." She pulled a glass of champagne off the tray of a passing waiter and took a few fortifying sips.

A couple of businessmen stopped them and started talking about the new acquisition of Holt with an enthusiasm that only those in the acquire and assimilate game could convey over that kind of topic.

Normally, Leah would have got in on the conversation. She was interested in business and particularly in Holt. Right now though, all she could really do was nod along while she forced champagne down her throat. A delicate balance. Don't drink too much, inhibitions might lower. But a certain amount was required to weather something like this.

She knew this game, this game of putting on armor. Playing polished and playing tough. But things were slipping when she was with him. And it sucked. Old feelings were getting stirred up, getting a second life thanks to all of the close proximity. And she didn't want that.

I want you. In my bed, every night.

Yes, she'd really said that to him.

She kept on smiling. Why was she doing this now? Why was she breaking down now? With him on her arm and people all around them?

She sucked in a breath and held it. She was fine. She would be fine. She'd spent her life proving herself. She hadn't excelled in school, but she'd been able to shine in business, and shine she had. No, she wasn't the most beautiful Holt heiress, but she had her own charisma. And she had business savvy. And she'd done whatever was necessary to get herself to the point where the media no longer called her an ugly duckling, but a socialite turned businesswoman.

She hadn't done those things by being sweet and open and leaving candy on people's desks. She'd changed. She'd learned to protect herself. And she would keep on doing that.

But she *would* have him. Because she wanted him. Because there had to be a perk to being trapped in this marriage with him, and if access to his body was the perk? She was more than happy with that.

Yes. She was. Indeed.

It wasn't about emotions. It wasn't about the ache in her chest that had shown up the day before the wedding and had insisted on sticking around.

Sex wouldn't hurt. It would feel good. At least, she imagined it would.

It was probably best they were waiting. She needed to get hold of her virginal nerves and beat them into submission. She'd shown him enough of her vulnerability when she'd been a lovelorn teenager. No, he didn't get any more. She was *taking* now.

So there.

The men, who had been droning all through her drinking and nodding along and fake smiling at whoever passed, were done now and were headed away from them. She was pretty sure she'd forgotten to say goodbye, but she'd been too lost in her own thoughts.

"So what now?" she asked. "Make more small talk? Smile for the camera? Do a dance for all of our admirers?" She gestured out toward the dance floor.

"I don't dance," he said, straightening his shoulders.

Just looking at him hurt. He was the epitome of masculine beauty in his tux, dark hair short and neat, not a hair out of place. And yet, there was something about him, no matter how contained he looked, that hinted at something darker beneath the surface. Something frozen in a block of ice. All it would take was a little heat and...

"We should dance," she said, lifting her chin, feeling defiant. Feeling angry. At herself mostly, for being such a stupid... girl where he was concerned. A look at his powerful physique and she got all fluttery. If he flashed ab she'd probably die.

Pathetic, woman. Pathetic.

"I already told you," he said, his voice hushed, "I don't..."

"But I do. And you deprived me of a dance on our wedding day since you were so eager to have me alone." She arched a brow. "You wouldn't deny your bride her first dance with her husband, would you?"

Something, she didn't know what, compelled her to push further, harder. Maybe it was the fact that he was acting like the wounded party. Like this wasn't a major deal for her. Like it was okay to just turn her down in front of all these people. She took a step toward him, placed her palm flat against his chest.

He didn't feel like ice. No, not even close. He was fire

against her skin, and with very little trouble she knew he could melt her.

"Dance with me," she whispered, keeping her eyes trained on his.

He caught her wrist, a strange look in his eye, one of curiosity. Detached, but present. He bent his head, his eyes never leaving hers, and lifted her arm to his lips, pressing a kiss to the sensitive underside of her wrist.

It sent a shiver over her veins, back to her heart, which jolted in response. Her stomach tightened to the point of pain, breathing a luxury her body couldn't afford. Not at the moment, not when all of her was focused on Ajax's lips against her bare skin.

"I think it would be best if I waited to hold you like that until we're in private," he said, his tone intimate, husky, and yet, she was aware of the people that were standing close, potentially overhearing. "I do not trust myself where you're concerned."

Everything in her shook. Breathing becoming impossible. "All right then," she said, her voice a choked whisper. More weakness. She hated it. "But you'd better make it very worth my while when we're in private. Don't make promises you can't back up."

"Never, *agape*. Never."

The evening wound down with more small talk, more champagne, more little touches that were dissolving her cool by inches.

And by the time they were driving back to his villa, she was just exhausted. Emotionally. Physically. She wasn't sure how she was supposed to endure this…this marriage. Two days in and she was sure she'd aged ten years.

It was tiring to have to cling to her armor so tightly. Over the years it had become a second skin. Effortless to wear. But now? Now it felt like she was clinging to it for dear life.

She closed her eyes and rested her head on the seat as Ajax maneuvered the car out of the city and onto the back roads. She tried to just breathe steadily. She tried the whole way back.

She tried when he pulled the car up to the house and killed the engine. She tried as they walked inside, side by side, not touching at all.

It was dark in the house. She noticed that Ajax kept a minimum of staff, and that they all clocked out at the end of normal workday hours. Dinners were delivered. Ajax seemed to isolate himself as much as possible, and not by accident.

Weird that he'd wanted to get married at all, but then, that was love for you.

It was why she'd sworn off it so long ago.

Feelings. Feelings were stupid. Feelings were awful. She didn't want to think about feelings. Not the emotional kind.

She turned to look at him, and the heat that had been on a low simmer in her blood all night started firing again, anger stoking the flame, sending the simmer into a rolling boil that she could hardly contain.

She curled her hands into fists as they passed through the entryway, both heading toward the stairs and to their separate rooms. And then she stopped.

"Ajax," she said.

He stopped and turned to look at her, and then the world burned down to nothing but him. There was no time to think, to doubt, to worry. None of that stupid, aching emotion. Because this wasn't desire anymore. It was need. The need to gain some control. To make him react.

To make him desire like she did. Because she couldn't stand that he seemed so cool. Couldn't stand that he was so unshaken.

She took a step toward him and planted both her hands on his shoulders, pushing him back against the wall at the same moment she rose up on her tiptoes to capture his lips in a kiss.

He was still for a moment, and then, with a feral growl, his arm came up to wrap around her waist.

Ajax Kouros was not an easy man to shock, and yet, he had been shocked more than once in the past two days. First by his runaway bride, then by his replacement bride, and now, by the kiss she was giving him.

A kiss that seemed to include her entire body. Maybe more than that. Not just skin and flesh, but her very soul.

It wasn't like anything in his experience. It didn't taste like booze and simple lust. It was passion given breath. And for a moment, there was nothing but the heat, the taste of her lips, the softness of her breasts pressed against his chest. And the intensity that fueled each movement.

He held her close to his body, feeling the shape of her, every inch of her, against him. And then, because it seemed right, because it seemed natural, he raised his other hand and slipped his fingers deep into her thick, wavy hair.

It was like silk, sliding through his fingers, tangling around his hand. He made a fist, trapping the strands in his grasp, holding her to him, keeping her from stopping the kiss. Keeping her from moving away.

This was new. A taste of a woman in a way he'd never before experienced.

Sex, applied in the wrong way, was simply another vice. One he didn't indulge, one he didn't even flirt with. Not anymore. Not now.

But this…this was the shot of whiskey he hadn't had on his wedding day. This was every glass of alcohol, every invitation to a hotel room, every line of cocaine he'd ever refused.

In his life, he'd had every sin laid out before him. And there had been a time when he'd indulged himself in them. But there was a point where he had made the choice to turn away. Not because he was a saint, but because in him lived the darkest of tendencies. To embrace temptation. To drown in excess.

And so he denied it. Because he knew that was the long, dark path to hell, and though he'd started his life on that path, he'd done his damnedest to find a new place to walk.

But for the moment, he was out of restraint. Because of Leah.

She parted her lips and kissed him deeply, his tongue sliding against hers. And because it seemed right, because he wanted to, he nipped her lush bottom lip, soothed away the pain.

The little sound that escaped her wasn't one of pain but of pleasure, and the encouragement spurred him on. He was consumed with this new craving, to have his fill of her taste, sweeter than candy, twice as tempting.

Dark and sweet.

Holding her tightly, he reversed their positions, put her back against the wall, both of his hands now deep in her hair, holding her to him. Her hands were everywhere. His shoulders, his back, down farther. She pulled him in tightly, his growing erection pressing against her stomach.

He was no detached observer to this kiss. He was drowning in it. Overtaken by it.

Shaking with it.

"Ajax," she whispered his name, her breath on his cheek.

Leah. He had Leah pressed up against a wall. Leah who had only agreed to marry him to save her business.

Leah, who made his defenses weak.

Leah, his wife. And yes, he would have an intimate relationship with her. At some point. But when he did, it would be on his terms. Not with him shaking like an addict denied his fix.

He pulled away from her, looked at her lips, swollen, red, not from the lipstick anymore, but from his kiss. He wanted to trace her lush lips with his thumb, follow the line with his tongue. Kiss her again.

Instead he dropped his hands to his sides, curled them into fists to disguise the tremor in them.

"That is enough for tonight, I think." He backed away from her, headed to the stairs.

"You think so?" she asked. "Because I think it was only the start."

He should give in. He should pull her into his arms, carry

her up the stairs, take her to his room and throw her on the bed. Give them both what their bodies wanted now.

Because it shouldn't matter to him. He shouldn't feel edgy and beyond himself. Shouldn't feel like he was about to lose himself, his control, utterly and completely.

He had been prepared to sleep with Rachel, after all, and the idea hadn't made him feel like he was losing his mind.

He tried to conjure a picture of the woman he loved. And he found it was hard. Tried to pick a fantasy he'd had of her, and realized there wasn't one. There had never been fantasies of Rachel, not like that. He'd known they would sleep together, and that had been enough. Because it would happen in the right time, according to the plan.

Because then…then everything would be complete. It would be right. But there had been no fantasies.

Even when working his body to the point of exhaustion before bed didn't keep sleeplessness or arousal at bay; when he took himself in hand, he never imagined a specific woman. No, he did his best to banish images, for fear that he would call up the wrong ones. Images of a past stained beyond the point of ever washing clean.

In those moments he imagined softness, heat, a breathy sound of desire in his ear. Like Leah had made tonight.

No. He wouldn't do this. He wasn't a slave to his body.

Then why the hell can't you stop shaking?

"I'll let you know when I'm ready to start with you, Leah," he bit out. "And when I do, you had better be certain, because when it happens, there will be no stopping."

If he let it go, if this feeling roaring inside of him ever slipped its leash, he knew there would be no way he could stop.

Flashes of memory went through his mind. Women's hands on his body. Practiced kisses. And then a girl, crying in the corner of the bed as though a monster were after her.

He had to stop now. He had to get his control back.

If he didn't, he would become a slave to it.

CHAPTER SIX

AJAX DIRECTED EVERY curse he knew, and there were many, at the media the next morning. Were it not for the media, he could escape his new bride for a little while, since pressing business demanded his presence at Holt Headquarters in New York.

But the media prevented it.

Though, in truth, it was not just the media. Leah would be badly missed by everyone on staff, from the woman at front desk reception to the man who cleaned the wastebaskets at night, if he showed up, newly married to the beloved heiress, without her in tow.

Yes, he was well and truly stuck.

He needed distance, a chance to regain a firm grip on himself, and he wasn't getting it.

He stormed into the study to find Leah, legs curled up beneath her, her laptop in front of her, a piece of red licorice dangling from her lips.

The combination of items brought him straight back to last night. Candy. Red. Lips.

The kiss.

He ran through another string of multilingual curses in his mind.

"We have to go to New York," he said, his words harsher than intended.

She arched her brows and sucked the piece of candy into her mouth, chewing thoughtfully before speaking. "Do we?"

"Yes. It seems your quality control issues weren't the only ones. Nothing like starting the takeover of a business with serious problems. So, I have to go and figure out where the weak link in the chain is, personally, or there will be no more Holt to worry about."

"You're being dramatic."

"A little," he said. "But I do not want to lose ground within my first week of ownership, and preferably not ever. Wouldn't Christofides love that?"

"I'm sure."

"That means I need to be there now. And you need to come with me."

"I suppose it would look wrong if I didn't go."

"Almost as bad as not showing up for a wedding. It would start to appear I couldn't do anything but repel women."

She laughed. "I doubt anyone would think you *repel* women. Although, sometimes you do have bad manners."

"Bad manners?"

"And you're a little hard to deal with."

"Am I?"

"If you don't know that, then you're out of touch with reality."

"I like things the way I like them. I like them to go according to plan."

She stood and stretched, rounded breasts pushed against the fabric of her T-shirt. And he couldn't stop his eyes from going there. Couldn't stop the memory of what it had felt like to have them pressed against his chest.

So soft. So feminine. So utterly different from him.

"And when things don't go according to plan you get completely surly."

"I cannot deny it. But then, in my defense, in my adult years very little has gone against my plan, and I'm out of practice in dealing with improvising."

"Nothing would dare go against you normally…you're far too scary."

"Scary?" He found the descriptor odd. More than that, he didn't like it. It made him remember things that were best left buried.

He didn't go out of his way to be scary. Neither was he particularly fun, and he knew that. But the things in life that so many people seemed to find fun had a dark underbelly that he'd spent his early years trapped beneath.

If a rich guy wanted to go and get high at a party, the drug had to come from somewhere. If someone wanted to pay for a little sex, or watch a graphic video, those women, those men had to come from somewhere.

He had seen those people. Their pain. Worse, he had been a part of it. He had caused it.

A mansion had to be paid for. The money had to come from somewhere.

As a boy he hadn't known that. He'd wandered around that mansion, unsupervised, and had taken all that was on offer. Whatever food was in the kitchen. Whatever substance was left unlocked.

And later, whatever woman was available.

But then he had learned that for every bit of fun there was a price. All that glittered was dark and tarnished beneath.

He knew.

Other people might be able to stick their head in the sand and pretend it wasn't true. They might be able to indulge themselves in the meaningless things in life, spending money, worthless paper, on what had cost others their souls.

But he couldn't do it. And yes, that made him a bit un-fun. But the alternative was depravity. And he had run from that. Had run away at sixteen, had changed his name, had changed islands.

"You're a bit severe," she said.

"I'm practical, which I realize is difficult to take for some people. People who lead with emotions rather than with logic."

"Logic doesn't explain everything. It doesn't have all the answers," she said, bending down and picking up another piece of licorice from the coffee table, lifting it to her lips. "Candy isn't logical. It's not very good for you. It can rot your teeth. But we like it." She took a bite and smiled.

If anyone made him want to forget the rot and taste the sweet, it was her.

The realization jolted him.

"Because people are stupid," he bit out. "And again that's feeling and not logic. You like candy so even though it's bad for you and contributes nothing to your life, you eat it."

"I don't just eat it, I sell it. I create it."

"So, your entire life's work is based around something wholly unnecessary."

"But something people like, Ajax. I make people happy."

"And give them cavities."

She laughed. He'd always liked the sound of her laugh. It wasn't genteel or restrained. It was just…feeling. Funny how, though he stripped down his feelings to the bare essentials, he'd always enjoyed watching hers.

Because she'd never had them stolen. Because she didn't know about all the horrors in life.

A woman like Leah didn't need to know.

A strange surge of protectiveness ran through him. The urge to protect her from that darkness, and from anything that had touched it was so strong he nearly doubled over with it. The urge to protect her from himself.

But that was an impossibility. She was his wife. He was her husband. He would touch her with his hands, and it would spread to her….

And they had to go to New York.

"Scary or not," he said, "you are coming to the States with me."

She shrugged. "Great. It is great, actually. Most of my things are there and all. And I need to pay a visit to the shop there. I like to frequent the stores. Especially the big ones."

"A working trip for both of us."

She nodded slowly, her eyes rising to meet his, as if she was trying to read his thoughts.

"What?" he asked.

"What what?"

"You are concentrating so hard I can hear you thinking."

"I'm thinking about last night." She took another bite of licorice.

"What about it?"

"That scintillating conversation with those two businessmen. Except no, not that. Our kiss."

The thought of it sent a rash of heat across his skin. He would have to stop and examine that later. How that could happen when the temperature in the room was constant. How he could feel that without giving himself permission?

The simple answer was that it was Leah's fault. She was doing things to him. And he had no idea how she held that power. How, when he had thought himself in love with another woman. When he'd held on to his control for so long.

"What about it?"

"I'm wondering why we're bothering to defer anything. I think it was pretty clear last night what we both wanted."

"And we'll have it, but when we have time to focus on that." Again, he felt edgy, restless. Not ready to confront the physical part of their relationship.

It was because of her, he decided. Because it had been rushed. Because what she'd done, for the company, and for him, was very much like selling herself. And he felt uneasy about it. If he had a doubt that she wanted him, wanted to be in the marriage, it would make him feel like he was one of his father's henchman after all. And that was why he'd run away in the first place. To escape that fate, no matter what.

You. In my bed. Every night.

She'd said it, but the vows were spoken. And whether or not she would ever admit it, she was bound to him. And that put her in his care. And if he didn't care for her, then it put her under his thumb, and he would be damned if he was ever that man.

"When?"

"On our honeymoon. I did have one planned. It's in two weeks. That should give ample time to get everything sorted out at Holt, for you to deal with any issues your stores are having due to the quality control glitch, and for us to have convinced the press that everything is, in fact, fine in our relationship."

It would give him time, so that he didn't feel like a marauder, mindlessly claiming husbandly rights simply because she was his bride. And whether or not she cared if he thought of another woman while they were in bed together, he found he did.

He didn't have the stomach for using people. And that was, in his mind, what it would be.

He'd had his fill of using people. He couldn't use Leah, too. Not like that. He could not make her a prostitute, paying her in the form of safety for her company.

And he couldn't make love to her while he had feelings for someone else.

Although, it was becoming harder to picture Rachel. With the memory of his and Leah's kiss burned into his mind, a watermark over his every thought for the past twelve hours, it was hard to think at all.

And that made it harder to pretend it was the reason he hadn't touched his wife. He pushed the thought aside. Of course it was a reason. It was practically *the* reason.

"Two weeks? And then we just start…living as a real married couple."

"It has to happen sometime. Preferably when we can focus on each other."

"I see…and…and besides sex, what is marriage to you,

Ajax? Is it love? Is it companionship? Friendship? What will I be to you?"

"I…I will share your bed," he said, his voice rough. "I will protect you. I will give you children. If you reach out in the dark…I will be there."

These were his real marriage vows. His promises to her. And he found he meant them. That he would carve them onto the remains of his soul if necessary.

He was changing direction, but this was still a path he could walk. Love wasn't necessary. There was no need for a heavy, emotional attachment. Not when there was honesty. Not when there was faithfulness. Loyalty.

He wasn't even certain now if he knew what love was. Rachel had been the symbol of his dreams. His finish line in so many ways. She had come to mean so much to him in what she had represented that it had been easy to imagine it was love.

But now he wondered. Leah had accused him of seeing Rachel as an ideal, not as a woman. Perhaps that was true.

Perhaps he was simply incapable of love. In a strange way, he found that comforting. Love was an awfully big emotion, one he imagined was hard to control. He couldn't have such a thing.

"Nothing more?" she asked.

"That is everything, Leah. From me, that is everything."

She looked away from him, lifted her hand and scrunched her ponytail, the curls springing back the moment she released it. And he remembered sifting his fingers through it last night. It had been straighter then. He wondered how it felt with all the curl in it. She bit her lower lip, and he remembered doing the same last night. And the little sound of pleasure she'd made.

His stomach tightened, and so did his groin. His lack of control stunned him enough that it took a while to get any back. All he could do was look at her, look at her and focus on the heat that was coursing through his body.

"I am giving you everything," he said slowly, "because

you're my wife. And there is no other woman who holds that position now or ever. No matter how the marriage started."

"Thanks, Ajax," she said, her voice a whisper, sadness in her eyes.

He wanted to offer her more. To offer her comfort. The problem was, he was the last person on earth who should ever be allowed to offer comfort. To give tenderness.

Because if he ever let the walls down, the darkness would start to bleed out.

Normally going back to Holt felt like coming home. But Leah didn't feel at home when she walked through the glass revolving doors and into the familiar, gray-marble lobby.

It was the same, but everything had changed. Her father wasn't here. He was in Rhodes. And while there was nothing too unusual about that—ever since her father had first visited the island, he'd been in love with it and had made it a second home—there was no longer a desk here with his name on it, and that did make it different.

Holt Enterprises had always been Joseph Holt's domain. Now it belonged to Ajax. And it belonged to her. Interesting because she'd never imagined that happening. Now that it had…now that it had she realized how much she valued being a part of it.

Because Holt was important. To her, to her future children, to the people who worked here. And to Ajax. Ajax loved Holt. She couldn't fault him there. He would do the very best he could by it, and if the success of Ajax's personal corporation was any indicator, the best he could do was very good indeed.

His husband skills were a bit more murky.

But the vow he'd made to her in the study at his home, where he had made plain the importance he put on her position as his wife…that gave her hope at least. Hope that things could be good. Better than they were. And it made her want to lower her defenses a little bit.

It made her want to try.

As they walked through the reception area, almost empty at this hour of the night, most of staff gone home, she had a strange sense of déjà vu. How often had she followed him like this back when she'd been a teenager? Before she'd put up her walls. Before she'd been aware of how she looked to other people.

Trailing behind him, gabbing about something or another, soaking in every ounce of attention he gave her. Trying to get him to look at her. Trying to make him smile.

At the time, she'd felt like he was her friend. Like he might have feelings for her. As an adult, she saw herself for what she was: a delusional, chubby girl, following around an older, sophisticated man who had no time to listen to her drone on about her plans for her future candy shop.

And yet he had. He had never once been unkind or made her feel unwanted. If he had, she probably wouldn't have retained her crush for so long.

Even now she wasn't immune to him.

That kiss...

She followed him into an elevator and crossed her arms beneath her breasts while he pushed all the appropriate buttons. She'd had fantasies about him and elevators. All the times they'd ridden up in them together. In her very fevered teenage imagination she'd pictured him pulling her into his arms and bending her backward, kissing her neck, her lips.

All very impassioned at the time, but her imagination could do better than that now.

Yes, the fantasies she could spin about an elevator now were not half so innocent. They picked up where they'd left off the night before. With her against the wall. And her skirt shoved up around her hips—never mind that she was wearing dress pants at the moment—and him putting his hands between her thighs to help answer the pounding ache that was threatening to...

"So," she said, overly bright, trying to blot out the images running rampant through her mind, "do you have any artwork picked out for your office yet?"

He gave her a strange look. "No."

"Well, you'll want to…personalize it, right?"

"No. I won't be working from here. Someone else will be put in charge."

"You'll have an office, though."

"Yes, but I won't be spending much time in it."

"Your lack of desire for frivolous things is sort of annoying, Ajax. Do you have any idea how obnoxious it is to try and make small talk with someone when they don't seem to think about anything small?"

"I'm sorry I can't accommodate your need for me to care about trivial things."

"You suck at conversation—do you know that?"

"It's not this hard with everyone."

"It didn't used to be this hard with me. What changed?"

He arched a brow. "You stopped talking to me."

Oh. Right. So she had.

"I suppose I did." She followed him down the hall, and she was assaulted by another punch of the familiar. How many times had they walked like this? And how had she missed that even though she was walking with him, she was walking alone.

He didn't need her there. He didn't want her there. He just… accepted her presence. It seemed like there had to be more. Like they needed to find more. But she was trapped between her desire to protect herself, and her need to make more from her marriage than just two people who could barely make eye contact.

That was why the candy she'd bought him was in her purse, and not already sitting on his desk. Because she hadn't decided what she was going to do with it yet.

He pushed open the door to what had been her father's office. The pictures on the wall were gone. His nameplate on his desk, gone. She swallowed, or at least she tried to. A lump stopped her accomplishing it.

"Wow. I guess it really is yours now."

"He was prompt in removing his things," Ajax said, looking around the space.

"Ajax…" She bit the inside of her cheek, trying to stop the question, the random, stupid, insistent question that wanted to come out at this, of all times, but she couldn't stop it. "Did you sleep with my sister?"

His focus zeroed in on her, his expression one of shock. Well, shock for Ajax, which meant a raised brow and deeper frown than normal. "Why would you ask that?"

"Morbid, oh Lord is it ever morbid, curiosity. I know you told me never to compare myself to her, but in this instance… well, I need to know if you'll be comparing us." She flinched, because really, what were the odds that Ajax had never slept with Rachel? They'd been together for a long time, and Ajax was an incredibly sexy, virile man. Leah never, ever, ever in a million years would have been able to keep her hands off him for all that time.

Hell, she'd attacked him and pushed him against a wall after two days of close proximity.

"I told you that?" he asked, turning back to the desk, then back to her, as if he wasn't sure where he was supposed to be looking.

"Not to compare myself? Yes. Don't you…do you remember that?" She looked at his expression, his eyes blank. He didn't remember. How stupid to think that he would. That one of the defining moments in her life, in deciding how to act in public, how to deal with the press, would even register on his radar. So very, very telling.

"Anyway… I just… I wanted to know," she finished, her words hollow in the silence.

"We didn't."

"What?" The admission pushed the air from her lungs. "How is that even possible?"

"We were going to wait until we married," he said, the words tugged from him, the topic clearly one he wasn't interested in addressing.

"I…I didn't expect that."

"Why not?"

"Most men would pressure a girl to get sex as quickly as possible. Why should I believe you're any different?"

"I am," he said, his tone light, a dark glint in his eyes that told her his voice was fraudulent. "I am not like most men." He moved toward her, his expression unchanging. Her heart stopped, her stomach folding in on itself. His eyes never wavered from hers, and she wondered, she hoped, that he would touch her. Kiss her. He dipped his head, traced her jaw with the tip of his finger. "I am much, much worse."

He pulled away from her and her breath left her body in a rush. She blinked, feeling dizzy, feeling like she was coming out of some sort of trance.

He wasn't going to answer her. She felt like there was a wall between them. Made of ice and his feelings for another woman. And she wanted to scream at him. For not being the man she'd wanted him to be. The man she'd thought he was.

And that wasn't really fair, was it? To be angry at him for not being like she imagined. And it really didn't make sense that it should hurt so much.

She reached into her purse, her fingers curling around the little box of truffles she'd put in there. Her olive branch. Her attempt to make things work better between them.

But not now.

She knew better than this. Knew that you had to protect yourself, or all of your insides would get pulled out and put on display for the public. Ridiculed. She wasn't dropping her shields for him.

She wasn't going to expose herself to that kind of pain. The idea of letting him in, of putting herself out there and trying to make their marriage more than just a plan, had obviously been a stupid one.

She released her hold on the box and turned away from him. "I'm going to go back to my penthouse and try to make arrangements for my things."

"Good. Be back at my house tonight."

"Why?"

"Appearance, *agape,* why else?"

"Oh, no. Yeah. Of course." She wanted to say something tart. To lash out at him. Certainly not so he could be with her. Or something like that. But her throat was too raw and her head hurt. And she wouldn't risk revealing that to him. "See you later then. I'll try to make some sort of big hand gesture and maybe do a pantomime of being trapped in a box so I get the paparazzi's attention as I go back to the house. Wouldn't want them to miss me being there. For appearances."

"Whatever you feel you need to do."

Yell at you until I forget how confused I am. "Great. See you later."

Ajax watched Leah leave, a strange weight settling in his stomach. She'd looked…upset, and that was an understatement. But he hadn't wanted to have a conversation with her about sex, not when his body still burned from their kiss.

And he hadn't wanted to admit that he'd never slept with Rachel. Pride? He'd never thought he would suffer from male pride in quite that way. He'd made his choices. Very deliberately and he was hardly going to regret them now.

He looked down at his desk. It looked empty. Because Joseph Holt wasn't here. He'd removed his presence, and Ajax found that he missed the presence of his mentor.

If there was ever a man he wanted to imitate, it was him.

Unlike his own father, Joseph Holt was a good man. He cared for his family, for people, his staff. He worked hard and found a reward in it. There was an honesty to him, a humanity that had been completely foreign to Ajax when he'd first shown up at the estate, a lost boy with scars inside that would never heal properly.

And Joseph Holt had taken him in and shown him there was another way to live, another way to act than the way he'd seen all of his life. Than the dirty, disgusting hell he'd been brought up in. A hell he'd nearly jumped into with both feet.

He sat down at the desk. *His* desk now. And he only hoped that with the absence of Joseph, and all of his things, he would still be able to be the man he'd taught him to be.

And then it suddenly hit him why his desk looked so empty. A strange memory from the past that seemed prominent now.

Leah hadn't left him any candy.

CHAPTER SEVEN

THE DAYS IN New York were basically miserable. Leah avoided Ajax to the best of her ability. She spent time at her shop and her lab, experimenting with flavors.

She didn't do a lot of hands-on candy creation, not at this stage in her career, but when she was feeling stressed it was a nice distraction.

But her two weeks was coming to an end. In just a few minutes. And that meant it was nearly honeymoon time. Romance time.

With a man she was barely speaking to. Yay. That was just freaking spiffy.

She was meeting him at the airport, because they'd both been too busy to get a car together. Well, no, that was a lie. She could have made time, but she'd lied and said she didn't have it so she could avoid him for a few extra moments.

Now she was sitting there in the private lounge, waiting for him to come, with bags of candy wrapped in ribbon scattered around her feet. She always took the surplus stock, and this time she'd ended up with a bunch of irregular chocolate shoes thanks to the factory snafu.

It would be really nice if the honeymoon was severely depressing. Binge eating easily accessed. She honestly had no idea what to expect from Ajax, so she'd come prepared.

The door to the lounge opened, and Ajax walked in, looking unbelievably sexy in a black suit with a black tie. The man was buttoned up and knotted to perfection, short hair in place. Everything about him shouted control freak. And she had no idea what it was in her that found it so attractive. She just wanted to loosen that tie, undo his buttons and run her fingers through his hair and get it all messy.

She sucked in a sharp breath and bent down, trying to gather up her candy. "Hi," she said, scooping the cellophane bags up, the packaging crinkling as she pulled them in tight to her chest. "I'm just… I got all this candy and I have to, get it now.…" She picked up a few more bags and nearly lost one. He took a step toward her at the same time she took one toward him. "Here." She dumped the bags into his arms. "Take. Please." Then she bent down and grabbed the rest, and her purse. "Ready?"

He arched a brow at her. "Everything is ready. Your bags are on board."

"Great. Thanks. So…where are we going?"

"Did I not mention?"

"No, it's one of those silly little incidentals we've never talked about. Like what your favorite color is, the real nature of your relationship with my sister…that kind of thing."

"Are you really bringing that up again now?" he asked, holding the door open for her. She walked out in front of him and started through the terminal, headed to the exit where the private planes were parked, ready for takeoff.

"I guess so. I hadn't planned to. But I hadn't really planned to the first time. I'm suffering from a case of terminal honesty at the moment."

"It's not as charming as one might think."

"Oh, I don't think it's charming. I think it's hideously embarrassing. I aim to stop it as soon as possible."

"Anytime you see fit."

She led the way out onto the tarmac. "Which plane is yours?"

"The big one," he said, without a trace of humor. All she could hear was the potential double entendre.

She arched a brow. "Indeed." She walked up the stairs that led to the interior of the jet. They'd flown in it on the way to New York, but still, to her, a plane on the runway looked like a plane on the runway.

The inside, however, was what truly distinguished it from anything she'd ever seen before. Plush carpets, leather furniture, a flat-screen television and a bedroom made it more comfortable than most Manhattan apartments. And twice as big as some of them, too.

She'd been raised wealthy, and she was used to opulence. To a degree. Ajax's version was on a whole other level. It wasn't showy, not in an obvious way. No gold-plated toilet paper roll holders.

It was in the quality of the leather on the couch, the type of wine being served. The glass the wine was in.

Ajax set her bags down on the couch and took a seat next to them. So she opted for the chair across the room from him. Safer.

"Now, tell me where we're going," she said.

"You don't want to be surprised?"

"The wedding was my surprise," she said dryly. "Let me in on the honeymoon destination."

"St. Lucia."

"Oh, wow." For some reason, the image of the beautiful island, one she'd never been to, but had seen pictures of, made her throat close up. Maybe because she knew he'd planned to take Rachel there. And it was easy to see Rachel happy in a place like that. Lounging on the beach, smiling at her new husband. Holding his hand while they walked through the surf.

He'd planned that for her.

Why did the thought sneak up on her like that sometimes? Why did she care? Why did she care about him or the honeymoon or anything? It would be so much easier if she could just be like him. With a big fat vacancy sign hanging on her chest.

She could be married to him, run her business, go to events

with him and get him naked at the end of the night and never care who he was thinking of or what he felt.

But that wasn't her. It wasn't how she was. She'd had to get tough when she'd made her leap into the world of business, had had to change the way she behaved in public and in private, really.

But with Ajax…sometimes he made her feel like the girl she'd been. He made her feel soft. Exposed. She didn't like it. Especially not when she'd just purposed to double down her efforts protecting herself.

She felt like she had a knot of confusion living in her stomach. Which made eating difficult. Well, eating anything but candy.

Good thing she'd brought a bunch with her.

Ajax pulled his laptop out of his briefcase and turned his focus to the screen. The conversation was clearly over.

Well, that was fine. She could just sit there and eat candy. And think about their honeymoon, which, now that she knew where they were going, she knew was sure to be filled with sun and sand.

And for now, she wouldn't think of anything else.

The rich blues and greens of St. Lucia felt even more vibrant and saturated after spending two weeks in the gray of New York City. Leah had always liked the city, but the ocean had always felt more like home to her.

This felt more like home.

Ajax had rented them a private villa for the duration of their stay, a massive structure made of rough-hewn wood, with a wide stretch of white sand to the front of it, backed by mountains and dense trees.

It was straight out of a fantasy. Too bad she was no longer under the delusion that her husband was, too.

"How long were you planning on this being your honeymoon destination?" she asked. Why had she asked? She didn't really want to know. Curse her stupid curiosity.

"More than a year. When we set the wedding date, I booked this place."

"You do like your plans, don't you?"

"Without a plan, how do you know if you're on the right path?"

"I don't know. If you adhere so tightly to a plan, how do you know you're not missing something really great that's just a hair to your left?"

He shrugged and walked up the steps that led into the villa. "It isn't worth the risk," he said. "Not to me."

He pushed the door open and went inside; Leah followed, scanning the surroundings. It was a giant, open room with a vaulted ceiling, accented by exposed beams. The floor was made from wood, too, rough and unfinished, giving the impression of something rustic in the midst of the polished luxury. The bedroom was only partitioned off from the main living area by a swathe of gauzy fabric. And beyond the veil, a large, plush bed that was certainly built for two.

And they weren't going to need separate sleeping quarters. She looked ahead, at Ajax's broad back, his trim hips and… well, yeah the way his black dress pants fit over his muscular butt. That was a perk to walking behind Ajax chatting his ear off she'd discovered a little later into her teens. The view from back there was good.

"What risk? The risk of failure?" she asked.

"No. Failure would not be half so bad. There are much bigger things, much darker things to fear." He set down the bag he'd been carrying and walked toward the far end of the room. "Let me ask you a question, Leah."

"Go for it."

"Do you think you're a good person?"

She blinked. "Yes. I…suppose so. I make candy, not war,

and I smile at people when I walk by them on the street. Never took money from my grandma's purse. Yes."

"All right, but do you trust that if your circumstances changed, you would remain a good person? That you would have morals, morals that took hold deep inside of you, that would keep you from ever changing?"

"I'd like to think so," she said, sensing she wouldn't like where he was leading her.

"I trust that I am not a good person. Not just that I might not be if things were to change, but that if I ever take my eyes off the prize in front of me, if I let myself slip up, I will go right back into the darkness I came out of, and I'm not willing to do it. Not just for me. For everyone I might hurt. Emotion, need, lust—those things distract. They are unpredictable. I don't trust them."

She laughed a little, not because anything he said was funny but because it was the only way she could release the tension, the unease, building inside of her.

"You wouldn't…hurt anyone, Ajax."

He laughed, and his was obviously not born of humor, either. "Oh, you say that, Leah, but you don't know anything about me, not really. You think you do. You think I was born the minute I appeared on your family's estate? No. By then… by then I had lived more life in sixteen years than a girl like you will have lived at the end of her days. And that's not an insult. You don't want to have seen what I've seen. To know what I've done. I don't want to know it. But I do. And the memory is what keeps me going this way. It's what reminds me, every day, of how important it is to keep your eyes on the goal."

"Ajax…"

"We're done talking about this."

"No, we aren't," she said. "You told me yesterday that you were worse than most men. Today you're telling me you've done things… I think I deserve to have an idea of what I'm dealing with here."

"Why? I thought you knew me so well?"

"No. I knew your mask. And I liked it better."

"Everyone does," he said. "And they should. On that note—" he reached for his tie, loosened it and then pulled it off "—I think I'll go for a swim." Then he started undoing the buttons on his shirt, stripping so he was bare to the waist. Oh...my.

It was so easy to forget how angry she was, how hurt and confused when she saw that lean, well-defined torso. All olive skin with a bit of dark hair over his chest. Broadcasting just how masculine he was. As if she needed the reminder.

He headed toward the bedroom area, and she just stopped, staring. He was behind the curtain, but she could see, easily, the silhouette of him through the thin gauze. He opened one of the bags that had been delivered ahead of them and pulled out swim shorts, then he pushed his pants and underwear down his thighs.

And as he stripped the clothes away from his skin, the armor was ripped from her body.

She should look away. He wasn't putting on a show for her. She had no right or reason to stand there staring at all that skin, hard, well-defined thighs, the butt...and...and...her brain stopped working when she caught a small glimpse of the front of him, still heavily obscured by the fabric. But the dark shadow there at the apex of his thighs was enticing nonetheless.

He raised his gaze, his eyes clashing with her as he tugged his swim shorts up and over the place she was currently ogling, then he stepped out from the behind the curtain.

"See anything you like?" he asked.

She puckered her lips. "Lots, actually. But then, that's a good thing, right? All things considered?"

"Am I supposed to blush and stammer now?" he asked, his tone dry.

She'd seen Ajax in swim shorts plenty of times, but this was different. They were alone. There was a bed. And she'd just seen his very naked silhouette. "I wouldn't dream of that," she said. "After all, you've seen things I can't even imagine."

"Don't forget." He walked past her and out the door. And then she realized what he was doing. He was avoiding her. Avoiding the potential intimacy of the moment.

He was so not getting away with that.

She stalked back into the bedroom area and opened her suitcase, rummaging around until she found her swimsuit. It was a one-piece, black. Serviceable. It was not what she wanted. He wasn't allowed to be the only one who could inspire lust-fueled brain failure.

She ignored the voice that told her she probably wasn't capable of inspiring it. That voice could suck it.

She needed to make a quick trip to the resort shops.

A swim did a little to cool the burn in Ajax's blood. But the water wasn't as cold as he needed it to be. It wasn't arousal. At least, it wasn't only arousal that was firing through his system.

But the moment he'd walked into that room, looked at Leah and that bed, he'd realized that it was going to happen, and that he wanted it to. And with that had been a collision with reality. Leah had been manipulated into being here. This place had been chosen for another woman. And he had simply brought her here as if she and Rachel were interchangeable, and he knew full well they were not.

For a start, Rachel hadn't made him feel like his blood was going to boil over and reduce to nothing. Leah on the other hand was testing the bonds of his control. Was making him want things he hadn't craved in years.

He'd been so close to pushing her down onto that bed when they'd first walked in. To kissing her until she lost that sad look, until he made the room theirs and exorcised the ghost of the woman he'd intended to bring into it.

And then he'd had to remind himself why he must keep control. Why he had to remember what sort of man he was.

Of course, with Leah there would be no drugs involved. Of course not. He hadn't touched them in seventeen years. Not even tempted to. Not after the last time.

Still, he couldn't separate sex from the chaos and shame that lingered in the air at his father's home. Couldn't separate it from that last night there. From that haze, that feeling of being out of control. Of everything being skewed and confused. And one frightened woman. A woman he had frightened.

No, he didn't want to think about it. But he had to. He had to remember. So he would remember why control was so important.

"Oh, good, you're still here."

He turned around at the sound of Leah's voice and his throat went dry. The memory he'd been replaying was wiped out completely. Now all he could see was curves, soft, pale skin.

And a red bikini that should be illegal. It tied at her rounded hips, and it seemed, to him, that it would be the easiest thing to release those ties. The top was the same, barely covering her breasts. Her stomach wasn't cut or defined like many of the women he saw at the beaches at the exclusive resorts he frequented, compliments of exercise or a skilled surgeon. No, she was simply Leah. Simply a woman.

In that moment it was her softness, her roundness, that made her seem wholly, purely female. There was a natural quality to her shape, to her movements.

For a moment, just a moment, his view of sex, the things he'd seen, the things he'd done, were erased. And there was only Leah.

"Yes, I am. Where have you been?" he asked, willing his body under control before he took a step out of the water and started toward where she stood on the white sand beach.

"Shopping."

"For?"

"All kinds of things," she said. "Mainly this." She put her

hand on her hip, indicating the bikini, he imagined. Not that there was much of it to indicate.

"What else?"

She met his eyes. "Underwear. The kind you want someone to see."

Heat shot through him, starting in his stomach, pooling in his groin. "Really?" His voice sounded rough. Not like his own.

"Yes. You seem interested."

There was no lying about it. It would be too obvious. And anyway, why should he? She was his wife. She wanted him. He wouldn't be forcing himself on her.

She did want him. And not just because she had to be here with him. She'd made her choice. She had.

"I am." His voice was unsteady, a stranger's voice.

"I'm glad."

"Does that mean you're ready? Here? Now?" He wasn't. Not while he felt like this.

"No. It's nice to have a little buildup, don't you think? Nice to anticipate."

She had no idea how damn long he'd been anticipating.

"I don't know if *nice* is the word I'd use."

She took a step toward him, her steps unsteady as her feet sank into the deep sand, her breasts bouncing with the motion.

And he felt like he was a teenage boy. Not the teenage boy he'd been with unlimited access to sex. Sex that had been, at its heart, twisted, one-sided, a commodity. Sex in his world was used for the pleasures of the rich, powerful and debauched.

There was something dark to his encounters in the past, to lust as he knew it. It wasn't this jittery feeling in his veins, this shot of anticipation and pure excitement. This desire to give, not just to take. To caress, not just possess.

And also uncertainty. She made him feel off balance. A side effect of things not going according to his plan. Or maybe just a side effect of her beautiful figure.

She extended her hand, touched his face. "I don't know—

it's nicer than fighting, which is the only other thing we seem to be able to do. Fight and kiss."

And the reins holding him back snapped. He dipped his head and captured her lips, quick and hard, too desperate for a taste to wait. When he broke the kiss, her eyes were round, her mouth swollen.

"Oh," she said.

"What?" he asked, afraid for a second he'd overstepped his bounds. But he'd been sure this was what she was here for. Flirtation. Seduction.

He knew what it looked like when women wanted him. Women had always wanted him, especially since he'd started earning money. He turned them down, but it didn't mean he didn't recognize what it looked like when a woman had sex on her mind.

"Sorry, you just knocked all my thoughts out of my head."

"Is that…good?" he asked.

"Yeah. Just… I don't think I can think of anything witty to say for at least a minute, so maybe you could just look away from my shame and leave me and my mushy brain in peace?"

"Are you going to swim?"

"I think you're supposed to wait a half hour to swim after having your brain scrambled."

"Is that a scientific fact?"

"No idea."

He smiled. Not because he wanted her to see him smile, not because he was conscious of needing to project an emotion. He smiled because he couldn't help himself. "I think…I think I should take you to dinner tonight."

"Romance?"

"Yes."

"You don't have to do that."

"I know. But I want to."

"Coming from you, Ajax, that's romance all by itself."

CHAPTER EIGHT

IT TOOK LEAH only an hour after the encounter on the beach to decide that she wasn't letting Ajax take her to dinner. And she had reasons and her own plan. A plan she was going to ambush him with. She didn't necessarily want romance. What she wanted was to feel as if she had some control. To feel like she wasn't simply being led around.

If there was one thing she'd learned about Ajax since their marriage a couple of weeks ago, it was that he lived in his head. To look at him, you wouldn't think it.

Tall, broad, muscular, he looked like a man who dealt in the physical. Like the promise of sex and sweat. But he was controlled by his mind. And he liked it that way.

And she didn't want him calculating his way through their marriage consummation. It would give him too much control.

One thing she did know: as strong as her feelings for him had been when she was a teenager, she hadn't loved him. There was a certain freedom in that. The kind of freedom that made her feel that maybe she didn't have to guard herself as closely as she'd thought.

She'd never really known Ajax. She'd imagined who she'd thought he might be because of polite conversation they'd made. Because he'd smiled at her, accepted her gifts. But she knew better than that now. You couldn't love a man you didn't know.

Of course, not loving him didn't mean not wanting him.

She did. She was so attracted to him her teeth ached. Among other things.

And she didn't want his restraint. She wanted him just as vulnerable as she was. Just as raw. Now her being a virgin put her at a massive disadvantage but she was just not going to think about all the thin sexy beauties, possibly including her sister, who had graced his bed. No, she was not.

Anyway, he wanted her. She'd seen the look in his eyes.

She'd picked the bikini as a challenge, and as a test, for her own benefit. Because the last thing she'd wanted was for him to get her naked and for her to see shock and horror over her shape. She looked all right, but she didn't have that popular stick shape happening. She wasn't a runway model. She wasn't even a swimsuit catalog model, in spite of the boobs.

But he'd seen, and he wanted.

There was victory in that.

Now she planned on taking his control while his defenses were down.

Her evil plan to seduce the Greek billionaire was in full swing. And when she did…when she did maybe she could exorcise the feelings inside of her. Maybe it would give her some power. Or maybe it would just dull the intensity of feeling she had around him.

Even without the feelings, she was the backup bride. The second choice. The less-beautiful, less-written-about, less-celebrated Holt heiress.

She loved her sister. She truly did. And having to share media adoration, or rather split it 70/30 was fine. But to let Rachel have her husband's heart? That just felt unfair. She didn't love him. He didn't love her. But she did not want him to love someone else. Seemed reasonable to her.

But tonight, tonight wasn't about crushes. Or love. Or being second best. Tonight he was going to want *her*. And that was just about control. And sex.

As soon as he came back from the very urgent business he was taking care of down in the resort's main building.

She reached into the neckline of her dress and leaned forward, giving her breasts a quick boost. Hey, she knew her greatest assets, and she wasn't above trying to display them to their best effect. Basic seduction technique. She was pretty sure. She'd never seduced anyone before.

But then, she'd never been in a loveless, or any other kind of marriage, either. So all new territory.

She looked in the mirror and let out a slow breath. Yeah, she looked…almost not like herself. Lots of eye makeup, her breasts putting on a great show over the neckline of her dress, a dress that was super skintight. She was just going to go with the bombshell look. And yeah, when she turned sideways, her stomach didn't look totally flat, but oh well.

She was her. And she was going to seduce the man with what she had. Because she wasn't like the other women he probably preferred. But not even a good pair of control-top panty hose would make it so.

And when she was naked they wouldn't have helped anyway. No point in false advertising, not when he was going to be seeing the woman behind the curtain, so to speak.

Anyway, the bikini had showed him what he was getting. And the look in his eyes…it was burned into her mind. It was what was giving her confidence now.

The front door to the villa opened, and she turned. She could see him in the doorway, his silhouette clear through the curtain that partitioned off the living area.

"You're back," she said.

"Yes." She couldn't see his face in detail, and his voice was monotone. His expression was, in all likelihood, monotone, too, and probably wouldn't give her any more clues than his voice. "Are you ready to go out?"

She swept the curtain aside. "Not really."

"You look ready."

She put her hands on her hips, on the dress that was practically shrink-wrapped to her curves. "This isn't the kind of thing I normally wear out."

"Why not?" He looked her over, appraising, and a rush of heat went through her body.

"Because…well, it's just not."

"Are you going to change?"

"Are you going to play obtuse?"

He nodded slowly. "Perhaps."

"Don't." She crossed to him, until she was standing close enough to him that she could feel the heat radiating from his body. "It doesn't suit you. You're not the kind of man who can pull it off. You're far too experienced."

"Experienced? I don't know if that's the word I would use," he said, his expression like granite. "Jaded? Maybe."

"Either way, playing dumb isn't your game."

"Perhaps not, but you do make it hard to think."

"Do I?"

Ajax stood, his hands at his sides, fighting the urge to pull Leah into his arms, to strip off the chains that held him, once and for all. To say to hell with control and simply take what he wanted, what he was starving for.

Somehow, in all of this, Leah had started to become an obsession. A desire he couldn't shake or ignore. Somehow, the feelings he'd had for Rachel on what would have been their wedding day had been consumed by the flame of need he felt for Leah.

Sweet Leah. Who had grown into a sharp-tongued temptress with curves that called to fantasies pushed into the darkest corners of his soul. Fantasies that had never been given the chance to play in his mind, not completely. They'd hovered around the edges of consciousness, a mist that he'd kept from creeping in. But now he was overtaken by it.

It was easier to simply let it flood in now, block the path. Block the view of everything behind and everything ahead.

He'd never felt like this. Had never been a slave to his desires in the way he was now. He'd experienced sexual arousal—of course he had. But the truth was, he hadn't had sex in seventeen years. And desire, adult desire, a man to a woman, was utterly foreign to him. He'd ensured that it was.

Because he'd always believed, since he'd been awakened to the reality of who he was, what he was capable of becoming, that he had to wait until he could be sure he would have control. That it was in the right context.

That the woman was not simply there, allowing herself to be used in exchange for something. That the woman wanted it.

But in this moment nothing mattered. Because there was something about Leah that made the past feel not just foggy, but nonexistent.

He wanted to drown in that feeling. Be baptized in it. Come out clean and new.

An illusion, he knew it, but he wanted to cling to it. Just for a while.

She reached up and traced his cheek with her fingertip, her whiskey eyes on his. Tempting him in a way alcohol never had.

He wanted it. Wanted to taste what he'd denied himself for so long. To let the memories of the women in his father's mansion burn so that there was only this. Sweet, heady and clean. He wanted everything, and suddenly he felt like he couldn't get it fast enough.

Seventeen years of self-denial, and on his worst night, with need, repressed and hot coursing through him, he had never felt this close to the edge. Had never felt anything this urgent. But now he was shaking, felt like he needed her more than air. He tried to look at her and see the girl she'd been, tried to look and remember why there was a time he hadn't wanted her. Now he wasn't certain if there had been a time.

How could he have ever not seen this? How could he have ever not wanted?

A whisper of something, desire, fear, washed over his skin.

And a memory. A memory of a girl who always left him gifts. Who told him everything that was happening in her life. A girl who had made his heart, a heart he'd put on ice years ago, feel warm in a way no one else had.

Not even the woman he'd thought he'd loved.

He touched her face, softly, then traced her lower lip with his thumb. He had never touched a woman like this before. With reverence. With respect.

The memory of past encounters left him ashamed. Women in his old world, in his father's world, had been treated as objects. Some men had, too. But it was the women he'd had experience with. Women who had probably only said yes to him because he was the boss's son. Because they didn't want to find themselves thrown out of the mansion with no access to drugs. Or worse, sold off to another corner of the world with a "master" who would be less kind.

And his last encounter with a woman…it had been so rough. Horrifying in the end. The haze of drugs clouding him badly. He'd had more that night than he'd had before.

And why not? His father had given them to him. A birthday present. And it was so rare that his father ever paid any attention to him.

Why not enjoy his gifts? The fruits of their labor, his father had said. The evidence of just how good their product was. It wasn't the first time he'd sampled the drugs. He was human, a young man with endless access to excess, and he'd taken it. But not the variety or amount he'd had the night of his birthday.

And his father had encouraged him to sample their other product. Women. Yes, he'd dabbled with the prostitutes that were around the mansion before. But never the women his father had taken into human trafficking. He'd barely seen any of those women before.

You can break her in, boy. A virgin, I think. A gift for you. She might say no, but she doesn't mean it. I've paid her well to spread her legs. She'll give it up whether she wants to or not.

He pulled back from Leah and took a deep breath. He didn't want to think about that. Not now. Not ever. He'd atoned for that particular sin, or he'd at least done his best to make it right. He could still remember, though. Her face. Her fear. The tears. But as soon as he'd realized…as soon as he'd gotten a moment of clarity…

And then they'd both escaped. He'd seen her back to her family, mostly untouched. The only scars on her, the only man to try to do anything to her had been him. Her scars were created by his hand. But at least…at least he'd stopped.

Control had won in the end. And he had to see that it always did.

Leah was his wife. Leah had made vows. Leah wanted to be here. She hadn't been kidnapped. She hadn't been sold.

Wasn't she? For shares in her own company? For the ownership of Holt?

No. It wasn't the same.

It wasn't.

"Tell me you want me," he ground out, his voice rougher than intended. "Tell me."

Her eyes opened, her expression dazed. "I want you."

"With my name." He was desperate to hear it. Consent was essential. Not consent under duress. Not consent that was heavy with the weight of duty. He required desire.

She touched his face. "I want you, Ajax. What other man would I want?"

"Why did you marry me?"

"For Holt. For my business. And for you, because you worked too hard to lose it all."

"But you made the decision. You *wanted* to."

"No one forced me. You were there. My father was there. He would never have made me do it. No one even hinted about me marrying you. I did. It was my idea." She put her finger on his lip, traced it as he'd done to her. "And if you'll recall, I demanded intimacy as a part of my terms and conditions."

"I do. But why?"

"Women have hormones, too, Ajax, and I don't want to go satisfying things with someone who isn't my husband. If this marriage is real, we honor our vows."

"Something we agree on."

"You'll be faithful to me, too?"

"Of course."

"No matter what?"

"Who would I break my vows with?"

She let out a shuddering breath. "All my life, Ajax, I have felt like I was just behind her. Everyone who's compared us has found me lacking next to her. And you preferred her, too. You said you loved her."

He was going to say something about emotion. About how he wasn't sure he'd ever had any. He'd directed everything he had at loving Rachel because marrying her had seemed like such a good idea. But he wasn't sure he'd truly loved her. Once she was taken away as a goal, his feelings had gone, too.

He was sure he *hadn't* loved her. He felt nothing when he thought of her now, not a twinge in his heart, not even a tug of lust. He felt more when he thought of that girl with the tear-streaked face from seventeen years earlier than he did when he thought of the woman he'd meant to marry just a few short weeks ago.

And he started to tell her that. But it wasn't what came out. "You are not sharing my body with any other woman."

Something in her expression turned feral, fierce. "Damn right I'm not. You're married to me."

"No, that's not what I meant." Why was he saying this now? It didn't matter. If he explained, he would have to give hints about his past. But it had been so long, and this was different. A few rushed, youthful couplings that had left him feeling dirty were nothing like this. "I have not been with a woman since I was fifteen."

Her mouth dropped open, her lips rounded into an *O*. "What?"

"So it's closer to eighteen years, in truth."

"That…that's an entire legal adult worth of time," she said, taking a step back. "I don't believe you. Your…your abs are like…begging to be licked, and you're telling me that no woman in the past…all that time, has ever taken them up on that?"

"They have offered. I've refused."

She gaped for a moment, short, half words coming out of her mouth, then cutting off partway. Then she finally spoke. "No offense, but why? You're a man. Men like sex. Men don't usually say no to sex."

"No, Leah, they often don't. And I find the atmosphere that surrounds irresponsible sexual behavior to be something I want no part of."

"Not all sex is irresponsible."

"No. It's not. But…I always thought that it was best in the context of a relationship. As I was never in the position to have them, I…abstained. I already told you that I wanted to wait until marriage to be with Rachel."

He wouldn't tell her the whole story now. Not now. Not while she still looked at him like this.

"And you *could* wait?"

"Yes. Easily. I prize my control over everything else, Leah. If I decide to do something, I do it. If I decide not to, I don't."

"You should win a control trophy or something," she said. "But then…I guess you've never felt very passionately about anyone."

"No." It was the truth and he realized it now. If Rachel had made him feel like this…like Leah did, if she'd made him shake…could he have held himself back?

"Because…because if you had, well…if she'd wanted you, I don't think you would have said no."

"Maybe that's true." A disquieting thought.

"But…but now?"

"We're married," he said. "This is…right."

"Right," she said, her amber eyes glistening. "Why did you tell me?"

He frowned. "Because it is honest."

"You're practically a virgin."

"I'm not," he said, his voice hard. "I am no innocent."

The conversation made him uncomfortable. Maybe that was male pride. Maybe he wasn't as different from other men now as he'd imagined. Not as immune to the stupid things men measured success by. He knew that there was nothing greater in following your base urges. Nothing more respectable. Any man could have all the sex he wanted. Control was the real strength, and he knew it. Yet, he still felt a measure of shame admitting his status to his wife.

"You don't look like one, that's for sure," she said, looking at him closely.

"Do I not?"

"You've seen too many things. It's reflected in your eyes." She reached out and traced the line of his brow before pulling away. "What have you seen, Ajax?"

He shook his head. "Things you have not. I won't burden you."

"But like you said…you weren't born the day you showed up at my father's estate."

"The man I am now is. And that man is the one who's going to make love with you tonight. Not the one I was. Not the one I might have become."

"But I want to know what made you who you are."

"No. Leah, you cannot want that. Please, the way you're looking at me now, the way you looked at me before, I will have that for tonight. Please."

She nodded slowly. "Okay. I'll take what you can give. For tonight."

"I do not know where to begin. I look at you…and there is so much I want."

A deep rose stained her cheeks, but her eyes never wavered from his. "Then we may have a problem, because I look at you and…I ache. And I really don't know where to start. Because I'm not just practically a virgin. I am one."

"Now that seems impossible to me."

"What?"

"How so many men didn't see your charms."

"It's more like…I didn't see theirs."

"Fair enough. You do not look like an innocent to me."

"What do I look like to you?"

He put his thumb on her chin. "A seductress."

"That's…almost sweet." She kissed his thumb. "Are you seduced?"

Utterly. He was ready to get on his knees and beg. He had waited long enough for this moment. He had waited forever to feel something like this.

This was different. Different than a lust that cared only for feeding itself. This was like the first time.

Oh, *Theos,* how he wished it was the first time. How he wished those other moments, those other women, those cold, selfish encounters, had not been. But he could not erase his past from reality. Only from his mind.

"I don't think we have as much to worry about as you might imagine."

"You don't?" she asked.

"No. I have always believed in making plans. When I decided to marry, I knew I would need to have the skills a husband is required to have to satisfy his wife. More than a teenage boy would need with a woman who was not even a lover. So I have done some reading. I am also gifted with singular focus. When I am in bed with you I will apply both my knowledge and my focus to you entirely, at the exclusion of everyone and everything else. A man who has had a lover every day for the past eighteen years, but only has a tenth of my focus and perfectionism could not come close to satisfying you as I will."

Her eyes darkened, irises shrinking to a gold line around a pool of black. Her breath shallow, the pulse at the base of her delicate throat pounding. Yes, she was a woman aroused. A woman who wanted this. Wanted him.

A virgin.

Strangely he found that revelation to be disturbing. A vague and unsettling parallel. Considering that he felt his very touch was a violation of her innocence. Emotional innocence was all he'd been betting on. It seemed especially disturbing, underlining the point, that she was innocent in this way, as well.

He was not. No matter how many years stood between him and those other women, him and that time in his father's house, he carried the evidence on his soul. Dirt that would never come clean.

And he had tried. He'd expected some sort of feeling of absolution. Sins washed white as snow when he'd helped to destroy the wicked empire his father had built. When he'd helped to free countless women and men from the trade. And yet, even when that was finished, he'd looked inside of himself and he'd still seen the monster.

There was nothing clean in him. Some stains stayed forever. And he had to be mindful of that. Of the fact that no matter how much had changed around him, not enough had changed in him.

But he wouldn't back out now. He couldn't. Not when she was looking at him like he was the best present she'd ever got.

Another testament to her innocence. Her naïveté. She didn't know what she was asking for. Didn't know the man that she was about to make love with. He *should* tell her. Who he was, where he was from. About all the life he'd lived before he'd walked through the wrought iron gates of the Holt Manor and became Ajax Kouros, leaving his real name, his life, his connections with Greece's most notorious drug and human trafficker far behind him.

He should tell her how he hadn't been a captive of that man, no, he was that man's son. He shared his genetics. He'd lived in the mansion, worn suits, driven cars, bought with money dripping with the blood of innocents.

No, he hadn't known better. But it didn't matter in the end. It was still what had created him.

And that night, he'd come face-to-face with a choice: embrace the monster, or leash him, shoving him down and moving forward, half a man, but a decent human being. He'd chosen to be decent.

But it didn't mean the monster wasn't there. It didn't mean it didn't prowl inside of him, waiting for a chance to escape and devour everything in its path. The monster who remembered what it was like to live only for yourself, to taste excess. He would kill it if he could. Instead, he'd spent years trying to choke it out, making it weak. Leaving it forgotten. Starving its appetites.

But tonight, it was just beneath his skin. Claws digging in, threatening to tear its way through his flesh. And he didn't want to put it back in the cage. Tonight he wanted to let the beast free. Wanted to sate that appetite.

No. He would not. It would be unthinkable.

"Do you think you can handle me?" he asked, putting his hands on her cheeks, looking at her eyes.

A smile curved her lips. "I was going to ask you the same question."

He hesitated, unsure of where she would want him to start. What he should do. Still, a part of him wanted to protect her. Give her something sweet and unchallenging. A few moments in bed to consummate the marriage, dispense with her virginity and his celibacy and move on.

But then there was the beast. And Ajax feared if he made

the wrong move he wouldn't be able to hold that part of himself back any longer.

Leah took the choice from him.

She kissed him, hard, deep, devouring, her tongue sliding against his, teeth scraping his bottom lip. Her fingers were forked through his hair, her body pressed hard against his.

He put one arm around her waist, and with the other he did what he'd been longing to do since…it felt like forever. It felt like a need that had been building in him long before he'd ever recognized it.

He cupped her breast, so soft, so incredibly sexy, sliding his thumb over her nipple. She arched into him, her soft flesh filling his palm. So perfect. So incredibly perfect. A fit he could only find with Leah.

Things were burning hot and fast, her hands creeping beneath the hem of his shirt, fingertips skimming over the muscles on his back, his stomach, his chest. This wasn't the sweet and easy first time he'd imagined.

And it felt like the first time for him, too. The first time he might have had.

But he couldn't stop to ask for something else. Not when this was what he really wanted. This moment of freedom. This moment of satisfied need in what amounted to a lifetime of self-denial.

She pulled away from him and stood back, her lips swollen, her eyes sultry, tempting. Then she reached behind herself and tugged the zipper on her dress.

"Stop," he said, his throat tight. "Let me."

She turned slowly, sweeping her hair to the side, exposing her back. He put his arm around her, his hand resting on her stomach. Then he lowered his head and kissed the back of her neck, resting his forehead there for a moment. He felt a shiver go through her body and she arched back, her bottom coming up against the hard ridge of his erection. He pulled her into his body even tighter, thrusting against her.

A raw sound escaped her lips. Passion. Need. Not fear. Everything he needed to keep going.

Although, he was so far gone now, he feared he was past the point of needing encouragement. He was lost in his desire, lost in the sensations coursing through his body, a body he never let make decisions. A body he denied pleasure on a daily basis.

He lifted his hand and gripped the tab on the zipper, drawing it down slowly, the fabric parting. He slid his hand down over the wedge of pale exposed skin, skimming his knuckles over her silken flesh. Then he lowered his head and kissed her, just between her shoulder blades.

"Oh, yes, Ajax."

"See? I think we'll muddle through."

She nodded, and he laughed. And in that moment, time seemed to freeze. He looked in her eyes, and saw a flash of the past. Not of the past at his father's house. The past in the offices at Holt. Leah looking at him, smiling, putting a piece of chocolate on his desk.

One he would eat later, though something in him felt it was wrong to do it. That it was wrong to encourage the growing connection between them. A connection that seemed to start at his chest, tendrils weaving through to the rest of him, slowly, unbidden.

Then, he'd turned away from it. He'd had to. But now…now he wouldn't look away.

He pushed the dress from her shoulders, letting it fall off her body, pooling at her feet. He could only stare. At her curves, highlighted by the black lace bra and panties.

Her small waist, the dramatic flare of her hips, the shape of her buttocks. He couldn't stop himself from putting his hand on her hip, from inching it around so that he could palm her ass. So perfect.

There was a beauty that radiated from her, so rare, so incredible, that he felt humbled by it. Shamed by it. He was not worthy to put his hands on her, and yet he couldn't resist the chance to.

"I want to touch you," he said, his voice so unlike his own. There was no control. There was no civility. There was barely any trace of the man left. It was more of a growl. More like a beast.

"Where?" she asked, her voice soft.

"Everywhere. And then I want to taste you. Everywhere."

"I like that promise."

"It's one I can keep."

He unhooked her bra and she tugged it down from her shoulders, tossing it aside. He wrapped his arm around her again, cupping her bare breasts, her skin so soft, nipple tight against his palm. His first time touching a woman this way. Need, shocking, hot, and like nothing he'd ever felt before, burst through him.

"I need to see you," he said, kissing the top of her shoulder. "I have waited for so long."

She turned to face him, eyes glistening. "So have I. Ajax... you don't know how long."

There was no shyness, no timidity in her gaze. And he looked his fill. He had never seen anything more beautiful than the sight of Leah, standing there, her breasts bared, raspberry nipples dark against her pale skin. He let his eyes travel farther down, to the little scrap of fabric that covered her most intimate place from his gaze.

"Take them off," he said, and this time, it was a growl.

She never took her eyes off his as she hooked her fingers in the sides of her panties and dragged them down her legs.

He looked at her, desire, desperation, clawing at his throat. He had just enough breath to issue a warning. "I'm about to skip some steps," he said.

He dropped to his knees, pressed a kiss to her stomach, just beneath her belly button. And lower. He was shaking, dying for his first taste of her. He wanted, needed, in a way he couldn't remember ever needing. It was visceral, as necessary as breathing.

He parted her thighs slightly, widening her stance, and covered her with his mouth, sliding his tongue through her slick folds, over the little bundle of her nerves he knew would bring her the most pleasure.

She gasped and bent forward, her hands clinging to his shoulders. And he continued to taste her, deeper, faster. He couldn't get enough of her. He never would. Her taste, the way she coated his tongue, the way she breathed his name, the way her nails cut into his skin, even with the fabric of his shirt as a buffer.

This was a first for him, something he'd never done. Because he had never cared about the satisfaction of the women in his father's house. They were prostitutes, and he had been taught to treat them in a certain way. Taught that their pleasure came from whatever they got in trade.

He shoved the thought aside and focused on Leah.

She filled his senses. Sustained him. How had he lived without this?

He gripped her hips and pressed her more firmly against his lips, lost in the act, lost in her.

"Ajax…" She said his name like a plea, like a prayer, and when her release broke over her, almost like a curse, her body trembling as he held her up, he rested his head against her thigh, trying to catch his breath, and she laced her fingers through his hair. The gesture was shockingly sweet, coming on the tail end of something so raw and uncontrolled, and yet it felt right.

His hands were shaking, so much that he found it hard to undo the buttons on his shirt. But Leah took over. Her hands left a trail of fire over his skin, testing him, pushing him to the limit, and when she cupped him, stroked him through his jeans, he caught her wrist and pulled her hand away.

"Careful," he said.

"What?"

"Too much."

It certainly hadn't been eighteen years since he'd had an orgasm, but in that time, he'd only had them alone. He had been convinced that he would have control, much in the same way he did with his own hand. That sex would feel familiar due to years of self-gratification.

But he had left out the variable.

The woman. His partner.

Leah was an active participant, and she wasn't keeping his pace. Wasn't letting things go down the path he'd imagined. Wasn't allowing him to keep to his plan.

She was forging her own, and bringing him with her.

"I like that you're on edge," she said, putting her hand against him again. "I like that you want me so much."

"Leah," he bit out.

"Yes." She sighed, squeezing him. "Say it again."

"Don't."

"Not that. My name."

"Leah," he said again, on a feral growl.

"I like it."

And he liked it, too. Too much to stop her, even though he should. Even though he should try to get control of the situation again. Control of his needs. He should be commanding this; he shouldn't be at her command.

"Stop touching me," he said. "Now."

She removed her hand from him, and he reached down and started to work his belt, undoing it and the button and zip on his pants, shoving them down his legs and kicking them aside.

"Not fair," she said. "I want to touch."

"No."

If she touched him it would be over. Not the sex. He wouldn't come. But he didn't know what he would do. If the fire got too hot. If the beast slipped its chains.

"Go into the bedroom," he said. Because he had to assert authority. He had to find his control. Hold it tight.

"Is that how we're going to play?"

He took her chin between his thumb and forefinger and dropped a light kiss on her lips. "If you want to play, *agape,* then you play by my rules. Now go to the bed and wait for me like a good girl."

He hadn't known it would be like this. Hadn't known he would be like this. But this, the demands, the orders, made for an easy reminder. An easy role to slip into that would help him maintain control.

A smile curved her lips, but he wasn't fooled. He saw the steel shining through. "Of course, darling."

She turned and walked away from him, giving her hips an extra sway, a show for his amusement. He reached down and squeezed his erection, sucking a sharp breath through his teeth.

"Hey," she said, turning and looking over her shoulder, her focus lowering to where his hand was wrapped around his shaft. "Not fair. If I can't touch, you can't."

He lowered his hand, and she continued on to the bed, sweeping the curtain to the room aside and climbing on, leaning back against the pillows, her arms draped to the sides. She was inviting. She was certainly not a *shy* virgin.

He walked over to the bed and stood at the side, and she rose up onto her knees, her eyes locked with his. She leaned in and pressed a kiss to his chest, and he wove his fingers through her hair. She moved lower, lips skimming his abs, blazing a trail farther down. Then her tongue flicked over the head of his arousal. The pleasure, the heat, seared through his skin, rocking him, threatening to destroy him. He tugged her hair, pulling her head backward.

"We're not playing like that, *agape,*" he said, his voice strained. "Not tonight."

"But you did it for me. I want to taste you."

"No. Not tonight." He was too close to the edge, his control too tenuous.

And his control was everything.

"What do you want then?"

"This." He joined her on the bed and dipped his head, sucking one pink nipple deep into his mouth and flicking his tongue over the tightened bud. He ran through the instructions he'd read on how to pleasure a woman this way, text swimming before his closed eyes, the need for concentration the perfect counterbalance for the ache in his body.

And she was the one shaking now, her fingers locked in his hair. This was what he could handle. This was what he wanted.

He turned his attention to the other breast, sucking, licking, until she was panting beneath him, little sounds of pleasure escaping her lips. He raised his head and kissed her, hard, and she returned it.

He could feel her desperation now, her need.

"Are you ready?" he asked. In this he would ask, because he knew for her there would be pain. And he didn't like that. Didn't relish it.

"Yes. Oh, yes, please now."

She parted her thighs and he settled between them taking himself in hand and pressing against the moist entrance to her body. Then he pulled back, replacing his erection with one finger, sliding it in slowly until she sighed.

She was so tight. So wet. And he nearly lost it then and there. He gritted his teeth and moved his finger within her, sliding his thumb over her clitoris.

"Good?" he asked.

"Yes."

"More?"

"Yes," she said.

He added a second, stretching her gently, working them in and out of her until he felt her internal muscles tighten around him. His stomach was so tight he could hardly breathe; he was aching with the need to be in her. To feel her around him there. To be connected to her.

He withdrew his fingers, positioning himself again. He could feel her heat, the slick wetness of her desire against the head of his arousal. She kissed his neck, the corner of his mouth, her hands moving over his back. Touching. Tempting. Testing.

He tightened his hands into fists around the sheet as he slid inside of her, inch by inch, slowly, excruciatingly so, but more for him than for her. He was lost. For one blinding moment his mind was clear of everything. Of his need for restraint, control.

There was only this. Only her body. Only the feeling of her around him.

He pushed in deep, thrusting hard, and she gasped, a little note of pain in the sound that brought him sharply back to the present.

"Okay?" he asked.

She nodded, biting her lip. He bent his head and kissed her. "If you're going to bite someone's lip," he said, "make it mine."

He didn't expect her to oblige him, but she did, pinning his lip tightly in her teeth. And the pain was just enough to take the edge off the pleasure, just enough to help him regain some of his control.

He thrust into her again, establishing a rhythm, her nails scraping against the bare skin of his back, his shoulders. Her touch inflaming, the pain anchoring, necessary.

"Harder," he bit out, gripping her thigh and tugging it up over his hip as he continued to ride her. Her hold on his shoulders deepened, her nails digging in enough that he was sure she had to be drawing blood. "Harder," he said again. And she obliged.

Every time he entered her, she arched into him until finally he felt her go stiff beneath him, a soundless scream on her lips, her warmth pulsing around him. And he let go. The rhythm forgotten, the steadiness gone. Only a blinding race to the finish remained as his blood roared in his ears, the strength of his release savaging him, tearing him to pieces inside and leaving them scattered, impossible to collect. Impossible to ever be whole again in the way he'd been before this. Before his orgasm.

Before Leah.

Somehow, in one wrenching moment, his wife had changed everything. And he felt nearly desperate to find a way to change it back.

CHAPTER NINE

LEAH'S WORLD WAS rocked. Completely. Ajax in theory was one thing. Ajax in reality was another thing entirely.

He had been firm, gentle sometimes, commanding, and OMG those years where his sexual activity had been dormant had clearly not affected him adversely. He knew about hot buttons on the female body that she'd never discovered on her own, and he knew how to do just the right things to them.

She could hardly breathe. What had it been, ten, twenty minutes since they'd parted? Since her orgasm had shattered her? Or maybe it had been two hours. Or thirty seconds. She honestly had no idea.

Ajax rolled into a sitting position, his back to her, his muscular, *perfect* back, to her. She reached out and traced her fingers over the lines on his back.

Ajax's body was sculpted, well-defined, without a spare ounce of flesh anywhere. Almost like he worked out to the point of punishing himself. Or to the point of exhaustion so he couldn't want anymore. She knew a little something about that. If she was faced with the choice of rolling around, tangled up in her sheets, dying of sexual frustration brought about by Ajax fantasies, she often opted to go and run on the treadmill.

When she didn't opt for a shower to uh…alleviate things in a different way altogether.

Maybe he would shower with her later. That was an optimistic thought.

He stood and she cocked her head to the side, taking in the view. Oh, the view. She'd admired that view many times. When it was covered in denim, or black, well-fitted dress pants. But naked? Oh, that was its own pleasure. She would happily buy tickets to this show.

"Where are you going?" she asked, when he started to move away from the bed.

"I have some work to do," he said, bending down and picking up his pants from the floor, tugging them up, covering her peep show.

"What? You have…work? What kind of work could you possibly have to do after…after that?" Oh, no, she sounded so…needy. So raw and exposed. But she'd had to let her guard down for that, to be with him that way.

And she hadn't had a chance to protect herself again. Like she'd just shed her scales, leaving behind new, shiny skin that was tender to the touch. To Ajax's coldness.

He turned, the muscles in his stomach rippling. "The world didn't stop turning just because we had sex."

She could only stare at him, words frozen on her lips. Her world had stopped. It had been rocked, in fact, she'd just thought that it'd been rocked; and it turned out everything was going on just fine in Ajax land. No big deal. He had work.

Screw that.

"Well, I think the world should stop for a second," she said. "This is supposed to be a real marriage…this is supposed to be our honeymoon. I know we're trying to make it look like things are good for the press, but you said this was a forever kind of thing. And…and that means you need to get back here and start acting like a husband."

"I just acted my part," he said. "Were you not satisfied?"

"I am not satisfied," she hissed, sitting up, tugging the covers over her breasts.

"Your screams during your multiple orgasms tell a different story."

"You… You… That was uncalled-for. And rude. And anyway, sexual satisfaction and my satisfaction with this moment are not inextricably linked!"

"This is a real marriage, *agape,* as I said it would be. I was in your bed tonight as you requested, but what happens after that, that's up to me."

"This isn't how marriage is," she said, her throat closing on the last word, making it sound choked. Betraying her emotion. What was wrong with her? Her armor wasn't protecting her now. She was breaking apart behind the layer of protection she counted on. The damage coming from the inside out.

"It's how *our* marriage is."

He turned and walked through the curtain, down into the living area, and she just sat there, her knees drawn up to her chest, a shiver, a chill, working its way through her body.

For her, sex had changed everything. And it seemed to have changed things for him, too. But he didn't feel closer to her. It didn't make him want to hold her or be near her.

She'd given him her body. Let him run his hands over her bare skin, let him *into* her body.

She had given him absolutely everything. And it still hadn't made him want her. It had only made him want to put her at a greater distance.

And the very last bit of fantasy, the last little shaft of light in the darkness, the hope that she hadn't realized still lived inside of her, that someday he would feel something for her, was snuffed out.

She was very careful to avoid Ajax for as long as possible the next day. When she woke up, early the next morning, he was asleep on the couch. She had to fight the urge to go to him and cover him with a blanket, or smooth his hair back from his forehead, or try to move him into a more comfortable position.

He'd clearly fallen asleep while working, half sitting up, his laptop on the table in front of him, his neck turned at an angle that looked the opposite of comfortable.

But it worked out, because his obviously exhausted state allowed her to sneak out undetected. She spent the day wandering around the private beaches and swimming, stopping at the bar for a fruity drink and some lunch.

Yes, for being a small, exclusive island, there were a lot of ways and places to avoid her new husband, and to get a grip on what had happened between them last night. Try to figure out a way to rebuild the walls inside.

But she didn't know how to do that. Didn't know how to protect herself when it felt like he was in her.

She sighed and let her wrap drop around her ankles. Then she started to half jog down to the waves. She stopped, adjusted her bikini top and rethought the jogging. There was not enough support in that itty-bitty red top for that much bouncing up and down.

"How are you doing?"

She turned around, midadjust, her hand stuffed down her top, and saw Ajax. She slowly removed her hand and tried not to die of embarrassment. "Morning," she said.

"I asked how you were."

"I don't know... How are you? You were practically a virgin, and don't virgins get all emotional after sex?"

"Leah, I'm being serious."

"So am I."

He shrugged his broad shoulders, his loose white shirt tightening across his chest. "Fine."

"Oh, yeah, good. Me, too. Fine. Totally fine. I'm glad you're fine because I'd hate to feel all guilty over any wounded virtue."

"I haven't got any."

"So you've said."

"And you?"

"My wounded virtue? Fine. Fine."

"That's what I was asking about."

"Okay," she said, putting her hands up. "I'm not fine. I don't want you sleeping on the couch."

"Why?"

"Because it feels wrong. Don't you think a married couple should share a bed?"

"Often in history married couples haven't."

"So? Often in history people died of dysentery, but that's not really a trend I want to continue."

"You don't know what it will be like…to spend so much time with me. Perhaps you should worry about something other than sharing a bed all night. Like if you'll be able to stand having breakfast with me in the morning."

"Or maybe, since it's our honeymoon, we see how much of each other we can stand. Why not have a little immersion therapy?"

"Why not keep us both from *needing* therapy?"

"Ajax, why don't you want to share a bed with me?"

"It's not what I do, Leah."

"You admitted to me you hadn't done anything like this in a long time, so how is it you have formed opinions on how you should be in this situation?" She looked out at the water, trying not to cry or do anything similarly humiliating. Like smacking him over the head. "Would you have shared a bed with Rachel?"

"No," he said, his voice rough.

"But I thought you loved her."

"I didn't, Leah, obviously."

The admission stunned her, left her feeling hollow. "What's that supposed to mean? You've been telling me all this time that you loved her. You weren't with another woman from the time you met her."

He put his hands on his head. "None of this ever had anything to do with her. I made a plan. I decided marrying her would be the best thing for my life, marrying into the Holt fam-

ily would be the best thing for my life, and feelings…followed."
He dropped his hands back down to his sides, curled them into
fists. "But I have hardly thought of her since our marriage, and
I would be shocked if you could find a man who would think
of her, when he had you, naked and underneath him."

His voice got deeper, rougher, the light in his eyes changing.

"Well…then," she said. "I guess there's…that."

"You do not like the thought of her with me," he said.

"Brilliant observation there, Sherlock, I really don't."

"Why?"

"Well, answer me this, Ajax, and whatever the answer is,
make it honest. What do you think about another man touching me? Kissing me like you did? Touching my breasts the
way you did."

A muscle in Ajax's jaw jumped. "I think…I think I would
have to kill him. And when I say that, I don't say it lightly. Or
metaphorically."

She swallowed. "Oh." She believed him. Somehow, she
believed him. "Ajax…who were you before you came to our
home? Before you came to work for my father?"

"This discussion is not…necessary. I don't…"

"You told me that last night. As if by keeping it from me
you were protecting me, but honestly? Real honesty here, not
protecting myself, not putting on a happy face. Not hiding
tears. You destroyed me. Your reaction to what happened between us. Leaving me like you did. You can't just pretend that
by closing yourself down and giving me nothing you won't be
hurting me."

"Leah, you don't know what you're asking."

"No, I don't. So tell me. It hardly seems fair. You've known
me most of my life. You know my family. You saw me all
through my hideous awkward stage, which, in my opinion,
gives you way too much power. I know you didn't just appear
one day. I know you got your scars from somewhere. Tell me
so I understand."

"You don't want to understand."

"I do."

"No." He turned, his expression fierce. "I'm not going to stand here on a beach with you in that ridiculous bikini and tell you all the sordid details of my life."

She let out a growl and reached behind her, undoing one of the ties on her bikini. Then she yanked off the top and threw it into the sand. "There. Half the ridiculous bikini is gone. So tell me part of the story." She waved her hand over her mid-section. "Half, even. You could tell me half."

He looked around them, then back at her. "What the hell are you doing?"

"My bikini was a problem. I have removed the problem. Half of it anyway. Tell me."

"You can't just…stand there like that."

She put her hands on her hips, anger, adrenaline, coursing through her. Because her defenses weren't holding. They weren't rebuilding. The only other option was to get him to bare himself, too. And if she had to stand there, half-naked to get him to do it, it was a small trade.

"Can. Am. Tell."

Ajax sucked in a sharp breath, his eyes glued, no matter how hard he tried to get them not to be, to Leah's breasts. She pushed him. Brought him to the brink, so that the monster tugged at his chain, begging to be released. And if he wasn't careful, the chains would break completely.

He could do this. She was testing him, and he wouldn't fail.

"You don't want to know this, Leah. This is…the kind of darkness you've never seen."

"I can handle your darkness, Ajax," she said, whiskey eyes burning into his.

The look in his eyes was that of a man ready to go into the torture chamber. "I don't want you to have to handle it."

"Tough. I married you. That means it concerns me. I'm not a child. I'm not a sheltered flower… Ajax, my whole life has been lived in front of the world. I have had total strangers leave the most hideous comments about me on blogs, in news stories, all because…because when you have any kind of public face, whether you want it or not, people feel like they own you. And that showed me a lot about people. A lot of really horrible things about people. So maybe to you I seem innocent or unaffected, but the simple truth is that I've seen more than you think. You can trust me with your story. With your darkness. I won't run."

"But maybe you should."

"I won't."

He paused for a moment, the words sticking in his throat. "My father was…is, I imagine, I doubt he's changed his name… Nikola Kouklakis. And no, we don't share a name. No, it is not by accident. But by my design."

He could see her thinking, could see her processing, wondering where she'd heard the name.

"He is a criminal. The most notorious criminal in Athens. One of the worst in the world. Doubtless you've heard his name on the news. He is a drug lord and human trafficker, and I was born and raised in his compound. My mother was never there. I don't even know who she is. I was raised by my father, the most violent, reviled man in Greece. And before I left, I nearly became him. It's what I was being groomed for. To take the place of a man who sold drugs and women. And do you know what, Leah? I would have. I could have."

She shook her head, her eyes glittering. "No, Ajax, you couldn't have."

"Yes, Leah, I could have. Why do you think it's so important I keep control? Why do you think I have to plan everything, keep my eyes on the prize ahead. Because if I don't…greed, corruption, murder, all of that is in my blood. It's who I am. Bred into me, raised into me. Nature or nurture? Doesn't matter, I have both on the side of darkness, and it is all still in me. If I don't keep it chained, if I don't keep it under control…."

"That's ridiculous, Ajax. You aren't a criminal any more than I am."

"If you run through the alleyways in the middle of the city, you make two right turns, then pass two buildings. At a third, you take a left. You knock on the door, and someone answers, usually a kid. Say whatever the word of the night is, and they show you to the back. They open up your backpack, inspect the packages. You take the money, and you go home." He swallowed. "You have to know it like that. Memorize it. Because you make the trip in the dark. And it's scary, especially when you're a little kid. So you need to know it. Know what to do, know what to say. And you have to be damn fast so you don't wind up with a slit throat. Or worse."

"What's worse?" she asked, her voice hoarse.

"Being sold. Trust me. It's worse. People who want to buy boys…it's not for anything good." He looked at her, at the horror etched onto her lovely face. "I am a drug runner. Is that not criminal activity?"

"You were a mule. A child."

"Call it what you will, there was an age when I knew what I was doing and when I continued to do it. Family business and all." He thought back, to the opulent mansion on the hill, overlooking the city. To the halls, filled with people, women, who were like wraiths, hollow eyed and desperate. Hungry looking. Willing to sell any and everything for a taste of their drug of choice.

"It is the most hideous business," he said. "Drugs turn people into ghosts. They steal everything vital from them. Everything alive. The color goes from them. They have one drive, and one drive only—the next fix. And they will sacrifice anything to get it. We—my father, me—we capitalized on that."

"Not you. You were a child."

"I lived in the mansion. I wore custom suits bought with that money."

"Yes, but you aren't there now."

"Stop trying to excuse it. I ran drugs when I was a boy, but I took them as a teenager. And I used the women who were addicted to them. I suspect…" He hesitated. "I have long suspected that Alexios Christofides was the child of a prostitute who lived in my father's compound. I don't know it for sure… but he hates me, and it's with enough ferocity that I know it goes beyond business."

"But you wouldn't have done anything to him, you were a boy…you."

"I was part of the problem. Do you want to know how I lost my virginity, Leah? To a prostitute. Not the kind that were kidnapped and sold, one of the ones who hung around waiting for her favored poison." She wanted to close her eyes. To block out his face, to block out the words, as the pieces of the puzzle that was Ajax Kouros came together. As the boy she'd cared for, the man who stood before her, merged into one. Merged with this new truth. "I traded her. She took my virginity, I gave her an ounce of cocaine. Generous, really. And that's not all. That's not everything. It's not even close. You can't begin to understand it. I was a boy, wandering around a massive mansion filled with vice, and none of it was locked to me. Some days I didn't eat, because no one prepared food for me. It was there, but do you think anyone spared me a thought? Not until I learned where the power was in the little class system my father built for himself. Sex and drugs."

"I don't… I didn't…"

"You didn't imagine it was that, did you? Because you're so…lucky to have been given what you were given. And I have spoiled it now. I shouldn't have tried to make you understand. I should not have forced this on you."

A flash went before his mind. A girl crying. Her dress torn. A piece of fabric in his hand. Proof *he* had done it. That her tears were his fault. That her fear was because of him. And clarity from the haze of drugs his father had given him, just enough clarity, to look up and into the mirror that hung on the wall in the bedroom and see the monster. And recognize that it was him.

"I asked."

"Cover yourself," he said, his voice rough.

"Why?"

"Because I...I can't think with you standing there like that." With his past bleeding into his present. The darkness covering all the beautiful light Leah had given him last night.

"Maybe you don't need to think."

She took a step toward him and he reached out and grabbed her wrist. "Did you hear nothing of what I just told you? Of who I am?"

"The son of a violent horrible criminal. And maybe if I hadn't known you for most of my life, maybe it would affect me. But I have seen your actions, Ajax, for years. I watched you work your way from the doing grounds work, to being an assistant to my father. Then, a trusted advisor before you were eighteen. I saw how my father believed in you, sent you to school, brought you on as an intern at Holt. I saw his faith in you, and I saw you never disappoint that faith. And my sister...you never laid a hand on her. Never hurt her. You wanted to honor her with marriage vows. And me. A silly kid who followed you around and talked about candy...you listened to me. No, Ajax, when I look at you I don't see a monster."

"You've never seen me without my plan. My control."

"Sure I have. Our wedding day."

She leaned in, her lips brushing his, and he leaned back. "Not now." He could tell her. He could tell her what it looked like when he really lost control. Or he could show her.

He was tempted. To lay her down in the sand and claim her, hard, fast, taking and satisfying the never-ending hunger in him. To try to fill the blackness with her light.

But he would not. Because if he let it go, even for a moment, with her, he might never get it back. Might never be able to subdue it, subdue himself, again.

"Don't," he bit out.

"Why?"

For one moment, his mind was moving too fast, his blood flowing too hot to formulate an answer. And then she reached out and put her palm flat on his chest, the heat and fire that assaulted him nearly too much to endure.

And he was pulling her against him, breasts crushed against his chest, his mouth crushed against hers. And he needed. Blind need, deeper, more all-consuming than anything had ever been.

Like the craving for a drug. Altering, impossible to resist. It pushed him to the edge, held him there, threatening to send him over. Into the abyss. He wanted to jump. Wanted to follow this desire straight to hell and drag her with him if he had to, so long as he could get what he needed.

So long as he could get his fix.

He pulled back, his chest rising and falling with each harsh breath. He started to speak but he couldn't form any words. So he just turned and left her there, on the beach, in nothing but her bikini bottoms.

And for the first time in his memory, he had no plan.

CHAPTER TEN

AJAX SAT AT the foot of the bed, a scarf stretched between his fists. He'd been thinking, all afternoon and until the sun went down, about what he would do with Leah. What he could do with her. She was his wife—there was no getting around that. A wife he'd promised to make a marriage with...but when she touched him it all went blank.

He couldn't see the path up ahead anymore. All he could see was those whiskey-colored eyes. Eyes that had tested him years ago. Had enticed him into something he hadn't identified. Something he'd forced himself to turn away from. And now, he was bewitched by them again. And couldn't hold on to his control. He could only see her.

The problems really started when she touched him. It had to stop.

If he could just keep some of the control. If he could take the variables away and have all the power. All the power and Leah's naked body, spread out before him. To take pleasure in, to give pleasure to.

One time with her and he was on his way to obsession.

She'd asked him if he would have shared Rachel's bed. He was pretty certain he'd lied. That he would have shared Rachel's bed because it was something a husband did with a wife.

And because Rachel wouldn't have challenged his control in the same way that Leah did. He had always known that.

Leah walked in the front door of the villa, dressed in her

swimsuit and cover-up, and the truth hit him full on. He had always known it would be like this. That Leah was the one who would wake up the monster.

She tugged at the flowing fabric on the cover-up, stretching it over her breasts. He'd been half hoping she would come through wearing nothing but bikini bottoms but he was disappointed on that front.

Was he disappointed? Yes. No point in pretending he didn't want her. He did. More than he could remember wanting anything or anyone. The acquisition of Holt seemed like nothing now, not compared to the need to join his body to Leah's.

She kept comparing his celibacy to her innocence. As if it united them somehow. As if they shared something. But she did not share in his darkness.

They were nothing alike. And she didn't know what she was tempting.

And if he had his way, she never would.

He wrapped the scarf around his fist and tugged it so that it was taut, watching her through the curtain as she approached the bed, her hips swaying gently, each step she took tightening the desire in his stomach further.

"Where have you been?" he asked.

"And you care why?"

"I'm your husband," he said, the words scraping his throat raw.

"Oh, really. Well, you can't just be my husband when it suits you, Ajax. You can't shove me away on the beach and walk away then expect that you get to know the details of my whereabouts."

"If something had happened to you?"

"I lived the first twenty-three years of my life without you in my pocket, I'm pretty sure I can handle the next twenty-three without you there, too."

"Tell me, Leah, knowing everything you know about me—"

he wrapped the scarf around his fist again, drawing his hands more tightly together "—do you still want me?"

She lifted her chin. "Yes."

"Tell me," he said, "exactly what you want from me."

"I already told you."

"Tell me again," he said. "Restate your terms." He had to know. He had to hear it again.

"You. In my bed. Children," she said, adding more now, "support of my business. The expansion of Leah's Lollies should be a priority."

He pulled his fists as far from each other as he could, the fabric straining between them. "Done."

"And what has this deal cost me? My soul?"

"I don't want your soul, darling girl, I want your body."

"I offered it. Freely."

"On my terms."

"And what," she asked, her voice breathy, "are your terms?"

"You can't touch me during sex."

"That's impossible," she said.

"No, it's not. When you touch me, when you push me too far too fast, I start to lose control, and that is unacceptable."

"And you have a solution?"

"You said you could handle my darkness." He stood from his position on the bed, the scarf still wrapped around his hands.

Her eyes fell to the scarf and shock flickered in the golden depths. Then, she raised her gaze to meet his, her tongue darting out slowly to moisten her lips. "Are you offering to show me the darkness?"

"No," he said, his voice rough, "I aim to protect you from it."

"How?"

"I need control."

"How much?"

"All of it. Can you give me that? In bed, I need all of the control."

Leah's heart thundered in her head, her hands shaking, her

entire body shaking, from the inside out. She felt like she might really be in over her head. Like she might have miscalculated. For the first time, when she looked at Ajax, she felt like she was looking at a stranger.

"Tell me what you want to do," she said, knowing instinctively what it was he wanted. What he needed.

"I want to tie your hands."

"And then what?"

"I'm going to pleasure you until you can't think straight. Until you can't string together a sentence. And then…and then I want to part your legs and lose myself in you."

He was a stranger now. This raw, sexual part of him was something she'd never seen before. And it hit her, on the heels of the first thought, that this raw, sexual part of him was probably something no one but her had ever seen.

That it was probably something he'd never experienced, not when what he'd spoken of had been inexperienced couplings with prostitutes.

And she'd caused it to emerge.

Ajax was her dearest fantasy, her longest-held desire. He'd broken her heart, piece by piece for most of her life. With his obliviousness to her as a woman. The attention he gave to her sister. His engagement to her sister. His staunch refusal to show her any affection, any romance in their marriage.

And so right now, the need to have all of his attention focused on her, to be at his mercy, to be the subject of his dominance, was an answer to a fantasy that she couldn't say no to.

Because in that moment, she saw it clearly. His need for the ties was a concession to her power. To her ability to shake his control.

She recognized the power in his need for her to submit.

No, Ajax would never love her. The disconnect between the man he was and the man she'd imagined him to be was a chasm so wide there was no bridge that could cross it.

But she could have this. Enjoy this. Why not? Why not at

least get something out of this stupid obsession? These feelings that had done so much to define her life.

It felt like he owed her. In so many ways.

If she couldn't have it all, if he couldn't be the man she wanted, then maybe she could have this. She would have this. She would let him have total control, total command of her body, of her pleasure. She would have to stop protecting herself so much. Because there was no way to take everything he was giving if she was hiding behind a wall.

The reality that he couldn't love her. That she shouldn't love him…it should be protection enough.

She would take the pleasure he gave and she would keep it for herself.

She held her hands out in front of her. "Take me," she said.

A dark light, like a black flame, flared in his eyes. He unwound the length of silk from his fists, slowly, achingly so. Then he started wrapping it around her wrists. Slow. Sensual. He made it tight, made it so she couldn't move her hands. But she wanted the game. She didn't need freedom. Didn't want it. Not when captivity meant this.

"Tell me again," he said, his hands moving, strong and sure, securing the knot.

"Take me."

"Because?"

"Because I want you." She knew he needed to hear that, even if she didn't know why.

"On the bed," he bit out.

She obeyed, sitting on the edge, her bound hands in her lap. He stroked her face with the back of his hand, along her jaw, slow, sweet. Possessive.

He moved his hands to the knot of her bikini top, and untied it in one deft motion before removing her bathing suit wrap, letting it fall to her waist, along with the top of her swimsuit.

She was bare to him again, but instead of looking shocked, he looked hungry.

"Do you want to see the sort of thing a man who hasn't had sex in eighteen years is capable of?" he asked, his voice rough. "Do you want to see all that innocence you thought I had?"

And she knew he was going to make her pay for her comments on the beach. Make her pay in the best possible way. He lowered his head and drew her nipple deep into his mouth, sucking hard, and just like that, she couldn't think. Couldn't breathe.

She wanted to close her eyes, to sink into oblivion where there was only this, this pleasure, this feeling that ran deep and hot. But she forced her eyes to stay open, forced herself to look at him. To see Ajax, her dearest, most long-held fantasy, pleasuring her like this.

But he wasn't done. He abandoned her breasts and tugged her bathing suit cover down her thighs, getting onto his knees before her. Then he took her bikini bottoms and undid the ties, sending the scrap of fabric to join her wrap on the floor.

"Open your legs," he said.

And she was powerless to do anything but obey.

He settled between her thighs, pressing a kiss to her sensitive skin. The first touch of his tongue was like fire, white heat licking along her veins, a gasp catching in her throat.

"Lie back," he said, commanding, "and put your hands over your head."

She followed his orders, putting her hands over her head, her legs dangling over the bed. Then he gripped her legs and hooked them over his shoulders, pulling her against his mouth. The onslaught of sensation, of pleasure ripped through her. She was desperate to touch him, but she couldn't, her hands held captive, just as he held her soul captive.

Everything in her was poised on the brink, waiting for release, sobbing for it, desperate for it.

He shifted and started to pleasure her with his hands as well as his lips and tongue, sliding a finger inside her, sending a shock wave through her. She was close, so close. And every time she would get ready to go over the edge, he would pull back, just enough, before starting again, pushing her higher each time.

"Ajax…I can't. I can't…"

"Yes, you can," he said, sliding the flat of his tongue against her in time with the thrust of his fingers.

She rocked against him, trying to get herself the rest of the way there.

Then he moved away from her, leaving her buzzing and unsatisfied. "Not yet," he said, his hands going to the buckle on his pants.

She was dying. She needed to touch him, to taste him. And she knew he wouldn't let her.

He worked the belt through the loops slowly, then the button on the slacks, and the zipper. He tugged his shirt off over his head before shoving his slacks and underwear down lean hips, leaving him completely naked for her enjoyment.

Except she couldn't touch him. Dammit. She was desperate, and she had a feeling he was enjoying it.

So much for feeling powerful. But, while she didn't feel like she was in control, she definitely felt turned on. A good-enough quality of turned on, with the promise of a big-enough release that she was okay with feeling out of control.

In fact, part of her, a part of her she hadn't known existed, relished it.

"Do you approve?" he asked.

"More than," she said, sounding all breathless and shaky.

"Are you ready?"

"Not yet. I want to…I want to taste you," she said, her eyes on his erection.

"No. Sorry, *agape*. That's against the rules."

"I want to break the rules," she said.

"You will follow the rules, or I won't allow you to come," he said, his tone hard.

Her breath caught. "Oh."

"Will you be good?"

"Yes," she said, swallowing hard, her stomach tightening.

She noticed his hands didn't shake quite so much as they had last time when he joined her on the bed. His fingertips grazed her cheekbones, the gesture surprisingly gentle considering the game they were playing.

He pulled her up all the way onto the bed, strong arms locked around her, holding her tight. She inhaled deeply. She was surrounded by Ajax, and she had never felt so at peace. Everything from before, the bindings on her wrists, melted away for one fleeting moment.

And then he was poised over her, her arms above her head, thrusting her breasts toward his lips. And he made the most of it, pleasure arrowing from her nipples down to the apex of her thighs.

"Now," she said.

"No," he said, "that's not how this works." He pressed his length against her slick folds, sliding it back and forth. She gasped, arching into him.

"Please."

"That's better." He thrust his hips against her, the contact on her clitoris just right.

"Please," she said again, knowing that if she made a command, he would only deny her again.

He pressed the head of his erection against the entrance to her body and pushed inside her slowly. Tears stung her eyes, tears of relief. She needed him. Needed the release.

And then she was caught up completely, drowning in his kisses, in the rhythm of his body moving against hers. Her blood was roaring in her ears, pleasure building in her, so much, too much. She didn't think she could survive it.

"Please," she whispered again, the word barely making a sound on her lips.

He thrust into her one last time, stiffening above her, his arousal pulsing inside of her as he spent himself, his orgasm taking him over at the same moment hers broke through her and dragged her under.

When she came back to herself, her hands were still over her head, her arms starting to fall asleep. And so was she.

"Would you?" she asked, lifting her bound hands.

He sat up quickly, untied her, then he stood. He looked…she couldn't even quite put a word to it. Haunted maybe. Scared.

"I have work to do," he said, an echo of last night. "I'll join you when I'm finished."

Leah lay back down, rubbing her wrists, watching him walk naked down into the living area. He sat on the couch that way, his forearms resting on his legs.

And that was when she realized that as much as he'd been demanding of her, as out of her element as she was, Ajax was no better off.

Ajax had neatly severed his past from the man he'd become. All of the years she'd known him, she'd never seen his darkness.

She'd seen drive. Intelligence. Hunger. She just hadn't realized what had spurred the drive. That he'd been running, not just toward something, but from something.

From the darkness.

And she saw it now. Saw it in his eyes. And she was worried that he was getting too tired to keep running. She wanted to throw her armor onto him. To strip herself bare so she could protect him from it.

But she honestly had no idea how to hold the darkness at bay.

CHAPTER ELEVEN

THE HONEYMOON WENT by too quickly. She and Ajax were together every night. Every night, he bound her wrists, and every night he showed her a world of pleasure she hadn't imagined possible.

But they weren't closer during the day. Not any closer at all. In fact, she felt more distant from him than she ever had before.

During the day.

She closed her eyes as the plane touched down on the tarmac in New York. And she saw flashes of their time together in St. Lucia.

Her hands bound to the bedpost, her back to him. Candles the only light in the room. He'd skimmed his hand over her back, gripped her hips before thrusting in deep. And his voice…so desperate, so rough, in her ear, telling her how good it felt, words in broken Greek, some of which she'd never heard before.

She opened her eyes and looked out the window. It was cold and gray out there. Gray runway, gray skyline, gray sky.

"Good to be back," she said, waiting for the plane to stop before she stood up and stretched.

"You sound so enthused," he said.

"I am." She wasn't.

This was weird. She felt like she was talking to a stranger. A cold, detached stranger, not the man she'd had hot, erotic sex with all night, every night, for the past week. He was her lover, her only lover. There was no mistaking him. There could have been no other man with her those nights. And yet…and yet the Ajax sitting in front of her, all cool and calm and… bored, wasn't that man.

He wasn't the man brought to the edge by her body. By their conversation.

She wanted to touch him. But she wasn't allowed to.

Her fingers curled into fists at her side. It wasn't so much his command that she was obeying, but her self-control she was testing.

She didn't want to be enslaved to her need for him. She knew this wasn't going to be a great love match. More and more, she questioned whether or not he could actually love.

Because she was seeing parts of him, glimpses into his soul, that frightened her now.

Always, Ajax had been a constant presence in her life. Serious, studious, kind. Now he was her husband, and as her husband he was distant, angry. As her lover he was dominant, generous, sexy. And as a man…she wondered if she knew who he was at all. If the person she'd always known was nothing more than an illusion, than a careful facade he'd put on as a scared, runaway boy from the kind of past she couldn't have ever imagined.

As a girl, she hadn't seen it. She'd been blinded by his physical beauty, by his careful kindness to her. As a teenager, it had been those small smiles. The accepting of her gifts, that had held her in thrall. He hadn't said anything about his past, and she hadn't asked. She'd filled in the blanks, seen what she'd wanted to see. Thought what she'd wanted to think about him.

But nowhere in there had she imagined he would look at her with flat, black eyes. So closed off. So emotionless.

Never had she imagined him binding her hands and having sex with her. It was really the best way to describe it. They didn't make love. Ajax was demanding, and in terms of the physical, he gave her everything. But his eyes were hollow. He held himself back from her.

There was something about being tied up that she liked. His dominance was arousing, his skill was wonderful. And if it had been a game, nothing more than a power play between lovers, she wouldn't have had a complaint.

But Ajax was using it for something else. Using it to keep control. To hold himself at a distance.

She wasn't an equal in it. Wasn't able to give back.

Like the conversations they'd had when she'd been a teenager. Only this was their bodies. He was doing all the talking, all the work. But her hands were tied. Literally.

He wasn't letting her give. Wasn't letting her add herself to the mix. It was all him. All what he wanted, even though what he seemed to want was to give her endless, blinding orgasms, which seemed sort of petty and stupid to have an issue with, but it was the principle.

She'd never been less sure of anything in her life. She was married to Ajax, only to discover she didn't know him. To have the security of fantasy and her notion of love ripped away from her, when she was bound to him for life.

She really felt like she needed a drink.

Although, since she'd been having unprotected sex with Ajax for a week, maybe she shouldn't. Oh, jeez, that had to stop. Yes, she wanted children and she knew he did, too, but honestly, she was so messed up at the moment it just wasn't a very good idea.

Her phone pinged, and she looked down at the new message that was displayed on the screen. "Oh, Ajax, I have to stop by the store. Do you mind?"

He lifted one shoulder. "If it's an emergency, of course we should go."

The little show of support made her feel not quite so alone. "It's not really an emergency—my manager just wants me to check something out, but…I appreciate it."

"Of course. I'm investing in this company, so I need to make sure everything is running well."

Ouch. "Right. Of course."

She might not love him, but he was her lover, and she wished they had a little something personal between them. She wasn't just his lover, either, she was his wife. Lifelong family…acquaintance. Up until the past few weeks she would have called him a friend, but friends *knew* each other. They only knew each other in the biblical sense. And even then, that was only provided she followed his rules.

There had been a time in her life when she'd imagined that being with Ajax would solve all of her problems. Instead, he'd just introduced her to a whole new set of them she hadn't even known existed.

Leah's Lollies was a pop of color in the middle of the city. The floor was set up like a game board, brightly colored squares leading you down different paths. There was the road to the candy cane forest, which boasted huge candy canes spread around like trees, dusted in crystal. Every sort of mint was there. And then there was chocolate cove, with chocolate sculptures that were rotated out every season, and at least three hundred varieties of chocolate candy.

It was the lightest, frothiest excess Ajax had ever seen. And in some ways, he found it refreshing. He was all too familiar with the dark side of human appetites.

A little sugar seemed harmless in comparison.

As soon as they'd walked in, Leah had scurried to the back to speak to the manager, leaving Ajax standing in the middle of the fruit patch, where all the fruity treats lived. A girl, no older than sixteen, approached, wearing a white-and-red-striped uniform and an overdone smile.

"Welcome to Leah's. Lolly?" She held up a small lollypop that matched her uniform.

"No."

She looked a little bit crestfallen. But he wasn't a candy person. Except when Leah had left him candy. He'd always eaten that because he hadn't wanted to hurt her feelings.

Something he'd done constantly since their marriage, he was sure of that.

"Actually," he said, "No lollypop, but…do you have a red hard candy?"

"Tons. Cinnamon or fruity?"

"Fruity."

"Over this way."

Leah's candy expert helped him pick a bag of small red, round candies. Cherry. They reminded him of her. Of her red lips. The color they'd been the first time he'd kissed her for a reason other than show. The first time he'd kissed them just because he wanted to.

And they reminded him of her bikini. The one she'd worn the first night they'd made love.

Leah appeared a few moments after he'd paid for the candy and stuck the bag in his jacket pocket.

"Did you get bored?" she asked.

"How could anyone get bored in here?"

"I feel the same way," she said, a dreamy smile on her face. "I think my favorite store is the one in France, though. I'm test-driving a bakery. You should see all the macaroons set out every day. In every color you can possibly imagine. So far they've sold out by midday every day."

Leah's expression took on a dreamy quality, her enthusiasm obvious. Enviable.

He wondered what it must be like to love something so much. To have so much passion for your work, for anything in life.

He didn't know. He would never know. The nature of things, of himself, required that he keep too much of himself chained. Passion was very much in chains.

Except when you're with Leah. Then it's her in chains.

Chains or a silk scarf. That was passion tugging at its leash, getting close, but not getting free. A dangerous, dangerous game, but one he couldn't bring himself to give up. And not because of their agreement. Not because they both wanted children.

But because he craved the taste of her. The feel of her.

So deadly. So close to the edge. And yet, he couldn't stop himself. He didn't even want to. Leah had always had a way in. She had always mattered to him. And that foothold she'd made in his soul, early on, was now threatening to be the undoing of all of his efforts.

Was threatening to pull him back into darkness. A man who was a slave to his passions. A man who barely deserved life, much less the soft, sweet touch of Leah's hands.

The man he feared most.

At least during the day he could put things back to normal. At least with her wrists bound he had some form of control. At least the safeguards were holding.

He thought about the bag of cherry candies in his pocket and wondered what he was thinking. Wondered why he'd bought them.

Then he pushed the thought to the side. He would worry about it later. Everything was fine. His barriers were firmly in place. It was the perfect arrangement, really. He had Leah, beautiful—how had he ever missed how beautiful?— exciting Leah, in his bed every night. He had a wife by his side, one who understood his devotion to his work and was just as devoted to her own. One who made it possible for him to acquire Holt. One to keep his competitor well and truly foiled. Yes, things were absolutely perfect.

"Ready to go?" he asked, already thinking of how he would tie her hands tonight. How he would bury his face between her thighs until he'd satisfied them both. He craved her, the taste of her on his tongue.

Oh, yes, he had plans tonight. Plans that were much more

pleasurable than any he'd ever made before taking Leah as his wife.

"Uh, yeah, sure. If you don't want anything."

He lifted a shoulder, not sure why he didn't want to tell her about the candy in his pocket. "No. I don't need anything."

"Oh. Okay."

Not touching, they stepped out of the store and onto the sidewalk. And flashbulbs exploded in front of them. He was blinded by the harsh light, bright spots in the dark that marred his vision so it was all he saw everywhere he turned. He tried to look at Leah, to see her expression, but her face was obscured by spots dancing before his eyes.

"Where have you been for the past week?" One of the reporters shouted a question, and the others took it to mean it was a field day.

"Ajax! Ajax! How do you respond to allegations that your ex-fiancée left you for another man?"

"Ajax! Why the charade?"

"Leah! What's it like to be the backup bride?"

Ajax gripped Leah's arm and pulled her in tight to his body. "No questions," he growled, dragging her toward the car.

He'd always commanded a fair bit of interest from the media, but nothing like this, not ever. It was Rachel, of course, his association with Holt and what had happened at the wedding. But mainly Rachel. She was the darling of the press. Of the society world in general.

And she had, no doubt, been indiscreet with her lover. And now suddenly, he and Leah were much more fascinating than they'd been when they'd simply made up the story about the amicable split of him and Rachel, and his discovery of feelings for Leah.

As he ushered Leah into the limo, he heard one last question rise up over the others. "How does it feel to have the swan get away while you get left with the ugly duckling?"

He slammed the door shut and shouted at his driver in Greek

to drive. And then remembered his driver didn't speak Greek. The man seemed to get the gist of it, though, even if he didn't understand the exact words.

And in that spirit, Ajax let loose a string of profanity he doubted even Leah was familiar with.

His vision started to clear, slowly, and he could see Leah's face, revealed by strips of light as the car passed buildings, still open, even though it was late. Each bar of light illuminated a glittering tear on her cheek. She didn't make a sound, her face didn't crumble, she sat, stoic, with moisture tracking down her face.

The car pulled up to his penthouse, and Leah was out before the vehicle had stopped all the way. Ajax followed.

"Leah," he said.

"Don't," she said, walking on ahead of him, stopping when at the doors, waiting until he entered the building code, and then charging ahead of him again.

"What they said…"

"Was true. I am your backup, and we both know it. But it was my choice. I knew what I was getting into. But that doesn't mean I have to like hearing crap like that shouted at me in public."

"Damn right," he growled, following her into a waiting elevator. "I won't allow it to run, Leah. I won't allow a headline like that to exist."

"Control the press now, do you, darling?" she said, her tone brittle. "You're more powerful than the president."

"I have connections. And that," he spat, "isn't news. It's the lowest form of entertainment, given to people who have nothing better to do than to sit and enjoy the misery of others. The modern-day Greek tragedy."

"Yep. All the catharsis of Oedipus Rex without the incest," she bit out. "I'm so thrilled to be a part of it."

"I would have spared you from this."

"It doesn't matter, Ajax," she said, wiping a tear from her

cheek. "If they didn't print it, it wouldn't make it any less true. You wanted her…you got stuck with me."

"I didn't love her."

"But you wanted her."

He couldn't imagine taking Rachel to his bed, not even in the vaguest fantasy. He couldn't imagine having or wanting any woman other than Leah. He could picture her even now, her dark curls spread over his pillow, her arms raised above her head, pushing her breasts up. An offering. One he would always accept.

"I don't want her now." He didn't think he ever had really.

"I… That's good. But still… Backup Bride. Yay. That's catchy. That's going to stick."

"I will…"

"You will what, Ajax? Go in and be all mean and scary and demand retractions? Why? What's the point?"

He reached down and cupped her chin. "Because I will not have them hurt you like this."

"Why not? You hurt me all the time."

He dropped his hand down to his side, a strange, cold feeling spreading from his chest down to his fingertips.

The elevator doors slid open, and she walked out into the hall, standing by the door, waiting for him to open it. She pushed past him and into the living room. "So, great, I'm going to bed. And I think I'm going to let you off the hook tonight."

"Let me off the…?"

"Of our deal. Every night. My bed. I don't want to do that tonight."

"Why?" he asked, knowing it was a stupid question, and yet he had no idea how to fix the situation he found himself in. Leah had been different in the candy store. Softer for a moment. More like the Leah he'd always known.

But now her guard was up, walls strong and high around her. He couldn't reach her. Didn't know what to say or do.

"I have a headache," she said. "Something to do with over-exposure to flashbulbs. Good night."

She stalked out of the room, and Ajax walked to the bar. He kept a bar in his house, and it was fully stocked. He told himself it was for guests, but deep down he knew. He knew he was waving a red flag in front of the beast, tempting him.

And tonight…tonight he nearly took the bait.

He gritted his teeth and turned away from it. He was in control. No one would take that from him, not even Leah.

CHAPTER TWELVE

LEAH WOKE UP feeling horrible, and her mood lasted the whole day. Last night's encounter with the press had been the embodiment of her every past insecurity. Of her every current insecurity. So many people so certain she wasn't good enough. So confident in saying it. In reminding her that her husband, the man she made love with every night, didn't really want her.

She had ample time to get grouchier since Ajax spent the whole day at Holt and she spent the whole day replaying the press fiasco, and every lame encounter she and Ajax had had since their marriage, without the memory of recent good sex as a buffer.

She was digging through his freezer, looking for something for dinner, when he came back home.

"Leah," he said, coming into the room, "I hope you didn't eat."

"That was actually why I was spelunking through your freezer. I'm hungry."

"I don't have much of anything in this house. I'm not here often enough."

"Yeah, I noticed. Order a pizza?"

"No, I thought we might go out."

"Why?"

He held a newspaper out in front of him, folded open to the society pages. There was a photo, a huge photo, of her and Ajax, walking out of Leah's Lollies last night. They both looked strained, and they had a gap between their hands that looked extremely…significant. She imagined the facial expressions were from the camera. As for the not touching…well, she wasn't allowed to touch him. Not when he didn't want. So that was his fault.

The headline was *really* nice.

"Strain for Ajax Kouros and his Backup Bride as Holt Heiress Cavorts with Her New Lover. Gee. Charming." She sucked in a sharp breath and blinked against the sudden stinging in her eyes. "I'm actually a Holt heiress, too. She's not more of a Holt heiress than me. But I'm usually the Other Holt Heiress. And now I've been demoted further than even this. It's like I don't have a name. This backup bride title is bull—"

"And it's why we're going out," he said. "A show of togetherness is essential right now. I am not allowing this marriage to become a farce."

"This marriage is a farce, Ajax."

He grabbed her arm and pulled her up against him, his dark eyes blazing. "Is it? We seem to have some very real moments."

"In bed. And even then…it's a game."

"Nothing is funny about any of it, Leah. Nothing."

"I didn't say it was. But you aren't real. It's not real. You have rules, and you're like a naked referee. I can't do anything you don't want me to do."

"It's for your own good," he bit out.

"Really? And since when did you become an expert on my own good, Ajax, huh?"

"It's not you I need to know—it's me."

"And why is that?"

"Do you want to know why I haven't been with a woman in eighteen years? Do you want to know why I have to control myself. Why I have to tie your hands?"

"Yes," she said, not sure she did. Suddenly wishing she could stop the train, but it was too late. There was too much momentum.

"The night of my sixteenth birthday I nearly raped a woman."

Leah went cold. Starting at her lips, spreading through her face, down to her fingertips. The moment, and it could only have been a moment, stretched on and on. Forever.

"You…what? I don't believe you. I don't… Ajax, you didn't…"

"I did. My father never paid much attention to me. I never knew who my mother was, probably a whore, and I mean that in the literal sense. I grew up neglected, surrounded by excess. The night of my birthday, my father actually gave me a party. And drugs. A lot of drugs. Not the first time I'd ever taken them. I was, for lack of a better term, a kid in a candy store after all. But at that age, my father decided it was time for me to truly understand the products he sold, so that when I became a man I could take over the business. When I became a man like him. Not if. When."

"What…what…?"

"I was high out of my mind, I'd never had so much. And there was a party. It was so damn loud and hot. People screwing in every room in the house. In the hall. Women who were paid to be there, paid to service men, doing their jobs right there in public because they had no other choice. And then there was Celia. I know her name. I still remember it. My father shut me in a room with her, and I was…I was so certain in my own appeal, my own importance. After all, no woman had ever said no to me. Who would dare say no to the boss's son? She'd been given to me. And I wanted her. I saw nothing else but what I wanted. And hell, she'd been paid to be with me. She was my whore, right? So I was ready to just take her. And I very nearly did."

He could remember tearing her dress. Her sharp sob, fists hitting him. And everything suddenly becoming clear. Realizing what he was doing. Realizing for the first time that his pursuit of self-satisfaction had a cost for those he used.

Realizing for the very first time that other people mattered.

It was not what he had been taught. He'd been taught nothing. He'd been fighting for survival within the walls of his father's mansion. A mansion that was more of a compound. Taking what he needed, what he wanted with no consequences.

Except on one girl's tear-streaked face he suddenly saw every consequence. The weighty price of his brand of enjoying life.

"Ajax…you didn't, though. That's what matters."

"No, Leah, it's not. It's not. I…grabbed her arm and then I looked at her. I really looked. She was terrified. Crying. Because of me. Because of what I had been about to do to her. Because of what I was too blinded by myself to see."

"And the drugs. You were on drugs."

"That makes it better, Leah? I shouldn't have ever agreed to that. Much less agreed to sleep with a woman who was paid to be there. Do you know what my father said?"

She didn't want to know. "What?"

"Break her in. She's a virgin. You'll like her."

"Oh," Leah breathed, the one syllable filled with pain. For him. For Celia.

"She was just a girl. Sixteen like me, I found out later."

"How did you find out?"

"Because the minute I sobered up enough to do anything but lie on the bed and cry with her over what was happening in me, about what I'd nearly done, about what my father did, we ran. I took her back home. She wasn't a prostitute. She wasn't there because she wanted to be, or even there to get drugs. She'd been kidnapped. I couldn't go to the police. Because I knew well that many of them were on my father's payroll. How else does a man with such a transparent operation last so long? And for that betrayal…for that betrayal he would have killed me. He very possibly would have tracked down Celia's family and had her killed, too."

"Ajax that's…terrible. You had no help…no way to get out."

"She wouldn't have needed help if not for my father. If not for me."

"And you saved her."

"Do not turn me into the hero of this twisted story. There was nothing heroic about what I did. It was the absolute least that a human should do for another human. I will never…I will never be that man again. That man who felt like everything was for him. That man who threw off all control, who threw away everything good in him in pursuit of pleasure."

"Pleasure you didn't take."

"Stop trying to spin it so I come out looking good," he said. "A murderer might stop his knife just before it hits his victim. He might stop. But he is still, in his heart, a murderer."

"And you think you would hurt me if I pushed you too far?"

He took a deep breath, and looked at her, his black eyes blank, bottomless. "That's the thing. I have no idea what I would do. I have kept myself, so much of myself, chained for so long. All I know is that the beast is hungry. I don't know what it wants. And I damn sure will not find out at your expense."

"And this is why you were never with a woman?"

"Sex, in my mind, has a place. It is not the halls of a mansion where everyone can see. It's not with a frightened girl kidnapped from her home. Sex like that? It has a victim, Leah. I thought in marriage that dynamic would be erased." His skin turned ashen, his expression like stone. "I haven't made a victim of you, have I?"

She tilted her chin, trying to look confident, trying not to look as if she was breaking inside. Breaking for him. For all he'd been through. For how he saw himself. Ajax believed he had a beast in him. More than that, Leah thought he probably believed he was the beast.

"Ajax, I asked you to sleep with me. I told you I wanted sex. You have never done anything I haven't wanted you to. You tie my hands because I let you. I only submit because I want to. I'm strong enough to handle you."

"But I fear I'm strong enough to break you."

She shook her head. "I don't think so. Ajax…the man you are today, the man you are now…could you possibly be that man without that moment with Celia?"

"I don't understand."

"Without that moment of clarity, that moment where you first saw who you were, would you have ever changed?"

"I don't… Leah, I can't…"

"What is your father doing now?"

"He's in jail," Ajax said. "Because I used my connections to find a way to put him in there. I hope he's dead, Leah. I pray it's so."

"You put him behind bars?"

"Yes."

"And the women?"

"As far as I know, with access to all of his computers, they rescued a record number of people."

"Because of you. Because that's who you are."

"No. I'm not."

"Do you have to punish yourself?"

"I'm not punishing myself. I'm keeping those around me safe. Except you." He met her eyes, a knot forming in his chest. "I fear I'm not keeping you safe."

"Trust that I'm strong enough to keep myself safe. And to know what I want."

"And what do you want?"

"Dolmades. Take me someplace Greek."

Ajax's heart was about to wear a hole through his chest. He was still high on adrenaline after his confession to Leah. Dinner hadn't done anything to take the edge off. He wondered if he even deserved to have the edge taken off.

Because the truth was ugly. So ugly. And he deserved to burn for it.

The restaurant was small, a trendy, darkly lit place where people who were truly famous went. It was where people went who didn't want privacy. The perfect place to go to encounter the press. To have pictures taken.

The press. He had to think of the press now and not just his past. Not about the monster prowling around inside of him.

"Do you want to dance?" There was a small dance floor, near the stage. It was intimate and crowded. Just the sort of thing a newlywed couple would be drawn to. He supposed.

"I didn't think you danced."

"I don't," he said. "Now, would you like the dance or not?"

Leah cocked her head to the side, her curls spilling over her shoulder like a dark waterfall, her eyebrows locked together. "Yes. Yes, I'll dance with you."

"All right." He stood and offered her his hand. "Try not to look like I've asked you to join me in front of the firing squad, okay?"

She smiled then. "Aw, Ajax, are you trying humor?"

"Yes. Have I succeeded?"

"Almost." She took his hand. He curled his fingers around it, relishing her softness. Her warmth.

He took her down to where the other couples were, moving in time with the music and pulled her against him. Before he realized that he truly had no idea how to dance.

"I've never done this before," he said.

She laced her fingers through his, one hand on his shoulder. "That can't be. You've been to hundreds of events with Rachel."

"And I always told her what I told you that day after our wedding. I don't dance."

"So why are you dancing now?"

"Because you're right. I can't go storming into the newsroom and threaten to kill people. It wouldn't be appropriate."

"Not even a little."

"And I can't stop them from printing things like they did today. But dammit, I can work to kill the rumors. I can do my part to make sure no one, anywhere, ever assumes that you're a backup for anything."

She blinked and rested her head against his shoulder. "I am, though."

"I didn't know Rachel," he said. "Not really. We never once had a deep conversation. I never told her about my life at my father's compound. And she wouldn't have wanted to hear it. She was content to just have a facade, and that was fine by me. Preferable even. But I didn't know her. She didn't know me. I didn't know you, either. But I'm starting to. And I think…I think you now know me better than any other person on earth."

"Really?" Her words were muffled by his suit jacket.

"Yes. Really. Starting from when you used to come and visit me. Do you remember that?"

She laughed, a watery sound. "Of course."

"You brought me chocolate. It always made me… I felt like someone was thinking of me. Me, not my business acumen, or anything else. Just me. And now you're the only woman who knows about my past. The only woman who has ever been with me…as a man. As anything other than the stupid, selfish boy I was. So I think you officially know me better than anyone."

"I guess I do."

"And you're here with me. You didn't run. And now that I know you, now that I know you as a woman, a woman who will not hesitate to yell at me, to take a cut out of my ego with a sassy remark, I find that…I find that I don't believe another woman would be right for me."

"But am I right for you? Or is it just that anyone would be wrong?" She lifted her head and looked at him, golden eyes sparkling.

"I don't know. But we're together."

"After three weeks of marriage. Someone get us a medal."

"I don't know that I really understand love… I doubt I ever will. I thought I did, but it's become very clear that I knew an attachment for convenience, and not any sort of real affection or deep emotion. I don't know if I'm wired to…to know how to give it. My father didn't love anything but money and power. He taught me to view myself as the final authority, be my own god, worship myself and my needs and…that one moment in my life, when I saw her face…" It made his chest tight to think about it, even after all these years. "That was the first time I ever looked outside of myself. The first time I considered that other people had feelings and needs and hopes and dreams that were just as important as mine. More important. And that I possessed the power to destroy them if I had a mind to."

Her fingers curled around his suit jacket, her hold on him tight. He continued. "Just that bit of humanity was a lot of effort to achieve and beyond that…I try to keep my needs, my desires, under control so that I at least don't hurt anyone. I can't be everything a husband should be, but I won't be cruel. I won't ever hurt you or force you, or do anything that you don't want me to."

Leah's heart thundered, her hands shaking. She was holding on to Ajax as tightly as she could to keep from crumpling to the floor.

He was telling her about himself. Everything he believed about himself. And he was, in the same breath, promising never to hurt her. And his words were destroying every wall she'd built between them.

Didn't he know? Didn't he have any idea that marriage to a man who kept half of his heart, half of who he was, prisoner deep down inside himself would be able to do nothing but hurt her? Even if the hurt only came from watching him. Day after day, struggling with what he considered to be an inner demon, when it was simply Ajax. He fought against himself, waged a war on appetites most people embraced. The appetites most people found made life worth living.

Didn't he know that it would kill her to watch it?

She looked at him, at the horrible blankness in his eyes, and she pictured his fire, his life, pushed down deep in his body, crying our for release. For freedom.

She had spent her life idolizing Ajax Kouros. A man who she thought had it all. A man she thought to be perfect. But she hadn't known Ajax. Hadn't known the struggles he'd faced, where he'd come from, or why he was headed toward his final destination with such singular purpose.

She hadn't known how hard his fight was. Hadn't known that every day cost him more energy just to keep himself in line than most people would ever have to expend.

She had loved an illusion. And now before her was the man. Or part of him anyway. She wanted the rest. She wanted all of him. She wanted to know him. To know the things about him even he didn't know, the things he wouldn't acknowledge.

And she realized something suddenly. That she was selling them both short. Yes, she'd purposed not to protect herself quite so much. To view him with realism. To accept he couldn't love her. That he couldn't love.

And in turn, she wouldn't love him. She wouldn't be vulnerable to him. She wouldn't give what she couldn't get.

She was taking half willingly. Pushing him for nothing, because if she pushed him for emotion, for love, she would have to acknowledge that she wanted it. That she wanted more than sex and companionship.

She would expose herself to the kind of pain the media had never come close to doling out.

She had just thought of him as a man denying himself, but was she any better? She was protecting herself. Protecting herself by denying a piece of her that was bound up, gasping for breath.

The part of herself who believed she deserved to try for it

all, pain be damned. Who believed her happiness was worth risking her heart. Who believed Ajax's happiness was worth risking her heart.

"So…" She swallowed. "What you're saying is, if you could go back to the moment you proposed, knowing what you know now…you would ask me instead?"

He nodded slowly, still swaying, almost in time with the music. "Yes."

She sucked in a sharp breath. "I…I'm not sure I would say yes."

His brows locked together. "Why?"

It was time to let her guard down. Really. It was time to have expectations. To believe she could make him change. To believe she wasn't the Backup Bride.

"You give this big talk about knowing me, Ajax, but I don't feel like I know you. I can't even explore your body when we're in bed together. Which means…you don't really know me, either. You have me on a leash. Following your rules so you can hang on to that control you love so much."

"I don't mean to leash you, Leah. It's myself that I—"

"That might be what you mean to be doing, but the fact is, when you impose rules like that, stop me from doing what I want, from showing you what I want, you're only making me the person you expect me to be, the person you think you need me to be. Rather than the person I am. No wonder it's been so good for you. But you could have what you have with me with any other woman. Any obedient woman, that is."

He spun her out from his body, then pulled her back in, dipping his face close to hers.

"Not bad," she said.

"Thank you, I learn fast."

"Yes, you do."

"So you think I don't allow you to be who you are? Have I stopped you from saying…any and everything that comes to your mind? You, daily, take strips off me with your tongue, my dear, and I've hardly done anything about that, now, have I?"

Yes, she'd done that. Often. Self-protection. An attempt to push him away. To derail him. But she wasn't doing that now.

She gritted her teeth and pulled her fingers from his, took her hand from his shoulders and cupped his face. He stopped moving, his expression confused. She found it endearing. That big strong Ajax Kouros was confused by little ol' her.

"I'm sorry," she said. "I do that because sometimes when you hurt my feelings it's easier to yell at you than it is to show you that I'm hurt. And tonight, Ajax, just tonight, mind you—I can't put a moratorium on the sarcasm forever—I'm going to stop. But I need something in return."

"What?"

"I need you to play by my rules. Just for tonight."

"After everything I told you about me?" he asked, his voice rough.

"If you lose control are you going to hurt me?"

He looked scared. Haunted. "I don't know."

"I do. You won't. That isn't what you are. Men who delight in hurting women…it's not about desire. Or losing control because they're around a woman they can't resist. Those are lies. Those men want to hurt. They want to make themselves powerful. I have never seen those desires in you."

"Leah…"

"My rules, okay, not yours. Tonight. Come on, you're already dancing. It's nothing but a little quickstep to hell after this. We might as well have some fun on the way."

"What are your rules?" he asked. His face was like stone, immobile, unreadable.

She leaned in, her lips touching his ear. "I was thinking, my hands, untied. And I get to do whatever I want to you. And Ajax, my darling, I have about ten years' worth of fantasies stored up for you."

"Ten years?"

"All right, we'll skip the early years. That was a lot of running through meadows and you braiding flowers in my hair. But things started getting good about the time I was sixteen."

"Fantasies? About me?"

She smiled. "You didn't think I left candy on your desk just to be nice, did you?"

"I did, yes. It meant a lot to me, as I said. Are you telling me you were baiting me?"

"A little candy trail that I hoped might lead you to my bed."

"Subtle," he said. "Too subtle."

"I realize that now."

He frowned. "Why me?"

"Because I thought you were perfect. And gorgeous. I was wrong."

His frown deepened. "Were you?"

"Not about the gorgeous part, about the perfect part. I made you something in my head that I shouldn't have. You aren't perfect, Ajax. But the thing is, I'm not a girl anymore. And I don't need you to be perfect."

"What do you need?" he asked, an edge of desperation to his voice.

"I just need you. The man you are. The man you have become because of your mistakes. Because of your scars. Not the man you are with all those chains on, but the man you *are*."

"You say that, Leah, but you don't know."

"You told me."

"I told you who I saw myself becoming, and why, but I don't even know what would happen now…I don't even know if I could change the way I do things, the way I see things. And I doubt you would like me if I did."

"Here's the thing—I don't know if I would, either. But you have to give me a chance to know you. Give yourself the chance to be you. And I'll give you a chance to know me."

He lifted his hand, cupped her cheek, then slid his fingers

through her hair, letting the strands fall around her face. "But there is every chance that once you know me, you won't like me."

She took his hand and turned his palm toward her face, pressing a kiss to his skin. "Ajax, you danced for me. So that the press wouldn't say horrible things about me. I like what I know of you. A lot."

"Even knowing my past?"

"Your past breaks my heart. I can't imagine what it must have been like to be a child in a place like that. To have a father like that."

"What if…what if you dig so deep, Leah, deep inside of me, and you find out the darkness just keeps going? That there's no end to it. What if this is all I am?"

She blinked back the tears that were stinging her eyes. And she didn't try that hard to hold them back. Her heart ached, her throat burning.

Because she didn't know the answer to that question. If her husband could only ever give her this, what would it mean? If, after deciding to give it all, she could only get crumbs in return, what would she do?

It made her want to fold in on herself and start building new armor. To push him away. To retreat into a place where she was safe. From comparisons made by him, made by the media. From the deep fear that one day she would look into his eyes, searching for the truth of his feelings, and see nothing. From anything that might hurt her.

But she couldn't do that. Not now. Never again.

"Then I will take everything you are," she said, the words heavy on her tongue. The vow heavy in her heart, on her shoulders. Because in that moment she knew it was true. And she knew she couldn't go back on it.

But as she looked into his dark, fathomless eyes she wished she could. She wished some other man had claimed her heart years ago so that she wasn't so vulnerable to this one.

But there was no other man. There was only Ajax. It had always been that way, and she knew, beyond a shadow of a doubt, that it always would be.

Every muscle in Ajax's body was locked tight, ready to release at any moment. To pounce on Leah, maybe? Or to run. That was the other possibility.

They'd driven back to the penthouse in total silence, Leah wringing her hands in the seat next to him, looking out the window and most definitely not at him. And he wondered if she was already regretting what she'd asked of him.

He was at war. He wanted her. Wanted her hands all over his body, her mouth on him. But he knew that if that happened, in one blinding moment years of hard-won control could be undone, and he might never get it back.

That he could become the monster he had always feared he was.

The beast he kept chained inside of him, was him. He knew it, had always known it. And it terrified him down to his soul. That if he ever let it go, those parts of himself would meld back together, and there would be no more separating it.

That he would become the thing he hated most. Oh, he didn't think he would become a drug lord. But a man consumed by the desire for power? For success? At the expense of all else?

Yes, that lived in him. That horrible, conscienceless drive lived in him. Strong and black, seeking to devour whatever it could on the path to success. Not just success, to ultimate, unquestionable power, and damn who was hurt in the process.

He didn't want that to have free rein. Ever.

But now he was standing in the bedroom at his penthouse, and Leah was looking at him with wide golden eyes, fringed with dark lashes. Her lips were painted red, her dress, a deep green, molded to her curves, and he stood ready to trade everything in for the chance to taste her with no limits.

To have her with no ties to hold her back.

Yes, that was what he wanted. So badly he ached with it. And he didn't have the power to fight it anymore. Suddenly, having her seemed to be the most essential thing he could imagine. The embodiment of a dream, buried so deep, for so long, that unearthing it was nearly painful.

"Show me, Leah," he said. "Show me what you want. Show me who you are."

CHAPTER THIRTEEN

"You first." She tilted her chin up, her hip cocked to the side, her eyes glittering. "I feel like I've been doing a lot of giving here lately. Not that you don't…give admirably during our encounters—you do. But I feel like I'm the vulnerable one, so now it's your turn. Get naked, Ajax."

Her command felt like it was for more than skin. Like she wanted the kind of nakedness he was most afraid of. The kind that would reveal more than his body. The kind that would reveal what was left of his soul, and the state it was in.

But for her he would.

He started unbuttoning his shirt, then his pants, and he stood before her, naked. Shaking. She was unbound; she could do with him what she wanted. He was at her mercy, and he didn't regret it.

She approached slowly, a low flame burning in her eyes, gold flickering in the dim light. She reached out and put her hand on his bare chest, nails raking over his flesh, lightly. The slight pain was, as it had been their first time, a welcome gift to help temper the pleasure that was holding him by the throat.

And then she kissed him there, her lips hot on his neck, her teeth grazing him slightly. A testament of her power. That she held him in thrall using no force, only touch.

The beast rattled the chains.

"Careful," he said, his voice rough.

She bit him harder, scoring sensitive flesh. "I don't think I will be. I'm tired of being careful. I'm tired of holding back. I'm tired of being…I'm tired of trying to seem unaffected by the crap that gets written about me in newspapers. I'm tired of trying to keep my head down so I can avoid it. I'm tired of trying to make myself more attractive or more palatable to the public. I'm tired of hiding myself. Of changing myself to suit people who will always find me wanting no matter what I do. But most of all, I'm tired of not having my way with you."

"Then take me. But I can't be responsible for the consequences."

"Oh, I hope there are consequences," she said. "Don't make promises you can't keep."

He grabbed her wrists and pulled her forward, bringing her breasts up hard against his chest, his erection pressing against her belly. "There will be, *agape*. Make no mistake." He lowered his head and claimed her lips, sliding his tongue between them, delving deep.

When they parted, they were both breathing hard, Leah's face flushed, her eyes bright. She looked down at him, aching for release, her admiration open, her desire obvious.

"Right now, you're about to face some consequences of your own," she said. "I feel like I've been on a diet for years. And I am starving now."

She leaned in and kissed his chest, kissed a trail down his abs, lingering at his hip bone, biting him gently there, making him jump. She wrapped her fingers around his shaft, squeezing him gently, and he jerked beneath her hand.

"Are these my consequences?" he asked, his throat constricted.

"I'm just getting started. I have really, really fantasized about this. You have no idea." She leaned in and touched her tongue to the tip of his length, and a shot of heat scorched along his veins. Too much. It was too much.

He could feel something breaking loose inside of him. Could feel the walls starting to crumble. Chains starting to break.

When she slid her tongue along his length, he nearly lost his grip. On his control. On everything.

He pulled away from her, his heart pounding, his breath ragged. "I can't… Leah, stop."

"Why?" she asked, sounding dazed.

"It's too much. I can't…I can't breathe."

"Now you know how I feel. All the time. Every time I'm with you. Let me." She leaned in and pressed her lips to his hardened length, then her tongue. Then she sucked him deep inside of her mouth, and he was plunged into darkness, a world of absolute pleasure. Of nothing beyond what she made him feel. It roared through him, consuming him.

He clung to her, his fingers buried in her hair as she licked and sucked him, poured out her desire to give him pleasure. It humbled him. Sent him to the edge of reason, of thought.

And when he felt his climax surging through him, he pulled back.

"Not like that," he said.

"Why not?" she asked. "You've done it like that for me plenty of times."

"I know. But I want to be in you," he said, watching her face as he told her in blunt, descriptive terms, just what he wanted from her. "I want you to ride me." One position they hadn't been able to accomplish with her hands bound.

She smiled, a vixen's smile. Leah was pure seductress. A woman. And he felt for her what a man should feel for a woman. But beneath that was a warmth he couldn't explain. One that had always been there, one that had built and built from the moment he'd first met her. When she'd left candy on his desk.

The reason he'd turned his focus somewhere else as soon as possible. The reason he had never, ever seen her as a woman before the wedding.

Emotion. Passion.

That warmth, added to the desire, made a fire so hot he thought it might consume them both.

And then he remembered the candy.

"Lie down on the bed," he said.

"I thought I was giving orders."

"No. We just got rid of the rules."

"What are you planning?"

"You just have to find out. But you won't, if you don't obey."

"My consequences?"

"You could say that."

She got onto the bed, and heard rustling behind him as he turned to get the bag of candy out of his jacket pocket, where he'd left it the night before.

When he turned, she was lying on her back, her elbows propping her up. She'd discarded her shoes, her dress, her underwear. Everything. And she looked like a fantasy, created and come to life just for him. Nothing could have been more perfect; no one else could have even come close.

"You're a step ahead of me."

"I take initiative," she said. "It's one of my better qualities."

He approached the bed, the bag in his hand.

"Why do you have a Leah's Lollies bag?" she asked, eyes narrowed.

"I bought these a few nights ago. I wasn't sure why then. But I am now." He opened the bag and reached in, pulling out one red, round candy and placing it on her thigh. He leaned in, pressed his lips to her, then took the candy between his teeth. Then he licked her skin clean, the cherry flavor mingling with the taste of her. "Lie down."

He didn't have to ask her twice. Her hands were at her sides, her breasts rising and falling rapidly with each breath. He placed one candy just below her belly button, then another next to it, and another. Until he made a crimson, winding trail over her stomach, to her breasts, three pieces going just between them.

Then he placed one on her lips.

"Hold it there," he said.

She nodded slightly.

And he looked down at the trail of temptation on her beautiful body. "I always thought you were sweet," he said.

He lowered his head and flicked his tongue over her clitoris, and she bucked beneath him, a short, muffled sound escaping her lips. "Careful," he said. "Don't lose my reward."

He moved to the candy that rested low on her stomach, just above the triangle of curls at the apex of her thighs, taking it with his teeth as he'd done with the first, then lapping at her skin, taking in the flavor of cherry and Leah.

Ajax followed the trail, to her breasts, pausing to trace her nipples with the tip of his tongue before sucking them deep, savoring them as he'd done the candy. No extra adornment was needed there, not at all. They were delicious enough without adding any sugar.

He moved to the valley between her breasts and lapped up the remaining treats before moving to her mouth, his lips hovering over hers. He traced the seam of her lips with his tongue and captured the candy before kissing her deeply.

"You taste like cherry," she said at last, her voice breathy.

"So do you."

She laughed. "Funny how that works."

He gripped her hips and flipped their position so that she was sitting on top of him, straddling him, her hair forming a silken curtain around them, his cock resting against the slick entrance to her body.

She put her hands on his shoulders, moved herself into position, taking him in, inch by inch. And he watched her face, watched the expression of pure pleasure as it took her over. And then he was too far gone to do anything but feel.

He was at her mercy, her tight, wet heat surrounding him, her rhythm, slow and steady, driving him to madness. And suddenly he felt desperate. Desperate and starving, a gaping pit opening up inside of him, of need, of desire, that he feared could never be satisfied.

He reversed positions again and closed his eyes, pounding into her, the sheets fisted into his hands, sweat breaking out over his skin. And blood roaring through his veins. The beast unleashed. His need so overpowering, so violent and intense that Ajax lost control completely, his entire being one with the hunger, with the drive to claim her, make her his, find the ultimate pleasure with her. In her.

His woman. His wife. Leah.

A hoarse cry escaped her lips, her back arching, internal muscles pulsing around him. And he let go, spilling himself inside of her, his orgasm a flame, weaving itself through every fiber of his body, burning him from the inside out, the white wash of heat so intense he thought there would be nothing left of him when it was all over.

And finally it passed. And there was nothing left but him, and Leah. And the realization that all of his walls were gone. That he was torn open. Bloody. Defenseless. He had unleashed the beast on Leah.

He pulled away from her, scrambled into a standing position, his heart pounding hard, his breath coming in harsh gasps. He looked at Leah, at her swollen lips, her round eyes, filled with shock, confusion.

And he turned and walked out of the room.

Leah was stunned. Devastated, really. Her world was completely shaken by her encounter with Ajax. There wasn't cold darkness down deep in him. He was full of black fire, hot and dangerous, destructive and amazing.

She would never get enough of him, of how it felt to have all of his passion unleashed on her. The way it had started, the way he'd responded to her tasting him, the sexy playfulness of the candy. And then…oh, and then. That moment when he'd lost all control and put every ounce of his power into pleasuring them both. That moment when he'd unleashed himself on her.

She felt raw. Sore in the absolute best way. She liked him when he was rough. When he was uncivilized. When he was the man beneath the veneer.

What she didn't like was him walking away while her world was shattered around her feet.

She stood up and put his shirt on, buttoning it as quickly as she could, on her way out to the living room.

"Hey," she said. "What the hell? Unless you're just getting a glass of water, in which case I'll have one, too."

Ajax was pacing up and down the floor like a caged tiger, his posture tense. And he was still completely naked. He was beautiful, even like this. Tense and upset, and clearly on the edge.

"What's up, Ajax? Walk me through your thought process here. Because we were making love and doing this whole 'get to know each other' thing and then you…left."

"Are you okay?" he asked, his voice rough.

"Fine. A little wobbly, but I think you should be after something like that. Means you did it right."

"Stop. Stop trying to make a joke out of everything," he said, the words torn from him. "I was rough with you. I don't even know… I can't even remember what I did."

"Let me refresh your memory." She walked down to the center of the room. "You lost control. You thrust into me so hard it took my breath away. And it gave me pleasure that went… way beyond anything I've ever experienced before."

"Did I hurt you?"

"No. Well, I mean I'm sore in places, but the good kind."

"There's no good kind of pain. Dammit, Leah, if you had told me to stop I might not even have heard you. I don't know if I could have stopped. That's the kind of monster I am."

His words hung in the air, stark and revealing.

"You didn't hurt me, Ajax, and you never would. It's…it's

just…don't you trust that I know what I want? That I know what I like? That I would never in a million years lie to you if you hurt me just to salve your conscience? You know me. You know I would never do that to you, to *us*. I have been honest with you," she said, and then bitterly regretted saying it.

Because she hadn't been honest with him. She hadn't even been honest with herself. She'd pushed at him, had tried to cover up the growing, expanding emotions inside of her with layers of protection.

So that she wouldn't fall in love.

So that she wouldn't have to be in love alone.

She'd walked into her marriage with an impression she had of Ajax based in fantasy, not in reality. Thinking that she was in no way susceptible to this man. The man she hadn't known.

And since then, she'd met the reality. She'd seen how far down his damage had gone. She'd had to face who he was, where he came from. That he wasn't a shining beacon of male perfection, but a damaged, wounded soul who was starving for love, for affection, and to find some kind of peace within himself.

Because the inside of Ajax was a war zone. A place without rest. A place where he stood vigil against any desire he possessed. She doubted he even let go in his own mind. He was enslaved, in bondage.

He had tied her hands at first when they'd made love, but he was really the one that was bound.

And faced with that, with all he was, all he had been, and all he might not be, she knew her feelings had changed.

And she couldn't keep them in anymore. Not now, not after everything they'd shared. She couldn't protect herself when the victory over his demons might depend on her honesty.

"I love you," she said. It was true now. Truer than it had ever been. And the risk didn't matter. The possibility of him never returning it didn't matter. It would hurt, but sharing it was so much more important than protecting herself.

In Ajax, she'd seen the danger of holding it all in, and she wouldn't do it. Not anymore. Not ever again. It didn't matter that the press didn't think she was the pretty Holt Heiress, or that it must suck for Ajax to have her instead of Rachel.

It didn't matter. All that mattered was how she felt. That she loved him.

"What?" He looked at her with black, blank eyes, and the lack of emotion in them nearly broke her then and there.

"I love you," she said. "I have…well, I've loved you, or at least I thought I did, for most of my life. And there was a time when…when I tried to dig it out of my chest. To make it go away. Because I needed to protect myself. Because you chose her. Because the press told me who I was. That I wasn't special or pretty, and I thought… I was sure I couldn't ever be enough for you. But you know what? I could keep it inside then because I didn't *really* love you."

"I would think not," he said, his voice hard.

"I didn't know you. I didn't know you'd been raised in a drug house and brothel. I didn't know you felt like you were a monster, that you kept so much of yourself in chains. I didn't know you lost your virginity to a prostitute. That you'd run from a certain position of power and wealth into nothing to save the life of a girl. To save your own soul. I didn't know you hadn't touched a woman for eighteen years for fear you might relinquish hold on your control."

"You're quite fixated on that."

"Yeah, well, I think it's kind of hot. Really hot, actually. I'm glad I was your first in so much time. I'm glad you were my first ever. And that's the thing, really, I'm glad that I know you. Even if the truth isn't easy. Even if it's not pretty. Because now that I *know* you, Ajax…everything you were, everything you are, *now* I love you."

"You just said…"

"That I didn't love you before. I loved the idea of you, but not you. Not the broken mess you are."

"You shouldn't love the mess I am. I'm…I'm…"

"You're a monster, so I've heard. A monster who has not once done anything to hurt me physically. A monster who spent all these years giving nothing but respect to my family. A monster who dismantled one of the world's most insidious crime rings. Yeah, you're a monster."

"You don't understand," he said.

And then she saw it. The terror in his eyes, the depth of fear, and she did understand.

"I do," she said. "I do understand."

"If you did, you wouldn't be standing here offering me anything but a divorce. If you really knew…"

"Ajax, you are a damn coward," she said.

"Because I want to protect you?"

"Because you want to protect *you!*" she said. "I know because until tonight, I was doing the same thing. This is the honest truth of it, Ajax. You aren't afraid of what will get out. You're afraid of what will get in. I know your life was hard. I know it was…more than I can possibly imagine. I know that. And I know that you had to go down deep to forget, to protect yourself."

He closed the distance between her and grabbed her arms. "You think I'm afraid? That I'm some sort of victim? Was I the one huddled on a bed crying while some asshole who was high out of his mind tried to force himself on me? No. Don't try to make me out to be anything other than what I was. What I am."

"It was a terrible thing, Ajax. The whole situation. But in the end, when that woman looks back on her life, how do you think she sees you? As a monster? Or as her savior? Because if it hadn't been you in that room with her, it would have been someone else. And would they have stopped when they saw her tears? Or would they have kept on? Would they have forced themselves on her without a thought? Would they have left her there in your father's compound? Would she have ever seen her family again?"

"Stop," he said, turning away from her.

"You need this lie, don't you? That you're somehow beyond redemption, because it gives you an excuse to cut yourself off from the world and then you don't have to admit how scared you are."

"This is all there is, Leah. This isn't a lie. This is just me. You can't possibly love this." He hit himself in the chest with his closed fist.

"Why not?"

"Because *I* don't!" he roared. "Because I *truly* know me. And I despise everything in there. I changed my name, I left my home. But none of that changes what I am on the inside, who I am. And if you...if you can somehow see past that? You're a damn fool, Leah Holt. I will do nothing but drag you down to hell with me, so if you have a brain in your stubborn head you'll get dressed and walk out the door."

Something in her broke. Her heart probably. Because there was so much truth in what he said. He hated himself, and she saw it now, could see just how broken he was, how sharp and jagged the pieces of him were. Always cutting, always leaving scars.

"No," she said. "I'm not going to leave. I'm not going to walk away just because it's hard." She wouldn't give up. She wouldn't hide. Always she was hiding. To avoid comparison, criticism, to avoid feeling vulnerable, but that had to stop. She wouldn't do it now. Not with him.

"This is as easy as it will ever be, *agape,*" he said. "This... this won't work."

"No way, Ajax." She shook her head. "No way. You are not doing this. I am your wife. I am the only woman you have ever been naked with, and I don't mean your body. Yes, there were women before me, but they didn't have your soul. I see you, and I think that's the thing that scares you the most."

"It should scare *you.*"

"Yeah, it scares me a little. Not because I think you would

ever do anything to hurt me. It scares me because I want you to love me, Ajax. I want you to open yourself up and take a chance. I want you to stop protecting yourself. Do you know how much it took for me to do it? To stand here and tell you that I love you? I want to mean enough to you that you would do the same for me."

"I don't love you," he said.

"No." Her throat started to tighten, her fingers going numb, tears stinging her eyes. "Don't...don't say that."

"You want me to lie to make you feel better?"

"I want you to tell the truth." Because this couldn't be it. How could he stand there and tell her he didn't love her after what had happened in the bedroom just a few moments before? A moment that had been so perfect? So incredible?

It had been love. It *had* to be love. Because it was for her. Truly. Deeply.

"I don't love you," he bit out, every word final, painful.

"Okay." She nodded and tried to swallow, blinking back tears. "Okay." It came out choked, weak. Utterly revealing. She felt like a little vulnerable sea creature that had been dragged out of its shell. So exposed. So naked and fragile.

She wanted to push at him. Shout at him. Do anything she could to cover up the pain.

But she wouldn't hide. She wouldn't. Not now. He deserved to see it, to see what life was like when you came out from behind the walls.

A tear slid down her cheek, and she sank down onto the couch, covering her mouth with her hand. Another tear followed the first. Then another.

"Leah?"

A sob shook her frame, and she put her other hand up, covering the first, as if it might keep her from flying apart completely. She was unprotected, for the first time in years. Hideously vulnerable. Coming apart.

"Leah," he said again.

She just shook her head.

"I refuse to be manipulated," he said, his voice low, harsh. "If you think tears are going to change my mind…"

She dropped her hands, wiped her arm over her cheek. "I have more pride than that!"

"Clearly you don't."

"Am I making you uncomfortable? If you were a real boy, you would know that this is normal. You see, Ajax, this is what people do when their hearts are broken. This is how people feel when they have their love thrown back at them!" Her voice broke, her words sounding hysterical. And she didn't care. "I'm so sorry this bothers you, because it's a picnic for me."

"Maybe that's why I don't understand. Maybe that's why I don't care. I don't have a heart." He walked past her back into the bedroom, and she just sat on the couch, staring ahead at nothing. He returned a moment later dressed in a T-shirt and jeans.

"I'm leaving," he said. "Because I have a feeling you're too stubborn to do it."

"Shall I expect something from your lawyer?"

"Yes."

"The business?"

"The least of my concerns at the moment."

That was more resounding than a slap in the face. That he would walk away from everything, from the reason they had been forced to marry in the first place, now, to get away from her.

"And if I'm pregnant? Because we haven't used a single condom."

"We'll figure out custody. I'm not going to leave you help-less."

She bit the inside of her cheek, took a deep, fortifying breath. "You couldn't. I have a successful business. I have millions of dollars. I've never been helpless. The simple truth is that I've never needed you. I just *wanted* you. I just love you. But I want you a lot less right now, so maybe you should just go."

He nodded, a muscle twitching in his jaw, like there were words built up, stopped in his throat. Words he wouldn't let out.

Then he turned and walked out of the room. The slam of the door the final word on the end of the marriage.

CHAPTER FOURTEEN

IT HAD BEEN the only thing to do. Ajax was sure of that. He'd had no other choice.

I love you.

They were the three most terrifying words he could think of Leah saying. Because that meant there was an expectation to give more than he could.

He gritted his teeth. Not more than he could, more than he wanted to.

He paced the hotel room, the one he'd got after leaving the penthouse, replaying those last moments with her. Wearing his shirt, the hem barely touching the top of her thighs. Her cheeks streaked with tears, her eyes filled with the kind of pain and misery he saw in his nightmares.

It would have been so easy to lie. To keep taking from her. To preserve his relationship, not just with her but with her father, the only good influence in his life when he'd been a teenager.

He'd been faced with this in the past. That girl who looked at him with such trust. A beautiful sixteen-year-old who was, yes, round, and a little frizzy, but, he knew, had the potential to become his entire world.

He hadn't even let himself complete the thought then. Hadn't let himself admit how much she could mean to him. Instead, he'd turned his attention somewhere else. Somewhere safer. Yes, it would have been easy to keep her. Letting her go, keeping her from being hurt by the monster, that had been the hard thing. The right thing. Because he couldn't give her what she needed. He didn't have it in him. The only thing he had in him was the potential to destroy her.

Liar.

Her words rang in his ears. Scared. Coward.

She had bared herself to him, given him everything. And still he hid.

You aren't afraid of what will get out, you're afraid of what will get in.

And then he let himself remember, really remember, the night at his father's house. That last night there. The terror of the girl. His own fear. The way the drug had twisted his thoughts, the way he'd been so sick after. The horror. The stark realization of what his father did. Of what he could become. Of the fact that there was good and evil in the world, and if he didn't do something soon he would be on the side of evil.

In one night, his world had been torn to pieces. Savaged.

He'd looked outside of himself, outside of the reality he'd been presented, and he saw all the pain, all the abuse, all of the ways a person could be destroyed, corrupted and perverted and he shut it all down.

Every desire. Every emotion. For fear he would have the wrong one.

For fear all of that horror, all of that pain, would get him.

He'd tried to get rid of the feeling. Had tried by taking down his father's organization, but it hadn't worked. He'd saved the damn world and he hadn't been able to save himself.

And so he'd built walls, shoved it all down deep, turned it all off. And walked away.

And then came Leah. She'd torn down the walls with her hands tied behind her back, quite literally. And he didn't like it. It burned. It felt like his skin had been stripped off. Like old wounds had been reopened, scars carved away, leaving all of his tender flesh exposed.

He stalked to the bar and pulled out a bottle of whiskey. Expensive. High quality. But that didn't matter. As long as it would take away his pain, for a moment. Just a moment.

He thought back to his wedding day, about how tempted he'd been to lose himself then, tempted to cover the disaster in a haze.

But he hadn't.

He stood for a moment, regarding the bottle. Then he took a glass out from beneath the bar and filled it.

He wouldn't find answers in the bottom of a glass of whiskey. He wouldn't find hope or salvation there. He wouldn't even find a meaningful salve for his pain.

But maybe, just maybe, he would find rock bottom. At least if he landed there, the only way would be up.

He smiled as he raised the glass to his lips.

There wasn't enough candy in the world to make her day any sweeter. And seeing those stupid cherry buttons, the kind Ajax had eaten off her skin, just made her want to cry all over again. And if not cry, throw things and sit in the corner with a bar of chocolate. Or twenty.

She hated this. She hated being away from him. She hated how badly he'd hurt her. She hated that, for one blinding moment in time she'd nearly had everything, and now it was gone.

She was an idiot. She should have shut up and kept her marriage. She should have kept sleeping with him every night and said *I love you* over and over again in her head as she fell asleep. She shouldn't have said anything to him.

No, she should have. Leah started opening boxes of candy and loading the big glass display jars in the window. As long as she was in New York she was going to spend some time in her flagship store. Working there was therapeutic. Working with candy was therapeutic. As was eating it.

Except those cherry buttons. She was getting rid of those.

She looked up from filling the jars and saw that one of the

big foam glitter lollies that normally stood up nice and tall in the display window was lying against the glass. She growled and dropped the candy bag, then stepped over her faux cotton candy mist that was placed around the display floor, trying to get to the lollipop.

She started losing her balance and braced herself, her palm flat on the window. She cursed under breath. Now it would need to be cleaned, and that was just extra work because she was a clumsy idiot who loved a man who just didn't love her.

Yeah, what if that was all it was. What if he wasn't lying? What if he wasn't scared? What if he just didn't love her?

She felt like she'd just been punched in the stomach. She sank down slowly, in the fake cotton candy, the big lollipop trees overhead. And she just felt sad. A tear slid down her cheek and she wiped it away.

Would there ever be a day she didn't cry over Ajax? Yes. There would be. Of course there would be. Because wounds didn't hurt like this forever. But some of them never truly went away. And this was more than a wound. This was like losing a part of herself, a part she hadn't realized she'd been missing.

A part she didn't think she'd ever be able to replace.

So no, she wouldn't always cry. But there would always be a piece missing from her heart.

She stood and exited the display, collecting her purse and coat, avoiding making eye contact with any of the store's employees or customers. She pushed open the door and went out into the chilly afternoon, tugging her jacket on as she did so.

She pulled up the collar of her coat, and as she did, a female reporter with a recorder advanced on her, along with two men, one of whom held a video camera, the other a microphone.

Every insecurity, every fear, flooded her, oozed from the soles of her shoes and kept her rooted to the spot.

"Ms. Holt, rumor is your husband checked into a hotel last night? Any comment? Is there trouble in paradise? What will you do if you lose him?"

She almost laughed. Because she *had* lost him. And then because she realized that nothing, after this, could ever hurt her again.

She raised her hand and indicated the building behind her. "I will go to work. Because I'm the owner of a very successful chain of candy shops. I'm an entrepreneur. A businesswoman. I am not simply another Holt heiress. I am not Ajax Kouros's backup bride. I have my own identity, my own success."

She was yelling now. She probably seemed completely unhinged. Years of pent-up rage at every member of the press who had ever abused her, pouring out onto this one woman. But she didn't care. She'd always thought this, but she'd never been bold enough to say it. Ajax had made her bold enough. He'd made her believe she deserved more. That she deserved better.

That she deserved, not to modify her behavior to suit other people, but to step out from behind her sister's shadow and demand respect.

"I am not defined by my family name," she continued, "or by how I compare to my sister. I am not defined by my husband. I have a name. I'm Leah Holt, and I'm second to no one. I'm simply myself."

Ajax stared at his phone from his position on the floor of his hotel room, at the hazy headline on the entertainment section of the paper.

Leah Holt Declares: I am not defined by my husband!

Good for her. He laughed and the sound sent a wave of pain through his head. Rock bottom was a real place. It was inside of him now. His chest felt torn to bloody shreds. His head felt like it was going to burst. But nothing, nothing matched the pain in his heart.

She'd been right about him. He was nothing more than a coward. He'd done nothing more than hide, than protect himself from any potential pain, any emotion, for so many years. Too many years.

Oh, those whiskey-colored eyes. He'd looked at them, even back when she'd been a teenager, and he'd known that she could destroy him. That she could have power over him, utterly. Completely. And so he had hidden.

He was still hiding. Hungover and hiding. Not anymore. No more.

He wanted to call Leah, but he didn't know what to say. He wanted to call her father, but he really didn't know what to say.

That left one number.

He dialed a number he hadn't used in a while.

"This is Rachel."

"Do you know where Leah is?" He didn't bother with a greeting.

"Yes. And if you don't, I don't think I'm in a position to tell you. Especially not given current headlines."

"I made a mistake."

"I know you broke my sister's heart. I can't forgive that, Jax."

"I don't want absolution from you," he growled. "I want my wife back."

"I had to walk away from you for my own reasons. Partly because I wouldn't simply be married to a man who saw me as a convenience. If Leah wants more than that, if she wants love, let her go. Let her have it."

"I love her," he said, his voice rough, his body shaking.

"You…you do?"

"More than anything. Please. I need to talk to her. In person. I have a lot of…groveling to do."

There was a long pause. "Okay, Jax. I'll help you."

There had always been something comforting about the Holt Estate in Rhodes. From the moment he'd first set foot on the estate as an emotionally battered boy, it had felt right. Now, when Ajax walked up to the door, he realized what it was. It felt like home. It felt like home in a way nothing else ever had.

Strange that he could connect it now. And it seemed obvious, too.

As did his feelings for Leah.

No, there were no answers in the bottom of a bottle of alcohol. There was just the headache from hell. But after that, when the pain in his chest hadn't lessened, when things had only got worse, he'd realized it was too late to protect himself.

And that he didn't want to anymore.

He only hoped that Leah really was here. That Rachel had been telling the truth and Joseph Holt wasn't waiting for him on the other side of the door with violence in mind.

When the door opened, he expected to see a maid. Instead, it was Leah, her mouth dropped open, her eyes round, her skin pale.

She started to close the door, and he put his foot in the way. "No. Leah, please."

"My father isn't here right now," she said.

"That's not why I'm here."

"Then my sister isn't here, either."

"I don't give a damn about where your sister is, and you know it."

She opened the door slowly. "Then what are you doing here?"

"I think the real question should be, why wasn't I here a week ago? Or maybe even, why wasn't I here to say this a year ago? Why wasn't it our wedding from the beginning?" He put his hand on her cheek. "Why didn't I see that it was always you?"

"Because…because…"

"Or maybe I did see. I think I did. I think every time you left me candy, I knew. Every time I listened to you talk about your dreams, I knew. But you were too much for me. For where I was at. So I ran. I made sure it wasn't you. Because I knew you would ask too much of me. I knew you would demand too much. I was right. You have. You have asked everything of me, and you've left me with no more defenses. You are right, you're second to no one, Leah Holt."

"You read my rant in the paper," she said, her voice choked.

"I did. And every word was true. You are not defined by me, by who you are in relation to your sister. You are beautiful. Like no one else. Like nothing else. You're so beautiful it's like staring into the sun. It burns through me. It shines a light in my soul. I wanted to hide from the light, because I knew it would expose me. Because I knew…it would show who I was, and if it did…how could you not turn away? How could anyone not turn away?"

All the years he hadn't felt, all the years he hadn't wanted, crashed in on him now. Threatened to pull him under. He was overwhelmed. By everything. By how much he loved the woman in front of him, by how much he wanted to make it all right.

"Leah, before you I was in chains. I was trapped in a prison I locked myself in so I could be safe. But a prison is still a prison, no matter whether or not you're there by choice. You set me free. You made me realize that all of the stuff on the other side, everything that could hurt was worth it, because the good outweighs it. What good is living life with no pain if I can't feel your arms around me ever again? What good is staying safe if I can never kiss you? What good is anything if I don't have your love?"

"Ajax…you…you said you didn't love me."

"Because I am everything you said. I'm a coward. But not anymore. I'm free of it. Of the fear. There's no room for it. There's just love. It's all that matters. You're all that matters."

"Ajax." She threw her arms around him, buried her face in his neck, tears leaving wetness on his skin.

He wrapped his arms around her, held her tight to him. His wife. The love of his life.

"I thought I knew love," he said. "But I was wrong. I chose to call something love because I found it comfortable. Because it was something I could control, but Leah, that isn't love. I've never known anything like this. So deep. So real."

"I thought I knew it, too. But I didn't really. Not until I *knew* you. Until I appreciated how strong you were. How amazing. Until I knew the hell you walked through, only to come out on the other side."

"Damaged," he said. "I came out damaged. But you…you make me feel new, Leah. You make me feel things in a way that I didn't know was possible. Before it was like I was looking at everything shrouded in darkness but now…now I see it. Now I understand. I thought I knew love, I thought I knew myself. But you found me."

Leah closed her eyes tight, held Ajax. Just held him. And he held her, too.

She was whole now. Her missing piece was back.

"Oh, Ajax. I feel like you helped me find me, too."

"I'm so glad," he said, "because without you, without all of those things you said to me. Without you loving me when I couldn't love myself, I wouldn't be standing here."

"I love you," she said. She pulled her head back, cupped his face with her hands and looked at his eyes. Looked at how they shone with emotion. Not flat, deep. Endless. "Now tell me how you feel."

"I love you," he said, his gaze never leaving hers. "I love you now and always."

"So…all things considered…what if we stay married?" She closed her eyes. "Ugh. I proposed to you again. I have to stop doing that."

He caught her chin with his thumb and forefinger. "No. Don't stop. I like all your propositions."

"Yeah?"

"Yes."

"So…will you?"

"Leah, I'm not perfect."

"I know, darling."

He laughed, then sobered again. "I will fail you. I will make mistakes. I will…I will still growl sometimes. But even then, I'll love you. And if you can take that, that little I have to offer, then I will be the happiest man in the world."

Leah leaned in and kissed him, poured her whole heart into it. When they parted, they were both breathing hard. "Ajax, that's the silliest thing I've ever heard."

"What is? The part about me failing you?"

"No. That sounds honest. You're human, after all. It's the part about you having so little to offer. Ajax, your love isn't a little thing. Your love is *every*thing."

"Oh, Leah, I'm so glad you think so. I feel the same way. Without your love, I would still be chained up inside myself. Without you, I wouldn't even be living. Not really. Your love took all the broken pieces in, and it put them back together. Put me back together."

And then Ajax Kouros, the man of her dreams, looked at her in a way that surpassed her dearest fantasies and kissed her. Kissed her as she'd spent so many days hoping he would. And she could feel it, down to her toes. Because that was the freedom of being exposed. She felt it all.

This was all so much better than any fantasy. Because this wasn't the perfect Ajax of her fantasies who kissed her, then rode off into the sunset with her. This was Ajax, the man, with every scar, every flaw. And more passion than she ever could have imagined.

"So," she said. "I have a silk scarf up in my room."

"I don't need that anymore."

"Who said anything about need? The only thing I need is you. The rest is just fun."

He smiled, the most genuine smile she'd ever seen on his face. "Fun. Something else I was missing, along with love. Leah, I have a feeling with you I'll never be without either one."

"That's a promise."

"IT's OFFICIALLY TIME to panic."

Leah walked out of the bathroom and into the bedroom at her father's Rhodes Estate where Ajax was sitting on the bed, waiting for her.

"Why?" he asked. "Is the bride missing again?"

"Rachel? No. As far as I know she's ready to walk down that aisle with Alex."

It had been a long time since the day Rachel had run out on the wedding that ended up being hers and Ajax's. The best day of her life.

"Then why are we panicking?"

"Well, I know how much you like to plan things. And I know that, after we got ourselves together and thinking straight, we decided to wait a few years to have kids...."

"And?"

"And, well, that's not exactly happening. I just took a test. I'm pregnant."

Ajax smiled, and her whole world brightened, the knot in her stomach dissolving. He stood up and put his arms around her, pulling her against his chest and kissing her, deep and hard, with everything he had. With no control. As he always did.

"That is the best news, Leah. The best gift."

"But...our plans."

"Who cares about plans? The greatest day of my life happened because all of my plans blew up in my face. That was when I found love. It was when I found you. Really found you."

"Thank you so much for not freaking out." She rose on her toes and kissed him again, then relaxed, pressing her forehead against his chin.

"You always surprise me," he said. "I'll never get tired of it."

"That's a relief. Because you're stuck with me for life."

"I always thought that I had to plan every step. That I had to know what was ahead, every facet, every detail, or I would get lost. But I know one thing now for sure."

"And that is?"

"I don't care where my path takes me. I don't need to know what's around every corner. All I need to know is that in the end, I'll be standing with you."

"I promise."

* * * * *

'Come on, you're dead on your feet.' Jack took her hands and hauled her up.

He'd either overestimated her weight or underestimated his strength, because she flew into his chest and her hands found themselves splayed across his pecs, warm and hard and...*ooooh*...her nose was pressed against his sternum. She sucked him in along with the breath she took...man-soap, man-smell...*Jack*.

She felt tiny next to his muscled frame as his hands held her loosely, fingers across her hip and at the top of her bottom. A lazy thumb stroked her hip bone through the chef's jacket and Ellie felt lust skitter along her skin. She slowly lifted her head and looked at him from beneath her eyelashes. There was a half-smile on his face, and yet his eyes were dark and serious...

He lifted his hand and gently rested his fingers on her lips. She knew what he was thinking...that he wanted to kiss her. Intended to kiss her.

Ellie just looked up at him with big eyes. She felt like a deer frozen in headlights—knowing that she should pull away, unable to do so. She could feel his hard body against hers, his rising chest beneath her palms. His arms were strong, his shoulders broad. She felt feminine and dainty and...judging by his hard body...*desired*.

Dear Reader,

For some reason I seem to love writing about things I know less than nothing about! This book is set in a bakery, which my friends found highly amusing because I have the baking skills of a dyslexic goat. But part of the fun of writing is falling into these alternate worlds and making them come alive. I hope you enjoy Ellie's eclectic beachfront bakery and the stunning scenery of the False Bay area of Cape Town.

I've wanted to write Ellie and Jack's story for a while and am so grateful that I was given the opportunity to do so. Ellie is, perhaps, not as feisty or gung ho as some of my previous heroines, but she has inner strength and a vulnerability that appealed to me. Standing in her famous war-reporter father's shadow, Ellie has never had his love or affection and even less of his time. Ellie thinks that she'd never fall in love with a war-reporting journalist, but when her father sends her a temporary, broke, homeless and beaten-up Jack, her promise to herself is tested.

I think I am, at heart, a nomad, and I love to travel, so I really identify with Jack's need to see new places and try new things. Emotional ties to houses, places and people all hinder his desire to keep moving, to sustain the thrill of his daredevil lifestyle. Girlfriends have come and gone because of his refusal to settle down, and I knew that Ellie had to be someone special to capture my very unique hero's transplanted heart!

A book is not really a book until it's in the hands of the reader. So thank you for reading mine. I hope you enjoy reading it as much I loved writing it!

With my very best wishes,

Joss
xxx

P.S. I love meeting new people, so please say hello via:
Facebook: Joss Wood
Twitter: @josswoodbooks
Josswoodbooks.wordpress.com

IF YOU CAN'T STAND THE HEAT...

BY
JOSS WOOD

First published in Great Britain 2013
by Mills & Boon, an imprint of Harlequin (UK) Limited,
Harlequin (UK) Limited, Eton House, 18-24 Paradise Road,
Richmond, Surrey TW9 1SR

© Joss Wood 2013

ISBN: 978 0 263 90703 2

Harlequin (UK) policy is to use papers that are natural, renewable and recyclable products and made from wood grown in sustainable forests. The logging and manufacturing processes conform to the legal environmental regulations of the country of origin.

Printed and bound in Spain
by Blackprint CPI, Barcelona

Joss Wood wrote her first book at the age of eight and has never really stopped. Her passion for putting letters on a blank screen is matched only by her love of books and travelling—especially to the wild places of Southern Africa—and possibly by her hatred of ironing and making school lunches.

Fuelled by coffee, when she's not writing or being a hands-on mum, Joss, with her background in business and marketing, works for a non-profit organisation to promote the local economic development and collective business interests of the area where she resides. Happily and chaotically surrounded by books, family and friends, she lives in KwaZulu-Natal, South Africa, with her husband, children and their many pets.

This and other titles by Joss Wood are available in eBook format—check out www.millsandboon.co.uk

For their love and support, I have so many friends to thank. Old friends, new friends, coffee friends and crying friends. Friends who know me inside out and friends I've just met. But, because we share a friendship based on raucous laughter, craziness, sarcasm, loyalty and love, this book is especially dedicated to Tracy, Linda and Kerry.

CHAPTER ONE

'*ELLIE, YOUR PHONE is ringing! Ellie, answer it now!*'

Ellie Evans grinned at her best friend Merri's voice emanating from her mobile in her personalised ring tone, then eagerly scooped up the phone and slapped it against her ear.

'El?'

'Hey, you—how's the Princess?' Ellie asked, sorting through the invoices on her desk, which essentially meant that she just moved them from one pile to another.

'The Princess' was her goddaughter, Molly Blue, a six-month-old diva who had them all wrapped around her chubby pinkie finger. Merri launched into a far too descriptive monologue about teething and nappies, interrupted sleep and baby food. Ellie—who was still having a hard time reconciling her party-lovin', heel-kickin', free-spirited friend with motherhood—*mmm*-ed in all the right places and tuned out.

'Okay, I get the hint. I'm boring,' Merri stated, yanking Ellie's attention back. 'But you normally make an effort to at least pretend to listen. So what's up?'

Her friend since they were teenagers, Merri knew her inside out. And as she was her employee as well as her best friend she had to tell her the earth-shattering news. Sitting in her tiny office on the second floor of her bakery and delicatessen, Ellie bit her lip and stared at her messy desk. Panic, bitter and insistent, crept up her throat.

She pulled in a deep breath. 'The Khans have sold the building.'

'Which building?'

'This building, Merri. We have six months before we have to move out.'

Ellie heard Merri's swift intake of breath.

'But why would they sell?' she wailed.

'They are in their seventies, and I would guess they're tired of the hassle. They probably got a fortune for the property. We all know that it's the best retail space for miles.'

'Just because it sits on the corner of the two main roads into town and is directly opposite the most famous beach in False Bay it doesn't mean it's the best...'

'That's exactly what it means.'

Ellie looked out of the sash window to the beach and the lazy ocean beyond it. It had been a day since she'd been slapped with the news and she no longer had butterflies about Pari's, the bakery that had been in her family for over forty years. They had all been eaten by the bats on some psycho-drug currently swarming in her stomach.

'Why can't we just rent from the new owners?'

'I asked. They are going to do major renovations to attract corporate shops and intend on hiking the rents accordingly. We couldn't afford it. And, more scarily, Lucy—'

'The estate agent?'

'Mmm. Well, she told me that retail space is at a premium in St James, and there are "few, if any" properties suitable for a bakery-slash-coffee-shop-slash-delicatessen for sale or to rent.'

After four decades of being a St James and False Bay institution Pari's future was uncertain, and as the partner-in-residence Ellie had to deal with this life-changing situation.

She had no idea what they—she—was going to do.

'Have you told your mum?' Merri asked quietly.

'I can't get hold of her. She hasn't made contact for ten days.

I think she's booked into an ashram…or sunning herself in Goa,' Ellie replied, her voice weary. Where she *wasn't* was in the bakery, with her partner/daughter, helping her sort out the mess they were in.

Your idea, Ellie reminded herself. *You said she could go. You suggested that she take the year off, have some fun, follow her dream...* What *had* she been thinking? In all honesty it had been a mostly symbolic offer; nobody had been more shocked—horrified!—than her when Ashnee had immediately run off to pack her bags and book her air ticket. She'd never thought Ashnee would leave the bakery, leave *her*…

'El, I know that this isn't a good time, especially in light of what you've just told me, but I can't put it off any longer. I need to ask you a huge favour.'

Ellie frowned when she picked up the serious note in Merri's voice.

'Anything, provided that you are still coming back to work on Monday,' Ellie quipped. Merri was a phenomenal baker and Ellie had desperately missed her talent in the bakery while she took her maternity leave.

The silence following her statement slapped her around the head. Oh, no…no, no, *no*! 'Merri, I need you,' she pleaded.

'My baby needs me too, El.' Merri sounded miserable. 'And I'm not ready to come back to work just yet. I will be, but not just yet. Maybe in another month. She's so little and I need to be with her…please? Tell me you understand, Ellie.'

I understand that I haven't filled your position because I was holding it open for you—because you asked me to. I understand that I'm running myself ragged, that the clients miss you...

'Another month?' Merri coaxed. 'Pretty please?'

Ellie rubbed her forehead. What could she say? Merri didn't need to work, thanks to her very generous father, so if she forced her to choose between the bakery and Molly Blue the bakery would lose. *She* would lose...

Ellie swallowed, told herself that if she pushed Merri to come back and she didn't then it was her decision...but she felt the flames of panic lick her throat. They were big girls, and their friendship was more than the job they shared—it would survive her leaving the bakery—but she didn't want to take the chance. Her head knew that she was overreacting but her heart didn't care.

She had too much at stake as it was. She couldn't risk losing her in any way. She'd coped for over six months; she'd manage another month. Somehow.

Ellie bit her top lip. 'Sure, Merri.'

'You're the best—but I've got to dash. The Princess is bellowing.' Now Ellie could hear Molly's insistent wail. 'I'll try to get to the bakery later this week and we can talk about what we're going to do. Byeee! Love you.'

'Love you...' Ellie heard the beep-beep that told her the call had been dropped and tossed her mobile on the desk in front of her.

'El, there's someone to see you out front.'

Ellie glanced from the merry face of Samantha, one of her servers, peeking around her door to the old-fashioned clock above her head, and frowned. The bakery and coffee shop had closed ten minutes ago, so who could it be?

'Who is it?'

Samantha shrugged. 'Dunno. He just said to tell you that your father sent him. He's alone out front...we're all heading home.'

'Thanks, Sammy.' Ellie frowned and swivelled around to look at the screens on the desk behind her. There were cameras in the front of the shop, in the bakery and in the storeroom, and they fed live footage into the monitors.

Ellie's brows rose as she spotted him, standing off to the

side of a long display of glass-fronted fridges, a rucksack hanging off his very broad shoulders. Week-long stubble covered his jaw and his auburn hair was tousled from finger raking.

Jack Chapman. Okay, she was officially surprised. Any woman who watched any one of the premier news channels would recognise that strong face under the shaggy hair. Ellie wasn't sure whether he was more famous for his superlative and insightful war reporting or for being the definition of eye candy.

Grubby low-slung jeans and even grubbier boots. A dark untucked T-shirt. He ran a hand through his hair and, seeing a clasp undone on the side pocket of his rucksack, bent down to fix it. Ellie watched the long muscles bunching under his thin shirt, the curve of a very nice butt, the strength of his brown neck.

Oh, *yum*—oh, stop it now! Get a grip! The important questions were: why was he here, what did he want and what on earth was her father thinking?

Ellie lifted her head as Samantha tapped on the doorframe again and stood there, shuffling on her feet and biting her lip. She recognised that look. 'What's up, Sammy?'

Samantha looked at her with big brown eyes. 'I know that I promised to work for you tomorrow night to help with the *petits fours* for that fashion show—'

'But?'

'But I've been offered a ticket to see Linkin Park and they are my favourite band…it's a free ticket and you know how much I love them.'

Ellie considered giving her a lecture on responsibility and keeping your word, on how promises shouldn't be broken, but the kid was nineteen and it *was* Linkin Park. She remembered being that age and the thrill of a kick-ass concert.

And Samantha, battling to put herself through university, couldn't afford to pay for a ticket herself. She'd remember it for for ever…so what if it meant that Ellie had to work a couple of hours longer? It wasn't as if she had a life or anything.

'Okay, I'll let you off the hook.' Ellie winced at Samantha's high-pitched squeal. 'This time. Now, get out of here.'

Ellie grinned as she heard her whooping down the stairs, but the grin faded when she glanced at the monitor again. Scowling, she reached for her mobile, hastily scrolling through her address book before pushing the green button.

'Ellie—hello.' Her father's deep voice crooned across the miles.

'Dad, why is Jack Chapman in my bakery?'

Ellie heard her father's sharp intake of breath. 'He's there already? Good. I was worried.'

Of course you were, Ellie silently agreed. For the past ten years, since her eighteenth birthday, she'd listened to her father rumble on and on about Jack Chapman—the son he'd always wanted and never got. 'He's the poster-boy for a new generation of war correspondents,' he'd said. 'Unbiased, tough. Willing to dive into a story without thinking about his safety, looking for the story behind the story, yet able to push aside emotion to look for the truth…' Yada, yada, yada…

'So, again, why is he here?' Ellie asked.

And, by the way, why do you only call when you want something from me? Oh, wait, you didn't call. I did! You just sent your boy along, expecting me to accommodate your every whim.

Some things never changed.

'He was doing an interview with a Somalian warlord who flipped. He was stripped of his cash and credit cards, delivered at gunpoint to a United Nations aid plane leaving for Cape Town and bundled onto it,' Mitchell Evans said in a clipped voice. 'I need you to give him a bed.'

Jeez, Dad, do I have a B&B sign tattooed on my forehead?

Ellie, desperate to move beyond her default habit of trying

to please her father, tried to say no, but a totally different set of words came out of her mouth. 'For how long?'

God, she was such a wimp.

'Well, here's the thing, sugar-pie…'

Oh, good grief. Her father had a *thing*. A lifetime with her father had taught her that a thing *never* worked out in her favour. 'Jack is helping me write a book on the intimate lives of war reporters—mine included.'

Interesting—but she had no idea what any of this had to do with *her*. But Mitchell didn't like being interrupted, so Ellie waited for him to finish.

'He needs to talk to my family members. I thought he could stay a little while, talk to you about life with me…'

Sorry…life with him? What life with him? During her parents' on-off marriage their home had been a place for her mum to do his laundry rather than to live. He'd lived his life in all the countries people were trying to get out of: Iraq, Gaza, Bosnia. Home was a place he'd dropped in and out of. Work had always been his passion, his muse, his lifelong love affair.

Resentment nibbled at the wall of her stomach. Depending on what story had been consuming him at the time, Mitchell had missed every single important event of her childhood. Christmas concerts and ballet recitals, swimming galas and father-daughter days. How could he be expected to be involved in his daughter's life when there were bigger issues in the world to write about, analyse, study?

What he'd never realised was that he was her biggest issue…the creator of her angst, the source of her abandonment issues, the spring that fed the fountain of her self-doubt.

Ellie winced at her melodramatic thoughts. Her childhood with Mitchell had been fraught with drama but it was over. However, in situations like these, old resentments bubbled up and over.

Her father had been yakking on for a while and Ellie refocused on what he was saying.

'The editors and I want Jack to include his story—he *is* the brightest of today's bunch—but getting Jack to talk about himself is like trying to find water in the Gobi Desert. He's not interested. He's as much an enigma to me as he was when we first met. So will you talk to him?' Mitchell asked. 'About me?'

Oh, good grief. Did she have to? Really?

'Maybe.' Which they both knew meant that she would. 'But, Dad, seriously? You can't just dump your waifs and strays on me.' He could—of course he could. He was Mitchell Evans and she was a push-over.

'Waif and stray? Jack is anything but!'

Ellie rubbed her temple. Could this day throw anything else at her head? The bottom line was that another of Mitchell's colleagues was on her doorstep and she could either take him in or turn him away. Which she wouldn't do…because then her father wouldn't be pleased and he'd sulk, and in twenty years' time he'd remind her that she'd let him down. Really, it was just easier to give the guy a bed for the night and bask in Mitchell's approval for twenty seconds. If that.

If only they were *normal* people, Ellie thought. The last colleague of her father's she'd had to stay—again at Mitchell's request—had got hammered on her wine and tried to paw her before passing out on her Persian carpet. And every cameraman, producer and correspondent she'd ever met—including her father—was crazy, weird, strange or odd. She figured that it was a necessary requirement if you wanted to chase down and report on human conflicts and disasters.

Mitchell's voice, now that he'd got his own way, sounded jaunty again. 'Jack's a good man. He's probably not slept for days, hasn't eaten properly for more than a week. A bed, a meal, a bath. It's not that much to ask because you're a good person, my sweet, sweet girl.'

My sweet, sweet girl? Tuh!

Sweet, sweet sucker, more like.

Ellie sneaked another look at Mr-Hot-Enough-to-Melt-Heavy-Metal. He did have a body to die for, she thought.

'Have you met Jack before?' Mitchell asked.

'Briefly. At your wedding to Steph.' Wife number three, who'd stuck around for six months. Ellie had been eighteen, chronically shy, and Jack had barely noticed her.

'Oh, yeah—Steph. I liked her…I still don't know why she left,' Mitchell said, sounding plausibly bemused.

Gee, Dad, here's a clue. Maybe, like me, she hated the idea of the man she adored being away for five of those six months, plunging into the situation in Afghanistan and only popping up occasionally on TV. Hated not knowing whether you were alive or dead. It's no picnic loving someone who doesn't love you a fraction as much as you love your job.

She, her mother and Mitchell's two subsequent wives had come second-best time after time…decade after decade. And she'd repeated the whole stupid cycle by getting engaged to Darryl.

She'd vowed she'd never fall in love with a journalist and she hadn't. But life had bust a gut laughing when she'd become engaged to a man she'd thought was the exact opposite of her father, only to realise that he spent even less time at home than her father had. That was quite an accomplishment, since he'd never, as far as she knew, left London itself.

She'd been such a sucker, Ellie thought. Still was…

Maybe one of these days she'd find her spine.

Ellie looked down at her mobile, realised that her father hadn't said goodbye before disconnecting and shrugged. Situation normal. She glanced at the monitor again and saw the impatience on Jack's face, caught his tapping foot. The muscles in his arms bulged as he folded them across his chest. Although the feed was in black and white she knew that his eyes were hazel...sometimes brown, sometimes green, gold, always compelling. Right now they were blazing with a combination of frustration, exhaustion and a very healthy dose of annoyance.

He was different from the twenty-four-year-old she'd met a decade ago. Older, harder, a bit damaged. Ellie felt an unfamiliar buzz in her womb and cocked her head as attraction skittered through her veins and caused her heartbeat to fuzz...

She tossed her mobile onto her desk and pushed her chair back as she stood up and blew out a breath.

It didn't matter that he was tall, built and had a sexy face that could stop traffic, she lectured herself. Crazy came in all packages.

'Jack?'

Jack Chapman, standing in the front section of the bakery—aqua stripes on the walls, black checked floors, white cabinets, a sunshine-yellow surfboard—whirled around at the low, melodious voice and blinked. Then blinked again. He knew he was tired, but this was ridiculous...

He'd been expecting the awkward, overweight, shy girl from Mitch's wedding not this...*babe*! This tropical, colourful, radiant, riveting, dazzling babe. With a capital B. In bold and italics.

Waist-length black hair streaked with purple and green stripes, milk-saturated coffee skin, vivid blue eyes and her father's pugnacious chin.

And slim, curvy legs that went up to her ears.

'Hi, I'm Ellie. Mitchell has asked me to put you up for the night.'

His pulse kicked up as he struggled to find his words. He eventually managed to spit a couple out. 'I'm grateful. Thank you.'

Whoa! Jack dropped his pack to the floor and resisted the

impulse to put his hand on his heart to check if it was okay. With his history…

You are not *having a heart attack, you moron! Major over-reaction here, dude, cool your jets!*

So she wasn't who he'd been expecting? In his line of work little was as expected, so why was his heart jumping and his mouth dry?

Jack rocked on his heels, looked around and tried not to act like a gauche teenager. 'This is a really nice place. Do you own it?'

Ellie looked around and the corners of her mouth tipped up. 'Yep. My mum and I are partners.'

'Ah…' He looked at the empty display fridges. 'Where's the food? Shouldn't there be food?'

Her smile was a fist to his sternum.

'Most of the baked goods are sold out and we put the deli meats away every night.' She fiddled with the strap of her huge leather tote bag. 'So, how was your flight?' she asked politely.

Sitting on the floor of a cargo plane in turbulence, with bruised ribs and a pounding headache? Just peachy. 'Fine, thanks.'

The reality was that he was exhausted, achingly stiff and sore, and his side felt as if he had a red-hot poker lodged inside it. He wanted a shower and to sleep for a week. His glance slid to a fridge filled with soft drinks. And he'd kill someone for a Coke.

Ellie caught his look and waved to the fridge. 'Help yourself.'

Jack grimaced. 'I can't pay for it.'

'Pari's can afford to give you a can on the house,' Ellie said wryly.

The words were barely out of her mouth and he was opening the fridge, yanking out a red can and popping the tab. The tart, sugary liquid slid down his throat and he sighed, knowing the sugar and caffeine would give him another hour or two of energy. Maybe...

He swore under his breath as once again he realised that he was stuck halfway across the world. He couldn't even pay for a damn soft drink. He silently cursed again. He needed to borrow cash and a bed from Ellie until his replacement bank cards were delivered. He grimaced at the sour taste now in his mouth. Having to ask for help made him feel...out of control, helpless. Powerless.

He hated to feel beholden, but he reminded himself it would only be for a night—two, maximum.

Jack finished his drink and looked around for a bin.

Ellie took the can from him, walked behind the counter and tossed it away. 'Help yourself to another, if you like.'

'I'm okay. Thanks.'

Ellie's eyebrows lifted and their eyes caught and held. Jack thought that she was an amazing combination of east and west: skin from her Goan-born grandparents, and blue eyes and that chin from her Irish father. Her body was all her own and should come with a 'Danger' warning. Long legs, tiny waist, incredible breasts...

Because he was very, very good at reading body language, he saw wariness in her face, a lot of shyness and a hint of resignation. Could he blame her? He was a stranger, about to move into her house.

'Funky décor,' he said, trying to put her at ease. Hanging off the wall next to the front door was a fire-red canoe; its seating area sprouting gushing bunches of multi-coloured daisy-like flowers. 'I don't think I've ever seen surfboards and canoes used to decorate before. Or filled with flowers.'

Ellie laughed. 'I know; they are completely over the top, but such fun!'

'Those daisy things look real,' Jack commented.

'Gerbera daisies—and I don't think there's a point to flower arrangements if they aren't real,' Ellie replied.

He'd never thought about flowers that way. Actually, he'd never thought about flowers at all. 'What's with the signatures on the canoe?'

Ellie shrugged. 'I have no idea. I bought it like that.'

Jack shoved his hand into the pocket of his jeans and winced when the taxi driver leaned on his horn. Dammit, he'd forgotten about *him*. He felt humiliation tighten his throat. Now came the hard part, he thought, cursing under his breath. A soft drink was one thing...

'Look, I'm really sorry, but I've got myself into a bit of a sticky situation... Is there any chance you could pay the taxi fare for me? I'm good for it, I promise.'

'Sure.' Ellie reached into her bag, pulled out her purse and handed him a couple of bills.

Jack felt the tips of his fingers brush hers and winced at the familiar flame that licked its way up his arm. His body had decided that it was seriously attracted to her and there was nothing he could do about it.

Damn, Jack thought, as he stomped out through the door to pay his taxi fare. He really didn't feel comfortable being attracted to a woman he was beholden to, who was his mentor's beloved daughter and with whom he'd spend only two days before blowing out of her life.

Just ignore it, Jack told himself. *You're a grown man, firmly in control of your libido.*

He blew air into his cheeks as he handed the money over to the taxi driver and rubbed his hand over his face. The door behind him opened and he turned away from the road to see Ellie lugging his heavy rucksack through the door. Ignoring his burning side, he broke into a jog, quickly reached her and took his pack from her. The gangster bastards had taken his iPad, his satellite and mobile phones, his cash and credit cards, but had left him his dirty, disgusting clothes.

He would've left them too...

'Here—let me take that.' Jack took his rucksack from her.

'I just need to lock up and we can go,' Ellie said, before disappearing back inside the building.

Jack waited in the late-afternoon sun on the corner, his rucksack resting against an aqua pot planted with hot-pink flowers. He was beginning to suspect—from her multi-coloured hair and her bright bakery with its pink and purple exterior—that Ellie liked colour. Lots of it.

Mitchell had mentioned that Ellie was a baker and he'd expected her to be frumpy and housewifey, rotund and rosy—not slim, sexy and arty. Even her jewellery was creative: multilength strands of beads in different shades of blue. He could say something about lucky beads to be against that chest, but decided that even the thought was pathetic...

He heard the door open behind him and she reappeared. She pulled the wooden and glass door shut, then yanked down the security grate and bolted and locked it.

Jack looked from the old-style bakery to the wide beach across the road and felt a smile form. It was nearly half-past six, a warm evening in summer, and the beach and boardwalk hummed with people.

'What time does the sun set?' he asked.

'Late. Eight-thirty-ish,' Ellie answered. She gestured to the road behind them. 'I live so close to work that I don't drive... um...my house is up that hill.'

Jack looked up the steep road to the mountain behind it and sighed. That was all he needed—a hike up a hill with a heavy pack. What else was this day going to throw at him?

He sighed again. 'Lead on.'

Ellie pulled a pair of over-large sunglasses from her bag and put them on, and they started to walk. They passed an antique

store, a bookstore and an old-fashioned-looking pharmacy—
he needed to stock up on some supplies there, but that would
raise some awkward questions. He waited for Ellie to initiate
the conversation. She did, moments later, good manners over-
coming her increasingly obvious shyness.

'So, what happened to you?'

'Didn't your father tell you?'

'Only that you got jumped by a couple of thugs and were
kicked out of Somalia. You need a place to stay because you're
broke.'

'Temporarily broke,' Jack corrected her. Mitchell hadn't
given her the whole story, thankfully. It was simple enough.
He'd asked a question about the hijackings of passing ships
which had pushed the warlord's 'detonate' button. He'd gone
psycho and ordered his henchman to beat the crap out of him.
He'd tried to resist, but six against one…bad odds.

Very bad odds. Jack shook off a shudder.

'So, is there anything else I can do for you apart from giving you a bed?'

Her question jerked him back to the present and his instinctive answer was, *A night with you in bed would be great*.

Seriously? *That* was what he was thinking?

Jack shook his head and ordered himself to get with the
programme. 'Um…I just need to spend a night, maybe two.
Borrow a mobile phone, a computer to send some e-mails,
have an address to have my replacement bank cards delivered to…' Jack replied.

'I have a spare mobile, and you can use my old laptop. I'll
write my address down for you. Are you on a deadline?'

'Not too bad. This is a print story for a political magazine.'

Ellie lifted her eyebrows. 'I thought you only did TV work?'

'I get the occasional assignment from newspapers and magazines. I freelance, so I write articles in between reporting for
the news channels,' Jack replied.

Ellie shoved her sunglasses up into her hair and rubbed her eyes. 'So how are you going to write these articles? I presume your notes were taken.'

'I backed up my notes and documents onto a flash drive just before the interview. I slipped it into my shoe.' It was one of the many precautionary measures he took when operating in Third World countries.

'They let you keep your passport?'

Jack shrugged. 'They wanted me to leave and not having a passport would have hindered that.'

Ellie shook her head. 'You have a crazy job.'

He did, and he loved it. Jack shrugged. 'I operate best in a war zone, under pressure.' He loved having a rucksack on his back, dodging bullets and bombs to get the stories few other journalists found.

'Mitchell always said that it's a powerful experience to be holed up in a hotel in Mogadishu or Sarajevo with no water, electricity or food, playing poker with local contacts to the background music of bombs and automatic gunfire. I never understood that.'

Jack frowned at the note of bitterness in her voice and, quickly realising that there was a subtext beneath her words that he didn't understand, chose his next words carefully. 'Most people would consider it their worst nightmare—and to the people living and working in that war zone it is—but it *is* exciting, and documenting history is important.'

And the possibility of imminent death didn't frighten him at all. After all, he'd faced death before...

No, what would kill him would be being into a nine-to-five job, living in one city, doing the same thing day in and day out. He'd cheated death and received a second swipe at life... and the promise he'd made so long ago, to live life hard and fast and big, still fuelled him on a daily basis.

Jack felt a hard knot in his throat and tried to swallow it down. He was alive because someone else hadn't received the same second swipe...

'We're here.'

Ellie's statement interrupted his spiralling thoughts and Jack hid his sigh of relief as she turned up a driveway and approached a wrought-iron gate. Thank God. He wasn't sure if he could go much further.

Ellie looked at the remote in her hand, took a breath and briefly closed her eyes. He saw the tension in her shoulders and the rigid muscle in her jaw. She wasn't comfortable... Jack cursed. If he had been operating on more than twelve hours' sleep in four days he would have picked up that the shyness was actually tension a lot earlier. And it had increased the closer they came to her home.

'Look, you're obviously not happy about having me here,' Jack said, dropping his pack to the ground. 'Sorry. I didn't realise. I'll head back to the bakery—hitch a lift to the airport.'

Ellie jammed her hands into the pockets of her cut-offs. 'No—really, Jack...I told my father I'd help you.'

'I don't need your charity,' Jack said, pushing the words out between his clenched teeth.

'It's not charity.' Ellie lifted up a hand and rubbed her eyes with her thumb and index finger. 'It's just been a long day and I'm tired.'

That wasn't it. She was strung tighter than a guitar string. His voice softened. 'Ellie, I don't want you to feel uncomfortable in your own home. I told Mitch that I was happy to wait at the airport. It's not a big deal.'

Ellie straightened and looked him in the eye. 'I'm sorry. I'm the one who is making this difficult. Your arrival just pulled up some old memories. The last time I took in one of my father's workmates I was chased around my house by a drunken, horny cameraman.'

He sent her his I'm-a-good-guy grin. 'Typical. Those damn cameramen—you can't send them anywhere.'

Ellie smiled, as he'd intended her to. He could see some of her tension dissolve at his stab at humour.

'Sorry, I know I sound ridiculous. And I'm not crazy about talking about my relationship with Mitchell for this book you're helping him write—'

'I'm *helping* him write? Is that what he said?' Jack shook his head. Mitchell was living in Never-Never Land. It was *his* book, and *he* was writing the damn thing. Yes, Mitchell Evans's and Ken Baines's names would be on the cover, but there would be no doubt about who was the author. The size-able advance in his bank account was a freaking big clue.

'Your father…I like him…but, jeez, he can be a pain in the ass,' Jack said.

'So does that mean you don't want to talk to me about him?' Ellie asked, sounding hopeful and a great deal less nervous.

Jack half smiled as he shook his head. 'Sorry…I do need to talk to you about him.'

He raked his hair off his face, thinking about the book. Ken's fascinating story was all but finished; Mitch's was progressing. Thank God he'd resisted all the collective pressure to get him to write his. Frankly, it would be like having his chest cracked open without anaesthetic.

He was such a hypocrite. He had no problems digging around other people's psyches but was more than happy to leave his own alone.

Jack looked at Ellie, saw her still uncertain expression and was reminded that she was wary of having a strange man in her house. He couldn't blame her.

'And as for chasing you around your house? Apart from the

fact that I am so whipped I couldn't make a move on a corpse, it really isn't my style.'

Ellie looked at him for a long moment and then her smile blossomed. It was the nicest punch to the heart he'd ever received.

CHAPTER TWO

JACK LOOKED UP a lavender-lined driveway to the house beyond it. It was a modest two-storey with Old World charm, wooden bay windows and a deep veranda, nestled in a wild garden surrounded by a high brick wall. The driveway led up to a two-door garage. He didn't do charming houses—hell, he didn't do *houses*. He had a flat that he barely saw, boxes that were still unpacked, a fridge that was never stocked. In many ways his flat was just another hotel room: as impersonal, as bland. He wasn't attached to any of his material possessions and he liked it that way.

Attachment was not an emotion he felt he needed to become better acquainted with…either to possessions or partners.

'Nice place,' Jack said as he walked up the stairs onto a covered veranda. Ellie took a set of keys from the back pocket of those tight shorts. It *was* nice—not for him, but nice—a charming house with loads of character.

'The house was my grandmother's. I inherited it from her.'

Jack glanced idly over his shoulder and his breath caught in his throat. *God, what a view!*

'Oh, that is just amazing,' he said, curling his fingers around the wooden beam that supported the veranda's roof. Looking out over the houses below, he could see a sweeping stretch of endless beach that showed the curve of the bay and the sleepy blue and green ocean.

'Where are we, exactly?' he asked.

Ellie moved to stand next to him. 'On the False Bay coast. We're about twenty minutes from the CBD of Cape Town, to the south. That bay is False Bay and you can see about thirty kilometres of beach from here. Kalk Bay is that way—' she pointed '—and Muizenberg is up the coast.'

'What are those brightly coloured boxes on the beach?'

'Changing booths. Aren't they fun? The beach is hugely popular, and if you look just north of the booths, at the tables and chairs under the black and white striped awning, that's where we were—at Pari's.'

'It's incredible.'

'Your room looks out onto the beach and the bathroom has a view of the Muizenberg Mountain behind us. There are some great walks and biking trails in the nature reserve behind us.'

Ellie nudged one of two almost identical blond Labradors aside in an attempt to get close enough to the front door and shove her key in the lock. Pushing open the wooden door with its stained glass window insert, she gestured for Jack to come into the hall as she automatically hung her bag onto a decorative hook.

'The bedrooms are upstairs. I presume that you'd like a shower? Something to eat? Drink?'

He probably reeked like an abandoned rubbish dump. 'I'd kill for a shower.'

Jack had an impression of more bright colours and eclectic art as he followed Ellie up the wooden staircase. There was a short passage and then she opened the door to a guest bedroom: white and lavender linen on a double bed, pale walls and a ginger cat curled up on the royal purple throw.

'Meet Chaos. The *en-suite* bathroom is through that door.'

Ellie picked up Chaos and cradled the cat like a baby. Jack scratched the cat behind its ears and Chaos blinked sleepily.

Jack thankfully dropped his backpack onto the wooden

floor and sat down on the purple throw at the end of the bed while he waited for the dots behind his eyes to recede. Ellie walked to the window, pulled the curtain back and lifted the wooden sash to let some fresh air into the room.

He dimly heard Ellie ask again if he wanted something to drink and struggled to respond normally. He was enormously grateful when she left the room and he could shove his head between his knees and pull himself back from the brink of fainting.

Because obviously he'd prefer not to take the concept of falling at Ellie's feet too literally.

Ellie skipped down the stairs, belted into the kitchen and yanked her mobile from her pocket.

Merri answered on the first ring. 'I know that you're upset with me about extending my maternity leave…'

'Shut up! This is more important!' Ellie hissed, keeping her voice low. 'Mitchell sent me a man!'

Merri waited a beat before responding. 'Your father is procuring men for you now? Are you *that* desperate? Oh, wait… yes, you are!'

'You are so funny…not.' Ellie shook her head. 'No, you twit, I'm acting as a Cape Town B&B for his stray colleagues again, but this time he sent me Jack Chapman!'

'The hottie war reporter?' Merri replied, after taking a moment to make the connection. She sounded awed and— gratifyingly—a smidgeon jealous. 'Well?'

'Well, what?'

'What's he like?' Merri demanded.

'He's reluctantly, cynically charming. Fascinating. And he has the envious ability to put people at ease. No wonder he's an ace reporter.' When low-key charm and fascination came wrapped up in such a pretty package it was doubly, mind-alteringly disarming.

'Well, well, well…' Merri drawled. 'It sounds like he has made *quite* an impression! You sound…breathy.'

Breathy? No, she did not!

But why did she feel excited, shy, nervous and—dammit—scared all at the same time? Oh, she wasn't scared of *him*—she knew instinctively, absolutely, that Jack was a gentleman down to his toes—but she was on a scalpel-edge because he was the first man in ages who had her nerve-endings humming and her sexual radar beeping. And if she told Merri *that*…

'You're attracted to him,' Merri stated.

She hated it when Merri read her mind. 'I'm not…it's just a surprise. And even if I was…'

'You are.'

'He's too sexy, too charming, has a crazy job that I loathe, and he'll be gone in a day or two.'

'Mmm, but he's seriously hot. Check him out on the internet.'

'Is that what you're doing? Stop it and concentrate!' She gave Merri—and herself—a mental slap. 'I have more than enough to deal with without adding the complication of even *thinking* about attraction and sex and a good-looking face topping a sexy body! Besides, I'm not good at relationships and men.'

'Because you're still scared to risk giving your heart away and having to take it back, battered and bruised, when they ride off into the sunset?'

Merri tossed her own words back at her and Ellie grimaced.

'Exactly! And a pretty face won't change anything. My father and my ex put me through an emotional grinder and Jack Chapman has the potential to do the same…'

'Well, that's jumping the gun, since you've just met him, but I'll bite. Why?'

'Purely because I'm attracted to him!' Ellie responded in

a heated voice. 'It's an unwritten rule of my life that the men I find fascinating have an ability to wreak havoc in my life!'

They dropped in, kicked her heart around, ultimately decided that she wasn't worth sticking around for and left.

Merri remained silent and after a while Ellie spoke again. 'You agree with me, don't you?'

'No, don't take my silence for agreement; I'm just in awe of your crazy.' Merri sighed. 'So, to sum up your rant: you are such a bum magnet when it comes to men that your rule of thumb is that if you find one attractive then you should run like hell? Avoid at all costs?'

'You've nailed it,' Ellie said glumly.

'I want to see how you manage to do this when the man in question has moved his very hot self into your rather small house.'

Ellie disconnected her mobile on Merri's hooting laughter. Really, with friends like her...

Returning to the spare bedroom with towels for his bathroom and a cold beer in her hands, Ellie heard a low groan and peeked through the crack in the door to look at Jack, still sitting on the edge of the bed, his hands gripping the bottom of his shirt, pale and sweating.

Hurrying into the room, she dumped the towels on the bed, handed him the beer and frowned. 'Are you all right?'

Jack took a long, long drink from the bottle and rested the cold glass against his cheek. 'Sure. Why?'

'I noticed that you winced when you picked up your backpack. You took your time walking up the stairs, and now you're as white as a sheet and your hands are shaking!'

Jack rubbed the back of his neck. 'I'm a bit dinged up,' he eventually admitted.

'Uh-huh? How dinged up?'

'Just a bit. I'll survive.' Jack put the almost empty beer bottle on the floor and gripped the edge of his shirt again.

Ellie watched him struggle to pull it up and shook her head at his white-rimmed mouth.

'Can I help?' she asked eventually.

'I'll get there,' Jack muttered.

He couldn't, and with a slight shake of her head she stepped closer to the bed, grabbed the edges of his T-shirt and helped him pull it over his head. A beautiful body was there—somewhere underneath the blue-black plate-sized bruises that looked like angry thunderclouds. He had a wicked vertical scar bisecting his chest that suggested a major operation at one time, and Ellie bit her lip when she walked around his knees to look at his back. She couldn't stifle her horrified gasp. The damage on his back was even worse, and on his tanned skin she could see clear imprints of a heel here and the toe of a boot there.

'What does the other guy look like?' she asked, trying to be casual.

'Guys. Not as bad as me, unfortunately.' Jack balled his T-shirt in his hand and tossed it towards his rucksack. 'The Somalians decided to give me something to remember them by.'

Jack sat on the edge of the bed, bent over and, using one hand and taking short breaths, undid the laces of his scuffed trainers. When they were loose enough, he toed them off.

Jack sent her a crooked grin that didn't fool her for a second. 'As you can see, all in working order.'

'Anything broken?'

Jack shook his head. 'I think they bruised a rib or two. I'll live. I've had worse.'

Ellie shook her head. 'Worse than this?'

'A bullet does more damage,' Jack said, standing up and slowly walking to the *en-suite* bathroom.

Ellie gasped. 'You've been *shot*?'

'Twice. Hurts like a bitch.'

Hearing water running in the basin, Ellie abruptly sat down. She was instantly catapulted back in time to when she'd spent a holiday with Mitchell and his mother—her grandmother Ginger—in London when she was fourteen. He'd run to Bosnia to do a 'quick report' and come back in an ambulance plane, shot in the thigh. He'd lost a lot of blood and spent a couple of days in the ICU.

It wasn't her favourite holiday memory.

Jack didn't seem to be particularly fazed about his injuries; like Mitchell he probably fed on danger and adrenalin... it made no sense to her.

'You do realise that you could've died?' Ellie said, wondering why she even bothered.

Jack walked back into the room, dried his face on a towel he'd picked up from the bed and shrugged. 'Nah. They were lousy shots.'

Ellie sighed. She couldn't understand why getting hurt, shot or putting yourself in danger wasn't a bigger deterrent. She knew that Jack, like her father, preferred to work solo, shunning the protection of the army or the police, wanting to get the mood on the streets, the story from the locals. Such independence ratcheted up the danger quotient to the nth degree.

There was a reason why war reporting was rated as one of the most dangerous jobs in the world. Were they dedicated to the job or just plain stupid? Right now, seeing those bruises, she couldn't help but choose *stupid*.

'So, before I go...do you want something to eat?'

Jack shook his head. 'The pilot stood me a couple of burgers at the airport. Thanks, though.'

'Okay, well, I'll be downstairs if you need anything...' Ellie couldn't resist dropping her eyes to sneak a peek at his stomach. As she'd suspected, he had a gorgeous six-pack—but her attention was immediately diverted by a mucky, bloody sanitary pad held in place by the waistband of his jeans.

She pursed her lips. 'And that?'

Jack glanced down and winced. With an enviable lack of modesty he flipped open the top two buttons of his jeans, pulled down the side of his boxer shorts and pulled off the pad. Ellie winced at the seeping, bloody, six-inch slash that bisected the artistic knife and broken heart tattoo on his hip.

'Not too bad,' Jack said, after prodding the wound with a blunt-edged finger.

'What is that? A knife wound?'

'Mmm. Psycho bastards.'

'You sound so calm,' Ellie said, her eyes wide.

'I *am* calm. I'm always calm.'

Too calm, she thought. 'Jack, it needs stitches.'

'This is minor, Ellie.' Jack looked mutinous. 'I'm going to give it a good scrub, slather it in the antiseptic I always carry with me and slap another pad on it.'

'Who uses sanitary pads for *this*?'

'It's an army thing and it serves the purpose. I'm an old hand at doctoring myself.'

Ellie sighed when Jack turned away to rummage in his rucksack. He pulled out another sanitary pad, stripped the plastic away and slapped the clean pad onto his still bleeding wound. She saw his stubborn look and knew that he'd made up his mind. If she couldn't get Jack to a hospital—he was six-two and built; how could she force him?—she'd have to trust him when he said that he was an old hand at patching himself up.

'When my bank cards arrive I'll go down to the pharmacy and get some proper supplies,' Jack told her.

Ellie sucked in a frustrated sigh. 'Give me a list of what you need and I'll run down and get it. I'll be back before you're finished showering.' She held up her hand. 'And, yes, you can pay me back.'

Jack looked hesitant and Ellie resisted the impulse to smack the back of his head. 'Jack, you need some decent medical supplies.'

Jack glared at the floor. She saw his broad shoulders dip in defeat before hearing his reluctant agreement. Within a minute he'd located a notebook from the side pocket of his rucksack and a pen, and he wrote in a strong, clear hand exactly what he wanted. He handed her the list and Ellie knew, by his miserable eyes, that he was embarrassed that he had to ask for her help. *Again.*

Men. Really...

The mobile in her pocket jangled and Ellie pulled it out, frowning at the unfamiliar number. Answering, she heard a low, distinctively feminine voice asking for Jack. Ellie's brows pulled together... How on earth could anyone know that Jack was with her? She had hardly completed that thought before realising that the jungle drums must be working well in the war journalists' world. Her father was spreading the news...

Ellie handed her mobile to Jack and couldn't help wondering who the owner of the low, subtly sexy voice was. Lover? Colleague? Friend?

'Hi, Ma.'

Or his mother. Horribly uncomfortable with the level of relief she felt on hearing that he was talking to his mother, Ellie scuttled from the room.

Jack lifted the mobile to his ear on an internal groan. He just wanted to go and lie down on that bed and sleep. Was that too much to ask? Really?

'I haven't been able to reach you for a week!' said his mother Rae in a semi-hysterical voice.

'Mum, we had an agreement. You only get to worry about me after you haven't spoken to me for three weeks.' Jack rubbed his forehead, actively trying to be patient. He understood her worry—after all that he'd put her and his father through how could he not?—but her over-protectiveness got very old, very quickly.

'Are you hurt?' his mother demanded curtly.

He wished he'd learnt to lie to her. 'Let me talk to Dad, Mum.'

'That means you're hurt. Derek! Jack's hurt!'

Jack heard her sob and she dropped the phone. His father's voice—an oasis of calm—crossed the miles.

'*Are* you hurt?'

'Mmm.'

'Where?'

Everywhere. There was no point whining about it. 'Couple of dents. Nothing major. Tell Mum to calm down to a mild panic.' Jack heard his mum gabbling in the background, listened through his father's reassurances and waited until his father spoke again.

'You mother says to please remind you to visit Dr Jance. Does she need to make an appointment for you?'

He'd forgotten that a check-up was due and he felt his insides contract. He did his best to forget what he'd gone through as a teenager, and these bi-yearly check-ups were reminders of those dreadful four years he'd spent as a slave to his failing heart. He tipped his head back in frustration when he heard Rae demand to talk to him again.

'Jack, the Sandersons contacted us last week,' she said in a rush.

Jack felt his heart contract and tasted guilt in the back of his throat. Abruptly he sat down on the edge of the bed. Brent Sanderson. He was alive because Brent had died. How could he *not* feel guilty? It was a constant—along with the feeling that he owed it to Brent to live life to the full, that living that way was the only way he could honour his brief life, the gift he'd been given…

'In six weeks it will be seventeen years since the op, and

Brent was seventeen when he died,' Rae said with a quaver in her voice.

She didn't need to tell him that. He knew *exactly* how long it had been. They'd both been seventeen when they'd swapped hearts.

'They want to hold a memorial service for him and have invited us…and you. We've said we'll go and I said that I'd talk to you.'

Jack stretched out, tucked a pillow behind his head and blew out a long stream of air. He tried not to dwell on Brent and his past—he preferred the *it happened; let's move on* approach—and he really, really didn't want to go. 'It's a gracious invitation but I'm pretty sure that they'd be happy if I didn't pitch up.'

'How can you say that?'

'Because it would be supremely difficult for them to see me walking around, fit and healthy, knowing that their son is six feet under, Mum!'

They'd given him the gift of their son's heart. He'd do anything to spare them further pain. And that included keeping his distance…

'They aren't like that and they want to meet you. You've avoided meeting them for years!'

'I haven't avoided them. It just never worked out.'

'I'll pretend to believe that lie if you consider coming to Brent's service,' Rae retorted.

His mother wasn't a fool. 'Mum, I'll see. I've got to go. I'll visit when I'm back in the UK.'

'You're not in the UK? Where are you?' Rae squawked.

Jack gritted his teeth. 'You're mollycoddling me, and you know it drives me nuts!'

'Well, your career drives *me* nuts! How can you, after fighting so hard for life, routinely put yourself in danger? It's—'

'Crazy and disrespectful to take such risks when I've been given another chance at life. I'm playing Russian Roulette with my life and you wish I'd settle down and meet a nice girl and give you grandchildren. Have I left anything out?'

'No,' Rae muttered. 'But I put it more eloquently.'

'Eloquent nagging is still nagging. But I do love you, you old bat. Sometimes.'

'Revolting child.'

'Bye, Ma,' Jack said, and disconnected the call.

He banged the mobile against his forehead. His parents thought that guilt and fear fuelled his daredevil lifestyle. It did—of course it did—but did that have to be a bad thing? They didn't understand—probably because he could never explain it—but playing it safe, sitting behind a desk in a humdrum job was, for him, a slow way to die. At fourteen he'd gone from being a healthy, rambunctious, sporty kid to a waif and a ghost, his time spent either in hospital rooms or at his childhood home. He'd just *existed* for more years than he cared to remember, and he'd vowed that when he had the chance of an active life he'd live it. Hard and fast. He wanted to do it all and see it all—to chase the thrills. For himself and for Brent. Being confined to one house, person or city would be his version of hell. His parents wanted him to settle down, but they didn't understand that he wouldn't settle down for anything or anyone. He had to keep moving—and working to feel alive.

Jack switched off the bedside light and stared up at the shadows on the ceiling, actively trying not to think about his past. As per normal, his job had thrown him a curveball and he'd landed up in a strange bed in a strange town. But, he thought as his eyes closed, he was very good at curveballs and strange situations, and meeting Mitch's dazzling daughter again was very much worth the detour.

On his second night in Ellie's spare room, Jack put aside the magazine he'd been reading, rolled onto his back and stared at the ceiling above his bed. The air-conditioning unit hummed softly and he could hear the croaky song of frogs in the garden, the occasional whistle of a cricket. It wasn't that late and his side throbbed.

Knowing that he wouldn't be able to sleep yet, he flipped back the sheet and stood up. After yanking on a pair of jeans he quietly opened the door and walked to the stairs. Navigating his way through the dark house, he walked into the front lounge, with its two big bay windows, leaned against the side wall and looked through the darkness towards the sea. Through the open windows he could hear the thud of waves hitting the beach and smell the brine-tinged air.

Ellie's distinctively feminine voice drifted through the bay window, so he pulled back the curtain. He looked out and watched her walk up the stairs to the veranda, mobile to her ear and one arm full of papers and files. She looked exhausted and he could see flour streaks on her open navy chef's jacket. Jack glanced at the luminous dial of his watch…ten-thirty at night was a hell of a time to be coming home from work.

'Ginger, my life is a horror movie at the moment.'

Ginger? Wasn't that Mitchell's mother? Ellie's Irish grandmother?

'Essentially I need Mum to come back but it's not fair to ask her. I'm chasing my tail on a daily basis, it's nearly month-end, I have payroll and I need to pay VAT this month. And I need to move the bakery but there's nowhere to move it to! And, to top it all, your wretched son has sent me a house guest!'

So she wasn't as sanguine about having him as a guest as she pretended to be. Jack watched as she balanced the stack of papers and two files on the arm of the Morris chair.

'No, he's okay,' Ellie continued. 'I've had worse.'

Only okay? He was going to have to work on that.

Ellie used her free hand to dig into her bag for her house keys and half turned, knocking the unstable pile with her hip.

The files tipped and the papers caught in the mild evening wind and drifted away.

'Dammit! Ginger—sorry, I have to go. I've just knocked something over.'

Ellie threw her mobile onto the seat of the Morris chair, then started to curse in Arabic. His mouth fell open. His eyes widened as the curses became quite creative, muddled and downright vulgar.

Jack thought that she could do with some help so he stepped over the sill of the low window directly onto the veranda and started to collect the bits of paper that were scattered all over the floor.

'Do you actually know what you're saying?' he demanded, when she stopped for ten seconds to take a breath.

Ellie sent him a puzzled look. 'Daughter of a donkey, son of a donkey, your mother is ugly, et cetera.'

Uh, no. Not even close. 'Do me a favour? Don't ever repeat any of those anywhere near an Arab, okay?'

Ellie slowly stood up and narrowed her eyes. 'They are rude, aren't they?'

He didn't need to respond because she'd already connected the dots.

'Mitchell! He taught me those when I was a kid.' It was so typical of Mitch's twisted sense of humour to teach his innocent daughter foul curse words in Arabic. 'I'm going to kill him! I take it you speak Arabic?'

'Mmm.' He'd discovered that he had a gift for languages while he was a teenager, when he'd been unable to do anything more energetic than read.

Ellie sent him a direct look. 'So, do you speak any other languages?'

Jack shrugged. 'Enough Mandarin to make myself understood. Some Japanese. I'm learning Russian. And Dari...'

'What's that?'

'Also known as Farsi, or Afghan Persian. Helpful, obviously, in Afghanistan.'

Ellie stared at him, seemingly impressed. 'That's incredible.'

Jack shrugged, uncomfortable with her praise. 'Lots of people speak second or third languages.'

'But not Farsi, Russian or Mandarin,' Ellie countered. 'I'm useless. I can barely spell in English.'

'I don't believe that.'

'You can ask Mitchell if you like. Nothing made him angrier than seeing my spelling test results,' Ellie quipped. 'Besides, English is a stupid language…their and there, which and witch, write, right, rite.'

'And another wright,' Jack added.

'You're just making that up,' she grumbled.

'I'm not. It's one of the few four-word homophones.' Jack's grin flashed. 'W.R.I.G.H.T. Someone who constructs or repairs things—as in a millwright.'

'Homophones? Huh.' Ellie heaved an exaggerated, forlorn sigh. 'Good grief, I'm sharing my house with a swot. What did I do to deserve that?'

Jack laughed, delighted. 'Life does throw challenges at one.'

After they'd finished collecting the papers Ellie sat down on the couch, rolling her head on her shoulders.

Jack sat on the low stone wall in front of her. 'Tough day?' he asked, conversationally.

Ellie slumped in the chair. 'Very. How can you tell?'

Jack lifted his hands. 'I heard you talking to your grandmother.'

'And how much did you hear?'

'You're pissed, you're stressed, something about having to move the bakery. You've had worse house guests than me.'

Even in the dim light he could see Ellie flush. 'Sorry.

Mitchell tends to use me as his own personal B&B… I didn't mean to make you feel unwelcome.'

'Am I?'

Ellie threw her hands up and sent him a miserable look. 'You're not. I'm more frustrated at Mitchell's high-handedness than at the actual reality of a house guest, if that makes sense.'

Jack nodded, hearing the truth in her statement, and relaxed. 'Mitch does have a very nebulous concept of the word *no*,' he stated calmly.

'And he's had twenty-eight years to perfect the art of manipulating me,' Ellie muttered. 'Again, that's not directed at you personally.'

Jack laughed. 'I get it, Ellie. Relax. Talking about relaxing…' Jack walked back into the house, found a wine rack and remembered that he'd seen a corkscrew in the middle drawer when he was looking for a bread knife earlier. He took the wine and two glasses back to the veranda. 'If I ever saw a girl in need of the stress-relieving qualities of alcohol, it's you.'

'If I have any of that I'll fall over,' Ellie told him, covering a yawn with her hand.

'A glass or two won't hurt.' Jack yanked the cork out, poured the Merlot and handed her a glass.

Ellie took the glass from him and took the first delicious sip. 'Yum. I could drink this all night.'

'Then it would definitely hurt when you wake up.' After a moment's silence, he succumbed to his curiosity. 'Tell me what that conversation was about.'

Ellie cradled the glass in her hand and eyed Jack across the rim. Shirtless, and with bare feet, he was a delectable sight for sore eyes at the end of a hectic day. 'You're very nosy.'

'I'm a journalist. It's a job requirement. Talk.'

She wanted to object, to tell him he was bossy—which he was—but she didn't. Couldn't. She needed someone to offload on and maybe it would be easier to talk to a stranger who was leaving… When *was* he leaving? She asked him.

Jack grinned. 'Not sure yet. Is it a problem if I stay for another night or two? I like your house,' he added, and Ellie's glass stopped halfway to her mouth.

'You want to stay because you like my house? Uh…why?'

'Well, apart from the fact that we haven't yet talked about Mitch, it's…restful.' Jack lifted a bare muscled shoulder. 'It shouldn't be with such bright colours but it is. I like hearing the sea, the wind coming off the mountain. I like it.'

'Thanks.' Ellie took a sip of wine. It would be nice to know if he liked her as much as he liked her house, but since she'd only spent a couple of hours with him what could she expect? Ellie couldn't believe she was even thinking about him like that. It was so high school—and she had bigger problems than thinking about boys and their nice bodies and whether they liked her back.

Jack topped up her wine glass and then his. He squinted at the label on the bottle. 'This is a nice wine. Maybe I should go on a wine-tasting tour of the vineyards.'

'That's a St Sylve Merlot. My friend Luke owns the winery and his fiancée Jess does the advertising for the bakery.'

'And we're back full circle to your bakery. Talk.' Jack boosted himself up so that he sat cross-legged on the stone wall, his back to a wooden beam.

His eyes rested on her face and they encouraged her to trust him, to let it out, to *talk* to him…

Damn, he was good at this.

Ellie's smile was small and held a hint of pride. 'Pari's Perfect Cakes—'

'Who was Pari, by the way?' Jack interrupted her.

'My grandmother. It was her bakery originally. It means "fairy" in India.' Pain flashed in her eyes. 'As you saw, Pari's is a retail bakery and delicatessen, with a small coffee shop.'

'It doesn't look like a small operation. How do you manage it all?'

'Well, that's one of my problems. We have two shifts of bakers who make the bread and the high turnover items, and Merri, my best friend, used to do the specialised pastries. I do special function cakes. My mum did the books, stock and payroll and chivvied us along. It all worked brilliantly until recently.'

Jack held up his hand. 'Wait—back up. Special function cakes? Like wedding cakes?'

'Sure—but any type of cakes.' Ellie picked up her mobile and quickly pressed some buttons. 'Look.'

Jack put his glass of wine next to him on the wall and leaned forward to take the device. He flipped through the screens, looking at her designs.

'These are amazing, Ellie.'

'Thank you.'

He looked down at her mobile again. 'I can't believe that you made a cake that looks exactly like a crocodile leather shoe.'

'Not any shoe—a Christian Louboutin shoe.'

Jack looked puzzled. 'A what?'

'Great designer of shoes?' Ellie shook her head.

'Sorry, I'm more of a trainers and boots kind of guy.' Jack handed the mobile back to her. 'So, what went wrong at the bakery?'

'Not wrong, exactly. Merri had a baby and started her maternity leave. She told me yesterday that she's extending it.'

'She *told* you?'

Ellie heard the disbelief in Jack's voice and quickly responded, 'She asked…suggested…kind of.'

Jack frowned. 'And you said yes?'

'I didn't have much of a choice. She doesn't need to work and I didn't want to push her into a corner and…'

'And you couldn't say no,' Jack stated with a slight shake of his head.

'And I suppose you've never said yes when you wanted to say no?' Ellie demanded.

'I can't say that I've never done that. I generally say what I mean and I never let anyone push me around…'

'She didn't…' Ellie started to protest but fell silent when she saw the challenging expression on Jack's face. This wasn't an argument she would win because—well, she *did* get pushed around. Sometimes. Would he understand if she told him that, as grown-up and confident as she now was, she still had intense periods of self-doubt? Would he think her an absolute drip because her habit reaction was to make sure everyone around her was happy? And if they were they would love her more?

'What else?' Jack asked, after taking a sip of wine.

Ellie swirled the wine in her glass. 'My mother has taken a year's sabbatical. She always had this dream to travel, so for her fiftieth birthday I gave her a year off. A grand gesture that I am deeply regretting now. But she's in seventh heaven. She's got a tattoo, has had at least one affair and has put dreadlocks in her hair.'

'You sound more upset about the dreadlocks than the affair.'

Ellie shrugged. 'I just want her home—back in the bakery. She managed the place, did the paperwork and the accounts, the payroll and just made the place run smoothly.'

And while I say that I want everyone to be happy I frequently resent the fact that she left, that Merri left—okay, temporarily—and I have to carry on, pick up the pieces. When do I get to step away?

'So, you're stressed out and doing the work of two other people?'

'And none of it well,' Ellie added, her tone sulky.

Jack smiled. 'Now, tell me about having to move.'

Ellie gave him the rundown and cradled her glass of wine in her hands. She felt lighter for telling him, grateful to hand over the problem just for a minute. She didn't expect him to solve the problem, but just being able to verbalise her emotions was liberating.

And, amazingly, Jack just listened—without offering a solution, a way to fix it. If he wasn't ripped and didn't have a stubble-covered jaw and a very masculine package she could almost pretend he was a girlfriend. He listened like one. *Keep dreaming*, she thought. Not in a million years could she pretend that Jack was anything but a hard-ass—literally and metaphorically—one hundred per cent male.

Ellie yawned, curled her legs up and felt her eyes closing. She felt Jack take the glass from her hand and forced her eyes open.

'Come on. You're dead on your feet.' Jack took her hands and hauled her up.

He'd either overestimated her weight or underestimated his strength because she flew into his chest and her hands found themselves splayed across his pecs, warm and hard and...*ooooh*... Her nose was pressed against his sternum. She sucked him in along with the breath she took...man-soap, man-smell...*Jack*.

She felt tiny next to his muscled frame as his hands loosely held her hips, fingers on the top of her bottom. A lazy thumb stroked her hipbone through the chef's jacket and Ellie felt lust skitter along her skin. She slowly lifted her head and looked at him from beneath her eyelashes. There was half a smile on his face, yet his eyes were dark and serious...

He lifted his hand and gently rested his fingers on her lips. She knew what he was thinking...that he wanted to kiss her. Intended to kiss her.

Ellie just looked up at him with big eyes. She felt like a deer frozen in the headlights, knowing that she should pull away, unable to do so. She could feel his hard body against hers, his rising chest beneath her palms. His arms were strong, his shoulders broad. She felt feminine and dainty and...judging by the amount of action in his pants...desired.

He stepped back at the same time as she pushed him away. She shoved her hands into her hair, squinting at him in the moonlight. This was crazy... She was adult enough to recognise passion that could be perilous—wild, erratic and swamping. But lust, as she'd learnt, clouded her thinking and stripped away her practicality. Lust, teamed with the brief emotional connection she'd felt earlier, when she'd opened up a little to him, had her running scared.

Bum magnet.

Jack cocked his head. 'So, not a good idea, huh?'

Ellie bit her lip. 'Really not.'

Jack lifted a shoulder and sent her a rueful smile. 'Okay. But you're a very tempting sight in the moonlight so maybe we should go in before I try to change your mind.'

When she didn't move, Jack reached out and ran a thumb over her bottom lip.

'You can't just stand there looking up at me with those incredible eyes, Ellie. Go now, before I forget that I am, actually, a good guy. Because we both know that I could persuade you to stay.'

Ellie erred on the side of caution and fled inside.

CHAPTER THREE

EVERY TIME HIS foot slapped the pavement a hot flash of pain radiated from his cut and caused every atom in his body to ache. It was the morning after almost kissing Ellie, and he was dripping with perspiration and panting like a dog.

He placed his hand against his side and winced. He shouldn't be running, he knew that, but running was his escape, his sanity, his meditation. And, thinking about things he shouldn't be doing, kissing Ellie was top of the list. Why was he so tempted by his blue-eyed hostess? Especially since he'd quickly realised that she wasn't into simple fun and games, wasn't someone he could play with and leave, wasn't a superficial type of girl. And he didn't do anything *but* superficial.

But there was something about her that tweaked his interest and that scared the hell out of him.

He started to climb the hill back home and—dammit! He *hurt*. Everywhere. *Suck it up and stop being a pansy*, he told himself. *You've had a heart transplant—a cut and a beating is nothing compared to that!*

Jack pushed his wet hair off his forehead and looked around. Good Lord, it was beautiful here...the sea was aqua and hunter-green, cerulean-blue in places. White-yellow sand. Eclectic, interesting buildings. He was lucky to be here, to see this stunning part of the world...

Brent never would.

Brent never would. The phrase that was always at the back of his mind. Intellectually he knew it came from survivor's guilt—the fact that he was alive because Brent was dead. In the first few months and years after the op he'd been excited to be able to do whatever he wanted, but he knew that over the past couple of years the burden of guilt he felt had increased.

Why? Why wasn't he coming to terms with what had happened? Why wasn't it getting easier? The burden of the responsibility of living life for someone else had become heavier with each passing year.

The mobile he'd borrowed from Ellie jangled in his pocket and he came to an abrupt stop. Thankfully he was back at Ellie's place. He didn't think he could go any further.

'So, what do you think of Ellie?' Mitchell said when Jack pushed the green button on the mobile and held it up to a sweaty ear.

'Uh…she's fine. Nice.'

She was…in the best sense of the word. A little highly strung, occasionally shy. Sensitive, overwhelmed and struggling to hide it. Sexy as hell.

'So, have you talked to her about me yet?'

Jack lifted his eyebrows at Mitchell's blatant narcissism and felt insulted on Ellie's behalf.

'Ellie's well, but over-worked. Her bakery is fabulous; she's running it on her own as her mum is overseas,' he said, his tone coolly pointed as he answered the questions Mitch should have thought to ask.

'Yeah, yeah… But how far have you got with the book? Did you get my e-mail? I sent it just now.'

His verbal pricks hadn't dented Mitchell's self-absorbed hide. Jack wished he could reach into the phone and slap Mitchell around the head. Had he always been so self-involved? Why hadn't he noticed before? Jack sighed and looked at his watch. It wasn't quite seven yet. Far too early to deal with Mitchell.

'Firstly, my laptop is still in Somalia, and, contrary to what you think, I don't hover over my laptop waiting for your e-mails,' Jack said as he made his way into the house, up the steps and into his room. Jack heard Mitchell splutter with annoyance but continued anyway. 'And, by the way, why did you teach Ellie such crude Arabic insults when she was a little girl? They are, admittedly, funny as hell, because she gets them all mixed up, but really...'

'She still remembers those, huh?'

Jack pulled his T-shirt over his head, walked into the bathroom and dropped it into the laundry basket. Yanking a bottle of pills out of his toiletry bag, he shook the required daily dosage into his hand, tossed them into his mouth and used his hand as a cup to get water into his mouth.

Those pills were his constant companions, his best friends. He loved them and loathed them in equal measure.

'And why did you tell Ellie that I'm *helping* you write this book?'

As per normal, Mitch ignored the questions he didn't want to answer. 'So, have you spoken to Ellie yet about *me*?'

'No. The woman works like a demon. I haven't managed to pin her down yet.' Jack frowned. 'And she's not exactly jumping for joy at the prospect.'

Mitchell didn't answer for a minute. 'Ellie and I have had our ups and downs...'

Ups and downs? Jack suspected that they'd had a lot more than that.

'She didn't like me being away so much,' Mitchell continued.

Jack rolled his eyes at that understatement. As he walked over to the window his eye was caught by two frames lying against the wall, behind the desk in the corner. Pulling them out, he saw that they were two photographs of a younger Ellie and a short blond man in front of the exclusive art gallery

Grigson's in London. Jack asked Mitch who the man in the photograph was.

'Someone she was briefly engaged to—five, six years ago.' Jack heard Mitchell light a cigarette. 'She wanted to get married. He didn't.'

Jack felt a spurt of sympathy for the guy. He'd had two potential-to-become-serious relationships in the past ten years and they'd both ended in tears on his partner's face and frustration on his. They'd wanted him to settle down. He equated that to being locked in a cage. He'd liked them, enjoyed them, but not enough to curtail his time or freedom for them.

'Jack? You still there?' Mitchell asked in his ear.

'Sure.'

'I spoke to most of our commissioning editors today and told them that you've been injured. They will leave you alone for three weeks. Unless something diabolical happens—then all bets are off,' Mitchell stated.

That was enough to yank his attention back, and fast. Jack felt his molars grinding. 'You do know I get very annoyed when you interfere in my life, Mitchell?'

Mitchell, never intimidated, just laughed. 'Oh, get over yourself! You haven't taken any time off in two years and we all know that leads to burnout. You've been flirting with it for a while, boyo.'

'Crap.'

'If you don't believe me, check your last couple of stories. You've always been super-fair and unemotional, but there's a fine line between being unemotional and robotic, Jack. You are drifting over that line. Losing every bit of empathy is every bit as problematic as having too much.'

'Again…crap,' Jack muttered, but wondered if Mitchell had a point. He remembered being in Egypt six weeks ago and watching a paramedic work on a badly beaten protester.

He'd been trying to recall if he'd paid his gas bill. Maybe he was taking the role of observer a bit too far.

'I'm going to courier you my notebooks, my diaries,' Mitchell told him. 'Get some sun, drink some wine. But if you don't get cracking on my book...'

Mitch repeated the most gruesome of Ellie's Arabic curses from the night before and Jack winced.

Jack tossed the mobile onto the bed, slapped his hands on his hips and stared at the photographs he'd replaced against the wall. Ellie... Maybe he should think about leaving, and soon. Almost kissing her last night had been a mistake...

Sure, he was attracted to her—she was stunning; what man wouldn't be? If she was a different type of girl then he could have her, enjoy her and then leave. Unfortunately he wasn't just physically attracted, and he *knew* that mental attraction was a sticky quagmire best avoided. And, practically, while Mitch wouldn't win any Father of the Year awards he might not approve of them hooking up, and he didn't want to cause friction between him and his subject, mentor and colleague.

Ellie, with her cosy house and settled lifestyle—the absolute opposite of what he liked and needed—was also far more fascinating than he generally liked his casual partners to be. Because fascination always made leaving so much harder than it needed to be.

'Morning.'

Ellie jumped as he entered the kitchen, looking tough and rugged and a whole lot of sexy. She could see that his hair had deep red highlights in the chocolate-brown strands. He'd scraped off his beard and the violet stripes under his eyes were almost gone. He did, however, still have that glint in his eyes—the one that said he wanted to tear up the bedcovers with her.

Ellie cursed when she felt heat rising up her neck.

'Can I get some coffee?'

Jack's question yanked her out of her reverie and she nodded, reaching for a mug above the coffee machine to give her hands something to do.

'You're up early,' she said when she'd found her voice.

Jack took the cup she handed him and leaned against the counter, crossing his legs at the ankles. 'Mmm. Good coffee. I went for a run this morning along the beachfront. It was… absolutely amazing. It's such a beautiful part of the world.'

'It is, but should you be exercising yet?'

'I'm fine.'

Yeah, she didn't think so—but it was his body, his choice, his pain. Ellie shook her head, picked up her own cup and sipped. She echoed his stance and leaned against the counter. Tension swirled between them and Ellie thought she could almost see the purple elephant sitting in the room, eyebrow cocked and smirking.

Maybe it would be better just to get it out there and in the open. But she couldn't get the words out… How she wished she could be one of those upfront, ballsy girls who just said what they felt and lived with the consequences.

She was still—especially when it came to men—the shy, awkward girl she'd been as a teenager.

Jack's eyebrows pulled together. 'The wariness is back in your eyes. Why?'

'Uh…last night. Um—' Oh, great. Now her tongue was on strike.

Jack, no slouch mentally, immediately picked up on what she was trying to say. 'The kiss that never happened?'

Ellie blushed. 'Mmm.'

'Yeah—sorry. I said I wouldn't hit on you and I did.' His tone didn't hold a hint of discomfort or embarrassment.

Ellie bit the inside of her lip. That wasn't what she'd expected him to say. Actually, she had no idea *what* she'd thought he'd say. The purple elephant grinned. 'I just… It's just that…'

Jack scratched the underside of his jaw and looked at her with his gold-flecked eyes. 'Relax, Ellie,' he said. 'It won't happen again…'

Ellie lifted her eyes to meet his and swallowed. In his she could read desire and lust and a healthy dose of amusement… as if he could read her thoughts, understand her confusion.

'Well…' he drawled as his finger gently pushed back a strand of hair that had fallen over her left eye. 'Maybe I should clarify that. I'll try not to let it happen again. You're very, very kissable, Ellie Evans.'

Ellie's eyes narrowed. She might not be the most assertive person in the world but that didn't mean he could look at her with those hot eyes and that smirky expression. Or presume that whatever happened between them would be solely *his* decision. Ellie narrowed her eyes, gripped the finger that had come to rest on her cheek and bent it backwards.

Hating personal confrontation, but knowing she needed to do this for the sake of her self-respect, she took a deep breath and forced the words out. 'There's only one person who will decide what happens between us and that will be me—not you.'

Jack grimaced and yanked his index finger out of her grip. He shook his finger out and sent her a surprised look. But, gratifyingly, there was an admiration in those hazel eyes that hadn't been there before and she liked seeing it there.

Jack sent her an approving smile. 'Good for you. I was wondering if you could stand up for yourself.'

Ellie narrowed her eyes. 'When I need to. No casual kissing.'

'Can we do *non*-casual kiss…?' Jack held up his hands at her fulsome glare. 'Joke! Peace!'

'Ha-ha.' Ellie rolled her shoulders. 'Would you like to go to work for me today?' she asked, blatantly changing the subject. 'I could do with a day off.'

'Okay—except my sugar icing and sculpting skills are sadly lacking. I can, however, make a mean red velvet cake.'

Ellie lowered her cup in surprise. 'You can bake?'

Ellie thought she saw pain flicker in his eyes. When he spoke his voice was gruff.

'Yes, I can bake. Normal stuff. Not pastries and croissants and fancy crap.'

Fancy crap? Well, that was one way to describe her business.

'Who taught you?' Ellie asked, openly curious.

'My mother.'

Ellie lifted her eyebrows. 'Sorry, I can't quite picture you baking as a kid. On bikes, on a sports field, camping—yes. Baking...no.'

Jack placed his cup on the counter and turned his face away from her. 'Well, it wasn't from choice.'

He sipped his coffee and when he looked at her again his face and eyes were devoid of whatever emotion she'd seen. Fear? Anger? Pain? A combination of all three?

This time it was Jack's turn to change the subject. 'So—breakfast. What are we having?'

Ellie looked at her watch and shook her head. 'No time. I need to go. I was supposed to be at work an hour ago.'

Jack shook his head. 'You should eat.'

'I'll grab something at the bakery.'

Well, she'd try to, but she frequently forgot. There just wasn't time most days. Ellie sighed. One of these days she'd have to start eating properly and sleeping more, but it wouldn't be any time soon. Maybe when Merri came back she could ease off a bit...but she probably wouldn't.

After all, she had a business to save.

Ellie looked at Jack, who was pulling eggs and bacon out of her fridge. Her mouth started to water. She'd kill for a proper fry-up...

Ellie pulled her thoughts away from food. 'So, I've given you keys to the house and I've just paid the deposit for you to hire a car. It should be delivered by eight so you won't be confined to the house any more.'

'The receipt for the deposit?' Jack sent her a level look.

Ellie rolled her eyes. He was insistent that she kept receipts for everything she spent so that he could repay her. 'In the hollow back of the wooden elephant on the hall table. With all the others.'

The annoying man wouldn't even allow her to buy milk or bread without asking for a receipt.

'Thanks.'

Jack slit open the pack of bacon and Ellie whimpered. She really, really didn't have time. She picked up her keys and bag, holding her chef's jacket in one hand.

'Pop down to the bakery later. I'll show you around. If you want to,' she added hastily.

Jack's smile had her melting like the gooey middle of her luscious chocolate brownies.

'I'll do that. See you later, then.'

Ellie bravely resisted the arc of sexual awareness that shimmered between them and sighed as she walked out of the kitchen.

In your dreams, Ellie. Because that was the only place making love to Jack was going to happen.

And even there her heart wasn't welcome to come to the party. Her heart, she'd decided a long time ago, wasn't allowed to party with *anyone* any more.

Later, dressed in denim shorts, flip-flops and an easy navy tee, Jack slipped through the front door of Pari's and looked over Ellie's business.

There were café-style tables outside, giving patrons the most marvellous view of the beach while they sipped their coffee and ate their muffins, and more wrought-iron tables inside, strategically placed between tables piled with preserves and organic wines, ten different types of olive oil and lots of other jars and tins of exotic foods with names he barely recognised. The décor was bohemian chic—he'd noticed that before—and all effortlessly elegant. Huge glass display fridges held a wide variety of pastries and cakes, and in another layer thick pink hams, haunches of rare roast beef and dark sausages.

It looked inviting and happy, and there was a line of people three deep at the wide counter, waiting to be served. The place was rocking, obviously extremely popular, and Jack suddenly realised what effort would be needed to move the bakery. If Ellie could find a place to move it to…

'Jack!'

Jack whipped his head up and saw Ellie approaching a table in the back corner of the room, a bottle of water in her hand. A good-looking couple sat at the table and Ellie motioned him over. Jack threaded his way through tables and people and ended up at the table, where a fourth chair was unoccupied.

'Paula and Will—meet my friend Jack. Take a seat, Jack,' Ellie said.

After shaking hands with Will, Jack pulled out the chair and sat down.

'I'm just about to chat to them about their wedding cake, but before we start does anyone want coffee?' Ellie continued.

Jack wasn't sure why he was sitting in on a client consultation, but since he didn't have anything better to do decided to go with the flow. He ordered a double espresso and noticed that Will was frowning at him.

'Do I know you?' Will asked, puzzled.

This was one of the things he most liked about Cape Town—the fact that people hardly recognised him. While he wasn't famous enough to attract paparazzi attention in the UK, his face was recognisable enough to attract some attention.

'I have one of those faces,' he lied.

Ellie sent him a grin. 'I'm just going to run through some ideas with Will and Paula, then I'll show you around.'

She placed her notebook on the table and switched into work mode, outwardly confident. Jack listened as the couple explained why they now wanted a Pari's cake—their cake designer had let them down at the last moment—and watched, amazed, as Ellie took their rather vague ideas and transformed them into a quickly sketched but brilliantly drawn concept cake. He sampled various types of cake along with the couple, and when they asked for his opinion confirmed that he liked the Death by Chocolate best. Though the carrot ran a close second. Or maybe the fudge…

If he hung around the bakery more often Jack decided he'd have to add another couple of miles to his daily run to combat the calories and the cholesterol.

Ellie watched her clients go as she gathered her papers and shoved a pencil into the messy knot of hair behind her head.

'Today is Monday. Their wedding is on Saturday. I'm going to have to do some serious juggling to get it done for them.' Ellie rubbed her hand over her eyes.

'So why are you doing it, then?' Jack asked, curious.

'They are a sweet couple, and a wedding cake is important,' Ellie replied.

'Sweet? No. But they sure are slick.'

Ellie looked puzzled. 'What do you mean?'

She might be confident about her work but she was seriously naïve when it came to reading people, instinctively choosing to believe that people put their best foot forward.

Jack leaned his forearms on the table and shook his head. 'El, they were playing you.'

'What are you talking about?'

'They decided to come to you for their wedding cake—but it wasn't because their cake designer let them down. They knew there was no chance you'd make their cake at such late notice if they didn't have a rock-solid reason and they appealed to the romantic in you.'

'But why would you think that? I thought they were perfectly nice and above-board.'

'She doesn't blink—at all—when she lies, and his eyes slide to the right. Trust me, they were playing you.'

'Huh…' Ellie wrinkled her nose. 'Are you sure?'

Of course he was. He'd interviewed ten-year-olds with a better ability to lie. 'So, what are you going to do?'

Ellie stood up and shrugged. 'Make them their cake, of course. Let's go.'

Of course she was. Jack sighed as he followed her to the back of the bakery. She was going to produce a stunning, complicated cake in five days and their guests would be impressed, not knowing how she'd juggled her schedule to fit it in.

'I'm beginning to suspect you're a glutton for punishment,' Jack told Ellie as she pushed through the stable door leading to the back of the bakery. And a sucker too. But he kept that thought to himself.

She threw a look at him above her shoulder. 'Maybe—but did you notice that they didn't ask for a price?'

He hadn't, actually.

'And that order form they signed—at the bottom it states that there is a twenty-five per cent surcharge for rush jobs. Pure profit, Jack.'

Well, maybe not so much of a sucker.

Ellie walked over to a stainless steel table and tossed her sketchpad onto it. She scowled at the design they'd decided on. 'There's a standard surcharge for rush jobs,' she admitted. 'But I really don't need the extra profit.'

'And now you're angry because they played you?' Jack commented.

'I was totally sucked in by Paula's big blue eyes, the panic I saw on her face. Will played his part perfectly as well, trying to reassure her while looking at me with those *help me* eyes!'

'They were good. Not great, but good.'

'*Arrgh!* I need the added pressure of making a wedding cake in five days like I need a hole in my head!'

'So call them up and tell them you can't do it,' Jack suggested.

That would mean going back on her word, and she couldn't do that. 'I can't. And, really, couldn't you have given me a heads-up *before* I agreed to make their damn cake?'

Jack cocked his head. 'How?'

'I don't know! You're the one who is supposed to be so street-wise and dialed-in… Couldn't you have whispered in my ear? Kicked my foot? Written me a damn note?'

Jack's lips quirked. 'My handwriting is shocking.'

'It is not. I've seen your writing!' Ellie shoved her hands into her hair. Her shoulders slumped. 'Useless man.'

'So I've been told.' He reached out and laid a hand on her shoulder, his expression suddenly serious. 'Sorry. It never occurred to me to interfere.'

She looked at him, leaning back against the wall, seemingly relaxed. But his eyes never stopped moving… He hadn't said anything to her because he was an observer. He didn't get involved in a situation; he just commentated on it after the fact. She couldn't blame him. It was what he did. What journalists did.

She would have appreciated a heads-up, though. *Dammit.*

Ellie heard a high-pitched whistle and snapped her head up, immediately looking at the back section of the bakery, where the production area flowed into another room. Elias, one of her head bakers, stood at the wide entrance and jerked his head. Something in his body language had Ellie moving forward, and she reached her elderly staff member at the same time Jack did.

'What's wrong, Elias?' Ellie asked when she reached him.

Ellie felt Jack's hand on her lower back and was glad it was there.

Elias spoke in broken English and Ellie listened carefully. Before she had time to take in his words, never mind the implications, Jack was also demanding to know what the problem was.

'One of the industrial mixers is only working at one speed and the other one has stopped altogether,' she explained.

'That's not good,' Jack said.

'It's a disaster! We have orders coming out of our ears and we need cake. *Dammit!* Nothing happens in the bakery without the mixers… Elias, how did this happen?'

Elias shifted on his feet and stared at a point behind her head. 'I did tell you, Miss Ellie…the mixers…they need service. Did tell you…bad noise.'

Ellie scrubbed her face with her hands. He was right. He *had* told her—numerous times—but she'd been so busy, feeling so overwhelmed, and the mixers had been working. It had been on her list of things to do but it had kept getting shoved to the bottom when, really, it should have been at the top.

Ellie placed her hands over her face again and shook her head. What was she going to do?

When she eventually dropped her hands she saw that Elias was walking out of earshot. Jack had obviously signalled that they needed some privacy. He placed his hands on the mixer and lifted his eyebrows at Ellie.

'Dropped the ball on this one, didn't you?' he remarked.

Ellie glared at him, her blue eyes laser-bright. 'In between juggling the orders and paying the staff and placing orders for supplies, I somehow forgot to schedule a service for the mixers! Stupid me.' She folded her arms across her chest as she paced the small area between them.

'It was, actually, since this is the heartbeat of your business.'

Did he think she didn't know that? 'I messed up. I get it… It's something I'm doing a lot of lately.'

'Stop feeling sorry for yourself and start thinking about how you're going to fix the problem,' Jack snapped.

She felt the instinctive urge to slap him…slap *something*.

'You can indulge in self-pity later, but right now your entire production has stopped and you're wasting daylight.'

His words shocked some sense into her, but she reserved the right to indulge in some hysterics later. 'I need to get someone here to fix these mixers…' Ellie saw him shake his head and she threw up her hands. 'What have I said wrong now?'

'Priorities, Ellie. What are you going to do about your orders?'

'You mean the mixers,' Ellie corrected him.

Jack shook his head and reached for the paper slips that were stuck on a wooden beam to the right of the mixers. 'No, I mean the orders. Prioritise the orders and get…what was his name…Elias…to start hand-mixing the batter for the cakes that are most urgent.'

That made sense, Ellie thought, reluctantly impressed.

Ellie took the slips he held out and a pen and quickly prioritised the orders. 'Okay, that's done. I'll get him working on these.'

Jack nodded and looked at the mixers. 'Are these under guarantee or anything?'

'No. Why?'

'Got a toolbox?'

'A toolbox? Why? What for?'

'While Elias starts the hand-mixing I'll take a look at these mixers. I know my way around machines and motors. It's probably just a broken drive belt or a stripped gear.'

'Where on earth would you have learnt about machines and motors?' Ellie demanded, bemused.

'Ellie, I spend a good portion of my life in Third World

countries, on Third World roads, using Third World transportation. I've broken down more times in more crappy cars than you've made wedding cakes. Since I'm not the type to hang about waiting for someone else to get things working, I get stuck in. I can now, thanks to the tutelage of some amazing bush mechanics, fix most things.'

Ellie shut her flapping mouth and swallowed. 'Okay, well… uh…there's a basic toolbox in the storeroom and a hardware store down the road if you need anything else.'

Jack put his hands on his hips. 'And get on that phone and get someone here to service those mixers. I might be able to get them running but they'll still need a service.'

Ellie looked at him, baffled at this take-charge Jack. 'Jack—thank you.'

'Get one of the staff to bring me that toolbox, will you?' Jack crouched on his haunches at the back of one of the machines and started to work off the cover that covered the mixer's motor. 'Hell, look at this motor! It's leaking oil…it's clogged up…when was this damn thing last serviced?'

Ellie, who thought that Jack wouldn't appreciate hearing that she hadn't the faintest clue, decided to scarper while she could and left Jack cursing to himself.

CHAPTER FOUR

ELIAS LAUGHED WHEN Jack messed up the traditional African handshake—again—and slapped him on the shoulder. 'We'll teach you yet, *mlungu*.'

'Ma-lun-goo?' Jack tested the word out on his tongue.

'"White man" in Xhosa,' said the old Xhosa baker.

'Ah.' Jack stared at Elias and a slow grin crossed his face. 'I heard you talking Xhosa earlier. I love the clicking sound you make. If I were staying I would want to learn Xhosa.'

'If you stay…' Elias grinned '…I teach you.'

'There's a deal,' Jack said, before bidding him goodnight and turning back to the rear entrance of the bakery.

Ellie looked up as he walked towards her and ran the back of her hand over her forehead. 'Bet you're regretting ambling down the hill this morning,' she said with a grateful smile.

'It's been an…interesting day,' Jack said, conscious of a dull headache behind his eyes. 'A baptism by grease, flour, sugar and baking powder…'

'I never expected you to help with either the fixing or the mixing, but thank you.'

He'd resurrected one of the mixers, and when a part arrived for the other mixer in the morning he'd have that up and running within an hour. While he'd been working on the mixers he'd watched Elias and his assistant falling further and further behind on the orders, and had instantly become their best friend when he'd got the one mixer working.

'Elias really battled physically to do that hand-mixing.'

Ellie cocked her head. 'So that's why you stepped in to help him?'

He shrugged. 'I thought he was going to have a heart attack,' Jack admitted.

He'd mixed the batter for more than a hundred and twenty cupcakes and, under Elias's beady eye, also mixed the ingredients for two Pari's Paradise Chocolate cakes and more than a few vanilla sponge cakes. His shoulders ached and his biceps were crying out for mercy...

'He's stronger than he looks. He should've retired years ago, but he doesn't want to and I can't make him.' Ellie sighed. 'He's worked here since the day the bakery opened. It's his second home, and as long as he wants to work I'll let him. But maybe I should try to sneak in another assistant.'

'Sneak in?'

'It took me six months to get him to accept Gideon in his space.' Ellie grinned. 'He's a wonderful old gent but he has the pride of Lucifer. I'm surprised he let you do anything.'

'Yeah, but I *did* get his beloved mixer working.'

'That you did,' Ellie agreed. 'And I'm so grateful. You worked like a dog today.'

Which raised the question...*why* had he bust his gut to help this woman he barely knew? He was an observer, not a participator, and her bakery wouldn't have gone into bankruptcy if they'd waited for a mechanic to fix the mixers. But he'd felt compelled to step up and get stuck in, to help her, to...

Aargh! He must have taken a blow to the head along with the stabbing and the beating, because this wasn't how he normally rolled.

Jack, frustrated at not recognising himself, thought that he'd kill for a beer or two. He stood next to Ellie's table and leaned his shoulder against a wall, watching her work. She'd been in the bakery for nearly twelve hours and she was still working on another cake. The nightshift of two more bakers were starting their shift and Ellie would probably be there to see them off in the morning.

She might tend to panic when she hit a snag but he admired her work ethic.

And her legs… Who would've thought that a chef's jacket over shorts and long tanned legs could look so sexy? Jack swallowed, uneasy at the realisation that he wanted…no, *craved* her.

He'd never had this reaction to any woman before. Generally it was easy come, easy go. Nothing about Ellie so far had been easy, and he suspected that nothing would be. Jack shifted on his feet as desire flared. It would be easy to seduce her, but that would make leaving in a couple of days that much more complicated. Because somehow he instinctively knew that he couldn't treat her as a casual encounter. There was something about Ellie that tugged at him—some button that she pushed that made him suspect that this was a woman worth getting to know…

And that was more terrifying than being caught in the crossfire in any hot zone anywhere in the world. They had yet to make flak jackets to protect against emotional bullets.

Ellie looked up from the bare cake in front of her, which had been cut into the vague shape of a train and was covered in rough white icing. She sent him a tired smile. 'I'm wondering what I can give you for supper.'

Jack pried himself off the wall and walked away from the table she was working at. 'Something simple…let's order pizza.'

Ellie sighed and Jack saw relief flicker on her face.

'Okay. I just need to finish this and we can go home. Or you can go home and I'll follow in a bit.'

Jack hooked a stool with his foot and rolled it towards him, sinking down onto it with a groan. 'I'll wait for you.'

Ellie pulled out a ball of fire-engine-red dough from a container and started to knead it with competent hands.

Jack stretched out his legs. 'What are you making with that red dough?'

'It's not dough. It's fondant icing. It's for a train cake,' Ellie explained. She gestured to what looked like a big pasta roller on the table next to hers. 'It goes in there to flatten it out, then I'll drape it over the cake.'

'Does it have to be done tonight?'

'It should be. Luckily, I can make this in my sleep.' Ellie slapped her hand into the fondant and caught his look. 'What? Why are you looking at me like that?'

'I was just thinking about your business, what you do here.' He hadn't been, but he suspected that she wasn't ready to hear what he'd really been thinking...which involved her being naked and sliding all over him.

Oh, Lordy-be, there was that smile that made her womb vibrate. It was a combination of schoolboy naughtiness and sex-on-a-stick, and Ellie thought that stronger women than her would have trouble resisting it. She opened her mouth to ask what he was smiling about and practically bit her tongue in half to keep the words from escaping.

The hell of it was that while she'd initially thought that Jack might be all flash, today he had proved that he was more than just a hot body with a reasonably sharp brain. How many men of her acquaintance would have jumped in to help, tinkering with a motor and getting splattered with grease and then patiently mixing endless batches of batter—a thankless, back-breaking, horrible job to do by hand—without a word of complaint?

Ellie smoothed icing over the front of the train. The ability to give without asking for something in return, to jump into a situation and offer help when it was most needed, was a rare quality and unfortunately deeply attractive. Even more so than his hot body and masculine face.

Ellie's hand stilled on the cake as a panicked thought jumped into her head. She wanted him to go—now—tonight. She wanted him to go before she started imagining him in her bakery, in her life…before she started dreaming of a clear mind to keep her focused, a steady hand to prod her along, a hard body to touch and taste, then to curl up against at night.

Ellie fisted her hand and had to stop herself from punching the cake. She was suddenly ridiculously, outrageously angry at herself. Why was she even letting thoughts like those into her head? Considering what-ifs and maybes? Yes, he was a good-looking guy who gave her a buzz, a man nice enough to help her out, but there was no call to start thinking that he was anything more than a transient visitor. He was nothing but her father's friend, a brief acquaintance, and realistically she wasn't his type.

Oh, she was attractive enough for a brief fling, but she wasn't stupid enough to believe that she could ever be more than that. *Nobody will give up their freedom and time for monogamy with you…*

Jack had got up, rested his hand on her clenched fist and forced her fingers open.

Ellie twisted her lips and blew out a breath, but kept her eyes fixed on the cake.

'I think that's enough for now. We need pizza and beer and to chill,' he said.

Ellie pulled her hand out from beneath his and brushed her hair off her forehead with the tips of her fingers, leaving a trail of red icing on her forehead. 'This cake…'

'Will still be here tomorrow.' Jack took her hand again and pulled her away from the table. He leaned forward and his voice was low, seductive and sexy in her ear. 'Beer. Pizza.'

Ellie looked at the half-white, half-red train. Beer, pizza and conversation with an interesting man versus a stupid train cake...? No contest.

The woman amazed him, Jack thought. Twenty minutes ago Ellie had looked as if she was about to collapse, but now, sitting across from him at a table on the deck of an admittedly fake, slightly scruffy Italian restaurant, she looked sensational. She'd pulled her hair back into a sleek ponytail which highlighted her amazing cheekbones and painted her lips a glossy soft pink. She'd sorted out the smudged make-up around her eyes and she looked and smelled as if she'd just stepped out of a shower.

He, on the other hand, felt as if he'd spent the day hauling hay and cleaning out stables. He took a long sip of his beer and sighed as the bittersweet liquid slid down his throat. The night was warm, the surf was pounding, he had a beer in his hand and a pretty girl across the table from him.

The only scenario that sounded better was if he'd had pizza in his belly and the girl was naked beneath him.

'There's that smile again,' Ellie murmured.

'Huh? What smile?'

Ellie rested her chin in the palm of her hand. 'You get this secretive, naughty, sexy smile...'

'Sexy?' The light on the deck was muted but Jack grinned as he saw her blush.

'Yeah, well...anyway. So, I'm starving.' Ellie looked around, not trying to hide the fact that she was looking to change the subject. 'Where's that pizza?'

Jack decided to let her off the hook—mostly because flirting caused his pants to wake up and start doing its happy dance.

He looked around and narrowed his eyes. 'Have you had any more thoughts about the bakery?'

Ellie wrinkled her nose. She took a sip from her glass of wine and glanced at the ocean. 'Moving it, you mean?'

'Mmm.'

'I have an idea that I'm working on,' Ellie said mysteriously.

His curiosity was instantly aroused. 'You can't leave me hanging!' Jack protested when she didn't elaborate.

Ellie smiled. 'There might be a property that could work.'

'You don't have much time,' Jack pointed out.

'I know. Six months.'

Under the table Jack felt Ellie crossing her legs and he heard her sigh.

'I want to hyperventilate every time I think about it.'

'Call your mother and tell her to come home. It's her business too, El. You don't have to carry this load alone. Tell her about having to move. Tell her that you need help.'

'I can't, Jack. She's been working in that bakery for ever, never taking time off. Now she's living her dream and having such a blast. I can't ask her to give that up. Not just yet. And…and I feel that if I do I'm admitting failure. That I need my mummy to hold my hand.'

Jack shook his head. 'So you'd rather work yourself to a standstill, knocking yourself out, instead of asking your friend to come back to work and your mother to come back and help you?'

'Making sure that the people I love are happy is very important to me, Jack.'

'Not if it comes at too high a price to *you*.'

She'd inherited Mitchell's irritable, don't-mess-with-me stare.

'You're really sexy when you're irritated,' he commented idly, unfazed.

'I suspect that you can be annoying…' she paused for a beat and bared her teeth at him '…all the time.'

Jack grinned at her attempt to intimidate him. She looked as scary as a Siamese cat with an attitude disorder.

Ellie rubbed her temple with her fingertips. 'Can we not talk about the bakery tonight? I'd like to pretend it's not there for five minutes.'

Jack agreed and sighed in relief when he saw a waiter heading their way with pizzas. It wasn't a moment too soon. He thought his stomach was about to eat itself.

'So, why war reporting?' Ellie asked, when they'd both satisfied their immediate hunger.

Ellie wound a piece of stray cheese around her finger and popped it into her mouth. Jack nearly choked on the bite of pizza he'd just taken. *Hell*... He quickly swallowed and pulled his mind out of the bedroom. She was getting harder and harder to resist. And he *had* to resist her...mostly because she *was* so damn hard to resist.

Ellie repeating her question wiped the idea of sex—only temporarily, he was sure—from his brain.

'When I was about fifteen I watched a lot of news, and Mitch and other war reporters were reporting from Iraq. I was fascinated. They seemed larger than life.'

'He was. Is.'

'Then he was interviewed and he spoke about the travelling and the adrenalin and I thought it was a kick-ass career.' Jack bit, swallowed and grinned. 'I still think it is.'

Ellie's eyes were a deep blue in the candlelight and Jack felt as if she could see into his soul.

'How do you deal with the bad stuff you've seen? The violence, the suffering, the madness, the cruelty? How do you process all of that?'

Jack carefully placed his slice of pizza back down on his plate. He took a while to answer, and when he did he was surprised to hear the emotion in his voice. 'It took some time but I've programmed myself to just report on the facts. My job is to tell the story—hopefully in a way that will facilitate change. I observe and I don't judge, because judgement requires an emotional involvement.'

'And you don't get emotionally involved,' Ellie said thoughtfully. 'Does that carry over into other areas of your life?'

Jack stiffened, wondering where she was going with that question. 'You mean like relationships and crap like that?'

'Yeah—crap like that.' Ellie's response was bone-dry.

He had to set her straight. Right now. Just in case she had any ideas...

'Like your father, my life doesn't lend itself to having a long-term relationship. Women tend to get annoyed when you don't spend time with them.'

'Yep, I know what that feels like. Any woman who gets involved with a war reporter is asking to put her emotions through a meat-grinder,' Ellie replied. 'God knows that's exactly what Mitchell did to me.'

She didn't give him time to respond and was frustrated when she changed the subject.

'So, how is the book coming along?'

Ellie pushed her plate away and Jack frowned. She'd barely managed to eat half her medium pizza and he had almost finished his large. 'Well, apart from the fact that I can't get a certain reporter's daughter to sit down and answer my questions, fine.'

He saw guilt flash across her face. 'Oh, Jack, I'm so sorry! You probably want to leave, head home, and I'm holding you up—'

Jack shook his head. Where did this need to blame herself for everything come from? She was so together and confident in some ways—such a train wreck when it came to her need to please.

'Ellie, stop it!' Ellie's mouth snapped shut and Jack thought that was progress. 'Firstly, if I wanted to leave I would've made a plan to go already. Secondly, as I said, I like your house, I like this area, and when I start feeling pressurised for time I'll tell you and we'll get down to it. As long as you do not want me out of your house we're good. *Do* you want me to leave?'

'No, you're reasonably well house-trained,' Ellie muttered. Jack grinned.

'So, why aren't you prepared to write your story? Mitchell said that you were asked to.' Ellie picked up the thread of their conversation again.

Because my story isn't just my story and it's a lot more complicated than people think. Jack swallowed those words and just shrugged.

Ellie picked an olive off her pizza and popped it into her mouth. They sat in a comfortable silence for a while, until Ellie spoke again. 'I think I know why you are reluctant to tell your story.'

This should be good. A little armchair analysis. 'Really? Why?'

'In light of what you said earlier, digging into your own story, analysing your life choices, would require emotional involvement. You can't stand back and just observe your own life. You can't be objective about yourself. Then again, who can?'

It was Jack's turn to stare at her, to feel the impact of her insightful words. He couldn't even begin to start formulating an argument. There wasn't one, because her observation was pure truth.

Jack drained the last inch of beer in his bottle and threw his serviette onto the table. 'You ready to go?'

Ellie nodded, pushed her chair back and pulled her purse out of her bag. He ground his teeth as she placed cash under the heavy salt cellar. Where the hell were his new bank cards? He was sick of not having access to funds.

He stopped at the cashier on the way out and asked for a

receipt, and he knew without looking at Ellie that she was rolling her eyes at him.

'Jack, you worked in the bakery. I'll pay for dinner.'

'No.' Jack took the printed bill from the manager and shoved it into his pocket.

'Stop being anal.'

Jack gripped her ponytail and tugged gently. 'Stop nagging. I thought we agreed that if I'm living in your house then I'll pick up the tab?'

She tossed her head. 'We never agreed on anything!'

Jack's grin flashed. 'It's easier if you just do it my way.'

'In your dreams.'

It was shortly after six the following evening when Jack returned from a trip to Robben Island, the off-coast prison that had housed Nelson Mandela for twenty-four years, and his mind was still on the beloved South African icon when he walked into Ellie's kitchen.

He kicked off his shoes, dumped the take-away Chinese he'd picked up on the way on the kitchen table and tossed his brand-new wallet containing his brand-new bank cards onto the table. Inside was enough cash to reimburse Ellie for everything she'd paid for so far. Thinking about Ellie, he wondered where she was.

Jack walked back into the hall and stood at the bottom of the stairs, calling her name. Her bag was on its customary hook and her mobile sat on the hall table. Jack walked back to the kitchen, onto the back deck, and finally found her, sprawled out on a lounger in the shade of one of the two umbrellas that stood next to her pool.

She was asleep, with an open sketchbook on her bare, flat stomach and a piece of charcoal on the grass below her hand. She was dressed in a tiny black and blue bikini and he spent many minutes examining her nearly-but-not-quite naked body.

Her long damp hair streamed over her shoulders and across the triangles that covered her full breasts. She had a flat, almost concave stomach, slim hips and long, smooth legs with fine muscles. The tips of her elegant feet were painted a vivid pink that reminded him of Grecian sunsets.

Very alluring, very sexy, Jack thought, sinking to the grass next to her chair. In order to stop himself from undoing those flimsy ties keeping those tiny triangles in place, he picked up the sketchpad and flipped through the pages.

The sketches were rough, jerky, but powerful, full of movement. She'd sketched her house, capturing its fat lines and bay windows, and there was a sketch of her dog, head on paws, his eyes soulful. There was a rather bleak landscape of cliffs and shadows which oozed sadness and regret.

Jack gasped at his likeness, grinning up at him from another white page. She'd captured his laugh and, worse, the attraction to her he'd thought he was hiding so well.

'Snoop.'

Jack snapped the book closed and looked up into her face. Her eyes were still closed and her eyelashes were ink-black on her face.

'I thought you were still asleep. I was trying to be quiet.'

'I'm a really light sleeper,' Ellie said, and held out her hand for her sketchpad.

Jack reluctantly handed it over. 'These are good—'

'It's something I do to pass the time.' Ellie tossed the pad on top of a box of charcoal sticks and sat up, covering her mouth as she yawned. 'Talking of which, what *is* the time?'

Jack looked at his watch. 'Half-six.'

Ellie looked horrified. 'I went for a swim around five and thought I'd take fifteen minutes to chill… I must've dozed off.'

Jack drew his thumb across the purple shadow under her eye. 'It looks like you needed it. What time did you finish last night? I saw your light was still on after midnight.'

'One? Half-one? I finished the VAT return and paid some creditors.' Ellie swung her legs off the sunchair, her feet brushing Jack's thighs. 'I've got a couple of hours' work tonight and then I'll be caught up. I shouldn't have fallen asleep…I meant to work after my swim.'

Jack clenched his fists in an effort not to reach for her. She looked so tired, so young, so…*weary* that all he wanted to do was take her in his arms and ease her stress. He shoved his hand into his hair. *She tries to hide it*, he thought, *but she's wiped out in every way she can be by the responsibilities of her business.* He wished there was something he could do for her. Dammit, was he starting to feel protective over her? He didn't know how to handle her, deal with her. He was used to resilient, emotionally tougher women, and Ellie had him wanting to shield her, shelter her.

'I need to think about what to make for supper,' Ellie said as she stood up, unfurling that long, slender body.

Her voice was saturated with exhaustion and he felt irritation jump up into his throat. 'Ellie, I am *not* another one of your responsibilities!' he snapped.

Ellie blinked at him. 'You don't want me to make supper?'

'No. For a number of reasons. The first being that I bought supper—Chinese. My replacement bank cards arrived,' he explained when she looked at him enquiringly. 'Also, I really think you need to learn that the world will not stop turning if you stop for five minutes and relax. You never stop moving, and when you do you're so exhausted that you can't keep your eyes open.'

Ellie picked up a sarong and wound it around her hips. 'Jack, please. I really don't want to argue with you.'

Jack nodded. 'Okay, I won't argue. I'll just tell you what to do. You're going to change into something that doesn't stop traffic and then we're going for a walk. On the way we'll stop and have a beer at one of the pubs on the beachfront. Then we'll come home, eat Chinese, of which you will have a reasonable portion, and then you're going to bed. Early.'

'Jack, it's hot. I don't feel like a walk and I can't take the time—'

'Yeah, you can,' Jack told her. 'And I know you're hot. You're standing there in a couple of triangles cooking my blood pressure. So this should help both of us cool off.'

Jack scooped her up, ignored her squeal and stepped, still dressed, into the deep end of her gloriously cold, sparkling blue pool.

CHAPTER FIVE

'It's such a stunning evening. Would you like to take the long route to the beachfront?' Ellie asked him as they stepped onto the road outside her house. 'It's a ten-minute walk instead of a five-minute walk but I'll show you a bit of the neighbourhood.'

'Sure,' Jack agreed, and they turned left instead of right.

He walked next to Ellie, his hands loose in the pockets of his shorts. The sea in front of them was pancake-flat and a patchwork quilt of greens and blues. It was make-your-soul-bump beautiful. The temperature had dropped and she was cool from the swim and the light, short sundress she was wearing.

She was really looking forward to an icy margarita and Jack's stimulating, slightly acerbic company.

A little way away from the house Jack broke their comfortable silence. 'By the way, I was contacted today by the Press Club. They've heard that I'm in town and have invited me to their annual dinner. I'd like you to go with me, but I know how busy you are. Any chance?'

Ellie's heart hiccupped. A date! A real date! *Whoop!* She did an internal happy dance. 'When is it?'

'Tomorrow. Tomorrow *is* Friday, right? It's black tie, I'm afraid.'

A date where she could seriously glam up? Double *whoop!*

'So, do you think you can leave work early for a change?' Jack enquired. 'It's a hassle going to these functions on my own.'

In a strange city where he knew no one of course it would be. And the world wouldn't stop turning if she left work a little earlier than normal. Besides, Merri would come in for an hour or two.

'Sure. That sounds like fun.'

'Great.' Jack moved between her and a large dog that was walking along the verge of a house with its gates left open.

Ellie appreciated his innate protectiveness but she knew Islay. He was as friendly as he was old.

Jack cleared his throat. 'Ellie, I was only supposed to spend one, maybe two nights in your house...'

'And tonight will be your fourth night,' Ellie replied quietly. 'Do you want to leave?'

Jack shook his head. 'Just the opposite, actually. Mitch, being Mitch, has put the word out to the network editors that I'm hurt and need some time off.'

Ellie flicked a glance at his hip. 'You *are* hurt.'

'Superficially.' Compared to what he'd gone through, his stab wound was minimal. 'Anyway, I'm off for a few weeks unless—'

She knew the drill. Journalists were only 'off' until the next story came along. 'Unless some huge story breaks.'

Jack nodded his agreement. 'So, I thought I'd stay in Cape Town for a bit longer.'

'In my house?' Ellie heard the squeak in her voice and winced. She sounded like a demented mouse.

'Well, I could move into a hotel, but I spend enough time in hotels as it is and I'd rather pay you.'

Ellie stopped in her tracks and turned to look at him. 'You'd pay to live with me?'

What exactly did he mean by that? What would be included in that deal? Not that she believed for one minute that he'd make her an offer that was below-board, but she just wanted to make sure… And really, how upset would she be if he suggested sleeping together? Since she was constantly thinking about sex with him…not very.

His grin suggested he knew exactly what she was thinking. 'It's a simple transaction, Ellie. Someone has to get paid to put my butt into a bed and I'd prefer it to be you and not some nameless, faceless corporation.' Jack stepped forward and his thumb drifted over her chin. 'A bed, food, coffee. No expectations, no pressure.' Damn.

'Oh.' Ellie dropped her head and thought she was an idiot for feeling disappointed. *You don't want to get involved, on any level, with any man—remember, Ellie?* Especially a man like Jack. Too good-looking, too successful, too much. Rough, tough, unemotional and—the big reason—never around.

But she wanted him. She really did.

Jack dropped his hand and Ellie was glad, because she didn't know for how much longer she could stop herself reaching up and kissing him, tasting those firm lips, feeling the rasp of his stubble under her lips, her fingers. She watched him walk away and after two steps he turned and looked back at her.

He must have seen something on her face, because his steps lengthened and then his hands were on her hips, yanking her into him. His mouth finally touched hers sweetly, gently, before he allowed his passion to explode. His quick tongue slipped between her lips, scraped her teeth and tangled with her own in a long, deep kiss that had no end or beginning.

One hand held her head in place and the other explored her back, her hip, the curves of her bottom, the tops of her thighs. Ellie slid her hand up his back, under his loose T-shirt, and acquainted herself with his bare flesh, the muscles in his back, that strip of flesh above his shorts and the soft leather belt. He was heat and lust and passion in its purist, most concentrated form; causing her nipples and her thighs to press together to subdue the deep, insistent throbbing between them.

He kissed her some more.

Ellie wasn't sure how much time had passed when he finally lifted his head and rested his forehead against hers. 'I'm burning up, on fire from wanting you. That's why I haven't kissed you before this.'

'Why did you kiss me now?' Ellie whispered back, her hands gripping his sides.

'Because you looked like you wanted me to—really wanted me to.'

She really had. And she wouldn't object to more.

Jack stepped back, linked his hands behind his head. The muscles in his arms bulged. 'I can't take you to bed… I mean of course I *can*. I want to. Desperately. But it would be the worst idea in the world.'

It didn't matter that she agreed with him. She wanted to know why he thought so. 'Why?'

Jack's mouth twisted. 'I'm not good for you. I'm hard and cynical, frequently bitter. I have seen so many bad things. You're arty and creative and…innocent. Untainted.'

'No, I'm not.' Ellie pursed her lips. He made her sound like a nun. 'You're not a bad man, Jack.'

'But I'd be bad for *you*.' Jack dropped his arms and stared out to sea. 'I am not a noble man, Ellie, but I'm trying to do the right thing here. Help me out, okay?'

Ellie lifted her hands in puzzlement. 'How am I supposed to do that?'

Jack glared at her. 'Well, for starters you could stop looking at me as if you want to slurp me up through a straw. Sexy little dresses like that don't help—and you're *very* lucky that you kept possession of that thing you call a bikini this afternoon. Short shorts and tight tops are out too…'

'Would you like me to walk around in a tent?' Ellie asked

sarcastically, but secretly she was enjoying the fact that she could turn him on so quickly. It was a power she'd never experienced before, a heady sensation knowing that this delicious man thought that she was equally tasty.

'That might work,' Jack replied.

Ellie pulled in a breath as he stepped forward and took her much smaller hand in his. His expression turned sober.

'El, I like you, but I think you have enough going on in your life without the added pressure of an affair with me. I need to write your father's life story and I don't know how objective I'm going to be if I am sleeping with his daughter.'

Ellie kept her eyes on his and gestured him to continue. Everything he'd said so far had made sense, but she could still feel his lips on hers, his big hands on her skin. Taste him on her lips.

'It's been a long time since I just liked a woman, enjoyed her company. Can we keep this simple? Try to just be friends? That way, when I leave, there won't be any...stupid feelings between us.' Jack stared down at her fingers. 'You know it's the smart thing to do.'

Ellie sighed and wished she could be half as erudite as he was. Sure, words were the tools of his trade, but he made her feel as thick as a peanut butter sandwich when it came to expressing herself. Only two words came to mind, and neither were worthy of this conversation.

'Yeah, okay,' she muttered.

Jack smiled and ran his thumb over her knuckles before dropping her hand. 'So, will you go to the camping store for a tent or shall I?'

'Make sure it's a pink one.' Ellie looked around and her expression softened. 'Oh, we're here!'

'Where?' Jack asked as she grabbed the edge of his shirt and tugged him across the road.

Ellie walked up to some wrought-iron gates and wrapped

her fingers around the bars, looking at the dilapidated double-storey building.

Jack tugged on the chain that held the gates together. 'What *is* this place?'

'It was a library at the turn of the century, then it was turned into a house, but it's been empty a couple of years. I've heard a rumour that old Mrs Hutchinson is finally considering selling it. Restored, this building would be utter perfection. Two storeys of whimsy, with balconies and bay windows galore. Its irregular shape reminds me of a blowsy matron in a voluminous skirt and a peculiar hat. Romantic, eccentric and very over the top.'

Jack immediately picked up where she was going with this. 'You're thinking of this place for the bakery?'

'It's just around the corner from the present location, with ample parking space. I took a box of cupcakes to the Town Planning office and...well, bribed them into letting me take a look at the building plans. There is a lot of space, but not too much...enough to hold the bakery, the delicatessen and a proper breakfast and lunch restaurant.'

Jack put his hands on his hips. 'It's difficult to comment without seeing the place. Let's go in.'

Ellie pointed at the sign on the fence. '"No Trespassers".'

'If I obeyed those signs I'd never get a story,' Jack said, and pulled at a rusty iron post on the fence. It moved, and he gestured Ellie through the gap he'd created. 'You're slim enough to climb through here.'

'And you?'

Jack grabbed the top of the fence with his hands, yanked himself up and held his body weight while he swung his legs onto the railing. Within seconds he was on the other side and his breathing hadn't changed.

Ellie shook her head as she slipped through the fence. 'If

you've split open your cut you're going to the emergency room,' she told him.

'Yes, Mum.' Jack grinned and led her up to the huge front door. He pursed his lips at the lock. 'No breaking in through *this* door.'

'We're not breaking in through any door!' Ellie stated as he pulled her away from the front door and around the house. 'Seriously, Jack, that's a crime!'

Jack peered through a window. 'Relax, there's nothing to steal, so if we get caught we can plead curiosity. I'm good at talking my way out of trouble.'

'Jack!'

Jack stopped at a side door. 'Good. Yale lock. Pass me a hairpin, El.'

'You are not going to… Hey!' Ellie slapped her hand against her head where Jack had yanked the pin from her hair. 'That hurt!'

'Sorry.' Jack opened the pin, inserted it into the lock and jiggled the handle. Within a minute the door swung open to his touch. 'Bingo.'

'I cannot believe that you picked that lock! Who taught you that?'

'You really don't want to know.'

Ellie looked curious. 'No, tell me. Who?'

'Your father, actually.'

Ellie rolled her eyes and Jack just grinned as he placed a hand on her lower back and pushed her inside.

'I *so* didn't need to know that!' she muttered.

'Relax.' Jack placed his hands on his hips and looked into the room to his right. 'Kitchen through here—an enormous one, but it needs to be gutted. God, Ellie, the ceiling is falling down!'

'I never said it didn't need work. Look at these floors, Jack. Solid yellow-wood.'

Jack looked at the patch of direct sunlight on the warped wood and at the hundreds of holes in it. 'White ants, Ellie, white ants. I bet the house is infested with them.'

'Are you always this pessimistic?' Ellie asked as she opened doors on either side of the passage.

'I just think you should slow down to a gallop. I can see the look in your eye. If you could you'd slap the deposit down,' Jack said. He picked at a piece of wallpaper and a strip came off in his hand. 'Before you even consider doing that I suggest you get an architect to look at the place, and a civil engineer to check that it's not going to fall down.'

It was sensible, unemotional advice—but sensible was for later. Right now she wanted to feel, sense, imagine.

Jack ducked his head into another room and Ellie heard what she swore was a screech. 'Did you squeal?' she called.

Jack hurried out of the room. 'Girls squeal. Men...don't. A rat nearly ran over my shoe! I hate rats!'

'Well, you squeal like a girl, and I'd rather have rats than white ants,' Ellie replied as they stepped into a massive hallway which was dominated by a two-storey-high ceiling and a thoroughly imposing staircase. Coloured sunshine from the stained glass inserts next to that imposing front door threw happy patterns onto the wooden floor.

'Okay, this is amazing,' Jack admitted.

'It's unbelievable,' Ellie said, falling hard.

Nothing had prepared her for the immediate visceral connection she felt to this property. She walked to the bay window behind the staircase and looked out onto the wilderness beyond, with its overgrown shrubs and trees. She could easily imagine the rambling, once stunning gardens that surrounded the house, like carefully chosen accessories on a red-carpet dress. Ellie walked the area downstairs and quickly established that the place could, without a huge amount of construction, be adapted to house the bakery.

It just took imagination—and she had lots of that.

'Why hasn't someone converted it into a restaurant? A bed and breakfast? An art gallery?' Jack asked when she rejoined him in the hall.

'Many have tried. Many have failed. Mrs Hutchinson hasn't ever been prepared to sell. She doesn't need the money and this building was her childhood home.' She shrugged at Jack's enquiring face. 'Basically, she's bats. The town fruitcake. She's refused offers—huge offers—for stupid reasons. Perceived lack of manners, not polishing your shoes. One man wore too much jewellery.'

'She sounds bonkers,' Jack said.

'That's one way of putting it,' Ellie said briskly, and tipped her head to look up at him. 'Let's finish with the breaking and entering. I could murder a drink.'

Jack followed her down the passage back to the side door, which he yanked open for her. 'Technically, it was only entering. We didn't break anything.'

'Semantics,' Ellie said as he pulled the door shut behind him and they headed back down the winding driveway to the road.

'You really are a bit of a pansy, aren't you?' Jack leapt over the fence and jammed his hands in his pockets as he waited for her to climb back through the gate.

She was just straightening up when she heard a car approaching and slowing down. Ellie looked up and straight into the eyes of the driver, who was looking at her curiously.

'Oh, *dammit*.'

Jack looked from her to the disappearing Toyota. 'Problem?'

Ellie slapped the palm of her hand against her forehead. 'That was Mrs Khumalo, the busiest of St James's busybodies. Soon it will be all over town either that I am having secret trysts with a married man, or that I am buying the property, or that I'm joining a cult and this is going to be its headquarters.'

Jack laughed as she stomped down the road. 'Cool. As the great Oscar Wilde said, "There's only one thing in the world worse than being talked about, and that is *not* being talked about".'

'Grrr.'

They fell into an easy silence on their walk home from the pub, and Ellie enjoyed the fact that they could be quiet together, that neither of them felt the need to fill the space with empty words.

Jack took the keys from her hand and opened the front door for her, nudging the dogs out of the way with a gentle knee so that she could walk in first. In the hallway Ellie dropped her bag on the side table and placed her hands on her back, stretching while Jack examined the life-size nude painting of a blonde on a scarlet velvet couch on the opposite wall. She wore only her long hair and a waist-length string of pearls... and a very come-hither grin.

'I can't stop looking at this painting.'

Since it was a nude painting of a gorgeous woman, Ellie wasn't surprised. Most men had the same reaction.

'Who *is* that?'

'My best friend Merri.'

Jack stepped up to the portrait and lightly touched the canvas with the back of his knuckle. 'I meant the artist. The way he's captured the blue veins in her pale skin, her inner glow... God, he's amazing!'

Ellie felt a spurt of pure, unadulterated pleasure. 'Thanks.'

Jack's mouth fell open. '*You* painted this?'

'Mmm. I studied Fine Art at uni and lived in London for a while, but I couldn't support myself by selling my art so I came home and started work at the bakery.'

'It's brilliant. But you left out quite a bit between uni and coming back to Cape Town.' He touched the frame with his fingertips. 'And this is more than something you pass time with.'

Ellie felt the familiar stab, the longing to immerse herself in a big painting that sucked her into a different dimension. 'It used to be my passion. It isn't any more.'

'Why not?'

'I painted that just before I went to the UK. I'd finished uni and was going to conquer the world. I was so in love with art, painting, creating. I was…*infused* by art.'

Jack sat on the bottom stair and patted the space next to him. Ellie sat down and rested her arms on her knees, looking at Merri's naughty smile.

'Were you always arty?'

Ellie shrugged. 'I think I started when I was about six. I remember the first time I fell into a drawing.'

'Tell me.'

Ellie felt her voice catch. 'Mitchell was home. He'd just come back from somewhere in Africa. He was working in his study—nothing strange there—and the door was open. He was reading aloud an article he'd written…he did that. He read all his articles aloud.'

'He still does.'

'It was a report on the genocide happening in Rwanda—Burundi—somewhere like that. The report was graphic, horrific…' Ellie shuddered and felt Jack's strong arm around her waist, his hand on her hip. This time there was nothing sexual about his touch. It was pure comfort. 'Mitchell called it like he saw it: women, old people, children. Severed heads, limbs…'

'I know, sweetheart. Skip that part. Tell me about the art.' Jack rested his chin on her hair, shaken by the idea of a little girl hearing that. Damn Mitch and his stupidity. The man was a talented journalist, but as a father…useless.

'I couldn't get the pictures his words conjured out of my brain and the only thing I could think of to do was draw.

Happy things—butterflies, princesses. I had nightmares for a while, and I'd wake up and hit my desk to paint or colour.' Ellie sighed. 'Mitchell could never censor himself. He had no conception of sensibility—that young kids didn't need to know that sixteen Afghan rebels had been executed and their decapitated heads paraded through the streets as a warning and that he'd witnessed it. It drove my mother mad that he couldn't keep his mouth shut in front of me.'

'But you had your art?'

'I did. He reported on brutality and war, violence, and I tried—still try—to counter that by producing beauty. It used to be through oils. Now it's through cake and icing.' Ellie shrugged and managed a smile.

Jack saw her staring at Merri's portrait and caught the pain and sadness in her eyes. There was more to this story or he wasn't a journalist. 'Why did you give it up?'

'Can we skip this part?' Ellie asked with a wobble in her voice.

'I'd really like to know.' Jack lowered his voice, made it persuasive.

'You ask me all these questions but you won't talk about yourself,' Ellie complained.

True. 'I know. I'm sorry. But tell me anyway.'

'Short story. He was the owner of an exclusive art gallery in Soho.' Grigson's, Jack remembered. The short blond from that photo in his room. 'He offered me an exhibition, told me I was the next big thing. I fell deeply, chronically in love with him. I found out later that was his *modus operandi*. I wasn't the first young artist he'd seduced into bed with that promise.'

Jack winced.

'I was swept away by him. He dealt in beauty and objects of art. He was a social butterfly—had invitations to something every night of the week. But he never took me along to anything. Like my father, he dropped in and out of my life. I kept asking him about the exhibition, spending time with me, taking me along, but he kept fobbing me off.'

'Bastard,' Jack growled.

'I told him that I wanted to break it off and he responded by proposing. I thought that meant that he'd change, but nothing did. I saw less of him than ever.'

'So what precipitated the break-up?' Jack briefly wondered why he was so interested in her past, why he felt the need to find the jerk and put him into a coma.

'I told him that I was done with waiting around for him. He responded by telling me that I was a mediocre artist who'd never amount to anything. That he'd just wanted to sleep with me occasionally but I wasn't worth the hassle…that it was, essentially, not worth my being around, him trying to keep me happy.'

Forget the coma. He now had the urge to put the guy six feet under. When Mitch had mentioned him he'd initially felt sorry for him, because he'd thought that she must have been pushing him into marriage, but he was the one who'd messed *her* around, messed her up. No wonder she tried so hard to be indispensable to the people she loved; she thought she had to try harder to be loved.

The two men she'd loved the most had hurt her, damaged her the most. God, the ways that love could mess up people. Just another reason why he wanted nothing to do with it…

'Anybody since then?' Jack asked, although he knew there hadn't been.

'No.'

Needing to move, to work off his anger, Jack jumped up and jogged up the stairs to inspect another painting. He placed his hands on his hips and looked around at the art covering the walls.

'Good grief, Ellie, some of these paintings are utterly fantastic. I'm trying to work out which ones are yours, because not all of them are.'

'Some are by fellow art students; others I've picked up along the way,' Ellie said, pride streaking through her voice. 'You like art?'

'I love art. Sculpture. Architecture,' Jack confirmed, quickly moving up the stairs to examine a seascape.

He placed a hand on his hip and winced at the movement. Ellie watched his body tense. His face was illuminated by the spotlight above his head. The violet shadows beneath his eyes were back and his face was pale beneath his slight tan.

Jack Chapman, she decided, had no concept of how to pace himself. He'd recently suffered a horrendous beating, had a nasty knife wound, and yet he'd spent the day sightseeing. She could see that he was exhausted and in pain, and she knew that he was one of those men who would carry on until he fell down.

He came across as easygoing and charming but there was a solid streak beneath the charm, a strength of character that people probably never saw beneath the good looks and air of success. His thought-processes were clear-headed and practical. While he'd challenged her decisions and her actions she didn't feel as if he was judging *her*.

He'd coaxed her past out of her and he was a fabulous listener. He listened intently and knew when to back away from the subject to give the guts-spiller some time to compose themselves.

Ellie caught his slight wince as he walked back down the stairs and she shook her head at him. 'For goodness' sake— will you sit down before you fall down?'

Jack's strong eyebrows pulled together. 'I'm fine.'

'Jack, you're not fine. You're exhausted and your body is protesting. Take a seat in the lounge, watch some TV. Do you want something to drink?'

Jack raked his hand through his hair. 'Nothing, thanks. Mind if I veg out on the veranda for a while?'

'Knock yourself out,' Ellie said. 'I'll plate up the Chinese.'

'Hey, El?' Jack called.

Ellie poked her head around the kitchen door. 'Yes?'

Jack rattled off an Arabic curse and Ellie wrinkled her nose. 'Something…something donkey. Sorry…what?'

'I just called your ex a bleeping-bleeping horse's bleeping ass.'

Ellie laughed. *Nice, Jack.*

After supper they headed back to the veranda and watched as dusk fell over the long coastline. Lights winked on as they sipped their red wine, sharing the couch with their bare feet up on the stone wall. Jack placed his arm along the back of the couch and Ellie felt his fingers in her hair. She turned to look at him but Jack was watching her hair slide between his fingers.

'It's so straight, so thick.'

Ellie felt his hands tug the band from her hair and felt the heavy drop as her hair cascaded down her back, could imagine it flowing over Jack's broad hand. She heard his swift intake of breath, felt his fingers combing her hair.

'I love the coloured streaks. They remind me of the flash of colour in a starling's wing.'

There was that creative flair again—this time with words. And there was that sexual buzz again. Ellie licked her lips. 'They're not my real hair.'

'Still pretty.' Jack lifted a strand of her hair and because it was so long easily brought it to his nose. 'Mmm…apple, lemon…flour.'

Ellie could not believe that she was so turned on by a man sniffing her hair. 'Jack…'

His eyes deepened, flooded with gold. He drifted the ends

of her hair over his lips before dropping it and sliding his big hand around her neck. 'Yeah?'

Ellie dropped her eyes. 'We weren't going to do this, remember?'

'Shh, nothing is going to happen,' Jack said.

He dropped his arm behind her back, wrapped it around her waist and pulled her so that she was plastered against his hard body. Ellie swung around and rested her head against his chest, deeply conscious of his warm arm under her breasts.

'Did you submit your piece on that Somalian pirate-slash-warlord?' Ellie asked, to take her mind off the fact that she wanted to move his hands to more deserving areas of her body. Her breasts, the backs of her knees, between her legs.

'Yes. I didn't get as much information from him as I wanted to, but it was okay.'

'Have you worked out what you said that set him off?'

She felt Jack shake his head. 'Nah. I think he was high… and psychotic.'

'That might be it.' Ellie rested her hands on his arm, feeling the veins under his skin. 'Tell me about yourself. Mother? Father? Siblings?'

'Like you, I was an only child. I'm not sure why,' Jack replied.

Ellie half smiled. 'Tell me what you were like as a kid.'

She felt him stiffen at her question. 'At what age?'

Strange question. 'I don't know…ten?'

Jack's laugh rumbled through his chest. 'Hell on wheels. Maybe that's why my folks didn't have another kid. They probably despaired in case they'd have another boy.'

Ellie laughed. 'You couldn't have been *that* bad.'

'I was worse. Before I was eight I'd broken a leg, had three lots of stitches and lost most of my teeth.'

Ellie's mouth fell open. 'How on earth did you manage to do that?'

'The broken leg came from ramping with my BMX. The ramp I'd built myself collapsed. The teeth incident was from a fight with Juliet Grafton. I called her ugly—which she was. She was also built like a brick outhouse and her father was a boxing champion. Her mean right hook connected with my mouth. Stitches—where do I start? Falling off bikes, roofs, rocks…'

Ellie raised an eyebrow.

'But I was cute. That counted for a lot.'

She wanted to tell him he was still cute, but she suspected he already knew that, so instead she just watched night fall over the sea.

CHAPTER SIX

ELLIE WALKED INTO the ballroom on Jack's arm and looked around the packed space, filled with black-suited men and elegant women. His appearance caused a buzz and Ellie felt the tension in Jack's arm as people turned to watch their progress into the room. To them he was a celebrity, and well respected, and a smattering of applause broke out.

Jack half lifted his hand in acknowledgement. When he spoke, he pitched his voice so that only she could hear him. 'Those are the most ridiculous shoes, Ellie.'

Ellie grinned at the teasing note in his voice. He'd already told her that he liked her shimmery silver and pink froth of a cocktail dress, and she knew that her moon-high silver sandals made her calves look fantastic. She *felt* fantastic; she was sure it had a lot to do with the approval in Jack's expressive eyes.

'And, as I said, that is a sexy dress. Very you. Bright, colourful, playful.'

Ellie looked around and half winced. 'Most women are wearing basic black.'

'You're not a basic type of girl. And colour suits you.' He touched the hair she'd worked into a bohemian roll, with curls falling down her back. 'Gorgeous hair…make-me-crazy scent…'

'So I'll do?'

Jack took her hand and his words were rueful. 'Very much so.'

Ellie smiled with pleasure, then lifted her eyebrows as a tall blonde with an equine face stalked up to Jack, took his hand and kissed his cheek. Jack lifted his own eyebrows at her familiarity as she introduced herself as the Chairperson of the Press Club. Ellie forgot her name as soon as she said it.

'I have people who'd like to meet you,' she stated in a commanding voice.

'I'd like to get my date a drink first,' Jack said, untangling himself from her octopus grip.

'Ellie?'

Ellie turned at the deep voice and looked up into laughing green eyes in a very good-looking face. 'Luke? What are *you* doing here?'

'St Sylve is one of the club's sponsors,' he told Ellie, after kissing her on the cheek. He held out his hand to Jack. 'Luke Savage.'

'You drink Luke's wine all the time at home, Jack,' Ellie told him after they'd been introduced. 'Where's Jess, Luke?'

Luke looked around for his fiancée and shrugged. 'Probably charming someone for business.'

'Jack, I really *must* take you to meet some people.'

The blonde tugged on Jack's sleeve and Ellie caught the irritation that flickered in his eyes.

Jack looked at Ellie and then at Luke. 'Will you be okay?'

Ellie smiled at him. 'Sure. I'll hang with Luke and Jess and see you at dinner.'

Jack nodded and turned away.

Ellie looked up at Luke and pulled a face. 'We're going to be placed at some awfully boring table, I can tell, with Horse Lady neighing at Jack all night.'

Luke grinned. 'Well, we're sitting with Cale and Maddie—'

Ellie squealed with excitement. 'They're here too?'

'Cale *is* a sports presenter and journalist, El.'

'I *so* want to sit with you guys!' Ellie fluttered her eye-lashes up at him.

Luke winked at her. 'We'll just have to see if we can make that happen.'

Ellie felt a feminine arm encircle her waist and turned to look into her friend's laughing deep brown eyes.

'Are you flirting with my husband-to-be, Ellie Evans?'

Ellie laughed and kissed Jess's cheek. ''Fraid so.'

'Can't blame you. I flirt with him all the time. Now, tell me—why and how are you here with the very yummy Jack Chapman?'

Luke had somehow organised that they were all at the same table, and Jack felt himself relaxing with Ellie's charming group of friends. They were warm and down-to-earth and Jack was enjoying himself.

He leaned closer to Ellie and lowered his voice. 'How do you know all these people?'

Ellie sent him a side-glance out of those fabulous eyes. 'Maddie and I went to uni together. I met Luke through her, and Cale—he and Cale are old schoolfriends. But I've known Jess for years and years—before she and Luke met. Her company does Pari's advertising.'

'So, El,' Luke said as he picked up a bottle of wine from the ice bucket on the table and topped up their glasses with a fruity Sauvignon, 'what's this I hear about you having to move your bakery?'

Ellie wiped her hands on a serviette and pulled a face. 'I have to find new premises in less than six months.'

'And have you found anything?' Cale asked.

'Maybe. There's an old building close to the bakery that might work. It's supposed to be on the market, but I need to find an architect—someone who can look at the house and tell me if it's solid and if I can do the alterations I'm thinking of—before I put in an offer.'

Luke looked at Cale and they both nodded. 'James.'

'Another friend from uni?' Jack asked with a smile on his face.

Luke and Cale laughed, but didn't disagree with him. Luke told Ellie that he'd send her his contact details and the rest of the table moved onto another subject.

'Are you seriously considering that building for the bakery?' Jack asked Ellie, resting his cheek on his fist.

'Maybe. Possibly.' Ellie fiddled with her serviette. 'I'll speak to James and see what he says. Then I'll have to run it by my mum.'

'Understandable, since Pari's will be paying for it.' Jack saw something flash across her face and frowned. *'You're* paying for it? How would you...? Sorry—that has nothing to do with me.'

'How would I pay for it? It's fine. I don't mind you asking. Ginger—my grandmother—set up a trust for me when I was little and she's pretty wealthy. Pari's would pay me rent. That's if I actually decide to buy and renovate the building.'

There it was again—that lack of confidence in her eyes. 'Why do you doubt yourself?'

'It's a lot of money, Jack.' Ellie twisted the serviette through her fingers. 'What if it's a disaster? What if I end up disappointing my mother, Merri, my grandmother Pari's memory...? God, my *customers*?'

'That's a lot of disappointing, El. And a lot of what-ifs.' Jack placed his hand on hers and held them still. 'You love that building. Yours eyes light up when you talk about it. When are you going to start trusting yourself a little more?'

Ellie bit that sexy bottom lip—the one he wanted so badly to taste again.

'Merri says that I'm too much of a people-pleaser. That I have this insane need to make the world right for everyone.'

He didn't think Merri was wrong. 'You need to start listening to yourself more and to underestimate yourself less.'

Ellie twisted her lips. 'And not to think that I'm indispensable and the world will stop turning if I say no... I'm a basket case, Jack.'

Jack sent her an easy grin. 'We're all basket cases in our own way. You're just a bit more...vulnerable. Softer than most.'

'I need to grow a bit more of a spine.'

'I think you're pretty much perfect just as you are.'

Jack sighed as the Master of Ceremonies started to talk. He'd much rather talk to Ellie than listen to boring speeches. He heard the MC introducing him and grimaced. His was probably going to be the most boring speech of all. He felt Ellie's hand grasp his knee and a bolt of sexual attraction fizzed straight through him.

'You didn't tell me that you were making a speech!' she hissed.

He stood up, buttoned his jacket and looked down at her. 'Yeah, well, for some reason they find me interesting.'

'Weird. I simply can't understand why,' Ellie teased.

Jack swallowed his laughter before moving away from her and heading for the podium, thinking that he could think of a couple of things he'd rather be doing than giving a speech. Top of the list was doing Ellie. In the pool, in the kitchen, in the shower...

Jack reached the podium, looked at the expectant faces and let his eyes drift over to his table. Luke raised his glass at him. Maddie rested her arms on the table and sent him a friendly smile. Ellie, being Ellie, pulled a quick tongue at him and he swallowed a grin.

There wasn't much wrong with the world if Ellie was in it, making him laugh.

* * *

It had been heaven to be in Jack's arms, even if it was just for a couple of slow dances around the edge of the dance floor. In her heels she'd been able to tuck her face into his neck, feel his warm breath in her hair, on her temple. There had been nothing demure about their dancing. They'd been up close and personal and neither of them had been able to hide their desire. Her nipples had dug into his chest and her stomach brushed his hard erection. Their breaths mingled, lips a hair's breadth apart. She was certain that someone would soon notice the smoke and call the fire brigade.

The music had changed now, from slow to fast, and Jack's broad hand on her lower back steered her back to their empty table. He pulled out a chair for her and looked from her to a hovering waiter.

'What can I get you to drink? G&T? A cocktail? Or do you feel like sharing a bottle of red wine?'

'That sounds good.'

Ellie crossed her legs as Jack took the chair next to her and flipped open the wine list he'd been handed. He held it so that Ellie could scan the selection with him.

Ellie tapped the list with her finger. 'I don't really care as long as it has alcohol and is wet. Any of Luke's wines are good. St Sylve's.'

She sounded nervous, Jack thought. So she should, even if she had only a vague idea of how close she'd come to being ravished on the dance floor.

Jack rubbed his forehead. *Ravished.* Only Ellie could make him think of such an old-fashioned word. Pulling himself together, he ordered the wine, then slipped off his suit jacket before loosening the collar on his white dress shirt and yanking down his tie in an effort to get more air into his lungs. Now, if only he could sort his tented pants out.

'That's better.'

Ellie touched her hair and smiled wryly. 'I wish I could do that to my hair.'

He wished *he* could do that to her hair. He'd spent many hours thinking about that hair brushing his stomach, about wrapping it around his hands as he settled himself over her... Jack shifted in his chair. What was *with* this woman and her ability to short-circuit his brain? He dropped his eyes to her chest, where the fabric of her dress flirted with her cleavage and showed just a hint of a lacy pink bra.

Kill me now, Jack thought.

Ellie draped a leg over a knee and looked across the room. He could see her rapidly beating pulse at the base of her neck and knew that she was just as hot for him as he was for her. Not that he needed any confirmation. The little brush of her stomach across his body on the dance floor had been a freaking big clue.

Their wine was delivered and their conversation dried up. Jack didn't care. He just wanted to drink her in, lap her up... He gulped his wine, thoroughly rattled at how sexy he found her. Deep blue eyes, that sensual mouth, the scent of her sweetly sexy perfume. She had such beautiful skin, every inch of which he wanted to explore, taste, caress...

Sitting there, looking at her, he became conscious of something settling inside of him... To hell with being sensible and playing it safe. He knew what he wanted and he was damn well going to ask for it.

He reached over and lightly rested the tips of his fingers on the inside of her wrist, smiling wryly when he felt her pulse skitter. He lifted his hand, pushed a strand of hair that had fallen over her eyes behind her ear.

He leaned over and spoke in her ear. 'I can't do this any more. I've tried everything I can to resist you but enough is enough. Let's go home. Let me take you to bed.'

He saw the answer in her eyes and didn't wait for her nod

before taking her hand and leading her—wine, function and friends forgotten—out of the room.

Jack waited while she locked the front door and then backed her up against it, his body easily covering hers. He'd removed his jacket and she could feel the heat from his body beneath his shirt. His chest flattened her breasts and her breath hitched in response. This was so big, she thought, so overpowering...

His hands were large and competent, stroking her waist and skimming her ribcage in a sensual promise of what was to come. His hands skirted over her bottom and he lifted her up and into him, forcing her to wrap her legs around his waist. His hands held her thighs, steaming hot under the frothy skirt of her favourite dress. One heel dropped to the floor and it took a slight shake of her other foot for her remaining shoe to drop as well. Jack's mouth finally brushed hers and his tongue dipped into her mouth in a long, slow slide.

Jack walked with her to the stairs and at the first step allowed her to slip down him. He cradled her head in his hands and rested his forehead on hers.

'Upstairs?' he whispered, and Ellie felt the word and his breath drift over her face.

She nodded, ordered her legs to move and lightly ran up the stairs. She turned into her darkened bedroom and realised that Jack was a second behind her. He yanked her to him and walked her backwards to her big double bed. She felt the mattress dip under her weight, and dip some more as she was pushed on her back and Jack crawled over her.

She felt one of the straps of her dress fall down a shoulder and Jack's lips on her smooth skin. He was everything she'd ever wanted, she thought: strong, sexy, amazingly adept at making heat and lust pool in her womb. She'd never felt so intimately invested in a kiss, an embrace...so desperate to have his mouth on her, his fingers on her, to touch him, explore him, know him.

This could mean something, Ellie thought. This could mean something...huge.

Jack sat back on his haunches and pulled her up, kissing her as his hands looked for the zip at the back of her dress. Cool air touched her fevered skin as his hands wandered and soothed, danced over her skin, while his tongue did an erotic tango with hers.

Then her dress fell to her waist and she half sat, half lay in her strapless bra, her torso open to his hot gaze.

It had been so long. She'd half forgotten what to do. Should she undo the buttons of his shirt, pull it over his head? Let him do it himself? Could she do that? Should she do that? Ellie brushed her hand over his hip and felt the padding of his dressing. Another thought dropped into her scrambled head. Should he even be doing this? What if he pulled the skin apart and he started bleeding again?

'Your cut...' Ellie murmured, sitting up in an effort to escape those searing eyes.

'Is fine,' Jack replied, stroking her from shoulder to hand.

Ellie rested her forehead on his collarbone and sighed. She wanted this, wanted to immerse herself in this experience with him, but suddenly her mind was jumping around like a cricket on speed, playing with thoughts that were not conducive to inspiring or maintaining passion. Thoughts like, What did this mean to him? To her? With all her previous lovers—okay, all two of them—she'd felt and given love and thought that that love was reciprocated to a degree. There was nothing like that with Jack. They had nothing more between them than a burgeoning friendship and a searing, burning passion.

It had been so long since Darryl, and she was so out of practice. Would she be enough for him? She had enough pride to want to get this right. Was she knowledgeable enough, sexy enough, passionate enough to make this something that he'd remember?

Jack pulled her dress over her head and ran his index finger above the edge of her bra, his finger tanned against her creamy skin. Ellie looked down at his finger and closed her eyes, confused and bemused. She wanted him, but she wasn't wholly convinced that she was ready…

She should say no. She needed to say no…

Jack looked down at her breasts spilling over her frothy bra and thought that he'd never seen anything as beautiful in his life. Her skin had a luminosity that he'd never seen before—the palest blush on a creamy rose. Her ribcage was narrow, her arms slim, and her fingers were still on his hip. He could feel the heat in them through his pants, as tangible as her very sudden, very obvious mental retreat.

Going, going…oh, crap…*gone*.

Jack knew that he could kiss her, could stoke those fires again, but if she wasn't as fully in the moment with this as he was—had been—then it wasn't fair to her or—*dammit*—to him. He wanted her engaged, body, mind and soul. He could have physical sex with other women. He wanted, *expected* more from Ellie. Why and how much more he wasn't sure, but still…

Jack ran his hand over her head and sat back, his knees on either side of her legs. Ellie looked at him with big, wide eyes the colour of blue moonlight and ran her tongue over her top lip. He really wished she wouldn't do that…it made him think of the plans he'd had for that tongue. Hot, wicked, sexy plans.

Dammit… He sighed.

There were a bunch of reasons why he shouldn't be doing this, he thought. All of them valid. He was here for a limited time and she wasn't the type of girl who indulged in brief affairs. They were already living in the same house, so if they slept together they'd step over from friendship into sex-coloured friendship which was the gateway for affection, which led to attachment and a myriad of complications.

And what if that happened and he found himself liking living with her and not wanting to leave? How could he reconcile that with the promise he'd made to himself and to others that he'd live life to its fullest? His hard, fast, take-no-prisoners lifestyle—a life spent on planes, trains and hotel rooms—was not conducive to a full-time lover and invariably led to disappointment and sometimes to disaster.

'Jack?'

Jack blinked and lifted his eyebrows. 'Mmm?'

'You're a bit...heavy,' Ellie said in a small voice.

Jack immediately moved off her legs and sat on the edge of the bed. 'Sorry,' he muttered.

'No, it's okay. Just...um...need to get my blood circulating,' Ellie said in a jerky voice.

Jack sat sideways on the bed and thought that Ellie looked breathtaking in the low light that spilled into the room from the passage. Her mouth was soft and inviting and her hair was mostly out of its elaborate style, falling in waves over her shoulders.

Jack, all concerns forgotten, started to lean forward, intent on kissing the life out of her, but he made the mistake of looking into her eyes. They were round and slightly scared—and utterly, comprehensively miserable. He wondered how long it would take for her to call it quits, how far she'd take him down the road before she realised that she wasn't mentally ready to sleep with him.

It turned out not to be long at all...

'I'm sorry.' Ellie's voice was jerky and full of remorse. 'I really can't do this.'

So, she did have guts. Good to know, Jack thought. And at least she was honest.

'Okay.'

Jack saw Ellie cross her arms over her chest so he stood up and walked over to her bedroom door, unhooked her dressing gown. He passed it to her and moved on to stand at her open window, looking out at the dark night. When he turned around again Ellie's gorgeous body was covered, chest to knee, in a silky wrap that was almost as heart-attack-inducing as the dress she'd worn earlier.

He had to get out of her room before he did something he would regret. Like haul her back into his arms.

So he walked over to her and dropped a kiss on her temple. 'It's late. Maybe we should get some sleep.'

He thought it was a tragedy when Ellie didn't try to stop him when he walked out of the room.

Ellie woke, dressed and stumbled down the stairs half asleep. The noise of the television from the lounge jerked her fully awake and immediately caused memories of the previous night to rush back with the power of a sumo wrestler. She groaned. Jeez, she'd had all the sophistication of a pot plant. It had been so long, and she'd been so nervous, so self-conscious and hadn't been able to stop the weird thoughts buzzing around her head. She'd been worried about him seeing her naked and she'd stressed about whether he would stay the night with her, how much foreplay he expected and whether he was enjoying himself.

She'd been unable to let go, and if she was so attracted to him shouldn't she be able to lose herself in him? Wasn't that what lust-filled lovers did?

Ellie stood in the doorway to the lounge and stared at her wooden floor.

'Morning,' Jack said from the corner of the room, where he sat in a violet chair, leaning forward, his hands loose between his knees.

Elle lifted her head and squinted at him. 'Morning. How long have you been up?'

'Not too long.'

Ellie rested her hand on the doorframe. 'I'll go and make coffee.'

Jack nodded to a steaming cup of coffee that stood on the coffee table. 'I heard you moving around as I came down the stairs so I made you a cup.'

'Thanks.' Ellie walked across the room to pick up her cup and wrapped her hands around it. The purple elephant was back and was laughing like a maniac. But she wasn't going to consider raising the subject. It was embarrassing enough thinking about it. Talking to him about it would be absolutely impossible!

And that was even before she realised how preoccupied and distant Jack looked.

'I thought I'd get caught up with what's happening in the world. Do you mind?' he said.

'No.'

He gestured to the TV. 'Your dad is in Kenya, reporting on the riots.'

Okay, she'd go with world politics if that was all he had. 'They are having elections soon,' he added.

She *so* didn't care. She wanted to know what he was going to do now, how she was supposed to act. Ellie bit her lip, walked further into the room and looked at her father's familiar face on the screen.

'He's looking tired.' Ellie sat down on the couch and tucked her legs up under her as Mitchell answered questions from the anchor in New York.

'He texted me earlier. He thinks there's big trouble brewing.'

Jack turned up the volume on the TV set and she listened with half an ear as Mitchell spoke about the situation in Kenya.

He's nearly sixty, Ellie thought, wondering whether he had any thoughts about retiring. Because that wasn't something he'd ever discuss with *her*.

'I'm going there.'

Ellie took a moment to assimilate his statement. 'Going where?'

'To Kenya. A massive bomb was found and defused and the country is on a knife edge. I have contacts there,' Jack explained. He lifted his cup. 'I'm going to head out as soon as I've finished my coffee.'

'Ah…'

'I'm the closest reporter, and if I can get on a flight now I'll be with Mitch within a couple of hours. He's going to need help covering this.'

'Why?'

Jack frowned. 'It's news, Ellie, and news is my job. I know Nairobi. I want to be there.'

Ellie's heart sank. Of course he did. It didn't matter that he was beaten up, hurt and tired, or that he'd kissed her senseless, there was a story and he needed to follow it. It was the nature of the beast.

The fact that she was acting like a nervous, awkwardly shy Victorian nerd was also a very good excuse for him to run from her—fast and hard. Could she blame him?

Ellie refocused as Jack answered his ringing mobile. 'Hey, Andrew. No, I managed to get a seat on the next flight out to Nairobi. I'll be at the airport in—' he looked at his watch '—an hour. In the air in three.'

It took forty-five minutes to get to the airport, which left fifteen minutes for him to pack up and walk out of her life, Ellie thought. Last night she'd been lost in this man's arms and this morning he was making plans to walk out through the door without giving her a second thought.

And that just summed up all her experiences with war reporters. Nothing was more important than the story...ever. *Ever.*

Jack leaned forward in his seat. He really didn't want to be on this plane, was unenthusiastic about going to Kenya, but all through the night, unable to sleep, he'd known that he couldn't stay with Ellie, that he needed to get some distance. From her...from the feelings she pulled to the surface.

Last night, for the first time in years, he'd allowed himself to become mentally engaged with a woman, and in doing so he'd caught a glimpse of all that he was missing by not allowing that intimate connection. The warmth of her smile, the richness of her laughter, her enjoyment of being with him all added another layer to the constant sexual buzz that took it from thrilling to frightening.

They'd been emotionally and physically in sync and he'd loved every second of the previous evening—even if she had called a halt to it. Hell, he'd loved every minute of the past few days. He could, if he let himself, imagine a lifetime of evenings drinking wine on the veranda, taking evening walks with her, making love to her.

Brent had never got to experience anything like this....

The thought chilled him to the bone. *Brent.* And, dear God, he needed to make a decision about going to that memorial service, to face his family...to face his demons, the never-ending guilt of being alive because that teenage boy was dead.

Jack rubbed his face. If he hadn't had a heart transplant, if he'd grown up normal, what would his life be like? Where would he be? What would he be? Would he be married yet? Have kids?

How much of his reluctance to get involved was his own reticent nature and how much was driven by guilt? Was he avoiding love and permanence not only because he felt that his job didn't allow it but also because he felt he didn't deserve it? That if Brent couldn't have it why should he?

He already had his heart—was he entitled to happiness with it as well? Jack let out a semi-audible groan.

The elderly lady next to him, with espresso eyes and cocoa skin, laid an elegant hand on his arm.

'Are you all right, my dear?'

Jack dredged up a smile. 'Fine, thanks.' He saw doubt cross her face and shrugged. 'Just trying to work through some stuff.'

She rattled off a phrase in an African language he didn't recognise.

'Sorry, I don't understand.'

'African proverb. Peace is costly but it is worth the expense.'

Indeed.

CHAPTER SEVEN

ELLIE SNAPPED AT one of her staff and, after apologising, realised that she desperately needed a break from the bakery. Taking a bottle of water from the fridge, she walked out through the front door into the strong afternoon sunlight. Checking for cars, she walked across the street and sat on the concrete wall that separated the beach from the promenade and stretched out her bare legs. She flipped open the buttons of her chef's tunic and shrugged it off, allowing the sea breeze to flow over her bare shoulders in her sleeveless fuchsia top.

It had been four hellish days since Jack's abrupt departure. She had the concentration span of a flea and her thoughts were a galaxy away from her business and her craft.

His memory should have faded but she could still remember, in high definition, her time spent with Jack. The way his eyes crinkled when he smiled, the flash of white teeth, those wizard-like eyes that made you want to spill your soul.

She missed him—really missed him. Missed his manly way of looking at a situation, his clear-headed thought-processes, and she missed bouncing ideas about Pari's off him. She missed her friend.

But more than missing him she was also now seriously irritated. Furious, in fact. Partly at Jack, for whirling out of her house like a dervish, but mostly at herself. How stupid was she to think that she could rely on him, that he wouldn't drop her like a hot brick for a story, for a situation?

The men she was attracted to always ran out on her, so why had she thought it would be different with Jack? He'd been in her life for under a week and she was livid that, sub-consciously at least, she'd come to rely on him in such a short time. For advice, for a smile, for conversation and company at the end of a long day. How could she have forgotten, even for one minute, that war reporters always, *always* left, usually at a critical time in her life?

She couldn't help the memory rolling back—was powerless against the familiar resentment. She'd been fourteen and she'd entered a drawing of a lion into a competition in a well-known wildlife magazine. Out of thousands of entries throughout the country she'd won the 'Young Teenager' category. She'd been due to receive her prize at a prestigious televised awards cer-emony. She'd spent weeks in a panic because Mitchell was on assignment, and the relief she'd felt when he'd arrived back home three days before the ceremony had been overwhelming.

Everything had been super-okay with her world. The thought of going up onto that stage in front of all those people had made her feel sick, but her handsome dad would be in the audience so she'd do it. She would move mountains for him.

Then someone had got assassinated and he'd flown out two hours before the event…which she'd been too distraught to attend.

Ellie straightened her shoulders. She was no longer that broken, defeated, sad teenager who'd flung her arms around her father and begged him not to go.

She sipped her water and narrowed her eyes. She'd looked up the political situation in Kenya, and while it was tense it wasn't exploding. Jack hadn't needed to high-tail it out of her house. He was running from her—probably looking for an excuse to get away from her hot and cold behaviour, her lack of confidence in that sort of situation and her disastrous bedroom skills. If Jack had bailed just because of that, if she never saw him again—and who knew if she would, since *she hadn't heard from him since he'd left*—then good riddance, because then he was an idiot. As angry and...she searched for the word...*disappointed* as she felt, she knew that she was worth far more than just to be some transient woman who provided him a bed and some fun in it.

Ellie heard a long wolf whistle and looked up to see Merri leaving Pari's, two bottles of water in her hand. She'd obviously left Molly Blue with someone in the bakery—probably Mama Thandi—and was sauntering across the road as if she owned it.

Merri handed her another bottle of water and sat next to her, stretching her long body. A car passing them drifted as the driver gaped at her sensational-looking friend. Merri, as per normal, didn't notice. Ellie was quite certain that the majority of motor car accidents in Muizenberg were somehow related to Merri and the effect she had on men's driving.

'Now, tell me, why are you looking all grumpy and sorry for yourself?'

Ellie cracked open the second bottle of water and took a long swallow. How did she explain Jack to Merri?

The best way was just to blurt it all out. 'I nearly slept with Jack.'

'Good for you!' Merri gaped at her. 'Wait...did you say *nearly*? What is wrong with you, woman?'

There was no judgement in Merri's voice, and Ellie knew that her 'almost sleeping with Jack' story wouldn't even create a blip on her shock radar. Merri was pretty much unshockable.

Unlike her, Merri was a thoroughly modern woman. Not a drip.

'Do you want to talk about it?' Merri asked.

Ellie shook her head. 'Yes. No. Maybe. Still processing. Very confused.'

'So it wasn't just sex, then?'

'We didn't get that far. I said that I wasn't ready and he backed off.'

'Nicely?'

'What do you mean?'

'Was he nice about it? No tantrums, accusations, saying you led him on?'

Ellie shook her head. 'Of course not. He just passed me my dressing gown and said goodnight.'

'Huh. I *really* have to start dating nicer guys,' Merri stated thoughtfully. 'So why couldn't you go through with it?'

Ellie looked out to sea and wondered if she could escape this conversation. As if sensing her thoughts, Merri hooked her arm in hers and kept her in place.

'It was fine—great. I was totally in the moment and then—' Ellie snapped her fingers '—like that, my brain started providing a running commentary.'

'Oh, I hate it when it does that,' Merri agreed. 'I remember being so caught up in the intensity of being with this one guy, and then he took off his shirt and he had a pelt of chest hair. And back hair. It was like he was wearing a coat...*ugh*. My brain started making jokes at his expense. Does Jack have back hair?'

'Uh...no.'

'Did he make animal sounds?'

'No.'

'Talk dirty?'

'No.'

'Have a really small—?'

'Merri!' Ellie interjected, cutting her off. 'He's fine—gorgeous, in fact! He didn't do anything wrong!'

'Then what was the problem?' Merri asked, puzzled. 'He's

gorgeous, nice, and you were into him.' She looked Ellie in her eyes and twisted her lips. 'Ah, *dammit*, Ellie!'

'What?' Ellie demanded.

'When you told me that Jack was staying with you we talked about you getting emotionally entangled with him.' Merri shook her head in despair. 'And you have, haven't you?'

'I'm not entangled with him. Or at the very least I'm trying not to get emotionally attached to him. When we were getting it on I had this thought that he could become a big thing if I let him.'

'And how is that *not* getting emotionally involved with him?' Merri demanded.

'The key phrase is *if I let him*,' Ellie protested.

Merri was silent for a while, and her voice was full of hope when she spoke again. 'Are you not just getting lust and feelings mixed up? Sometimes sex is just sex and it doesn't always have to be more.'

'I know that…and I tried to think that. Unfortunately I can't just think of him as a random slab of meat.'

'Try harder.' Merri sighed forlornly. 'Have I taught you nothing?' She narrowed her eyes in thought. 'Maybe you need to practise the concept of casual sex a bit more? I have a friend who is always up to…helping the cause.'

Ellie hiccupped a laugh at Merri's outrageous suggestion. 'Thanks, but no. Really.'

They both heard Merri's name being called, and across the street Mama Thandi stood with Molly in her arms, her face wet with tears. 'I'm coming!' Merri called back as she stood up.

She bent and kissed Ellie goodbye and a nearby jogger nearly ran straight into a lightpole.

Merri was right. She had to wrap her head around the concept of casual sex. And if—big if!—Jack came back, then she'd have to decide whether she could separate sex and emotion, because becoming emotionally attached to Jack would be a disaster of mega proportions.

They were fire and water, heaven and hell, victory and defeat. Maybe there *was* something fast and hot between them sexually, but fast and hot weren't enough to sustain a relationship. Relationships needed time and input, and at the very least for the participants within said relationship to be on the same continent for more than a nano-second.

Like Mitchell, Jack was the ultimate free spirit: an adventurer of heart and soul who needed his freedom as he needed air to breathe.

Apart from the fact that she didn't want to—was too damn scared to—become emotionally involved with a man who was just like her father, Ellie knew that she wasn't exciting enough, long term, for someone as charismatic as Jack. Darryl had put her childhood fears and suspicions into words five minutes before he'd left her life for good.

'You need to face facts, Ellie. You're not enough—not sexy enough, smart enough, interesting enough—for a man to make sacrifices for. Nobody will give up their freedom and time for monogamy with you. Nobody interesting, at least.'

It was something she'd suspected all her life, and having someone—him—verbalise it had actually been a relief. Even if it had hurt like hell.

Ellie watched the afternoon crowds walk down the promenade, smiling at the earnest joggers, the chattering groups of women walking off their extra pounds. Kids on bicycles weaved through the crowds and skateboarders followed in their wake. It was a typical scene for a hot day in the summer.

Ellie saw a taxi pull up across the road just down the street from the bakery before she half turned to look at the sea. A number of cargo ships hovered on the horizon and a sailboat zipped by closer to shore. Reaching for her bottle of water, she looked back at the bakery and saw a man climb out of the

taxi, his hand briefly touching his side. His broad shoulders
and long legs reminded her of Jack...but this man had short
hair, wore smart chinos, a long-sleeved white shirt with the
cuffs rolled back and dark, sleek sunglasses. Then the sun
picked up the reddish glints in his hair...

Jack?

Ellie yelped and dropped her water bottle as he paid the
driver and pulled that familiar black rucksack from the boot
of the taxi.

Jack... Jack was back.

Oh, good God... Jack. Was. Back.

As if he sensed her eyes on him Jack straightened and
looked across the road. Ellie folded her arms and bit her lip.
There was no way that she was going to run across the road
like a demented schoolgirl and hurl herself into his arms...as
much as she wanted to.

Ellie gnawed on her bottom lip as he lifted his rucksack
with one hand, dropped it over his shoulder and slowly walked
across the road. When he reached her he dropped the rucksack at her feet and sent her a small grin.

'Hi, El.'

Ellie's stomach plummeted and twisted as her name rolled
off his tongue. She tucked her hands into the back pockets of
her jeans and rocked on her heels.

'You're back. And you cut your hair...' Ellie stuttered and
her heart copied her voice.

The corner of Jack's mouth lifted as he brushed his hand
over his short back and sides. 'Seems like it.'

'I thought you would've headed home...' Ellie said, wishing she could hug him and also that she could finish a sentence. What *was* it about this man who had her words freezing
on her tongue?

His eyes didn't leave hers. 'I have a flat in London but it
certainly isn't home.' His mouth lifted in that teasing way that

she'd missed so much. 'Besides, I paid you for three weeks' board and lodging and I'd like to get my money's worth.'

Ellie grinned. 'That sounds fair.' She could smell him from where she stood: sandalwood and citrus, clean soap and sexy male. Ellie breathed him in and again wished she were in his arms.

She looked up into his face and sighed at the stress in his eyes, the deeper brackets around his mouth. 'Rough trip?'

He shrugged. 'I've had worse.' He took her hand and raised her knuckles to place a gentle kiss on them. 'I'm sorry I didn't call…I wasn't sure what to say.'

Ellie's eyes narrowed as she remembered that she was supposed to be cross with him. 'I have to say that when it's required you can vacate a house at speed.'

Jack pushed his hair off his forehead. 'Yeah, sorry. I'm not used to explaining my actions… I've been on my own for too long and I'm not good at stopping to play nice.'

Ellie pulled her hand out of his and tapped her finger against her chin. 'How's my dad?'

'He's fine.' Jack went on to explain what he'd done in Kenya, the outcome of the contact he'd made with his numerous sources. His words were brief and succinct but Ellie could hear the tension in his voice, saw pain flicker in and out of his eyes and wondered what he wasn't telling her.

'Something else happened. Something that rocked you.'

Shock rippled across Jack's face. Then those shutters fell over his eyes and he dropped his gaze from hers, looking down at the pavement. When he lifted his head again his expression was rueful. 'The sun is shining; it's a stunning afternoon. I want to go home, climb into my board shorts and hit the surf. I just want to forget about work for a while.'

Ellie wished she could join him but gestured to the bakery. 'I still have a couple of hours' work to do.'

'Of course you do. I'll meet you back here at closing time.'

Jack picked up his rucksack and slung it over one shoulder. 'It's good to be back, El.'

Ellie watched him cross the street and turn the corner for home. Jack was back and the world suddenly seemed brighter and lighter and shinier.

That couldn't, in *any* galaxy, be good.

'So, he hasn't made a move on you again?'

'No, not even close. Then again, he's barely spoken to me,' Ellie answered Merri, who was in for the afternoon, helping her make Sacher Torte for an order to be picked up that evening.

Princess Molly Blue, as beautiful as her mother, was fast asleep on Mama Thandi's back, held in place by a light cotton shawl wrapped around her back and Mama's chest. Ellie looked at Mama, who was quickly plaiting strips of dough for braided bread; it really was a very efficient way to carry on working and let your baby be close to you. Ellie hoped Merri was taking notes.

'What do you mean?'

'He's been back for two days and I've barely seen him.' Ellie shrugged. 'We eat supper together and then he disappears to his room to work.' She tightened the ties of her apron and frowned. 'There are friends, lovers and acquaintances. Jack left as a friend, was briefly—sort of—a lover, and he's come back as the last.'

Merri split a vanilla pod and scraped out its insides with a knife. 'What changed? Do you think it was because you said no?'

Ellie separated the whites and yolks of eggs as she considered the question. 'I don't know. Maybe.'

'If that's the reason then he's a jerk of magnificent proportions,' Merri stated, adding the vanilla to butter and sugar and switching on the beater.

'He might as well be a guest in my B&B, except that he packs the dishwasher, makes dinner if I'm working late and even, very kindly, did a load of my laundry with his own. I just want my friend back,' Ellie added.

'No, you don't. You want to sleep with him,' Merri said in a cheerful voice.

'No! Well, yes. But I can't. Won't.'

'Uh…why?'

'Because, as you said, I can't seem to separate the emotion and the deed,' Ellie admitted reluctantly. 'If I sleep with him I risk—'

'Caring for him, falling in love with him. Why would that be the worst thing that could happen to you?'

Ellie viciously tipped the egg whites into another mixing bowl and reached for a hand-beater. 'I don't want to talk about this any more.'

'Tough.'

Ellie shut off the hand-beater and checked on the chocolate that was melting in a *bain-marie*. 'We don't have enough time for me to list the reasons…'

'Yes, we do. Spill.'

'He has a job I hate. He's never around. I don't have time for a relationship—'

Merri pointed a wooden spoon at her. 'Quit lying to yourself, El. The biggest reason you are so scared is because he doesn't need you, and we all know that you live to be needed.'

Ellie looked at her, shocked. 'That's so unfair.'

'Ellie, you take pride in being indispensable. You *need* people to need you. You need to love more than you need love, and you recognise that Jack doesn't need your love to survive, to function. You're terrified of being rejected…'

'Aren't we all?' Ellie demanded.

'No. Some of us realise that you can't force someone to love you just because you want him to.'

'Bully for you,' Ellie muttered mutinously.

Merri stared at her, her eyes uncharacteristically sombre. 'I don't think I ever realised until this moment how much your father's lack of attention and Darryl's scumbag antics scarred you.'

Ellie wanted to protest that she wasn't scarred, that she was just being careful, but she knew it wasn't true. She'd suspected for a long time that she was emotionally damaged, and Merri's words just confirmed what she'd always thought.

So maybe it was better that she and Jack kept their distance, kept the status quo.

'Can we talk about something else? Molly Blue? Is she teething yet?'

Merri grinned at her. 'No, I don't want to talk about my baby.'

She'd been talking about Molly for six months straight and she didn't want to talk about her now? How unfair, Ellie thought.

'I still want to talk about you. Let's talk about your inability to say no...'

Ellie, past the point of patience, threw an egg at her.

Ellie rolled over and looked, wide-eyed, at the luminous hands of her bedside clock. It was twelve-seventeen and she wasn't even close to sleep. Throwing off her sheet, she cocked her head as she heard footsteps going down the stairs.

It seemed she wasn't the only person who was awake.

Ellie pulled a thigh-length T-shirt over her skimpy tank. It skimmed the hem of her sleeping shorts. Deciding against shoes, she flipped her thick plait over her shoulder, left the room and walked down the darkened stairs. She knew where he'd be: standing on the front veranda, looking out to the moonlit sea.

He wasn't. He was sitting on one of the chairs, dressed in

running shorts and pulling on his trainers. Ellie hesitated at the front door and took a moment to watch him, looking hard and tough, as he quickly tied the laces in his shoes. It was after midnight—why was he going for a run? It made no sense…

'What are you doing?' she asked, stepping through the open door.

Jack snapped his head up to look at her and she caught the tension in his eyes. 'Can't sleep.'

'So you're going for a run?'

Jack shrugged. 'It's better than lying awake looking at the ceiling.'

Ellie folded her arms and looked at the top of his head. For the past four days he'd been quiet, and tonight at dinner he'd said little, after which he'd excused himself as usual to do some work. Despite hoping that he'd come back downstairs, she hadn't seen him since he'd left the table.

Jack stood up and started to stretch, and Ellie wondered if this was Jack's way of expelling stress and tension. She might indulge in a good crying jag but he went running. Maybe, just maybe, she could get him to try talking for a change.

She crossed her arms as she stepped outside, then walked up to him and nudged him with her shoulder.

'Why don't you talk to me instead of hitting the streets?'

'Uh—'

'C'mon.' Ellie boosted herself up on the stone wall so that she faced Jack, her back to the sea. 'What's going on, Jack? Has something happened?'

Jack placed his arm behind his head to stretch out his arms and Ellie noticed his chest muscles rippling, his six-pack contracting, that nasty scar lifting. She forced herself to take her mind off his body and concentrate on his words.

'Nothing's happened…'

Dammit, he simply wasn't going to open up. Ellie felt a spurt of hurt and disappointment and hopped off the wall.

'Okay, Jack, don't talk to me. But don't treat me like an idiot by telling me that nothing happened!'

Ellie headed for the front door and was stopped by Jack's strong arm around her stomach.

'Geez, Ellie. Cool your jets, would you?'

Ellie whirled around, put her hands on his chest and shoved. Her efforts had no impact on him at all. 'Dammit, I just want you to talk to me!'

'If you gave me two seconds to finish my sentence then you'd realise that I am trying to talk to you!' Jack dropped his arms and pointed to the Morris chair. 'Sit.'

Ellie sat and pulled her feet up to tuck them under her, her expression mutinous. She'd give him one more chance, but if he tried to fob her off with 'nothing happened' again she'd shove him off the wall.

Jack sat on the edge of the wall. 'Kenya was a fairly routine trip in that nothing *unusual* happened. I hit the streets, found my contacts, got some intel, reported. I worked, hung out with the rest of the press corps.'

Ellie pulled a face. 'Sorry.'

Jack placed his hand behind his ear. 'What was that?'

Ellie glared at him. 'You heard me. So if the trip was fairly routine, then what's bugging you?'

'Exactly that…the fact that the trip felt so routine. Unexciting, flat.'

Ellie scratched her forehead. 'I'm sorry, I don't understand.'

'I'm not sure if I understand either. There are certain reasons I do what I do. Why I do it. I need the adrenalin. I need to feel like I'm living life at full throttle.' Jack must have seen the question on her face because he shook his head. 'Maybe some day I'll tell you why but not now. Not tonight.'

Not ready yet. She could respect that. 'Okay, so you need the thrill, the buzz of danger…'

'Not necessarily danger—okay, I like the danger factor

too—but in places or situations like that there's always a buzz, an energy that is so tangible you can almost reach out and taste it. I feed on that energy.'

'And there wasn't any this time?'

Jack closed his eyes. 'Oh, there was—apparently. Everyone I spoke to said that there was something in the air, a sense that the place was on a knife edge, that violence was a hair's breadth away. The journalists were buzzing on the atmosphere and I didn't pick up a damn thing. I couldn't feel it. I felt like I was just going through the motions.'

'Oh.'

'There are different types of war correspondent. There are the idealists—the ones who want to make a difference. There are the ones who, sadly, feed off the violence, the brutality. There are others who use it to hide from life.' Jack scrubbed his hands over his face. 'I report. Full-stop. Right from the beginning I knew that it wasn't my job to save the world. That my job was to relay the facts, not to get involved with the emotion. I have always been super-objective. I don't particularly like making judgement calls, mostly because I can always see both sides of the story. Nobody is ever one hundred per cent right. But I always—*always!*—have been the first to pick up the mood on the street, the energy in the air.'

'Do you ever take a stand? Get off the fence?' Ellie asked him after a short silence. 'Make a judgement call?'

Jack thought about her question for a moment. 'Personally or professionally?'

'Either. Both.'

'When it comes to political ideologies I am for neutrality. Personally, I've experienced some stuff…gone through a lot… so when bad things happen I measure it up against what I went through and frequently realise that it's not worth getting upset about. So I don't get worked up easily, and because of that I probably don't get involved on either side of anything either.'

Whoa! Super-complicated man. 'Okay, so getting back to Kenya…'

'I made an offhand comment to Mitch about feeling like this and that led to a discussion about me. He said that I've become too distant, too unemotional, too hard. He used the word "robotic". *Am* I robotic, El?'

Ellie stood up, sat on the wall next to him and dropped her head onto his shoulder. 'I don't think you are, but to be fair I haven't seen you in that situation or seen you report for a long time—six months at least.'

'He also said that I'm desensitised to violence, that I don't see other people's pain. That I'm becoming heartless.'

That was rich, coming from her father, Ellie thought, the King of Self-Involvement. Except her father was very good at what he did, so he might have a point. But Ellie didn't believe that Jack was as callous as he or her father made him out to be. It was more likely that he used his emotional distance as a shield.

'Is not caring just a way to protect yourself from everything bad you've seen?'

Jack shrugged. 'I have no idea. Mitch said that I'm burnt out, that it's affecting my reporting, that I'm coming across as hard. He said that I need to get my head in the game, take some time off to fill the well. We had a rip roaring argument…'

'He sent you home?'

Jack looked rebellious. 'As much as he likes to think he does, Mitchell doesn't *send* me anywhere. I left because there wasn't much more to report on except for rehashing the same story.' Jack stared at his feet.

'Is he right? *Are* you burnt out?' Ellie asked quietly, keeping her temple on his shoulder.

'I don't know.'

'I think you need to give yourself a break. You were beaten up in Somalia, stabbed, kicked out of the country. You've just come back from a less than cheerful city. When did you last take a proper holiday, relax…counter all the gruesome stuff you've witnessed with happy stuff?'

'Happy stuff?'

'Lying on a beach, surfing, drinking wine in the afternoon sun. Napping. Reading a book for pleasure and not for research. Um…sleeping late. In other words, a holiday?'

'Not for a while. Not for a very long time,' Jack admitted, placing his broad hand on her knee.

'Thought so. Maybe you should actually do that?'

'I don't know how to relax, to take it easy. It's not in my nature. I like moving, working, exploring. I need to keep moving to feel alive.'

'Maybe that's what you've conditioned yourself to feel… but it's not healthy.' Ellie yawned and reluctantly lifted her head off his arm.

Jack stood up and ran a gentle hand over her hair. 'Get some sleep, El. There's no point in us both being exhausted.'

Ellie didn't think about it. She just stood up, wrapped her arms around his waist and laid her cheek on his bare chest. 'Don't beat yourself up, Jack. Mitchell might think he's always right, but he's not.'

'I kind of think he might be this time.'

'Well, I hope you didn't tell him that. You'll never hear the end of it.' Ellie placed her forehead on his chest and kept one hand on his waist.

Jack stood ramrod-straight and for the longest minute Ellie held her breath, certain that he would push her away. Eventually his arms locked around her back and he buried his face in her hair. Ellie rubbed her hands over his back, met his miserable eyes and ran her hand across his forehead, down his cheek to his chest. Her hands dropped, brushed the waistband of his shorts, and she felt tension—suddenly sexual—skitter through his body. She moved her hands to put them on his hips and felt his swift intake of air.

'I missed you,' he said, his voice gruff.

'I missed you too.'

Jack closed his eyes and his arms tightened and his lower body jumped in reaction to her words. She could feel his heat and response through her light cotton shirt and sleeping shorts and she wanted him...

She didn't want to want him. She couldn't afford to want him.

She forced herself to say the words. 'I need to go to bed, Jack.'

Jack immediately released her and she suddenly felt colder without his heat.

'Go on up. I'm going for a run.'

Ellie nodded. 'Thanks, by the way.'

One eyebrow rose. 'For...?'

'Talking to me. I thought you were mad at me, so it was a bit of a relief. Sorry I jumped to the wrong conclusion in the beginning.'

Jack sent her a small grin. 'Next time you jump to conclusions I won't give you a second chance.'

Ellie patted his chest. 'Yes, you will.'

'I'm afraid you're probably right,' Jack said softly, and jogged down the stairs.

The night was warm and the streets were deserted, and the sea was his only companion as he ran along the promenade, his feet slapping against the pavement. Sweat ran down his temples and down his spine into the waistband of his shorts. His body felt fluid but his mind was a mess.

God, it felt good to run. Apart from the fact that it kept his heart working properly, it was easier to think when he was running.

He hadn't lied to Ellie—he *hadn't* connected with the story or the atmosphere in Kenya and that worried him—but he certainly hadn't told her the whole truth. How could he? How could he explain to her that he'd spent his days in Kenya missing her, thinking about her? He'd never allowed anyone to distract him from the job at hand, yet she had. He'd be walking the streets, seeing an old man whittling away at a piece of wood, and he'd think Ellie would crouch down next to him and demand to know what he was creating. He'd drink his morning coffee at the hotel and wish he was standing on her veranda, watching the endless blues and greens of the sea.

His nights were a combination of fantasy and frustration, thinking about what he wanted to do to and with her amazing body.

When he'd seen her on the wall that afternoon he'd come back his thumping heart had settled, sighed. And he'd known he had the potential to fall deeper and deeper in trouble. Emotional trouble.

He'd known her for only days and she'd stirred up all these weird feelings inside him. Why? What was it about her that made him feel as if he'd stepped outside of himself? He could talk to her. He wanted to talk to her. Take this evening, for example. He would never have spoken to any of his previous girlfriends like that…hell, he'd barely *spoken* to them. He'd just flown in from wherever, climbed into bed, kept said girlfriend in bed until he needed to leave and then left. He didn't know how to act as part of a couple on an on-going basis, and before he'd landed in Cape Town he'd never come close to being tied down by anyone or anything. He excelled in saying goodbye and never looking back. He'd had a second chance at life and he'd made a promise to live it hard, because he'd always believed it would be an injustice to live a small life… to confine himself to a humdrum job…to be shackled by a house or a lover.

His beliefs, so firmly held for so long, were starting to waver.

And that was why he'd scuttled out of Ellie's house last week. He hadn't needed to go to Kenya but it had been a damn good excuse to put some distance between them.

Jack stopped and, breathing heavily, placed his hands on his hips. In the low light of the sodium streetlights he stared out to the breaking waves as clouds scuttled across the moon. Little in life made sense any more… He could easily have gone back to London after Kenya but he'd headed south instead. What was happening to him?

He'd been shot, beaten up and stabbed. He'd sneaked behind enemy lines, walked into the compounds of drug cartels, through whorehouses filled with the dregs of humanity who'd slit his throat just for the fun of it—just to get a story. He'd seen the worst of what people could do to each other and yet he'd never felt fear like this before…

He was terrified he was becoming emotionally involved with her—would do practically anything to stop that happening. Ellie had hit the nail squarely in one of their many conversations; he was an observer, not a participator. Involvement with her would require a decision, taking a stand for her, sticking around, partaking in a life together.

He didn't want to do that—wasn't ready to do that. Wouldn't do that. He needed to find some perspective, reconnect with his beliefs, reaffirm his values. Jack nodded at the sea. He had to make sure that he kept some emotional distance, guarded against any deepening of their relationship. It was the sensible decision—hell, it was the only decision.

And while he was making major decisions he really needed to decide what he was going to do about Brent's memorial service. Go or not? He was starting to feel that he needed to, that he needed to honour Brent, to say thank you for the gift of his life. But would seeing him make the Sandersons' day worse? Would being there deepen the guilt he felt?

Maybe he shouldn't go.

Jack swore as he resumed running. This was why it was better not to examine his thoughts and emotions too closely. It just confused him. And, talking about being confused, what had Ellie meant when she'd said she had thought that he was angry with her? Why would she think that?

Jack intended to find out.

CHAPTER EIGHT

JACK POUNDED UP the steps and flung open her bedroom door. He knew she wouldn't be asleep and she wasn't. She was sitting up in bed, working on her computer. Didn't she ever give work a rest?

'Why are you working?' he demanded crossly.

'I'm not. I'm catching up with friends.'

'At one in the morning?'

'Excuse me, at least *I'm* not the one running after midnight!' Ellie closed the lid of her computer and tapped her finger against it. 'Did you just burst in here to give me a hard time generally or was there a specific reason?'

Jack walked into the room and stood at the end of her bed. 'You said that you thought I was mad at you. Why, Ellie?'

Ellie plucked the sheet with her fingers and felt her face flaming in the dim light of her lamp. 'It's not important.'

Jack sat on the edge of the bed and placed his hand on her knee. 'I think it might be. Talk to me, El.'

Ellie shook her head and placed her computer on her bedside table. 'Jack, it really doesn't matter since you haven't made any…since we're not…'

'Sleeping together?' Jack sounded puzzled. 'Are you upset that I'm *not* sleeping with you?'

'Yes…no. I don't know. I thought you'd changed your mind about…me.'

Jack's expression was pure confusion. 'Let me try and decode that from girl-speak. Firstly, I couldn't run out of your house, not call you, then come back and expect to jump into bed with you. I thought we needed some time, and I've been dealing with all this other crap, so…' Jack rubbed the back of his neck. 'I changed my mind…? Hold on a sec—did you think that I didn't want to sleep with you? Why on earth wouldn't I want to sleep with you?'

'Good grief, Jack, you can't expect me to verbalise it!' Ellie cried.

'Well, if you want me to understand what's going on in that crazy head of yours, *yes*! Because I am lost!'

'I wasn't any good and it couldn't have been much fun for you,' Ellie mumbled. 'And I backed off midway.'

There was a long silence and Ellie felt Jack staring at her head. When he eventually spoke Ellie could hear the regret in his voice.

'Have you been worried about that since I left?'

'Mmm.'

Jack swore. 'And I left here with a rocket on my tail, not even thinking… Dammit!'

Ellie looked up at him. 'So you weren't mad that I said no?'

'Disappointed? Yes. Cross? Absolutely not.'

'Oh.'

Jack played with her fingers. 'Why *did* you stop, by the way? What happened?'

'My brain started a running commentary as soon as we got to my bedroom. I started to second-guess what we were doing—what I was doing. And whether I was getting it right.'

Jack cradled her cheek with his hand. 'Making love is not a test to be graded, sweetheart. Come on—cough it up. What else were you worrying about?'

'Whether I was enough for you. Whether I was practiced

enough. Cellulite…other crazy girl stuff.' Ellie stared at a point beyond his shoulder.

'You don't have a centimetre of cellulite, and if you do I *so* don't care. And if we're trading thoughts about that night then I should tell you that I'm sorry if I went too fast for you. I'd thought about having you so many times, in so many ways… and I guess I was nervous too.'

'Why were you nervous? You've had lots of sex before.'

'Yes, but I've never had sex with *you*!' Jack exclaimed. 'What? I'm not allowed to be nervous? I finally get the girl I've been fantasising about in bed and suddenly I'm a stud? It doesn't work like that, Ellie. The first time you make love to someone it's *always* the first time. I'm also worried about pleasing you. It never works out perfectly. We don't know each other's bodies, what the other person likes and/or doesn't like. It falls into place with time.'

Ellie continued to stare at her bedclothes.

'Sweetheart, I really need you to talk to me, to tell me what you're thinking,' Jack said quietly, his voice persuasive.

Ellie lifted her head and looked at him with sad eyes. 'Thank you for that—for saying all of that. And you're probably right. We just need time.'

'Exactly.'

Ellie held his gaze. 'But we have a problem. By my calculations, and from everything you've told me, you're staying another week at the most. Then you'll leave…probably around about the time we can start making mountains move. So my two questions are: how fair would that be to either of us? And, really, what would be the point?'

'It doesn't have to be love, Ellie. It doesn't have to be for ever. It can just be two people who are attracted to each other giving each other pleasure and company. The point can be…' Jack encircled her neck with his hand and smoothed his thumb over the tendons in her neck '…this.'

He touched the corner of her mouth with his.

'So sweet. Spicy.' He stroked her jaw and placed his lips on the spot between her jaw and her ear. 'Soft. The point can be that I think you have the most beautiful skin.'

Jack moved and dropped his other hand onto her bottom. In a movement that was as smooth as it was sexy, he pulled her onto his lap so that she straddled his thighs.

As sparks bolted down her inner thighs Ellie dimly remembered that she had to be pressing on his knife wound and tried to scramble off him. Jack's hand on her thighs kept her firmly in place.

'Nuh-uh—where are you going? I like you here,' he said.

'Your cut,' Ellie protested, her head dropping so that their noses were practically touching.

'I'm fine and you feel great,' Jack informed her, lifting his head to nibble on her mouth. 'I love your mouth…' he murmured. 'Love your eyes…fantastic skin…'

He lifted his hands from her thighs and placed them on her chest, holding the weight of her breasts in his hands. Ellie moaned as he thumbed her nipples into gloriously sensitive peaks.

'As for these…these are simply a point of their own.'

Ellie couldn't find any words, was drenched in the wet heat of his voice. She arched her back and rolled her neck as she pushed into his hands seeking more.

'You are so beautiful…' Jack dropped his hands down to her waist.

She shook her hair out and it spilled down her chest, over her brief tank top. Jack leaned back and just looked at her, his caress as bold as his eyes.

'Take it off,' he said, his voice hoarse. 'Let me look at you.'

Somewhere in some place deep inside her Ellie knew that she should probably say no, that she should climb off his lap and be sensible, but instead she arched her back, pulled her shirt over her head and held the garment in place against her chest. She hadn't thought it was possible for Jack's eyes to darken with passion, but they did and she saw his jaw clench.

She felt feminine and powerful and wondrously, wickedly wanton.

'You're killing me here, woman,' Jack growled and he lifted his hand to yank the shirt away. His nostrils flared as he took in her creamy skin now flushed with arousal. He held her face in his hands. 'Trust me, El. I'm going to show you exactly what the point of this is...'

Ellie walked into the bedroom from the bathroom, wrapped in a towel from waist to mid-thigh and towel-drying her hair. She looked from the clock to Jack, who was lying crossways across the bed, spread out on his stomach. 'We've wasted a good portion of the morning.'

'Hush your mouth, wench. A morning in bed is never wasted,' Jack said as he stood up and stretched. He was totally self-confident about his body and he had a right to be, Ellie thought. Apart from the nasty scar on his chest, he was perfect.

'How did you get that scar?' Ellie asked.

Jack lifted his hand up to his chest and immediately turned away. 'Operation.'

Ellie rubbed the ends of her hair between the folds of the towel. 'What operation?'

Jack walked past her and swatted her backside. 'The one I had in hospital.'

He stepped into the *en-suite* bathroom and Ellie heard water hitting the shower door. Well, that had gone well. *Not.* Obviously his scar-causing operation was not up for discussion. Ellie wondered why not. It couldn't be that big a deal, surely?

Jack raised his voice. 'This is such a waste of water...you should've let me shower with you.'

Ellie smiled at herself in the dressing table mirror. 'I couldn't trust you not to have your wicked way with me again.'

She'd thought about yanking him into the shower with her but she didn't think she could stand another bout of that sweet, sweet torture. Or maybe she could—in an hour or two, when all her nerve-endings had subsided slightly.

'You like my wicked ways.' Jack's voice was chock-full of self-satisfaction.

'I do? How can you tell?'

'Well, I think your begging was a huge hint,' Jack said dryly, before she heard the shower door open and close.

Ellie pulled fresh underwear out of her dresser drawer and quickly slipped into a matching aqua-green set. White shorts and a pretty floral top were perfect for a day to be spent at home…she had to stock up on cleaning products and dog food, spend some time on the internet paying personal bills, and she needed to finalise the arrangements for Jess's bachelorette party.

Maybe after that she could persuade Jack back into bed…

Jess! Jess and Luke! Oh, *man*! She'd forgotten that she was having lunch with them. She picked up her watch from the dresser and cursed again. She had barely ten minutes before they were due to pick her up. This was Jack's fault and his ability to make her forget everything when his clever hands were anywhere near her body.

Ellie stomped over to the bathroom and looked into the steam to the stunning body beyond. Tight buns, broad chest, a nice package…. A very nice package that knew exactly what it was doing…. *Concentrate, Ellie!*

'Jack?'

Jack, his head full of shampoo, turned around and lifted one eyebrow. 'Changed your mind? C'mon in. I'll wash your back.'

Ellie gestured to her clothes and tipped her head. 'No—no time. Listen, I just suddenly remembered that I made plans for today.'

She saw the disappointment on Jack's face before he rearranged his features into a blank mask. 'Okay. Have fun.'

Ellie tried not to roll her eyes and failed. 'I'm having lunch with Luke and Jess—I forgot. Want to join us?'

Pleasure, hot and quick, flashed in his eyes. 'Sure.'

Ellie thought she'd push her luck and try to satisfy her curiosity. 'So why won't you tell me about your scar?'

Jack tipped his head back under the stream of water. 'Because it's not important.'

'If it wasn't important then you'd talk about it,' Ellie told him, and sighed when she saw the shutters come down in his eyes. She was beginning to recognise that look. It meant that the subject was no longer up for discussion. Ellie blew out her breath. She'd made sweet love to him all night but that didn't mean she could go crawling around in his head. 'Okay, then, be all mysterious. But hurry up, because they'll be here any moment.'

Jack rinsed out the last of the shampoo, switched off the water and grabbed a towel that hung on the railing. He wrapped the towel around his waist and shoved his hair back from his face. Catching Ellie watching him, he placed his hand on her shoulder and leaned forward to drop a kiss on the corner of her mouth.

'You okay?'

'Fine.'

'Not too sore?' Jack placed his forehead against hers and his hands on her waist.

She was a little *burny* in places that shouldn't burn. 'A little.'

'Sorry.' Jack kissed her forehead and stepped back. 'I'm going to find something to wear. Jeans and open-collar shirt?'

'No, shorts and a T-shirt,' Ellie said, following him out of the bathroom. 'We'll probably end up on the rickety deck of some about-to-fall-down shack...'

Jack pulled a face. 'And that's where we'll eat?' he said, doubt lacing his voice.

'That's where you'll eat the most amazing seafood in the world. Luke knows all the best places to eat up and down the coast,' Ellie replied, and sighed when she heard the insistent pealing of her gate bell. 'That's them—early as usual. I'll see you downstairs.'

'Ellie?'

Ellie turned at Jack's serious voice. Oh, God, what was he going to say?

Jack's smile was slow and powerful. 'Thank you for an amazing night.'

Ellie floated down the steps. Ellie Evans, she mused, sex goddess. Yeah, she could get behind that title.

In the late afternoon Jess and Luke, seeing the old lighthouse a kilometre down the beach, decided that they should take a closer look at the old iron structure. Ellie and Jack, who were operating on a lot less sleep, shook their heads at their departing backs, took a bottle of wine and glasses to the beach, found an old log for a backrest and sat in the sand.

'How are you doing?' Jack asked, pouring wine into a glass and then handing it to her.

Ellie squinted at him. 'I'm utterly exhausted. I think we got about two hours' sleep.'

Jack covered his mouth as he yawned. 'I'm tired too. So, did you have fun?'

Ellie blushed. 'Yes, thanks. You?'

Jack laughed. 'I think the fact that I couldn't get enough of you answers that question better than I could with words.' He watched her face flush again and internally shook his head. Her confidence had really taken a battering at some point and never quite recovered.

'Tell me about your ex.'

Ellie looked as if he'd asked her to swallow a spider. 'Good grief—why?'

'Because I think that he messed up your head—badly. Dented your confidence.' Jack dug his toes into the sand as he looked at her. 'Did he?'

Ellie picked up a handful of sand and let it drift through her fingers. 'S'pose so. Not that I had much to start with.'

'And why would that be?'

Ellie tipped her head at him. 'Jack, you saw me. I was plump and very shy, and standing firmly in the shadow of my famous father—who was everything I wasn't. Good-looking, charming, erudite, confident. Then I went to art school.'

He loved that secret smile—the one that lit her up from the inside out. 'And…?'

'And I flourished. I found something I loved and excelled in. I was happy and the weight fell off me. Boys were asking me out on dates, and although I never went I *was* being asked.'

'Why didn't you go?'

'As I said, I was shy. They asked and I said no and I got the reputation of being hard to get. And, boys being boys, they thought that was cool, so I became more popular, which made me more confident and I finally started dating.'

'Where does the grim gallery owner fit in?' Jack asked, draping a possessive leg over hers.

'He was a friend of one of our final-year lecturers and he came to give a talk to the graduating class. On a whim he said that he'd look at our work in progress. He asked to see my portfolio, said that I had talent and told me look him up if I ever got to London, saying that he might offer me an exhibition.' Ellie watched a crab crawl out of a hole and scuttle towards the waves. 'A couple of months later I did meet up with him in London. We started a relationship and he slowly eroded every bit of confidence I'd worked so hard to acquire.'

'How?'

'My art wasn't up to standard.' Ellie shrugged as thunderclouds built in her eyes.

'Why did you stay with him?'

Ellie bit her bottom lip. 'Because he told me he loved me and said that he'd never leave. The two sentences I'd waited to hear all my life.'

Jack rubbed his eyes. 'Oh, sweetheart.'

'Then, during the little time he spent with me, he started on everything else. Clothes and hair. Weight. My cooking, my friends, my skill in the bedroom.'

Jack felt his mouth drop open with surprise, which was closely followed by the burn of fury. 'He said you were a bad lover?'

'No, he said that I was a damned awful lover and a blow-up doll would be more fun.'

If that...Jack swallowed the names he wanted to call Ellie's waste-of-skin ex. No wonder she'd frozen the other night. No wonder she seemed constantly to second-guess herself.

Ellie dug her bare feet into the sand. 'Merri thinks that he and my father scarred me emotionally.'

Well, yeah. 'What do you think?'

Ellie sipped her wine and dropped back so that her elbows were in the sand. 'Of course they did. I'm scared to get close to people because I don't want to run the risk of getting hurt and I know that they'll leave me. I tend to keep myself emotionally isolated. It's safer that way.'

'Safer isn't necessarily better,' Jack pointed out.

Ellie slanted him a look. 'You do the same thing, Jack Chapman, and don't think you don't.'

'What do you mean?' Jack asked, bewildered by her suddenly turning the tables on him.

'You observe, watch, report and walk away. You don't get involved, so you're as much as an emotional coward as me.'

Jack sighed as her well-made point hit him dead centre. He took a minute to allow his surprise to settle before placing his hand on her knee. 'Maybe I am, El.'

Jeez, he wished he could get the words out. It was a perfect time to tell her that they had no future, that she shouldn't expect anything from him, that he couldn't consider settling down with her—with anyone. That he couldn't afford to take this any deeper, to allow her to creep behind the doors and walls of his self-sufficiency.

Ellie's teasing voice snapped him out of his reverie. 'You awake behind those shades, Chapman?'

'Yep.' Jack hooked his arm around her neck, pulled her to him and dropped a hard kiss on her mouth. 'Just thinking.'

'Careful, you might hurt yourself,' Ellie teased, and yelped when his fingers connected with her ribcage. Her wine glass wobbled in her hand and she dropped it when his other hand tickled her under her arms.

'Jack! You wretch! Stop…please, Jack!' Ellie whimpered, and then her breath hitched.

He realised he was lying on her, her mouth just below his. Tickling turned to passion and laughter turned to need as he plundered her mouth.

Jack felt his heart sink into his stomach as he placed his head in the crook of her neck.

Dammit, Ellie, how am I ever going to find the strength to walk away from you?

'I hate hangovers,' Jack thought he heard Ellie mutter.

She was showered, teeth brushed and dressed, but she still looked headachey and miserable, huddled into the corner of the couch, tousle-haired and exceptionally grumpy. But, amazingly, still so sexy.

'Why did I drink so much last night?' she wailed.

Jack crouched down in front of her and smiled as he handed her a couple of aspirin and some water. 'Hey, in reply to every drunken text you sent at various times throughout the evening I suggested that you stop. You told me that you could handle it.'

'Well, I can't,' Ellie sulked.

'Tough it out, sunshine.'

It had been Jess's hen's party last night and Ellie had hosted the pre-clubbing ritual of cupcakes and champagne. When he'd run down the stairs at eight Ellie had been sitting on the edge of the couch and his eyes had rolled back in his head when he'd seen what she was—almost—wearing: a piece of sparkly scrap material covering her breasts, held in place by strings criss-crossing her back, tight jeans and screw-me heels. She'd pulled back her hair into a severe tail, and with dramatic make-up she'd looked dangerous and sexy.

She'd had 'trouble' written all over her face. He'd decided to leave the house before he carried her upstairs, made her change and lectured her on exactly what the men in the club would think, seeing her in that outfit.

When he'd heard her stumble in—with Jess, Clem Copeland and Maddie—it had been after two. The dogs had wandered upstairs at three, and at three-thirty he'd heard the shouted suggestion of skinny-dipping in the pool. He really deserved credit for not looking.

He'd known he must be getting old when he'd chosen to roll over and go back to sleep rather than spy on hot naked women cavorting in the moonlight.

He grinned as he placed his cup on the coffee table in front of them. Oh, he was enjoying this, he thought as he took the opposite corner of the couch and settled in, his laptop between his crossed knees.

Ellie held her head. 'What's with the computer?' she demanded. 'Oooh, I think there are a hundred ADD gnomes tap-dancing in my head.'

'You and I are going to talk about Mitchell,' Jack said pleasantly.

Ellie groaned. 'No, we're not.'

'Mmm, yes, we are.' Jack looked from his screen to her. His eyes were alert with intelligence, his fingers steady

on the keyboard. He was after a story and she was part of it.
'Jack, please…'

'It's just a couple of questions about your father.'

'Questions I don't want to answer,' Ellie said stubbornly.

'Why not?'

'Because it doesn't change anything!' Ellie shouted, and
watched as her head fell off her shoulders and rolled across
the room. 'He wasn't there for me, *ever*! He was a drop-in dad,
and I loved him far more than he loved me.'

Jack shook his head. 'How old were you when your parents got divorced?'

'Fifteen,' Ellie snapped.

'And how did your mother take it?'

'How do you think? She was devastated.' Ellie leaned forward to make her point, groaned and sank back. 'Do you know
she never fell in love again after him? He was her one love.
And he brushed us both off like we were nothing…'

Ellie felt a sob rise and ruthlessly forced it down. She'd shed
enough tears over her father, her ex, men in general. Hangover or no, she wasn't going to shed any more. But she wanted
to. She wanted to tell Jack how much it hurt, how much she
wanted to be loved, cherished, protected. She didn't *need* to
be—not as she had when she was a little girl—but she still
had a faint wish to be able to step into a strong pair of arms
and rest awhile.

Like now, when her head felt separated from her body and
her stomach was staging its own hostile rebellion.

'So you ran from an emotionally and physically absent father to an emotionally and physically absent fiancé. Why?'

'That's not a question about Mitchell,' Ellie retorted.

'Why, El?'

'Because it's what I deserved! Because my love was never
enough to keep someone with me! Because I choose badly!'

Jack sighed. 'Oh, El, that is off-the-charts crap. You had

a father who was useless and you had a bad relationship. It doesn't mean that *you* are useless!'

'Feels like it,' Ellie muttered. 'And might I point out that you dig around in my head, throwing questions at me, but you won't answer any of mine?' It wasn't fair that he wanted to delve into her life and emotions and he wouldn't allow her into his.

Jack's hands stilled on the keyboard and he sent her a shuttered look. His sigh covered his obvious irritation. 'What do you want to know?'

'You *know* what,' Ellie muttered. She gestured to his chest. 'Tell me about that scar. How did you get it?'

'Heart transplant,' Jack said, his voice devoid of inflection.

'Excuse me?'

'You heard what I said.'

Ellie sat up, her headache all but forgotten under this enormous news. 'But you look fine.'

'That's because I *am* fine! I've been fine for seventeen years!'

Ooooh, touchy subject. Even more touchy than her father issues. 'Hey, I'm still processing this—just give me a second, okay? How would you like me to react?'

'Well, for starters, I'd like you to take that look of pity off your face!' Jack picked his computer up and banged it down onto the coffee table. 'That's why I don't tell people—because they instantly go all sympathetic and gooey!'

Oh, wait… His sharp, snappy voice was pulling her headache right back.

'Stop putting words into my mouth! I never said that.' Ellie pulled her legs up and rested her chin on her knees, her eyes on his suddenly miserable face. His expression practically begged her to leave the subject alone, but he'd opened the door and she was going to walk on in. 'Why did you need a heart transplant?'

'I caught viral pneumonia when I was thirteen. It damaged my heart.'

'And how old were you when you had the transplant?'

'Seventeen.'

'Geez, Jack.' Ellie wanted to crawl into his lap to comfort him, but knew that any affection right now would be misconstrued, deeply unwelcome.

'Nobody outside of my family knows,' Jack warned her. 'It's not something that I want to become public knowledge.'

'Why not?'

'Because it doesn't define me!' Jack's eyes flashed with irritation.

'If it didn't define you to a certain point then you wouldn't keep it so secret,' Ellie pointed out. 'What's the big deal? So you were sick when you were a kid, and you got a new heart—?' Ellie sat up, curiosity on her face. 'Do you know whose heart you got?'

'Yes. It was another teenager. Killed in a car crash,' Jack said curtly. He nodded to his computer and glared at Ellie. 'Can we get back to the subject on hand?'

'No.' Ellie shook her head. 'I'm still trying to wrap my head around this. So you got viral pneumonia, which damaged your heart, and you were sick for a long time. Then you got a new heart and now you're fine?'

'I take anti-rejection pills every day and make a point of keeping myself healthy. Apart from that, and the scar, I'm as normal as anyone else.'

Physically, maybe, but Ellie suspected that there was a whole bunch of psychological stuff still whirling around in his head. She needed to understand how it had moulded the man in front of her. Because she had no doubt that it had. How could it not have? It was too big, too life-changing—in every sense of the word. 'Tell me about those years between falling sick and having the operation.'

'You're not going to let this go, are you?'

Jack rested his forearms on his knees in a pose she was coming to realise was characteristic of him and linked his hands.

'I became housebound, lacking energy, lacking breath. I got sick frequently. Sport, school, partying, girls were all out of the question…it was an effort just to stay alive. At the end stages just before the op, my heart was so damaged that I could hardly walk. I…*existed*.'

She could hardly imagine it—this vibrant, energetic, amazing man, who should have been an active, lively teen, restricted by his failing heart and deteriorating health. 'Frustration' and 'resentment' were words far too weak to describe some of the emotions he must have experienced at the time.

'And that time defined the rest of your life?'

'Yes.'

'How?'

'I hate being told what I can or can't do, that I have to stay in one place, that I can't pick up and leave. I lived a life of very few choices. I vowed to never limit myself again. For the best part of my teenage life I was so…*confined* that I promised myself I would never be again. And I promised Brent—'

'Who?'

'My donor. I promised him, and myself, that I would *live* life, not exist. Not try to protect myself. That I'd do everything he never had the chance to.'

Phew. Well, she'd asked.

Jack stood up abruptly. 'I need more coffee. Do you want another cup?'

The door slammed shut. Ellie shook her head and wished she hadn't. *Ow, my head!* How was she supposed to take in and think about Jack's monumental disclosure when her head was splitting apart?

No fair.

CHAPTER NINE

JACK LEFT THE room and Ellie stared at the spot he'd vacated and forced herself to concentrate. A heart transplant? Was he being serious? Of course he was, she'd seen his scar, but... *holy mackerel.* She'd expected to hear about a big operation, but a heart transplant was a very big deal. How could it not be?

Ellie heard Jack's footsteps behind her and sent him a wary look as he sat down beside her, another cup of coffee in his hand.

'You still want to talk about it, don't you?' Jack asked, his expression stating that he'd rather have his legs waxed.

Ellie leaned back and put her feet up on the coffee table. 'It's just another part of your history—like stitches or breaking a leg…though on a much mightier scale.'

'You laughed when you heard about those incidents. I can handle humour. I can't stand pity.' Jack glared at her.

'Sorry, I'm a bit short on heart transplant jokes,' Ellie shot back. 'And stop glaring at me! I didn't torture you to tell me.'

'You'd be surprised,' Jack retorted, looking miserable. 'I look into your eyes and I want to tell you…*stuff.*'

Ellie batted her lashes and Jack laughed. Reluctantly, but he laughed. 'You appear to be sweet but you are actually a brat, do you know that?'

'Sweet? *Ugh.*' Ellie wrinkled her nose. 'What a description. I prefer "amazing sex goddess".'

Jack's laugh was a lot easier this time. 'You are that too. But you'll have to keep proving it to retain the title.'

Ellie slapped his groping hands away and captured the hand closest to hers. 'I will, but I need to say something to you first.' His expression became guarded at her serious tone, but she decided to carry on anyway. She took a deep breath and spoke. 'I'm sorry for what you lived through but, although you probably won't believe me, I don't feel pity. If anything I'm in awe of what you've achieved, how you've refused to allow your past to limit you.'

Jack shoved a hand into his hair, squirmed, but Ellie ploughed on.

'You could've chosen to protect yourself, to hide out, to nurture yourself, and everyone would've understood. But because you're you you probably said to your heart, *Right, dude, we've both got a second chance. Hang on—we're going for a ride.* Am I right?'

'Yeah…I suppose.'

'I respect the hell out of you. You're also…well…not ugly… which doesn't hurt.'

Jack's laugh whizzed over her head as he reached for her and pulled her across his lap. Ellie looked up at him and swallowed. When she teamed her respect for him with his sharp intellect, his dry sense of humour and the fact that he was a very decent guy, her heart started doing somersaults in her ribcage.

Add their physical chemistry to the mix and she had a soupy mess that could blow up in her face.

Since they'd started sleeping together she'd refused to think of him as anything other than a brief affair. Whenever she found herself thinking about him in terms of more, she reminded herself that she only had tomorrow or the next day or the next and closed the door on those fantasies. She wouldn't think of him in any other context other than that of a short-term, big-fun, no-strings affair, because it would be so easy to allow him to slip inside her heart and her head and that way madness lay. He would leave—he'd told her he would—and she would be left holding her bruised and battered heart.

Jack's thumb brushed over her lips and he just looked down at her with a soft, vulnerable expression on his face that she'd never seen before. It was encounters like this that dragged her deeper into an emotional quagmire. He was so enticing, on both an emotional and physical level, that it was difficult to not slip over the edge into deeper involvement. She was teetering on the edge. But she had to step back…because thinking of anything else was, frankly, stupid.

There were a couple of things she was sure of: she could love him, really love him, but he didn't want or need her love. And he'd never need her, love her, as she needed him to.

Life was tough enough without having to compete with his job for his attention and his time. History had taught her that she'd end up either disappointing him or being disappointed. Both sucked equally, so why risk either? No, falling all the way in love with him was *not* an option, she thought as his mouth drifted across hers.

But it might be easier said than done.

It was the start of a new week and Jack, after spending hours at his computer, chipping away at Mitch's story, felt as if he needed a break. It was the middle of the afternoon so he walked down to the bakery and ducked behind the counter. Sliding behind Samantha, he shoved a mug under the spout and shot a double espresso into a cup. Yanking a twenty out of his pocket, he dropped it in the pocket of her apron and snagged a chocolate muffin before walking through the stable door into the bakery.

As was his habit, he spent a moment admiring Ellie's legs beneath the scarlet chef's jacket before walking over to her table and pulling at the ponytail that fell out of her baseball cap.

Ellie lifted her fondant-full hands, smiled at him and eyed his muffin. 'I'm starving—can I have some?'

Jack held the muffin to her mouth and sighed when Ellie took an enormous bite. 'Piglet.'

'I didn't have lunch,' Ellie explained. 'I got involved in this cake.'

Jack ran his hand down Ellie's back and popped the rest of the muffin into his mouth.

'You have people who slap together sandwiches for your customers not twelve feet from you—order something,' Jack suggested.

'Crazy day,' Ellie told him, and resumed working on a delicate cream rosebud that looked almost real.

He peered over her shoulder at the sugar-rose-scattered wedding cake. 'That's really pretty.'

'Thanks,' Ellie responded, her brow furrowed in concentration as she resumed work rolling a tiny petal.

Jack sat on a stool next to her table and watched her work. Her laptop stood open on the table in front of her and he gestured to it with his coffee cup. 'What's with the laptop?'

Ellie spared it a brief glance. 'I've been trying to talk to my mother about the having-to-move-the-bakery situation and she promised to find a place she could Skype from. I'm waiting for her call.'

Progress of a type, Jack thought, but he doubted that Ellie would share the full responsibility of Pari's with her mother. He could see the tension in the cords of her neck, in her raised shoulders. She didn't want to burden her mum and would find any excuse not to. And if he knew her—and he thought he did—she would downplay the situation she was in.

Sometimes Jack wanted to shake her. She had about five months to purchase the property, do the renovations and move the bakery if she didn't want to lose any trade. She was wasting daylight in so many ways…trying to charm the owner of the building into selling when she should be threatening to walk away…chatting to her mum via Skype when she should have demanded that she return home weeks ago… Jack sighed. He tried to negotiate, rather than confront people, but he could kick ass when he needed to. Ellie's confrontation style was that she didn't essentially *have* one.

Although she *did* have a way of making him emotionally vomit all over his shoes, Jack thought, thinking about their discussion yesterday. He couldn't believe that he'd told her about his operation, his life before he'd started living again. He'd never told anybody—never discussed his past. God, if it wasn't for his mother nagging him about his check-ups he wouldn't discuss it at all.

That would be the perfect scenario. How he wished he could erase the scar, the memories, the feeling that someone had him by the throat every time he thought about it. Ellie didn't understand how difficult talking about it had been for him. He'd felt as if he'd been giving birth while he was sitting on that couch, forcing the words through his constricted throat. He'd been catapulted back seventeen years to a place he'd never wanted to revisit. He'd always been reticent, self-contained, and being so sick had isolated him from his peers and made him more so. He didn't allow people into his mind or his heart easily.

Yet Ellie kept creeping in. Did that mean that they'd moved from being a casual relationship to something that mattered? If so, he sure hadn't planned on that happening…how had that happened? And when?

A day ago…a week ago…the first time he saw her in the bakery?

He'd thought that he'd be able to live with Ellie, sleep with Ellie and remain unaffected…*hah!* And some said he was a smart guy! He shoved his hands into his hair and tugged. Being in Cape Town was becoming a bit too complicated. He felt far too at home here in Ellie's house, among her things. He'd never meant it to be a place where he could see himself living…

Yet a part of him could. Maybe it was Ellie…okay, most of it *was* Ellie, but it didn't help that she lived in possibly one of the most beautiful places he'd ever seen. Mountains and sea, sunny days, aqua and cobalt water, a pretty town. She had nice friends, people he could see himself spending time with, an interesting job, a relaxed, comfortable house.

It was miles—geographically and mentally—away from his soulless, stuffy flat in London, with its beige walls and furniture…although he *did* miss his kick-ass plasma TV. If he ever moved here that would be the only household appliance he'd pay to ship out here…

Jack gripped the edge of the stool. He was allowing the romance of the setting, his sexual attraction to Ellie and the prettiness of this area cloud his practicality. He was going soft—and possibly crazy.

He needed to go back to work. Needed a distraction from his increasingly sentimental and syrupy thoughts. There was nothing quite like a conflict, a war or a disaster, to slap your feet back to the ground.

Jack's reflections were interrupted by a Skype call coming in on Ellie's computer. At her request, Jack hit the 'answer' button with his non-sticky finger and Ellie's brown-eyed mother appeared on screen. They could be sisters, Jack thought. A couple less laughter lines, long hair instead of short, blue eyes, not deep brown.

'*Namaste*, angel face,' said Ashnee, blowing her a kiss before wrapping her bare arms around her knees and grinning into the camera.

Ellie leaned on her elbows and stared at the screen. 'Mum, I miss you so much. You look fabulous!'

Ashnee fluffed her short hair. 'I feel fabulous. I see that I'm in the bakery. Busy?'

'Hugely,' Ellie said. 'And that's what I need to talk to you about.'

Jack listened as Ellie explained the situation to her mum, and from beside the computer watched the emotions cross Ashnee's face. There was sadness, regret and then resignation.

'And we definitely can't afford the new rent?'

Ellie shook her head. 'Nope.'

Ashnee looked down at her hands, beautifully decorated with henna designs. 'So we have to move? To the old Hutchinson place?'

'Mmm, if only I can get Mrs H to sell.'

Ellie looked up as the stable door opened and lifted her hand to greet Merri who, as per usual, had Molly Blue on her slim hip. She indicated that she was on a call and Merri nodded and wandered over to the table where she usually worked, where two less experienced bakers were making macaroons.

Ellie listened with half an ear as her mum repeated her words back to her. She knew it was Ashnee's way of thinking the problem through, so she half listened and watched the conversation between Merri and the other bakers. Merri looked cross and the bakers frustrated, and when Merri picked up a batch of baked macaroons and tossed them into the dustbin behind them Ellie felt her temper heat.

Merri had no right to do quality control when she wasn't even working on the premises. Right—she needed to sort this out before she ended up with no macaroons and no bakers.

'Mum...' Ellie reached out her hand, grabbed Jack's hard arm and pulled him into the camera's view '...meet Jack. Jack—Ashnee. Jack and I are kind of seeing each other... have a chat while I sort something out.'

'Uh...'

Jack looked from her to the screen but Ellie ignored his panicked face. Good grief, anyone would think she'd asked him to meet the Queen! Ellie rolled her eyes and walked across the bakery. One pair of annoyed and two pairs of mutinous eyes looked back at her.

'What are you doing, Merri?' she asked, keeping her voice low and even.

'The macaroons were lumpy,' Merri stated, allowing Mama Thandi to take Molly from her. Merri placed her hands on her hips. 'That means the mixture was under-mixed.'

Ellie walked over to the dustbin, opened it and grabbed one of the discarded macaroons. It wasn't Merri-perfect but they could have sold the product. And, dammit, Merri had wasted time and energy, electricity and ingredients, when she wasn't even supposed to be at work.

Ellie dropped the pastry back into the bin, closed her eyes and hauled in a deep breath. She felt like an old dishrag, with every bit of energy and enthusiasm wrung out of her. And the two people who'd always been her backstop, her support structure—the other two pillars of the bakery—were wafting in and out or, in her mum's case, wafting around the Indian sub-continent, while she buckled under the responsibility of keeping the bakery afloat.

It was her fault. She'd allowed them their freedom. But enough was enough. She was done, and if they didn't step up she'd collapse under the weight and Pari's would come crashing down.

She would *not* let that happen.

Ellie opened her eyes and as she did so took a step towards Merri, grabbed her wrist and pulled her across the bakery to her table.

'What is *wrong* with you?' Merri demanded when they reached Jack, rubbing at her wrist in irritation.

'You! *You* are what is wrong with me!' Ellie snapped back,

and then she pointed her finger to her mum, on the other side of the world. 'And you! Both of you are going to listen to me!'

Jack cocked his head and stepped back. *Clever man*, Ellie thought. Get out of the area about to be firebombed.

'You first.' Ellie looked at Merri. 'You either work here or you don't. You aren't allowed to walk into my bakery if you don't and do quality control.'

'I was just…' Merri's words trailed off.

Huh…Ellie thought. *My scary face is actually scary!* She steeled herself to say what she needed to. 'I love you, Merri, and I desperately want you to come back to work. Next week is the beginning of a new month. Either get your ass back to work on that day or get fired. Have I made myself clear?'

'Ellie, let's talk about this,' Merri replied, in her most persuasive voice.

'We're not talking about anything! That's the way it is. Be here or don't bother coming back.' Ellie held her stare until Merri turned away and flounced off.

Round Two, Ellie thought, and looked down at her mum. This next conversation would be just as hard, if not harder. She bit her lip and looked for the words. 'Mum, I know that I told you to take this time to travel, to live your dream, but I'm yanking you back. I need you here. I cannot do this alone.'

Ashnee looked at her for a long time and Ellie held her breath. What if she said no? Refused to give up her travelling? What would she do then? Ellie felt panic rise up in her throat at her mum's long silence. Just when she didn't think she could stand it any more Ashnee's huge smile filled the screen.

'Oh, thank God!'

Ellie blinked once, shook her head and blinked again. What was she so excited about?

'I didn't think I could stand another minute!' Ashnee cried. 'I've been desperate to come home! I'm sick of the heat and the crowds.'

'But… But…' Ellie looked at Jack, who was quietly laughing, obviously enjoying every minute of this drama. 'I don't understand.'

'Me neither!' Ashnee said cheerfully, dropping her bare feet to the floor. 'All I know is that I'm catching the first plane I can. Which might take a couple of days, since I'm somewhere near nowhere.'

Ellie sat down on her chair and looked bemused. 'Okay. Good. This is a bit overwhelming.'

'Love you, baby girl!' Ashnee blew her a kiss. 'I'll e-mail you as soon as I have some flight deets.'

And with a wink and a grin her mum was gone.

Ellie stared at the screen for a moment longer before looking up and around. Her mum was gone and Merri was nowhere to be seen. She rubbed her hands over her face, feeling slightly sick at her actions and her words. The impulse to go after Merri was overwhelming…what if she didn't come back? Ellie half stood and felt Jack's strong hand pushing her back into the chair.

'Don't you *dare* go running after her.'

Ellie looked up into Jack's laughing eyes and hauled in a deep breath. 'What have I done?' she whispered.

'Something you should've done ages ago,' Jack replied. He hooked a friendly arm around her neck and chuckled. 'And I have to say…when you finally decide to kick ass you don't take any prisoners.'

A few evenings later Jack wandered into the kitchen as Ellie took a plastic container from the fridge and placed it on the counter. After kissing her hello and getting a lukewarm response he sent her a keen look, trying to work out what was wrong—or more wrong than usual. He knew that she was super-stressed at work, and he suspected that their undefined relationship added another layer of tension to her.

They were reaching a tipping point, he realised. Soon one of them would have to fish or cut bait.

Leaning his forearms on the counter, he peered through the clear lid at tuna steaks covered in a sticky-looking marinade. In the past couple of weeks he'd had more home-cooked meals than he'd eaten since he left home, and fresh fish, properly done, was a treat he never tired of.

Ellie rolled her head and he knew that the knots in her neck were super-tight. 'Spit it out, El. What's wrong?'

'Apart from the normal?' Ellie tipped her head back and looked at the ceiling. 'Horrible day.'

'What happened?'

Ellie placed a strange vegetable on the wooden board and removed a sharp knife from the block of knives close by. He didn't recognise the vegetable and wrinkled his nose.

'Bok choy cabbage. It's good for you,' Ellie stated.

'If you say so. Your day?'

Ellie tossed the cabbage into a frying pan. 'Psycho bride, late deliveries, flood in the upstairs toilet. Samantha wrenched her ankle. Elias is sick.' Ellie took a huge sip of the wine he handed her and sighed with pleasure. 'I need this.'

Ellie pushed a tendril of hair back from her face as she heated another pan for the tuna. Working quickly and competently, she took the tuna steaks to the stove and tossed them into the hot pan. 'Will you get some spring onions out of the fridge, please?'

The steaks sizzled and the room was filled with the fragrant aromas of soy sauce, ginger and garlic. Grabbing his own knife, Jack sliced up the spring onions and asked her where she wanted them.

'In the pan with the bok choy,' Ellie replied. 'Can you get plates?'

Jack handed her the plates as directed. 'Did you manage to get to chat to your mum about the new premises at all?'

Ellie rubbed her eye with her wrist. 'I took her to see the place and showed her the plans that James the architect drew up. She likes it—likes the building, the plans. I'm not quite sure if it's the travelling or the jet lag or her spiritual journey, but she shrugged off the issue of me not having enough money in my trust fund to buy the building at Mrs H's price and do the renovations, insisting that it'll all work out.'

Ashnee had smiled, hugged her and told her that she just had to have faith—a commodity Ellie had run out of a long time ago.

She was also on the brink of losing her mind, and her life was a pie chart of confusion. The segment labelled 'Jack' was particularly large. Ellie looked at him, sitting at the kitchen table, savouring his wine, his long legs stretched out and his bare foot tickling a dog's neck. She knew that she had only days, maybe hours left with him, and every time she tried to envisage life without Jack in it, her breath hitched in her throat.

She'd never felt fear like this before... What she felt for him terrified her... This was true fear, being confronted with a life without Jack in it. He was only ever supposed to be a fling... when had he turned into someone so damn important? Someone she thought she was in love with?

Thought? Bah! Someone she was horribly, unconditionally, categorically in love with. Dammit...he had her heart in his hands and she knew that when he left he'd drop-kick it over a cliff. It was going to hurt like hell.

Ellie shoved her fist into her sternum and hoped like hell that she was confusing what she was feeling with indigestion. Well, she could always hope...

Ellie quickly plated the tuna steaks and sprinkled sesame seeds over the bok choy before putting them onto the plates.

She gestured to his plate. 'Eat. It's getting cold.'

Jack, looking thoroughly healthy and relaxed, eagerly took her advice and concentrated on his supper, which he ploughed through. He caught her look of amazement at his empty plate. She was barely halfway through hers.

'Hungry?'

'For food like that? Always.' Jack stood up and helped himself to the last piece of tuna steak and the other half of the bok choy cabbage.

'By the way, your mum phoned the bakery today, looking for you.'

Jack lifted his head and frowned. 'What? Why?' He picked up his mobile and shook his head. 'My mobile has a signal. What did she want?'

Ellie smiled. 'That's the odd thing...nothing, really. We had a perfectly pleasant chat about the bakery and what I do and...'

'And she was sussing you out. I told her I was staying with you.' Jack leaned back in his chair and sighed, frustrated. 'Sorry—only child, doubly over-protective mother because I was so sick for so long. She nursed me through it all and can't quite cut the apron strings.'

'I enjoyed chatting to her. Luckily I can talk and ice at the same time, because it was a long call. She said to remind you about Brent's memorial service. He's the donor of your heart, isn't he?'

'Mmm. He died when he was seventeen. It's been seventeen years...'

'Your mum said to let his family know if you can go. She said that they'd understand if you were on assignment.'

'That's code for *we'd rather not have you there*,' Jack sighed. 'It's a gracious invite, but I suspect that seeing me would be incredibly difficult for them. I imagine they'd feel guilty for wishing he was alive and not me. *I* feel guilty for being alive...'

'Oh, Jack.' Ellie rested her chin on her fist. 'Survivor's guilt?'

'Yeah. Are you going to say something pithy about me not needing to feel that?'

'I wouldn't dare. How could I, not having walked in your shoes?' Ellie toyed with her fork. 'So, are you going to go?'

Jack's eyes flickered with pain. 'I really don't know. But I do know that I have to be back at work some time next week.'

'Ah.' Ellie felt a knife-point deep in her heart. So he'd be gone within the week? Her heart stuttered and faltered and felt as if it would crumble. She had only days more with him. Days to make enough memories to last her a lifetime.

'El, don't look at me like that.'

'Like what?'

'Like you wouldn't say no if I took you right now,' Jack replied.

Ellie cocked her head, pretending to think as heat spread into her womb. She had such limited time to make memories that would have to last her a lifetime so she figured she might as well start immediately. 'I wouldn't say no.'

Jack's eyes widened and Ellie laughed at his shocked face.

'You're joking,' he said, his voice laced with disappointment.

Ellie fiddled with the edge of her top and sent him a slow smile. 'What if I'm not?'

Jack's fork clattered to his plate. 'I think my heart just stopped.'

He lifted his hand, leaned across the table and, as per usual, pushed back a strand of hair behind her ear. Ellie shivered as his finger rubbed the sensitive spot there and trailed down her neck.

'No going back, Ellie. Right here, right now,' Jack muttered, his eyes on her mouth.

Ellie leaned back in her chair and grinned at him as she pulled her tank top over her head to reveal a white, semitransparent lacy bra.

Jack clutched his chest. 'Heart attack imminent.'

She stood up and walked around the table, standing in front of him while she undid the button that held her soft wrap-around skirt together.

'Well, I will slap you later for joking about that—right after I've had my way with you.'

Jack's eyes dropped as the skirt fell to a frothy puddle on the floor, showing her amazing long legs and the smallest scrap of white lace. Placing his hands on her hips, he turned her around. His finger traced the line of her underwear.

'Good God, I'm a goner,' he muttered, placing his mouth on the sensitive dip where her spine met her bottom.

'No, but you will be,' Ellie promised as she turned back. She gave him an impish look. 'Are you game to see how much this table can actually take?'

'Next week' was here. Despite her not wanting it to, it had crept stealthily and inexorably closer and had finally arrived. Despite her every effort Ellie had not been able to hold back time, and Jack was booked on a flight to London later that morning.

It was time to face reality, pay the piper, face the music, bite the bullet...to stop using stupid idioms.

Jack's clothes were on her bed, his toiletries were in a bag and not on her bathroom shelves, and he was preparing to walk out of her life. Ellie sat on the edge of her bed, sipping a cup of coffee she couldn't taste and wondering what to say, how to act.

It was D-day and she knew that she would have to break through the uneasy silence or else choke on the words that she needed to verbalise. Because if she didn't she was certain she'd regret her silence for ever.

He was too important, too crucial to her happiness for her to let him waltz away without discussing what he meant to her, what she thought they had. Courage, she reminded herself, was not an absence of fear but acting despite that fear.

She had to do this—no matter how scary it was, how confrontational it could become, he was worth it. She was worth it. *They* were worth it.

Too bad that her knees were knocking together and her teeth were chattering. She'd practised this, she reminded herself—had spent the past few nights lying awake, holding him, while the words she wanted to say ran through her head.

All she could remember of those carefully practised phrases was: *I'm in love with you* and *Please don't leave me.*

Ellie put her coffee cup down on the floor next to her feet and crossed her legs. She sat on her hands so that he wouldn't see how much she was shaking.

'Jack…'

Jack looked at her and she sighed at his guarded expression. 'Mmm?'

'Where to from here?' Ellie asked. She winced, hearing the way that the words ran into each other as she launched them out of her mouth.

She saw him tense, caught his jaw hardening. He picked up a pile of shirts and shoved them into his rucksack. 'Between you and I? Ellie, I'm coming back. I mean, I'd like to come back between assignments. To you.'

Well, that was better than him saying goodbye for ever, but it wasn't quite enough. Ellie sucked in her bottom lip. 'Why?'

Jack's eyes flashed in irritation. She could see that he'd been hoping to avoid this conversation. *Tough luck, Chapman.*

'What kind of question is that?'

'A very reasonable one,' Ellie replied. 'Why do you want to come back?'

'Because there's something cooking between us!'

Ellie stood up and walked over to the window, staring out at the sunlight-drenched garden. '"Something cooking between us"? Is that *all* you can say?' Ellie demanded.

'I don't know what you want me to say!' Jack was quiet for a long time before he spoke again. 'Okay...I've never felt as much for anyone as I do for you.'

Ellie shook her head and her ponytail bounced. Seriously? That was all he could come up with? Where had her erudite reporter gone—the one who relied on words for his living? Where had he run away to?

Well, if he wasn't going to open up she would have to. *Courage, Ellie.*

'Jack, this has been one of the best times of my life. I've loved having you here, with me. I don't want it to end but I am also not prepared to put my life on hold, waiting for you to drop back in.' She pulled in a breath and looked for words, hoping to make him understand her point of view. 'I can't spend my life wondering if you're alive or dead, worrying about you constantly. I don't want to deal with crappy signals and brief telephone calls and even briefer visits home. Living a half-life with you, missing birthdays and anniversaries and special days!' Ellie stated. 'I've lived that life. I hated that life.'

'That was your father, not me! Stop judging me by what he did and said. We are nothing alike!' His expression was pure frustration. 'I am not your father and I don't make promises I can't keep! When I say I'll do something, I'll *do* it. And might I point out that technology has made it a lot easier to stay connected.'

Ellie sent him an enquiring look.

'We have mobiles with great coverage, and when I can't get a signal on my mobile I'll have a satellite phone. I could be on Mars and still be able to call you. There is internet access everywhere, and we could talk every day—hell, every hour, if that's what you needed. And I couldn't survive only seeing you every six weeks. A week, two at the most, and I'd be home.'

'But you can't *guarantee* that!' Ellie shouted.

'Nobody can, Ellie! But I'll do my damnedest!'

Ellie swallowed. She wanted to believe him. She really did. And she believed that he believed it—right now. But without a solid commitment, a declaration of love and trust, it couldn't last. Long-distance relationships, especially those tinged with danger, had a finite lifespan. If he couldn't make a commitment then she had to let him go now, while she could. Now—before she completely succumbed to the temptation of heaven and hell that loving him would be.

Heaven when he came back; hell when he was away.

No, that grey space in between the two, purgatory, was the safest place for her to be. It was the only place where she could function as a semi-normal person.

Ellie shook her head. 'I'm sorry, a mostly long-distance relationship is not an option. I…can't.'

Jack threw up his hands. 'I don't understand why not.'

'Because all you've told me so far is that I am somewhat important and that you'll come back when you can. How can you ask me to wait for you when that's all you can give me?'

Jack pushed both his hands into his hair and linked his hands around the back of his head, his eyes devastated.

'Ellie, I'm doing the best I can. There's never been anyone who has come as close to capturing my heart as you. Ever. But I won't tell you something you want to hear just because you want to hear it. I'm giving you as much as I am able to. Can't you understand that?'

Oh, God, how was she supposed to resist such a naked, emotion-saturated statement? But she had to. There was too much at stake.

'It's not enough for me, Jack. It really isn't.'

'Ellie—'

Ellie held up her hand. 'Wait, let me get this out.' When she spoke again her voice was rich with emotion. 'Over the past couple of weeks I've come to realise—*you* taught me!—that I'm worth making sacrifices for. I think *you* are worth making sacrifices for. But the reality is that you're the one who would always be leaving. I can't force you to change that, I can't force you to need me, and I certainly can't force you to love me. All I can be is a person who can be loved, and I am. I know that now. I want it all, Jack. Dammit, I *deserve* it all!'

'You're asking me to give up my career—'

'I've never asked you to do that. I'm asking you to look at your life, to adjust it so that there is space for me in it. I'm asking you to make me a priority. I'm asking for some sort of commitment.'

Jack's voice was low and sad when he spoke again. 'I need to be able to move, Ellie, breathe. I can't live a humdrum life. I can't be confined—even by you.'

'It's not good enough, Jack. Not any more.' Ellie felt her heart rip out of her chest. 'I can't be with someone who thinks life with me would be humdrum, tedious, boring.'

'I didn't mean—'

'Yes, you did!' Ellie shouted, suddenly pushed beyond her limits. 'You want to think that a life with me would be unexciting and dull because anything else would mean that you would have to get emotionally involved, take a stand, make a choice that could lead to pain. Don't you think you're taking this protecting-your-heart thing a bit too far? You've stopped *living*, Jack.'

'Of course I'm living! What the hell do you think I've been doing for the past seventeen years?' Jack roared, his eyes light with fury.

'That's not living—it's reporting! Living is taking emotional chances, laughing, loving.' Ellie shoved her hands into her hair. 'I'm in love with you and I'm pretty sure that you're the man I can see myself living the rest of my life with. Would you consider loving me, living with me, creating a family with me?'

He stared at his feet, his arms tightly crossed. His body language didn't inspire confidence.

'This is emotional blackmail,' Jack muttered eventually, and Ellie closed her eyes as his words kicked her in the heart. And here came the pain, roaring towards her with the force of a Sherman tank.

'I'm sorry that you consider someone telling you that they adore you blackmail. Goodbye, Jack.' Ellie turned away and folded her arms across her torso, gripping hard. 'Lock the front door behind you, will you?'

'Ellie—'

Ellie whirled around, fury, misery and anger emanating from every pore. 'What? What else is there to say, Jack? I love you, but you're so damn scared of feeling anything that you won't step out of that self-protecting cocoon you've wedged yourself into! Of the two of us, *you* are the bigger pansy-assed coward and I am done with this conversation. Just leave, Jack. Please. You've played basketball with my heart for long enough.'

She heard him pick up his pack, jog down the stairs. From behind the curtain of the bay window Ellie watched him storm to his car, his broad shoulders tight and halfway up to his ears, his arms ending in clenched fists.

I love you, she wanted to say. *I love you so much it scares me. I wish you knew how to take a real chance, how to risk your very precious heart.*

But two sentences kept tumbling over and over in her head. *Please don't leave me. Please come back.*

But he didn't stop, didn't turn around. When she saw his car back down her driveway and watched the tail-lights disappear down the road and out of sight, Ellie sank to the floor and buried her face in her hands.

It was over and she was alone. Again.

CHAPTER TEN

FIVE DAYS AFTER he'd left Cape Town Jack and his cameraman were standing next to a pile of rubble that had once been a primary school on the outskirts of Concepción, Chile. What had originally been a black car was buried under a pile of rocks. A massive earthquake had hit the region and Jack had been asked if he'd like to report on it. He hadn't even left transit at Heathrow. He'd just caught the first flight he could to Chile.

Behind them were mounds of bricks and twisted iron and the half-walls of the decimated school. Since the quake had struck early in the morning most of the children hadn't arrived yet for lessons, but Jack knew from talking to the family members who stalked the site that there had been an early-morning staff meeting and there were still a few teachers unaccounted for. Their relatives were still digging through the rubble, slowly moving piles of bricks to find the bodies of their loved ones. Few held out any hope for their survival. The devastation was too widespread, too intense, for hope to survive for long.

Jack rubbed his hands over his face as he prepared to link live to New York. He didn't want to be here, he thought. He wanted to go home to that bright house with its eclectic art and two rambunctious dogs. He wanted to run with the dogs on the beach, stretch out on the leather couch, listen to the sea at night and the wind in the morning.

He wanted Ellie.

But Ellie would mean giving this up, Jack reminded himself. He couldn't...this was what he did, what he was. He needed to work.... Jack blew out his breath. But was that just years of habit talking? He couldn't avoid the truth...he *needed* her. As much as his work. More.

Jack leaned back against a dusty car and lifted his head to the sunlight. He'd been seventy degrees of dim that last night in St James. He'd thought he was so strong, so in control. While she'd launched those emotional arrows at his soul he'd kept telling himself that it wouldn't hurt, that he'd be fine. Now, five days and too much horror later, he felt as if he'd taken a series of punches to his stomach and heart. He was doubled over in pain.

He was generally level-headed and unemotional, and in truth he'd never been a crier. He could count on one hand the amount of times he'd wept since he was a child. Even the bleakest times of his illness, the fear he'd felt when he'd had the transplant and the relief of being normal again had never reduced him to tears, but the fact that he'd lost Ellie had had him choking down grief more than once or twice. The early hours of the morning were the worst; that was when he felt as if his heart was being physically yanked from his chest.

What was he going to do? Sacrifice his job for her? Sacrifice her for the job? Be bored with a normal life with Ellie in it or miserable with an action-packed existence without her?

He didn't know—couldn't make a decision. All he was certain of was that he missed her, that his world had gone from bright colours to monochrome, that he was plodding through each day feeling adrift without his connection to her. He was fine physically. Mentally and emotionally he was a train wreck. He felt as if he'd been stripped of all his internal organs—heart included—that he was just a shell of a man, marking time.

Ted, his cameraman, told him he was about to go live so Jack stood up straight and waited for the signal. He greeted the anchorwoman and launched into his report. Death, destruction, the cost of rebuilding people's lives…

Jack was midway through when a commotion from the decimated building behind him caught his attention. He knew that noise—it was an indication that someone had been found. Still live to New York, he bounded with Ted over the rubble to where a lone man, his face ravaged with grief, was furiously tossing bricks and stones off a pile. Jack recognised his look of terrible excitement, of despair-ravaged hope. He'd found someone he loved…

Jack, forgetting that he was live on international TV, picked up his pace and scuttled across the rubble to where the man was sinking into a hole he'd dug. Jack saw a strand of long black hair flowing around a half-sheared brick and his heart stopped. He swallowed. It was exactly the shade of Ellie's hair…

The young man was sobbing as he yanked debris away from her. *'Mi esposa, mi esposa,'* he muttered frantically, tears streaming down his face.

His wife. All he could see was his wife's hair…

Jack swallowed and jumped into the small hole with him, started to throw bricks, planks and stones away from where he imagined her head and body was. The problem was that her hair was so long—she could be lying in any direction.

Minutes felt like hours and his back muscles and biceps were screaming in pain. His shirt was soaked onto his body but Jack refused to quit. There was no sound coming from the victim but Jack knew that didn't mean she was dead. He refused to believe she was dead…

What if this was Ellie? How would he be feeling? The thought kept hurtling through his brain. Desperate, out of control, terrified. He wouldn't be able to live without her…

Jack lifted a board up and away and there she lay, her beautiful face unmarked by the falling building. Her eyes were open, glassy, but Jack didn't need to check her pulse to see that she was still alive. The hand lifting up towards the young man was a solid enough hint.

Jack yelled at Ted to call for the medics and was surprised to see that Ted was still filming. Why wasn't he helping them? Surely the woman was more important than the story? He felt sickened by Ted's callousness, the fact that he could just observe and not participate, to report but not become involved.

Then again, he couldn't blame him either. Wasn't that what *he* did, story after story, situation after situation?

Jack caught the bottle of water someone threw down, cracked the seal and gently poured a tiny bit of water into the woman's mouth. He didn't want to lift her neck, he had no idea what injuries she had, and her legs were still pinned beneath the debris. Her husband had his face buried in his hands, sobbing uncontrollably.

Jack gently dripped water from the bottle into her mouth and they waited. The young man was now talking to his wife, and Jack felt the lump in his throat grow as he watched them interact, listened to their conversation. It was blindingly obvious that they loved each other so much, that they were ecstatic to be given a second chance.

All his life he'd avoided love, thinking that it equalled confinement. That he'd lose his freedom. That a love affair would hamper his individuality and compromise his independence. He now realised that, compared to losing Ellie, none of it meant a damn thing. His feelings for her scared him, but he knew he was a better man for loving her and that she was worth any emotional risk. He'd been so careful to control every aspect of his life and it was a revelation to discover that being out of control was the best feeling in the world. Being in love felt marvellous. He loved the way it made him feel...

With her he'd found the place he most wanted to be—the home he'd thought he didn't need. She was the one person, the one place, where he could be truly intimate and feel safe. Secure. Looked after. Loved. She had given him the gift of balance and stability and his throat swelled with emotion. He needed to get back to her...

Jack wet the corner of his T-shirt and wiped the victim's face. He saw relief and gratitude in her eyes.

'Muchas gracias,' she whispered between dry and swollen lips.

Jack swallowed, nodded and ran his hand over his head as he heard the rescue workers and medics approaching. He sent her a quick smile and backed away, lifting himself out of the small area to allow for medical assistance.

It was only as he walked away from them and Ted that he realised that his face and cheeks were wet with tears.

Across the world Ellie worked in her bakery, waiting for her staff to come in to work. Her heart was haemorrhaging, she decided, as a lone tear dripped off her chin and landed on the pale pink wedding cake beneath her. It had been nearly a week since Jack had left and she missed him with an intensity that astonished her. The memory of the night he'd left was on constant replay in her head, and she relived the moment of her heart ripping apart on a daily, hourly basis, causing pain to shoot through her system. There was no relief from the memories. Every room in the house made her think of Jack, and she hadn't been able to eat at her kitchen table since he'd left.

She wasn't eating, wasn't sleeping, wasn't thinking. Her hands shook. She felt constantly cold. Ellie looked at the tiny tearstain on the cake and felt grateful she could cover it with a sugar rose. Idly she wondered if she should be making wedding cakes with a scorched heart. Wedding cakes should be made with love and hope, not with sadness and regret.

Ellie looked up to see Merri in front of her, dressed in a bright pink apron. 'Reporting for duty, ma'am.'

Ellie just managed to smile. She'd totally forgotten her threat to fire her if she didn't arrive for work, and now a part of her wished Merri *hadn't* come back, so that she would be so busy she'd never have to think, feel, again.

'It's about time,' Ellie muttered, and held out her arms for a hug.

She stepped into her friend's arms and hung on. After a while she stepped back, felt Merri's hand between her shoulderblades and turned her head to look into her deeply concerned face.

'You okay?' Merri asked.

'Jack left.' Ellie shook her head and wiped her eyes with the corner of her apron. 'I can't seem to stop hurting. I think I'm okay, then it sneaks up on me and *wham*! Dammit—I'm dripping again.'

'God, El, how long have you been like this? Why didn't you call me?'

Ellie winced, feeling the headache pounding between her eyes. 'I couldn't—can't—talk about him.' She bit her lip. 'I feel like I've been eviscerated with a butter knife.'

'Oh, sweetie. You're fathoms deep in love with him.'

Ellie nodded.

Merri sat down on the chair next to Ellie's table and sent her a sympathetic look. 'I'm sorry you couldn't make it work, but sometimes love just isn't enough.'

'It's supposed to be,' Ellie whispered.

Merri's voice was laced with regret and loss. 'In books and movies. In real life...? Not so much.'

Ellie stared past Merri's head. 'I'm worried about him. My imagination is in overdrive.'

'Jack knows how to look after himself.' Merri put her arms

on the table. Her face was uncharacteristically serious. 'Ellie, I've never seen you so unhinged. I'm worried about *you*.'

'So is my mum.' Ellie stared at her flour-dusted shoes. 'She keeps telling me that I can't live like this, that I have to do something about him…but what can I do? Nothing! He's gone and he isn't coming back.'

'You need to try and relax. Get a decent night's sleep and find a way to work through this.'

'I'm trying—'

'Try harder. If you carry on like this you'll be on anti-depressants in a month, in a loony bin in three months.'

'I know that I'm a mess.' Ellie gripped the bridge of her nose with her thumb and forefinger. 'I feel like I am marinating in pain.' She flipped Merri a tiny smile. 'Does that sound desperately melodramatic?'

'Yes, but you're entitled.'

Merri draped an arm across her shoulder and they both looked down at the wedding cake. Merri tipped her head so that it touched Ellie's. 'Sweetie, I'll be here to hold your hand every step of the way, to talk to you and to cry with you. But this cake…?'

'What's wrong with it?'

Merri picked up a swatch of fabric off the table and held it against the cake. 'Wrong shade of pink, honey.'

Jack shoved his hands into his coat pockets as he left the church where Brent's memorial service had just ended. It was over, and yet he didn't feel the relief he'd expected to. He'd delayed his return to Cape Town to be here but he wondered if he'd ever manage not to feel guilty for being alive. He needed to get to Ellie. She'd understand, help him work through this.

Now he needed to avoid the Sandersons if he could. What could he say to them? He was sorry? He was…but it sounded stupid, seeing that he lived because Brent had died. There they all were—Mrs Sanderson hugging his mother by the gate, Mr Sanderson, his eyes pink from cold and tears, talking to his dad.

He should say something. Anything… But he really just wanted to walk away. They couldn't—wouldn't—want to talk to him.

Jack had made it halfway to his car when he heard his name being called.

'Jack!'

He felt the hand on his arm, turned and looked down into Brent's mother's elegant face. He winced internally.

'Where are you rushing off to?' she asked.

Jack, guilt holding his heart in a vice grip, looked around for a means of escape. 'Uh…'

'I'm so glad you came. *We're* so glad you came.'

Oh, Lord, now Mr Sanderson had joined them. Any moment his parents would join the party and he'd be toast. Jack forced himself to put his hand out and shake Mr Sanderson's hand. 'Sir. It was a nice service.'

'We're very happy you made it, Jack. And call me David.'

'I'm June.'

Oh, this was getting to be fun. *Not.* Jack jammed his freezing hands back into his coat pockets and reluctantly nodded when David asked him if he'd take a short walk with them through the cemetery. Jack sent his mother a miserable look over his shoulder and followed Brent's parents to Brent's headstone. June dusted some snow off the face of the stone and rested her gloved hand on top.

'We've wanted to talk to you for a while. We've been following your career,' David said. 'You've made quite a name for yourself.'

'Thank you.'

'You didn't want to come today,' June said. 'You didn't want to see us. Why not?'

Jack looked at a point beyond her face. 'I thought it would hurt you too much.'

'And? Come on—spit it out,' June coaxed.

Her eyes encouraged him to be honest, and for a moment he felt as if he was seventeen again and terrified.

'And it kills me to know that Brent had to lose his life so that I could have mine,' Jack said in a rush, scared that if he didn't get the words out he never would.

June's eyes filled with tears and her face softened. 'Sweetheart, his death had nothing to do with you. It was his time to go…'

'But—'

'But nothing. I'm just grateful that you had a second chance at life. Grateful that you haven't wasted his gift…' June took his hand between hers. 'Yet your mother tells us you have no home, no family, no partner. It worries her. It worries *us*. Why not?'

'Uh—'

'When we gave you our son's heart we expected you not to waste your second chance. We also expected you to make the most of your second chance,' David stated, his voice firm but gentle. 'But we never wanted you to feel guilty—only thankful.'

His mother must have had more than a few discussions with them about him for them to be having this conversation, Jack realised. He wasn't sure whether to be grateful or to wring her neck for interfering. He smiled inside. He'd go for grateful.

'So you think it would be okay if I fell in love? Had a family? Even knowing that Brent never had that chance and I do, with *his* heart?' he asked, holding his breath.

David placed his hand on his shoulder and squeezed. 'Not only do we think it's okay, we think it's important. It's another chance—another opportunity for you to be fulfilled—and that's all we ever wanted. For you to make the most of his gift, to wring out as much happiness as you can from life. Brent had a generous spirit and that would be his wish.'

'And it's ours...' June added.

Jack swallowed the tears he felt at the back of his throat as their words picked up the last of his guilt and flew away with it. He managed what he suspected was a watery grin. 'Well, there is this girl, and she's been giving our heart a run for its money...'

June grinned and put her hand into the crook of his elbow. 'Ooh, a feisty one. I like her already.'

Three days later Ellie sat cross-legged in the middle of the driveway and gazed at what she was privately calling Ellie's Folly. Fascinated, she rested her elbow on her knee and her chin in her hand and just looked. The house preened in the spotty sunlight that appeared now and again from between low black clouds, like an elderly showgirl remembering her former life.

Rolled up and sticking out of the back pocket of her shorts was the agreement of sale that Mrs H had finally signed an hour before.

'Enough is enough,' she'd told Mrs H, after carefully explaining what she intended doing with the property. 'Either accept my offer or I'm walking away.'

'But—'

'Permanently. Pari's will close down, jobs will be lost and St James will lose a landmark institution. I'm tired of your vacillations and games. I'm dealing with enough drama as it is and I don't need any more. The ball is in your court.'

Getting tough had paid dividends and the old lady had signed at a price that allowed her enough cash to do the renovations. She was now the owner of a gorgeous old building that needed lots of love and attention. Thank goodness—because she seriously needed the distraction of hard work.

It had been a good day. If she ignored the fact that she was still miserable and heartbroken and so, so sad.

Ellie felt something cold nudge her shoulder and looked sideways to see a large frappe in one of Pari's takeaway glasses. She'd told her mum that she'd be here and wasn't surprised by her presence.

'Isn't she stunning?' Ellie breathed, unable to take her eyes off the building.

'She is—but you are even more so.'

Ellie scrambled to her feet as that deep voice caressed her. She looked at him, wide-eyed with astonishment.

Jack was back and he was standing in front of her, looking fit and fantastic.

Ellie took a step back, feeling totally disorientated and more than a little scared. Why was he back? Oh, her battered heart had lifted at the sight of his wonderful face, but how it would hurt when he left again. How would she survive this? Would she ever get used to him dropping in and out of her life?

Yet…she didn't care. After the past days of hell on earth it didn't matter. None of it mattered. Because, as sobering and shocking as the concept was, there was nothing she wouldn't do for him. The reality was that she'd never loved anyone or anything as much as she loved Jack…she would give up Pari's for him, move to the ends of the earth for him…she'd even live through having her insides scraped out with a teaspoon every time he went on a dangerous assignment if it meant having him smile at her, laugh with her, hold her after making love to her.

He was back, she loved him and she'd do anything to be with him.

Ellie dropped her iced coffee to the driveway and only just stopped herself from flinging herself against his chest and weeping like a fool. Instead she put the heels of her hands to her temples and shrugged her shoulders. 'Okay, I surrender.'

'You surrender what?' Jack asked conversationally, his finger tapping his still full cup of coffee.

'Do you want me to leave Pari's? I can make cakes in London. I'll take Rescue Remedy and yoga and meditation classes every time you go on assignments to hellholes. I'll get through it.' Ellie stumbled to the low wall that ran parallel to the driveway, sat down and dropped her head into her hands. 'What do you need me to do?'

'Now, *why* would you do all that, El?' Jack asked.

She felt him sit down next to her. 'Because I love you and I can't live without you,' Ellie muttered to the concrete. She felt his big hand on the back of her neck as tears dripped onto the paving below.

Jack pulled her head to his shoulder and held it there as he continued to sip his coffee. 'That's a hell of an offer, El.'

Ellie looped her arms around his waist, still staring at their shoes. She sniffed, the reality of what she'd offered slowly sinking in. She'd miss Merri and her staff, her customers and this new building that she'd never have the chance to turn into something special. And her house—she really loved her house—but she'd take her pets. That wasn't negotiable.

She'd miss the beach and the city but she'd have Jack… Her racing heart settled. She'd have Jack sometimes and it would be all right. Anything was better than nothing.

She felt Jack's kiss in her hair before he let her go. Ellie wiped her eyes with the back of her wrist and sniffed.

'I have a counter-offer,' Jack said, his voice vibrating with emotion.

'You do?'

'As it happens, I love you too.' The corners of his mouth kicked up when her mouth fell open. He put his finger under her chin and pushed it up so that her teeth clicked together. 'I can't—won't—ask you to uproot your wonderful life. But I *can* ask you if I can share it.'

There went her jaw again. 'Sorry?'

Jack pulled his feet up, bent his legs and rested his arms on his knees. His cup was on the wall next to his feet. The late-summer breeze blew his hair off his forehead. 'I want to stay here, live in your house with you. On an on-going and permanent basis.'

'Uh—'

Jack managed to grin. 'Work with me here, darling. I'm trying, very badly, to propose.'

'Propose what?' Ellie said blankly, still stuck three sentences behind, on the 'I love you too' comment.

'I can't imagine my life in any form without you in it so… will you marry me?' Jack asked.

'Uh—what?'

'You? Me? Married?'

'You want to *marry* me?' Ellie squawked.

'That's what I keep saying. But the question is, do you want to marry *me*?'

Jack bit his lip, anxiety written all over his face. Ellie couldn't believe that her tough warrior—a man who'd faced untold danger, who'd lived through and overcome so much in his life—was scared of rejection, scared that her answer might be no.

Gathering her last two wits together, she leaned forward and placed her hands on his knees.

'Yes. Absolutely.'

Jack dropped his forehead to his chest in relief and Ellie rubbed her thumbs over the bare skin on the inside of his knees. He was warm and strong and vital and her world suddenly made sense again.

'I *do* love you, El,' Jack muttered, his voice hoarse as he looked at her with blazing eyes.

Her heart constricted and fluttered and, lifting her hands, she gently held his face. 'I love you too. Welcome home.'

* * *

Ellie sat sideways between Jack's legs, his arms loosely around her waist and his chin on her head. They'd been quiet for a while after his proposal, both happy to savour the moment.

She didn't want to break the spell, but Ellie knew that they still had a couple of issues to work through. 'What about kids, Jack? Do you want any?'

He looked down at her and half shrugged. 'Sure. When?'

Ellie blinked. 'Excuse me?'

Jack squeezed her waist. 'I don't think you really heard me before, or took in what I said, but I want it all. But it starts with you. If you want kids now, later, whenever... I just want to make you happy.'

Ellie blinked, swallowing as emotion—love—grabbed her heart. 'Oh, you slay me.' She pushed her hair back. 'I'd like your baby, Jack—hell, I'd *love* your baby. But not right now. I'd like us to take a little time for ourselves. Just to *be*, to get used to our new life together, before we throw another person into the mix.'

'We can do that.' Jack pulled up her T-shirt and put his warm hand on her bare skin.

Ellie shivered at his touch and hoped that she never stopped responding like this.

She tipped her head back and sideways to look up at him. 'You said that you just want me to be happy but I want *you* to be happy—how are we both going to be happy?'

Jack let out a joyful laugh. 'You really didn't hear me earlier, did you?'

Ellie blushed. 'I kind of tuned out after you told me you loved me. Tuned back in when you proposed. In between it's a bit blurry.'

Jack scooted backwards so that he could look down into her face. He was hers—a warrior soldier with a scarred body, warm smile and vulnerability in his eyes.

'Okay, are you concentrating?'

Ellie laughed. 'Jack!'

'El, I love it here—love your dogs, your city, your friends. I'm happier here than anywhere else.' He ran the edge of his thumb over her trembling bottom lip. 'I've been a fighter all my life but I'll fight hard for you—fight to share your sunshine-filled life.'

'But your career—'

Jack shrugged. 'I still want to do parts of it—with your support. But I can pick and choose my stories a bit better. I don't always need to go into hot areas, chase the conflicts. I can do human drama stories, crime, special reports. I might have to go away now and again, but I meant what I said. There are ways for us to communicate every day and I wouldn't want to be away from you for long.'

Ellie swallowed. How long was long? 'A month? Two?'

Jack laughed. 'Are you mad? I couldn't survive that long without you! A week—maybe ten days at the most. And that would be pushing it.'

Ellie grinned. Jack was not going to be an absent husband, a forgetful lover. He was right. He was nothing like her father.

She tapped his knee in warning. 'Do *not* get hurt again.'

She felt his lips smile against hers. 'Deal.'

Ellie toyed with his fingers. 'But, Jack, if you need to go into a situation that's dangerous, I meant what I said. I'll find a way to deal with it. I don't want you to miss it or feel cheated.' She needed him to understand. 'You were right. You are nothing like my dad or my ex. And I am nothing like that shy, plump insecure little girl. I can cope with you being away for short periods as long as we keep communicating…'

'Don't think this is only from your side. I need to connect with you as well, sweetheart. I missed you so much when I was in Chile. I felt…*bereft*.'

Ellie draped her thighs over his and scooted closer, so that she could link her hands at the back of his neck. 'Was it bad?'

'Yeah. It was.' Jack nodded.

'I saw the footage of you rescuing that woman,' Ellie said quietly. 'Merri caught it on the news and I downloaded the clip from the internet.'

'I guess they aren't calling me unemotional any more, since I was caught crying on camera.' Jack rubbed his forehead with the tips of his fingers. 'She looked like you. Long black hair, creamy skin. Gorgeous. Her husband was a train wreck and I kept thinking: how would I feel if this was you? Gutted, shell-shocked, scared witless.' Jack frowned. 'I've been scared in my life, El, but nothing compares to how terrified I was when I considered what it would feel like to lose you permanently.' Jack shuddered before he spoke again. 'I went to Brent's service—spoke to his parents.'

'That must have been hard. How was it?'

Jack smiled. 'It was…healing. For all of us. Me especially.'

'I'm so glad.' Ellie's breath hitched. 'I know that you're not into these mushy moments, but I just want to keep telling you how much I love you…'

'I don't mind hearing that.' Jack's mouth kicked up as his hand cradled the side of her head. 'And ditto for me. There's so much I still want to say…'

'Like?'

'Like my world has colour again now that you are back in it.' His eyes turned serious. 'El, I love my work, but I love you more. I'll never cheat on you. I promise to be faithful. And I promise, as far as I'm humanly able, to be here when you need me. I promise to be with you on the important dates, and if and when we have kids I'll look at my career and see what I can change to be an active, involved dad.'

Ellie opened her mouth to speak but Jack shook his head.

'You're my life. You're what makes me happy. I want to

wake up next to you, wander down to the bakery for breakfast, be with you at night. Unfortunately I have to earn money, and I do enjoy what I do. But if I have to choose between the two I'll choose you.'

'You don't have to choose.' Ellie gulped as Jack lifted his thumbs to wipe away her tears. His mouth lifted at the corners and his eyes darkened with emotion, and Ellie caught a glimpse of his soul, overflowing with love for her.

He took her hand and placed it on the left side of his chest. 'I've protected my heart in every way I can. Physically, emotionally, spiritually. It's on loan to me and now I'm giving it to you…this heart that saved my life—it's yours.'

Ellie gulped a sob and the stream of tears that she'd been holding back slid down her face. Leaning into him, she placed her cheek against his, and when she thought she could talk sensibly again she took his hand and echoed his action by putting it on her chest. 'Then take mine. Keep it safe.'

'I promise I will.'

And they both knew, in a way only lovers could understand, that their hearts were joined—married—on that low stone wall outside a decrepit house in the late-afternoon summer sun.

EPILOGUE

Six months later

ELLIE FELT HER mum's arm around her waist as she stood at the edge of the crowd, waiting to be called by the Master of Ceremonies to make her speech. Merri stood on her other side, with Molly Blue in her pushchair, sucking a doughnut.

It was the day of Pari's grand re-opening and the new building was restored to its formal splendour. The gardens might need a year or two to mature, but spring was almost upon them and she could see tiny shoots of new growth on the rescued rose bushes, on the trees and bushes.

The bakery had been operating for a week and there had been problems—but nothing insurmountable. Business was booming in the bakery, in the new restaurant, in the tiny art studio/gift shop she'd set up to display her artwork and some works by other artists from the area.

She only had one little issue… Her fiancé—the man she was due to marry in a month—was not yet home. He was nowhere to be seen. She had no idea why he was delayed because every time she called him his mobile went straight to voicemail, and he'd left his satellite phone at home. She could feel her mum and Merri's rising annoyance—this was her big day and he wasn't here. Ellie knew that her mum was trying to keep back all the 'I told you so' and 'war reporters—consistently unreliable' phrases that she desperately wanted to utter.

Ellie resisted looking at her watch. Jack would get here, and if he didn't he would have a damn good excuse for not being able to make it. Over the past six months he'd done everything he'd said he would and he loved her absolutely, intensely, ferociously. He'd never deliberately hurt her and sometimes things happened. *Life* happened.

'Relax, guys,' Ellie told them, sending them both a great big smile. 'I am.'

'Has he forgotten how to use a phone?' Ashnee demanded. 'I'm really quite annoyed with him—'

'You can read me the Riot Act later, Ash,' Jack said from behind them, and Ellie squealed in delight as she whipped around. 'Right now, I'd like to kiss my girl.'

Then his big hands were cradling her face, his lips were on hers and the tectonic plates deep in the earth shifted and settled. When he finally lifted his head he smiled down at her. 'Sorry—battery on my mobile died. And I got a speeding fine on the way here.'

'I *knew* you would get here on time.' Ellie smiled. 'Missed you.'

'Missed you too,' Jack replied.

Ellie pulled her bottom lip between her teeth. 'How did it go with the cardiologist?'

His heart transplant wasn't a secret any more. It wasn't something he discussed, but it was out in the open. 'Fine—situation normal. He says that you're looking after my heart beautifully.'

Her lips twitched. 'Good.'

'I'm sorry that I had to delay my return. I really wanted to be home sooner. But I decided to wait for your present.'

Ellie held his hand between both of hers. 'My present? What is it?'

Jack's eyes flashed with mischief. 'It's a few things, actually. Two of them are my parents, who insisted on being here for Pari's re-opening.'

Ellie and Ashnee, who'd instantly bonded with Jack's mother Rae, danced on the spot. 'That's fabulous news. I'm so happy they're here. Where are they?' Ellie demanded, looking around at the sizeable crowd.

'Over there. With your other present—Mitch. He flew back from New York with me.'

Jack gestured to the crowd to the right of them and Ellie's heart hitched when Mitchell raised his hand and waved it in her direction. Her dad was here…finally…at one of the most important occasions of her life. Ellie felt her heart stumble. This was Jack's doing, she knew. She *so* appreciated the fact that he'd gone to the effort of getting him here, that he thought that Mitch being here would make her happy. And it did— sort of. She'd invited Mitch but never expected him to come. It was such a relief to know that she didn't need her dad's approval any more; she'd finally accepted that her father wasn't father material and his lack in that department had nothing to do with her.

He was—had been—a shocking father, but she could forgive him anything since he'd sent Jack into her life.

'Thank you.' Ellie rose up on her toes to kiss Jack's mouth.

'Pleasure.' Jack ran a hand over her hair as the Master of Ceremonies began his speech. Jack bent his head to whisper in her ear. 'I love you. I'm proud of what you've done, and it's fabulous. But…'

'But?'

'But keep the speeches short, sweetheart, so that I can pull you into a pantry and kiss the hell out of you.'

'That's all you want to do?' Ellie looked at him and shook her head, eyes dancing. 'Damn, I must be getting boring! Got to watch that…'

Ellie grinned as Jack's shout of laughter followed her all the way to the podium.

True happiness, she decided, really was laughing and living and loving well. She tossed Jack a grin as she launched into her very, very, *very* short speech.

After all, she had her man to kiss…

* * * * *

A sneaky peek at next month...

MODERN™

INTERNATIONAL AFFAIRS, SEDUCTION & PASSION GUARANTEED

My wish list for next month's titles...

In stores from 20th September 2013:

❏ The Greek's Marriage Bargain – Sharon Kendrick

❏ The Playboy of Puerto Banús – Carol Marinelli

❏ The Divorce Party – Jennifer Hayward

❏ A Hint of Scandal – Tara Pammi

In stores from 4th October 2013:

❏ An Enticing Debt to Pay – Annie West

❏ Marriage Made of Secrets – Maya Blake

❏ Never Underestimate a Caffarelli – Melanie Milburne

❏ A Precious Inheritance – Paula Roe

Available at WHSmith, Tesco, Asda, Eason, Amazon and Apple

Just can't wait?

Wrap up warm this winter with Sarah Morgan…

Sleigh Bells in the Snow

Kayla Green loves business and hates Christmas.

So when Jackson O'Neil invites her to Snow Crystal Resort to discuss their business proposal… the last thing she's expecting is to stay for Christmas dinner. As the snowflakes continue to fall, will the woman who doesn't believe in the magic of Christmas finally fall under its spell…?

4th October

www.millsandboon.co.uk/sarahmorgan

1013/MB435

She's loved and lost — will she ever learn to open her heart again?

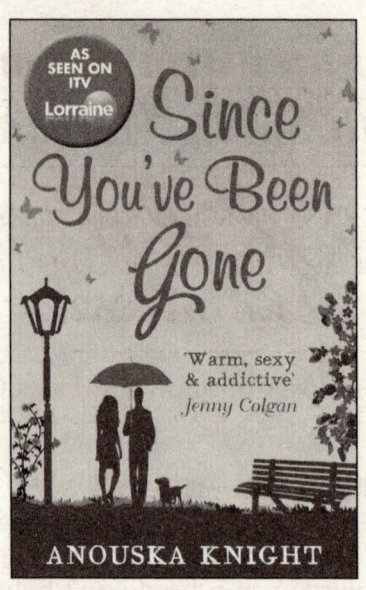

From the winner of ITV Lorraine's Racy Reads, Anouska Knight, comes a heart-warming tale of love, loss and confectionery.

'The perfect summer read — warm, sexy and addictive!'
—Jenny Colgan

For exclusive content visit:
www.millsandboon.co.uk/anouskaknight